COLEEN NOLAN

Denial

PAN BOOKS

First published 2011 by Pan Books
an imprint of Pan Macmillan, a division of Macmillan Publishers Limited
Pan Macmillan, 20 New Wharf Road, London N1 9RR
Basingstoke and Oxford
Associated companies throughout the world
www.panmacmillan.com

ISBN 978-0-330-51697-6

3 5 7 9 8 6 4

A CIP catalogue record for this book is available from
the British Library.

Typeset by Ellipsis Books Limited, Glasgow
Printed in the UK by CPI Mackays, Chatham ME5 8TD

Visit **www.panmacmillan.com** to read more about all our books
and to buy them. You will also find features, author interviews and
news of any author events, and you can sign up for e-newsletters
so that you're always first to hear about our new releases.

For all the women who were told
they couldn't or they shouldn't.
You can and you should.

Meet the Stars ...

Karen King: the star of a girl band turned presenter with a soft-heart and an unfortunate weakness for Pop Tarts who is separated from her philandering husband Jason and living with her much younger, sexy boyfriend Dave.

Julia Hill: ruthless and ambitious, she loves designer shoes, and is utterly paranoid about losing her looks – hence her love of cosmetic procedures. Currently in a coma after crashing her car amid fears her secret sex-change was about to be exposed.

Lesley Gold: big-haired sexpot with a racy past who loves a glass of bubbly or three, now married to drop-dead gorgeous Dan Kincaid. Never seen without her lipgloss, she is the only *Girl Talk* girl still working at Channel 6, presenting their new hit show, *Best Ever Sex*.

Faye Cole: a desperate single mum-to-be whose marriage to award-winning war reporter Mike Parry is on the rocks after her fling with her former *Girl Talk* co-presenter, Cheryl West, became public knowledge.

Cheryl West: feisty former world-class sprinter turned TV presenter, battling to find credible work following the demise of

Girl Talk; reduced to selling lurid kiss-and-tell stories about her fling with Faye Cole, and hoping the end justifies the means when it comes to getting her career back on track.

James Almond: self-important ex-Controller of Entertainment at Channel 6, responsible for axing popular late-night show, *Girl Talk*. Out in the cold after a kinky sex scandal involving his star daytime presenter ended up in the tabloids, and now plotting his comeback.

One

Tabitha Tate was in an edit suite at the back of the Channel 6 newsroom putting together the report that would lead that evening's main bulletin. She frowned at her notebook, where she'd scribbled a rough version of the script to go with the pictures the editor was now cutting together.

'I'm not sure about *ousted*.' Tabitha put a line through the word and stuck a foot up on the desk. Her cropped pants revealed a few inches of pale bare skin above a strappy peep-toe shoe, with a towering heel, that revealed a toenail painted a deep shade of damson. She chewed on the end of her pen, her green eyes narrowing in concentration. A strand of raven-black hair fell across her pretty face. 'I mean, is it entirely accurate to say James Almond was *ousted* as head of entertainment at Channel 6?' There was no trace of an accent, just an unmistakable hint of well-to-do.

Her editor, Lance, pasty-faced from spending too much time in darkened rooms staring at TV screens, snorted. Ignoring a sign that read *No Food or Drink to be Consumed*, he picked up the fried-egg sandwich going cold on a paper plate at the side of the desk and bit into it. Brown sauce oozed from the soft white sliced bread and dripped on to the plate. Still chewing, he said, 'Why don't you just say he was kicked out for being a dirty pervert?'

He shuttled through shots of James coming and going at the High Court where his privacy case against the *Sunday* newspaper was under way.

Tabitha snapped a flapjack in half. 'I suppose if I'm being strictly accurate, he *resigned*.'

'Only because they'd have kicked him out for being a dirty pervert if he'd stuck around.'

Lance parked up the tape on a shot of James in a well-cut, powder-blue suit and Ray-Bans, looking self-assured as he strolled along the Strand with his hands in his pockets, a press posse at his heels. 'Look at him, the shifty bastard. He's having a ball.'

Tabitha rocked back in her chair and studied the shot. 'He definitely looks like a man who knows he's going to win, that's for sure.'

The privacy case, packed with celebrity revelations, had been front-page news across all the tabloids for the last few days. When the *Sunday* had first run its exclusive a few months before, exposing a sordid affair between James, then entertainment supremo at Channel 6, and Helen England, the station's star presenter of its hit daytime show *Good Morning Britain*, it had caused a furore. With perfect timing, the story had broken as James was enjoying a romantic weekend break with his wife, and Helen was relaxing at the country pile she shared with her TV presenter husband and their baby – a few months old and as cute as a button – extolling the joys of family life to a celebrity magazine.

The pictures that had accompanied the *Sunday* splash were both sensational and sick-making. The head of entertainment, known for his sharp suits, was snapped in a man-sized nappy nuzzling the breast of his lover, who was kitted out in a saucy nurse's uniform. The fact that their kinky sessions had taken place during office hours and that James had used the Channel 6 cab account to get to what the *Sunday* called their 'seedy love nest' only made things worse.

'You've got to admire him in a way,' Tabitha said. She rolled up the sleeves of an expensive-looking tailored shirt and leaned forward. The hint of stretch in the fabric made it cling to her narrow waist and accentuated her fabulous boobs. 'Talk about bouncing back.'

'I'm telling you, he's loving every minute.' Lance tossed his greasy paper plate and balled-up napkin into the bin in the corner of the room and spooled through the tape again at high speed. He paused, rewound and hit the play button on a shot of James with the High Court behind him, flanked by his barrister as he faced a barrage of questions.

Tabitha heard her own voice off camera shouting over the rest. 'Is it true you're in talks with a major broadcaster?'

James gave her a crafty smile. 'Let's just say I have several irons in the fire. I'll have a clearer picture of where my future lies once proceedings conclude and there is a judgement in my favour – as I am confident there will be.' His smile broadened.

Another voice chipped in: 'Mr Almond, you seem almost *over*confident. Shouldn't you wait for the ruling?'

James fiddled with the cuff of his starched white shirt. 'There's no need when it's abundantly clear there has been a breach of privacy. What two consenting adults choose to do behind closed doors is entirely their business.' He glanced in the direction of Tabitha – was that a wink? 'I think we all need to understand that it is not the business of the tabloid press to seek to ruin a man's reputation when there is no public interest whatsoever at stake.'

Lance shook his head. 'Oh, I get it. It's all right to be a sicko, even if you're doing it on the firm's time. I'll remember that next time I need a company car to get me to the lap-dancing club after a late shift.'

'You've got to hand it to him – he's a cool customer. If he loses, he'll have to pick up all the costs – something like a million quid. It would bankrupt him.'

Tabitha had mixed feelings about James Almond. Clearly the man was a total creep, but he was also big news, and it was thanks to him that she was getting her break as a serious reporter. It was amazing how none of the so-called proper reporters at Channel 6 had been keen on taking on the story; all too scared it would somehow backfire on them, probably. Tabitha, however, didn't give a stuff. She wasn't in the least bit bothered what might or might not happen after the hearing. This was her chance, and all she cared about was letting everyone see what she was made of: live links from outside the High Court, the lead story on all the bulletins day in, day out. Nothing fazed her. As long as she did a decent job, all the boring showbiz stuff she normally got lumbered with would be a thing of the past. It didn't matter that she wasn't actually a journalist and didn't know the first thing about court reporting or restrictions on what she could or couldn't say. There was a helpful freelance bloke who helped her out with all that. Her job was to ooze confidence on screen and make sure she looked good.

She watched herself on the monitor, face serious, lip gloss perfect, recapping on the proceedings as the film cut to a shot of a curvy Karen King teetering along in skyscraper heels, paparazzi in pursuit, getting into a car. 'Karen King, who suffered a bruising encounter with Marcus Savage, the barrister representing James Almond, is no doubt relieved to be leaving the court,' Tabitha said on screen.

Analysing her performance now, she allowed herself a smile. No question about it – she was an absolute natural. Even the crusty old news editor had said as much. Still, you were only as good as your last piece. You only had to look at Karen King to know that. A few months earlier she had been one of five women hosting *Girl Talk*, an award-winning chat show on Channel 6. Each night, she and her co-hosts Julia Hill, Lesley Gold, Cheryl West and Faye Cole breathed life into the late schedule with a feisty dollop of live TV. The chemistry between the five, as well as their off-screen antics, meant they were huge stars and rarely out of the gossip magazines. *Girl Talk* was one of the most successful and high-profile shows in mainstream TV – or had been, until James Almond had unceremoniously axed it and all five women had lost their jobs.

There had been endless speculation in the press about a feud between the women and their former boss. When Julia Hill had crashed her car and ended up in a coma, some columnists hinted that James's shabby treatment of her was somehow to blame. Tabitha had found the whole story fascinating from the outset, so when one of the guys she knew on the *Sunday* showbiz desk let slip that the source of their original exclusive on James was in fact the *Girl Talk* presenters, she ran with it. She knew it wouldn't exactly make her popular with the women, but Tabitha couldn't afford to worry about that. You can't tiptoe round these things, she told herself. In the end, what counted was the story.

And it had turned out to be a hell of a story, just what she needed for the sniffy news lot to take her seriously. Tabitha was well aware they regarded her as eye candy, only fit for hanging round on the red carpet trying to grab a word with some Z-list celeb or other. Not any more. Now they could see she was made of sterner stuff. Though she couldn't help feeling a teeny bit sorry for the *Girl Talk* lot, since it was her revelations linking them to the *Sunday* exposé that had allowed James Almond to summon them as witnesses in his privacy case and given him the perfect opportunity to set about blackening their names. However, as the *Girl Talk* presenters had turned up in court one by one to do battle with James Almond's barrister, Tabitha had experienced a surge of pride, knowing that all the glamour and celebrity hoo-ha injected into the proceedings by their presence was down to her.

First to give evidence was Lesley Gold, blonde mane tumbling over her shoulders, a short bandage dress emphasizing her curves, tawny eyes hidden behind an enormous pair of filmstar shades. She told the hearing that James kept secret files on his staff for blackmail purposes. She wasn't in the least concerned when his barrister sought to discredit her by bringing up her reputation for drinking and promiscuity. Lesley stifled a yawn. 'I hardly think that's headline news,' she said. When CCTV footage that had been doing the rounds on the Internet got an airing in court and showed her having sex with famous male model Dan Kincaid in her dressing room at Channel 6, Lesley merely shrugged. 'Isn't that an invasion of *my* privacy?' she said, making the barrister flush. 'I mean,' she went on, locking eyes with James, 'I'd be interested to know who took that footage in the first place – wouldn't you?' As it happened, she and Dan had recently got married, so it was hardly a scandal that they couldn't keep their hands off each other. And it seemed that the tabloids agreed. The *Sun* quoted sources at

Channel 6 who claimed the whole building was riddled with secret cameras designed to spy on staff.

Faye Cole had the hardest time on the stand. Her life had pretty much fallen apart in the months since *Girl Talk* when the tabloids had revealed details of the secret lesbian affair she had been having with her co-presenter Cheryl West. Just when Faye had thought things couldn't get any worse, Cheryl appeared on the cover of *Attitude* magazine, followed a week later by a no-holds-barred account of the affair in the *News of the World*. When Faye saw the pictures of her ex-lover, sleek bob slicked-back, green eyes in contrast to her dark, velvety skin, posing in a mannish suit and puffing on a cigar, she felt sick. How had she ever fancied *that*? As for the timing – right when she was begging her husband, Mike, a heroic war reporter, to forgive her for the sake of their unborn child – it could hardly have been worse.

By the time she was called to give evidence, Faye was heavily pregnant. Even though her ankles were swollen, she dug out her highest heels and squeezed herself into a clingy scarlet wraparound dress. Her feet were killing her and her head was pounding as she stepped into the witness box. The courtroom felt airless and intimidating, and, as Faye pledged to tell the truth, a peculiar sensation made her catch her breath. Twenty minutes later, she had to reach for the edge of the stand as a bolt of pain made her double up. Without warning she keeled over, landing with a thump and banging her head. Tabitha felt awful doing a piece to camera live into the lunchtime bulletin as Faye was stretchered off into an ambulance behind her, but the rush of adrenalin that shot through her system more than made up for it. There was nothing like being at the sharp end of rolling news. She even managed to find out through a junior doctor chum of hers at St Thomas' Hospital that Faye had actually gone into labour and given birth to a 6lb 2oz baby girl. The news editor was in heaven. It was obvious Tabitha was a born reporter.

In the edit suite, Lance cut together a sequence of shots of the *Girl Talk* women arriving at court in their heels and huge shades, clutching designer bags, dropping in library footage of Julia (who was still in a coma) to go with Tabitha's voice-over. He searched for a decent shot of Karen King. She had certainly piled on the weight since *Girl Talk* had come off air.

Tabitha glanced at the screen. 'There's a better shot of her getting into her car on the other roll. Her behind looks huge.'

Lance shook his head and shuttled through the next roll of rushes. 'Shit, it didn't take you long to turn into a hard-nosed news bitch, did it?'

Tabitha grinned. 'She got all worked up in court, said the only reason James Almond axed *Girl Talk* was so he could clear the way to give all the best jobs to his bit on the side, the luscious Helen England.'

'Spot on, by the sound of it.'

'Thing is, Lance, it's not about being right or wrong – it's about being *strong*.' Tabitha flashed him a brilliant smile, hooked one of her long legs over the arm of her chair, and stretched. 'It's the business we're in – cut-throat. Ruthless. Dog eat dog.'

'Carry on like that and you could give James Almond a run for his money.'

Tabitha looked thoughtful. 'I don't suppose he's all bad. I mean, he's a brilliant programme-maker. You just have to look at all the awards he's won over the years.'

'He's a frigging weirdo.'

'Suppose.' Her brow creased in concentration. 'Who was it who said it's not what happens to you but how you react to it?'

'Christ knows – Nelson Mandela?'

Tabitha was silent for a moment. 'Actually, I think it might have been Patsy Kensit . . . or maybe Patsy Palmer. Not sure.'

Lance gave her a funny look.

She glanced at her watch. Less than fifteen minutes to transmission. Tabitha thrived on all the deadlines and last-minute tension, everyone getting agitated in the run-up to going on air. Any minute now the news editor would burst in, red-faced, wanting to know how much longer she was going to be. No, there was nothing like live telly. Correction. There was nothing like having the lead story on the teatime news for the fourth night running.

'Right, let's run through from the top, make sure the pictures match the words, then I'll lay the voice down,' she said. The door slid open to reveal the news editor, balding, sweaty-browed and red in the face. 'Keep your hair on, Charlie,' Tabitha said. 'Nearly done.'

Two

Karen was in the kitchen at midday tucking into her second Pop-Tart when her phone started ringing. She ignored it but managed to catch sight of herself in the mirrored tiles as she glanced towards the sleek black device vibrating on the counter. She shuddered and turned away, popping another tart in the toaster.

Bloody tiles, she thought, berating herself for not choosing non-reflective. That brief gaze had been enough for her to take in her chubby jowls, double chin and tired eyes. God, she felt depressed as she savoured the last bite of strawberry goo-filled puff pastry. It wasn't as if she was really annoyed about the tiles; she was annoyed at what she saw in them. Her ebony hair hung in a limp curtain around her shoulders, her face had a sallow, doughy look – where on earth were her cheekbones? – and her emerald eyes had lost their sparkle. There were dark smudges under each eye as if she hadn't taken off her mascara properly, which to her horror stayed put when she rubbed at them.

The moment *Girl Talk* had been axed she'd begun stuffing her face again. Being slaughtered in court a week ago had just made things worse. It had been hideous on the stand at the mercy of that vile barrister. He and James made a good team, no doubt about it. Somehow they'd managed to find out that she'd given up her baby for adoption when she was seventeen, which meant she had been an unmarried, teenage mum. That, and the news that she was now having an affair with her driver, who happened to be a lot younger than her, plus the fact that James pretty much made her out to be the most ruthless and desperate for the spotlight of all the girls, had thoroughly tarnished her image. No one would want to employ her now. Not that offers of work had exactly been flooding in these last few months. She had been thinking about taking a corporate job, a training video for a mobile phone company's call-centre staff, until they said they wanted her dressed as a dominatrix and wielding a whip. If that ever got out, she could kiss goodbye to any hopes of getting back into mainstream broadcasting ever again. But once she'd said no to that, it was as if her agent, Carla Charles, had given up on her.

No wonder her eating was out of control. She'd always been an emotional eater, and the last few months had been among the worst of her life. The toaster pinged and she went to take its latest offering. As she did, she looked down at her size 18 waist, wrapped in a fluffy pink dressing gown that barely met in the middle, and burst into tears. She just wanted this whole ordeal to be over so she could concentrate on getting her life back in order. Until she knew it was truly finished once and for all, she couldn't move on. She couldn't face going back into TV until her name had been cleared, and that would only happen once James lost his case and ended up bankrupt. Thank God the ruling was due by the end of the day.

Three

Faye Cole lay on her side in a scratchy hospital gown staring at a blank white wall. She was absolutely drained. A few days earlier she had come to in the back of an ambulance with an oxygen mask over her face and a sweaty bloke in a fluorescent jacket bending over her saying the baby was on its way and to keep calm. The oxygen mask had made her panic and she'd tried to rip it off, but he'd pushed it back into place and held it there. 'Easy, love,' he kept saying. 'Soon be there.'

She felt fuzzy-headed. She thought back to when she was in the witness box at the High Court with James Almond's smarmy barrister going into unnecessary detail about what he called her 'intimate affair' with Cheryl. As she shifted in the bed, a pain shot through her. The nurse had warned her the stitches would hurt. Even more painful was the memory of being torn to shreds in court. It was all coming back now. On the day of the hearing she had been so anxious she hadn't eaten all day. While she was waiting to be called, she had paced up and down the corridors in a pair of towering heels that had pinched her swollen feet. Her honey-blonde hair had been styled in a slick up-do and her wraparound dress had flattered her bump and seemed to make her eyes an even more intense shade of blue than usual. Come to think of it, she had been experiencing odd stomach pains even before she went into the courtroom, which she had put down to nerves. Perhaps those were contractions and she had been too worked-up to realize.

She had barely made it from the ambulance to the accident and emergency department before a young lad, who didn't look old enough to shave but seemed to be in charge, was telling her to push, and her baby was on its way into the world. She closed her eyes. She hadn't even held her daughter. They had whipped her straight into the special care unit as a precaution since she was three weeks early and a teeny bit jaundiced. Faye had been to see her but hadn't dared pick her up. She looked too small and fragile, with her wispy golden curls and a Babygro that seemed much too big. Although it was the right size for a newborn baby – Faye had checked – the nurses had had to roll up the sleeves to stop them swamping her tiny hands.

The idea of taking her home was terrifying. For the time being Faye just wanted to wallow. She felt awful, groggy. When she had dug out her compact to check her reflection, she had looked red-eyed and her face was blotchy from crying. The last thing she wanted was anyone seeing her in that state, so she had told the staff not to admit visitors. Not even the girls, and definitely not Mike. Not that he'd have been in a rush to see her anyway, the way things were between them. It was the baby he was bothered about, not Faye. According to the nurse who was monitoring her blood pressure, he had arrived soon after Faye had given birth and been in and out of the special care unit ever since. Whenever Faye paid a visit he was somewhere else having a coffee. The nurses must have been tipping him off.

According to the doctor, all being well, Baby Cole would be back on the ward with her mum in another day or so, and, assuming there were no complications, they'd be allowed home within forty-eight hours. Faye felt sick at the thought. How was she supposed to manage with a baby all on her own, without nurses bustling about and a panic button at the side of the bed? At least her parents were on their way back from their holiday in Madeira. Her mother would have to take over.

Faye sank back into her pillows. All she needed now was for the estate agent to say he'd found a buyer for the house. Just days before the privacy hearing had begun she had shown him round so he could measure up and take photos, all the while enthusing about what a perfect family home it was. 'It's a gorgeous property, great location,' he'd said, striding about the kitchen, admiring the bespoke units and gleaming state-of-the-art appliances. 'You've really looked after it.'

The truth was that the place had been in chaos until Faye had paid a company to come in and blitz it. The professional oven-clean was amazing. The cooker looked as good as new.

'I don't think you'll have any problems reaching full asking price,' the agent told her. 'We've got people on our books desperate for somewhere with this much space – and a decent garden. It'll be gone in no time.'

Faye's wretched expression had prompted him to look away and make some more jottings in his notebook as she muttered a few words about leaving him to it and made her way into the hall, his words cutting through her. He might as well have plunged a knife into her heart. It was meant to be *her* family that filled this house, the home she'd worked all her life to achieve, not some rich strangers who could waltz in and live the life she had waited so long for. She didn't want to move, but Mike was insisting they sell up, split the proceeds and move on with their lives.

She had walked through the hall, past walls clad in silk-embossed wallpaper she'd designed herself, and gone to sit on the bottom step of the stairs. As she ran her hand along the spindles Mike had painstakingly restored over the years, she had struggled to stop herself from crying out loud.

Now, lying in her hospital bed, it was almost unbelievable to think that only six months ago she'd had it all. She and Mike had patched things up and were so excited about starting a family. Now there was no Mike. OK, she had a healthy baby, a perfect little girl, but somehow she couldn't get excited about the next chapter of her life as an out-of-work presenter and single mum. The whole prospect filled her with terror. How could her life have fallen apart so fast? Her brain rolled the question over and over, but she already knew the answer. It was James Almond who had wrecked everything and robbed her of any chance of happiness.

She closed her eyes and tears ran down her cheeks. He thought he was too clever for all of them. Well, he was wrong. No one was untouchable. Whatever the outcome of the privacy case, one day she would make him pay.

Four

Cheryl finally sat down in Noel Harding's waiting room after searching for an hour for the building which he'd said was 'just off Oxford Street'. She only discovered it once a black cab had rescued her and driven her a long way north. As she reached the shabby building, she realized that this was only 'off Oxford Street' if you classed Soho as 'off Hertfordshire'.

Looking round the room, she felt deeply depressed as her eyes took in the faded pictures of stars of the past and reality 'celebs' which filled the walls. It was a far cry from her old agency; Mona had the lot – a beautiful office in the heart of Chelsea, A-list clients, and a trophy case crammed with BAFTAs and TV Dome awards displayed as if she were a proud mother showing off her offspring's successes. Cheryl had been with Mona Lewis since she was eighteen, so it had come as a major shock to get all her show reels and headshots sent back to her with a Post-it note that read, 'Been fun, darling, but no money in the L word, Mona x'. Bloody bitch, after all the money she'd made her. She had a good mind to sue, but another court case was the last thing she needed right now.

She looked at the tatty clock on the wall and checked her watch. God, even the clock was wrong. If Noel Harding's offices were anything to go by, he had to be a rubbish agent. Maybe she wouldn't sign up with him after all. She felt around in her bag and pulled out her BlackBerry. No messages. She felt sick inside as she thought about the James Almond ruling, due any time. She'd signed up for Google alerts on the case, so an empty inbox meant no news yet, but she wondered how it long it was going to be.

The door opened and Noel Harding, in crumpled grey suit-trousers, a short-sleeved shirt in some sort of cotton-viscose mix, and a cable-knit sleeveless pullover, stepped into the waiting area. Cheryl felt her stomach churn. If she was seriously considering this man as her agent, she really had hit rock bottom.

'Sorry to keep you waiting.' Noel Harding gave her a smile that revealed sharp yellowing teeth. 'It's just that I'm in the middle of a huge deal – on the brink of signing one of my darling ladies to be the face of a most prestigious brand.'

Cheryl managed a weak smile.

'It's taking all of my considerable powers of persuasion to get her to sign on the dotted, mind you. Can't think why. There's no shame in incontinence these days. Weakening of the bladder comes to us all.'

Cheryl swallowed again.

'Right, young lady, give me another minute and you'll have my full attention. Let's see what we can come up with for you.' Noel Harding looked her up and down and tapped the side of his nose. 'I've got an idea already.'

Cheryl waited for him to close his office door then got up and bolted for the exit.

In a private room at the St Genevieve Hospital in north London, surrounded by tubes and bleeping machines, lay an almost unrecognizable Julia Hill.

The perfect blonde hair was now an unruly dark mop, the
once porcelain skin was lined and pale, and the carefully remod-
elled nose had gone crooked. There was even the faintest hint
of fuzz around her top lip. Beside the bed stood a plain-looking
nurse who seemed to be having trouble changing Julia's catheter
bag. As she yanked at one of the tubes, Julia's fingers flexed
slightly. Noticing, the nurse stopped what she was doing and
went over to the monitors. Satisfied that all was normal, she
finished the procedure and began to undress her.

'Put Sky News on – quick,' Lesley said in a tone of urgency
that caused her husband Dan to jump. It was Lesley's day off
and they were still in their massive gold bed at lunchtime. He
rolled over, reached for the control and flicked the plasma over
from *Loose Women* to Sky in time to catch a report on rugby
players giving sex education to school children. He gave her a
curious look.

'Honestly, Lesley, getting married hasn't changed you one
bit!'

Lesley threw him a sarcastic look. 'Not *them*, you silly sod –
look at the caption.' The breaking-news crawler at the bottom
of the screen said that the judge in the James Almond privacy
case was expected to give his ruling shortly.

'Oh,' Dan mouthed as he pulled himself over towards her.
'Fingers crossed, darling,' he said, pulling her in for a cuddle
as Lesley's eyes remained fixed on the screen.

Five

James Almond selected a ginger nut from the assortment of biscuits on the china plate in front of him and dipped it in his tea. He had few weaknesses, but dunking biccies, as long as no one was watching, was now one of them. He put it down to the strain of the trial. He rested his elbows on the desk and propped his chin on his hands. The room, in the basement of the court building, was set aside for clients to meet with their legal representatives; its grubby off-white walls and tatty office furniture felt cold and gloomy.

If there was one bonus to being in court for a few days, it was having so much time to think and come up with ideas, mainly during the proceedings while the barristers were on their feet boring everyone to death. He had come to the conclusion that everything happens for a reason, and that the hearing would be the making of him. For one thing, media interest in the proceedings was massive – he had even managed to knock Cheryl Cole off the front page a couple of times – and had done wonders for his profile. He was truly a household name. For all the wrong reasons, some might argue, but not James. Every cloud has a silver lining, he reminded himself at moments of stress. At least he'd found out exactly who he could trust: no one.

He flicked a crumb off his shirt and checked his BlackBerry for messages. There were none, of course. Not a single word

19

of support from his so-called friends, although strictly speaking – and James was nothing if not strict – he had no friends. What he had was contacts. Colleagues. Acquaintances. Media hangers-on. The type constantly on the lookout for a free lunch, even if James knew only too well that there was no such thing. Always, somewhere down the line, there was a price to pay.

It wasn't very long ago that James had been a sought-after and popular figure in the world of broadcasting: a 'player', no less, with 'friends' practically queuing up to have coffee/lunch/cocktails/dinner with him. Going back only a few months, his diary had been crammed with appointments. Every once in a while his PA would take pity on him and leave the odd fifteen-minute window with nothing scheduled, but that had been about it. Otherwise, it was business, in one form or another, from wall to wall. He had been at the top of his game, well-connected. It had all changed, though, with a fairly spectacular fall from grace. Just one unfortunate exposé in the *Sunday* – the kind of tawdry newspaper he'd use to protect his hand-woven Persian rugs if he was toilet-training a puppy, frankly – had sent the very same people once so desperate to suck up to him scurrying for cover. It was most extraordinary. He narrowed his eyes. And exactly who had been behind all that? Those saggy bitches from *Girl Talk*, that's who. Still, he was a survivor, and there was such a thing as the right to privacy, as the *Sunday* was about to find out to its cost.

Now, on the final day of the hearing, as he waited for his lawyer Godfrey Black to brief him on the day's proceedings, James busied himself making notes, mainly a list of things to do once it was all over. He paused and smiled. All those losers who thought he was dead and buried would very soon be falling over themselves to get back into his good books.

He stuck out a long leg and examined his footwear, which was black and shiny, crafted from soft Italian leather, and had a pointy toe. The shoes looked perfect with his navy sharkskin suit, which he had teamed with a crisp white Paul Costelloe shirt and plain navy tie. He checked the inside pocket of his jacket where his shades were: tortoiseshell Wayfarers, naturally. When he emerged from court in a few hours a vindicated man, he wanted to look his best.

Behind him the door opened and a breathless Godfrey Black breezed in. 'I'm sorry I'm late,' he said, sinking into a plastic chair, which sounded ready to splinter under his weight, and shrugging off his overcoat to reveal a dark navy pinstripe suit. He raked a hand through his unruly silver thatch, then shook a massive cotton handkerchief from his trouser pocket and blew his nose. James winced.

Godfrey folded his handkerchief and stuffed it back into his pocket. 'I must say, James, you look remarkably relaxed for a man who might well be on the brink of financial ruin.'

'You must surely know by now, my dear Godfrey, that I am not the kind of man to shrink from the most testing of challenges. In fact, I welcome them. An untested man is an incomplete man. Who said that?'

'Well, I . . .'

'I did. I am that rarest of beings – at my best and most confident when my back is against the wall.' He looked thoughtful. 'You know, I honestly can't imagine what it might take to faze me. That's what Cambridge does for you – instills an unshakable sense of being the crème de la crème, equipped to deal with all that life throws up, good and bad. I don't suppose many of your clients actually relish having to appear in court, do they?'

'No, I—'

'Quite. That's what makes me different. To tell you the truth, Godfrey, I view this whole procedure as an opportunity to learn. That's all it is.'

'I think it's rather more serious—'

James held up a hand to silence him. 'Once I'm back at the helm of Channel 6's entertainment output, we'll have lunch, you and I. I'll get my PA to arrange something, perhaps at Rules. What do you say?' Godfrey was silent. 'I must say, it makes a change to be able to converse with an intellectual equal. Not too much of that in the world of television, I'm afraid, more's the pity.'

Godfrey Black nodded. Lunch at Rules indeed. Surely the man was deluded if he thought he still had a career at Channel 6 – or anywhere else, for that matter – after everything that had come out in the course of the hearing.

Six

Karen was still mooching around the kitchen in her dressing gown. Barely half an hour earlier she had polished off the last three Pop-Tarts in the packet – best to eat them and be done with it, remove temptation, she had reasoned – and she was still hungry. No, not hungry, exactly. It was more that she just wanted to keep eating, which wasn't quite the same thing. Her body was crying out for sugar, and no wonder. It was the stress of this James Almond business.

On the TV in the corner of the kitchen Tabitha Tate, in a flimsy dress and bulky jacket, a furry microphone in her hand, stood on the pavement outside the court delivering the latest on the case. Not that she had anything new to say as there still wasn't a verdict. She droned on anyway, pausing now and then for the studio anchor, a sallow-faced man with a sensible short back and sides, to ask an entirely pointless question.

'Oh, for heaven's sake,' Karen said, losing her patience with the pair of them. 'We know all this already. You told us the same thing about a hundred times this morning. All anyone wants to know is that the slimy bastard's going down.'

That was the thing with rolling news. Same old stuff over and over until you lost the will to live. Not that Karen dared switch channel, in case the ruling came through while she was watching a couple come to blows over a lie-detector test on *Maury*. That would be just her luck. Still, the waiting was killing her. No wonder she couldn't stop eating.

On screen, Tabitha Tate pushed a hank of raven hair off her face. The caption read 'Breaking News, *LIVE*'. Karen remembered seeing her around the building at Channel 6, hurtling along a corridor, rushing into the canteen for a coffee to go, always with that self-important look that seemed to go hand in hand with the newsroom lot. She was only young, but she was definitely making a name for herself. It was Tabitha Tate who had revealed that Karen and the others had tipped off the *Sunday* about James and Helen. Karen watched her with dislike. She let rip at the screen. 'Oh, shut up – what do you know about anything anyway?'

Steadying herself against the speckled marble counter of the breakfast bar, she took several long deep breaths, in and out, until her quickening heart rate calmed down again. No point getting all worked up. It wasn't helping, and it certainly wasn't hurting James, who swaggered in and out of court every day, smiling for the cameras, looking as if he hadn't a care in the world. He had to be the most insensitive and ignorant man she had ever encountered. She frowned. Actually, it was a close-run thing with Jason. Her estranged husband was definitely a contender when it came to crass insensitivity. For some strange reason, despite having run off with an airhead glamour model, it still didn't seem to have sunk in that their marriage was finished. O-v-e-r. She had been as clear as she could, spelled it out – literally – but to no avail. Jason still seemed to think she would forgive him, that it was simply a matter of time. If he sent one more bunch of white roses, she swore she would wrap them round his neck.

She felt her heart rate shooting up again. The fact that her body was full of sugar and caffeine probably wasn't helping. She had to get a grip, keep busy. At least James would be landed with crippling legal costs once his privacy case went belly up. That would wipe the self-satisfied smirk off his face. Karen allowed herself a wry smile. James Almond, so fond of telling everyone what goes around comes around, was about to discover first-hand the truth of his own mantra.

Tabitha Tate was still on screen, reduced to talking about James Almond's penchant for designer suits and speculating about the cost of his trial wardrobe. Good heavens above – did that really count as news?

'Of course, there has been speculation that James Almond could even return to Channel 6, either at the helm of entertainment again, or in some other senior capacity,' Tabitha Tate said, her expression cool and informed.

Karen's mouth fell open. '*What? No!*' She was shouting again and her head was thumping. Surely there was not the slightest chance he might swan back into his old job? Then again, there was a new owner in the picture these days, the Russian oligarch, Vladimir Vladislav. Hadn't he married some model whose three-in-a-bed exploits with a golfer had been all over the papers? Maybe Vladimir Vladislav didn't care what his staff got up to behind closed doors. Perhaps kinky sex was the norm for a wealthy oligarch with a stake in top-shelf magazines. He and James would no doubt get along like a house on fire. Karen felt her throat go tight. The thought of James rising phoenix-like from the ashes didn't bear thinking about.

She opened a cupboard and stared at the contents. A depressing collection of sugar-free breakfast cereals and organic porridge oats faced her. Dave had bought those. She sighed. Living with a health nut when she was in binge-eating mode made things very tricky indeed. Perhaps if she ate something wholesome it would break the awful habit she'd got into of picking at junk all day. She felt a surge of optimism as she reached for the oats, measured some into a cup and tipped them into a pan. Dave would be proud. Feeling virtuous, she gazed at the innocent health-giving flakes. Diet gurus were always going on about porridge, making out it was some kind of wonderfood. Wasn't it oats that reduced cholesterol and made you feel full up for ages? Karen studied the blurb on the back of the box which said something about oats being a *super*grain as opposed to a mere wholegrain. She wasn't entirely sure what that meant, but it sounded impressive – exactly what she needed.

She shook the pan, producing a fine cloud of dust. What a pity the kind of food that was good for you tended to be, well, a bit boring, if she was honest. You'd think a so-called superfood would look a bit less like the stuffing they used in old-fashioned Jiffy bags and a bit more . . . appetizing. Still, if she used water rather than milk, there'd be practically no calories, which was a bonus. Even better, one little bowl would keep her going until dinner and stave off more cravings. That was the beauty of porridge. It wasn't something you'd want to keep stuffing your face with, unlike Krispy Kremes, which seemed to have the opposite effect. She would make an effort, ditch the junk and get back into a proper routine of three meals a day. Starting tomorrow she would have porridge for breakfast, just like Dave. Her spirits soared as she fantasized about eating properly, the weight falling off. She stirred the gloopy mixture in the pan and vowed to turn over a new leaf.

If only it was as simple to shift flab as it was to gain it in the first place. It had been the easiest thing in the world to balloon from a svelte size 12 to a blubbery 18. She had piled on the pounds in no time and with barely any effort, yet reversing the process would require extreme willpower. She would have to give up all her favourite things. She might even have to start exercising, God forbid: go for a run on the common first thing with Dave. She watched the porridge bubble in the pan, took it off the heat and slopped it into a bowl. It didn't look edible. Perhaps if she sprinkled it with a bit of sugar and a spoonful of that nice yoghurt, the one that came with a fruity bit in its own little corner compartment, it might look a bit more appealing. She could add some honey – that was healthy, wasn't it?

She flung open another cupboard. Next to the honey was a half-eaten packet of chocolate digestives. They were probably off by now. She took one and nibbled at it to see if it had gone soft. Hmm, she wasn't sure. She took a bigger bite. It tasted fine. She finished it, put the rest into a food bag, sealed it, and returned it to the cupboard. A few seconds later she retrieved the food bag and ate another biscuit. That was the trouble with having stuff like that around. Once she knew it was there, it was fatal.

She tried a spoonful of the porridge. Dear God, it tasted awful – just what you'd expect wallpaper paste to taste like. Maybe she should have used milk after all. No point scrimping on calories if the result was inedible. She scraped the contents of the bowl into the bin and reached for another biscuit. Oh, go on, finish them, she told herself. Get all the crap out of the way now, and you can start your diet tomorrow.

Seven

James took off his shoes, slung his jacket over the banister and dropped his briefcase on the hall table. There were further delays to the verdict and he couldn't stand a moment more in the dingy back rooms at the court. He'd slipped out of a service entrance and taken a black cab home. The unblinking red light on the answering machine indicated that there were no messages. In the kitchen he took an ice tray and vodka from the freezer and poured a hefty shot. The liquid was dense, syrupy and clung to the sides of the glass. He sloshed it about in the tumbler, rattling the ice cubes. Until relatively recently he had been a single malt man, until he read a piece in *Esquire* or *Tatler* or one of those magazines about vodka being the drink of the moment. The single malt, it claimed, conjured up images of fusty clubs where old boys napped open-mouthed, drooling, in the library after lunch. That was definitely not how he saw himself. He had switched at once to Grey Goose, which seemed to be the vodka of choice among the trendy set. Now, though, he preferred Stolichnaya. Strange to think he had once looked down his nose at vodka as rocket fuel for peasants. He could not have been more wrong. It was actually extremely pleasant. Hit the spot, too.

He opened the fridge and took out a wedge of farmhouse

cheddar. There was no bread so he would have to make do with Bath Olivers. Not that he was very hungry.

James drained his glass and poured another shot. He was probably drinking too much, but it hardly mattered. It was depressing rattling about in a house that was far too big for him, but it couldn't be sold until his privacy case was over and the fuss had died down. It astonished him that ghouls actually drove up to the gates to gawp and take pictures. As for the paparazzi, a grainy picture of him on the doorstep in sweat-pants and an LA Galaxy shirt had made the tabloids a week or so earlier. The press persisted in calling it 'a house of death'. It made him sick. Still, let them have their fun. He had more important things to think about.

He loaded his snack on to a tray and took it into the sit-ting room, where he stretched out on the sofa. The room was vast, with just a few pieces of bespoke modern furniture and a rug inspired by Mondrian on the parquet floor in front of the fireplace. On the mantelpiece was a series of framed black and white photos of his late wife, Stephanie, on a beach, splashing about in the surf. James had taken them on holiday in Cornwall a year or so after they had first met. The biggest photo of Stephanie, thigh-deep in the water, laughing as a wave drenched her, was missing. She had flung it at him when he told her he had been seeing Helen England and their affair was about to be front-page news. There was still a dent in the wall opposite the hearth where it had smashed.

James cut a lump of cheese and balanced it on a Bath Oliver. As he bit into it, crumbs landed on his front. He brushed them away, not caring if they fell on the floor. The house, decorated with such care by his wife, no longer felt like home. It had become oppressive, a prison, despite its five bedrooms and subterranean pool. He drained his glass again. The door to the basement was kept locked now, off-limits. He could not bear to go down there. The black-tiled pool, illuminated with soft, shadowy beams, was once his favourite part of the house. It had been Stephanie's idea to put in a pool, and to start with he had baulked at the cost, but once it was done he was thrilled. He would go down there and do fifty lengths first thing in the morning and sometimes again before bed if he needed to unwind. It was the perfect place to clear his head: a silent chamber, womb-like and comforting.

That was before he had found his wife's body at the bottom of the pool. His chest tightened just thinking about it. He had jumped in and heaved her to the surface, waded through the water struggling to hold her in his arms. It was as if she had grown too heavy for him, and he had slipped and splashed and lost his footing and let go of her more than once. Her eyes were blank as he knelt, blowing air into her mouth, pumping her chest. It wasn't as if he knew what he was doing, not really. He had grabbed her shoulders and shook her and shouted her name as if she would somehow come round. Instead, she remained limp, flopping about in his arms, her face impassive. Finally, he had eased her on to the hard mosaic floor and covered her face with his shirt. It was the expression in her eyes he couldn't stand. He had been much too late to be of any use to her. She had been in the water for hours.

He looked at the photos on the mantelpiece, his face wet with tears, and wiped the back of his hand across his cheek. What was he supposed to do now, stuck here all by himself? He let out a noisy sob. It was all so unfair. He went into the kitchen, blew his nose on a piece of kitchen roll and returned with the bottle of vodka.

While Stephanie was sliding under the water, fully clothed, two floors below him, he had been lounging on the bed in the spare room, tipping single malt down his throat – this was before his conversion to vodka – watching *Gavin & Stacey*. There had been a row over dinner – the subject of Helen England had come up yet again – and he had stalked off, leaving his wife at the table knocking back red wine. Even though the bedroom door had been open, he hadn't noticed her go past. What had happened in the pool was anyone's guess. There was no suicide note. Perhaps she had just felt like a swim and hadn't realized how inebriated she was. Despite his being subjected to some gruelling questioning from the police, the inquest recorded an open verdict. The truth was he would never know what happened.

The strange thing was that he hadn't appreciated what Stephanie meant to him, how much she did and the extent to which he relied on her until she wasn't there any more.

He wiped his face with the kitchen towel. He needed to get a grip. He blamed the *Girl Talk* girls for the death of his wife. It was their interfering that had brought his affair with Helen England to light in the first place. He straightened his shoulders. Succumbing to self-pity was pointless. The only thing that would make him feel better would be finishing off those malicious bitches once and for all. In a few hours the judge would give his ruling and James could start putting his life back together again.

Eight

Karen rang her best friend, Bella Noble. 'I've just scoffed half a packet of chocolate digestives,' she wailed.

'That's good. It means you stopped yourself from eating the whole lot. Well done – you should be proud.'

Bella headed away from the Channel 6 coffee bar and found a quiet corner in the atrium, flopping on to a squashy leather armchair. Moments later a serious-looking man carrying a tray with a copy of the *FT*, an oversized drink and a muffin on it, threatened to plonk himself on the sofa facing her. When he clocked her frosty expression, he did a brisk U-turn and veered off towards a table next to the lifts. She pushed a blonde curl off her face and tore open a packet of brown sugar, stirring it into her cappuccino. 'It's OK to go off the rails once in a while,' she told her friend.

Bella, a producer at Channel 6, spoke to Karen every day. She knew exactly how much strain the James Almond trial was causing. Stuck at home with no work on the horizon, Karen was showing signs of going to pieces.

'You have to look on the bright side,' Bella said. 'I sometimes get through a load of biccies too. It's being able to stop before you wolf the lot down that's the main thing, so pat on the back.'

'I didn't stop, that's the point. There was only half a packet left and I ate the lot.' Karen's voice wobbled. She hated herself for turning into such a slob.

Bella took a deep breath. 'OK, no need to beat yourself up. We all have those moments of weakness. If you do cave into temptation, put it behind you and move on.'

Karen gazed at the tub of Chunky Monkey ice cream on the kitchen counter in front of her. 'I *have* moved on . . . to a large tub of Ben & Jerry's. The banana one with chocolatey bits and nuts. Seriously, Bella, I can't stop eating. I'm scared I'll end up too fat to get out of bed and they'll make one of those awful documentaries about me. You know – how junk food turned me into a blubbering wreck.'

'Right, that's enough of that. You're only a size 18, which is nothing to be ashamed of. A few weeks of sensible eating and a bit of exercising and you'll be back to your fabulous sylphlike self in no time. Right now you're stressed, which is why you're eating. Food equals comfort. The thing is not to get stressed about being stressed, if you know what I mean.'

Karen said, 'The last time I was stressed the weight dropped off.'

'That was different.' Bella's voice was firm. 'You'd had your heart broken. Love affairs gone bad lead to starvation. It's a well-known fact.' Bella thought back to Karen's ex, Jason, tossing aside their twenty-odd years together for some empty-headed model whose 'career' was built on flaunting her silicone-enhanced breasts.

'Heartache's different,' Bella said. 'You've got a decent bloke now and you're in love.'

Karen said nothing.

'You *are* still in love with Dave?'

'Yes. Of course I am.'

'And what does he have to say about you putting on weight?'

'He says he doesn't mind.'

'There you are, then,' Bella said. 'And if you want to shift the weight quickly, what about doing one of those boot camp things? They're all the rage.'

Karen had read about boot camps run by no-nonsense ex-Marines. They definitely worked, but she wasn't sure she liked the idea of being woken at the crack of dawn by thumping music, or of jumping off cliffs and wading through fast-flowing rivers and heaven-knows-what-else that seemed to be compulsory. No, it wasn't for her. Wasn't there some kind of space-age suit you could wear around the house these days that miraculously sucked up the flab, a bit like a vacuum cleaner? She was sure she'd read somewhere that Robbie Williams had one, and he was looking pretty amazing. She undid the belt on her dressing gown and breathed out.

'They're expecting the ruling today,' she said.

Bella glanced at the giant screen on the wall of the atrium, where a bedraggled Tabitha Tate, a strand of shiny black hair plastered to her lip gloss, was gesturing at the court building behind her. 'Well,' Bella said, 'once he's safely humiliated and financially ruined you'll feel much better.'

'I'll probably never work again after the way things went in court. You'd think *I* was on trial.'

Karen had told the court about James Almond's practice of creating secret and damaging dossiers designed to force out anyone he took against. Although she had had no qualms about saying what she knew, she had been a bundle of nerves when it came to taking the stand. The court felt small and oppressive, with everyone much too close for comfort. The public gallery, every seat taken, seemed to tower over her and the packed press bench was only a few feet away. As for James, he was right in front of her, leaning back in his seat, practically oozing swagger and self-confidence. He even had the gall to wink at her as she was taking the oath. Everywhere she looked there seemed to be critical eyes boring into her. It didn't help that she had put on so much weight – she felt like a lumbering elephant as she took to the stand. Before she had even confirmed her name her confidence was on its way out of the building. It was the most nerve-racking thing she had ever experienced.

James's snooty barrister, Marcus Savage, had managed to make her feel about an inch tall, and that was before he'd even opened his mouth. She'd had the feeling he was taking the mickey, poking fun at everything she said. As she answered his questions, her voice sounded small and unsure and sweat ran down her back. Her hair, which she had styled into a loose chignon especially for the occasion, stuck to the back of her neck and her dress, a formal grey shift, felt too tight. She wished she had worn a lightweight jacket instead of the wool dogtooth check, which was suffocating. She could feel her make-up sliding off.

'He played everyone off each other, spied on his staff, kept files on all of us.' She felt flustered and her voice had gone up by an octave or two. The barrister observed her over a pair of gold-rimmed glasses. 'You think you're very clever running rings round me,' she continued, 'but it doesn't change anything.' Karen had glared at James, her face flushed. 'I don't care what anyone says – he's an absolute disgrace.'

Marcus Savage, not in the least perturbed by Karen's outburst, had merely raised an eyebrow and aimed a bemused smile at the judge. 'I appreciate we live in a celebrity-obsessed society these days, Ms King – who better than you to remind us of that? – and that some celebrities have, shall we say, an over-inflated sense of their own importance.' He paused and gazed at her until she went even redder and looked away. 'However, for the time being, in this court at least, we still rely on the judge to decide on the ruling at the end of the day.'

There was a ripple of laughter. Karen glanced at the press bench, where they were all scribbling away. She felt light-headed, ready to pass out. Marcus Savage leaned on the desk and gave her a triumphant smile. She had never felt so humiliated.

The following day the papers seemed more concerned with her frumpy appearance than what she'd had to say in court. The showbiz reporters had ripped her to pieces. *Heat* magazine put her in their *What Were You Thinking?* spread next to a picture of Heather Mills in a shiny jumpsuit.

'What if he wins?' she said to Bella.

'He won't.'

'I heard the Channel 6 reporter say there was a chance he could get his old job back.'

Bella glanced at the screen facing her which was showing footage of James Almond getting out of a taxi that morning on his way into court, looking impeccable in a dark navy suit, one hand in his pocket as he strode along, his expression relaxed and amiable as the press pack jostled and scampered along beside him. He was loving the attention, it was obvious. She shook her head. Tosser.

'Never in a million years,' Bella said. 'Trust me, he's finished.'

Nine

Standing in the Strand with the High Court behind her, Tabitha Tate applied a fresh coat of lip gloss and pulled her coat tightly around her. Not so long ago she wouldn't have been seen dead on screen in the thick black parka that made her look like a Michelin woman, but now she couldn't care less. One thing she had learned was that practical clothing marked out the real reporters from the rest. Although it was late summer, the temperature had dropped as the afternoon went on and the wind was positively glacial, not that she minded, snug in her coat. She was way too excited to care what the weather was doing. The biggest media case of the decade had just concluded, and she was due to report live into the main teatime bulletin.

Tabitha checked her watch and looked around to see who else was there. Next to the railings close to the exit, one of the girls from Channel 5 News shivered in a slip dress and no coat. Tabitha smiled. Silly girl would soon learn once she'd had her first bout of pneumonia. She was in the worst spot too, because as soon as James came out she'd get pushed to one side and left behind. That's why Tabitha had moved back a bit. She was guaranteed to nab him for a final word after he'd said his bit – no way would James Almond leave without an impromptu speech – before he got into his car.

Tabitha took a deep breath and signalled to her cameraman,

Tim Wade. She drew back her shoulders, and as soon as the red light came on began to deliver an unrehearsed piece to camera. 'Seconds from now, here in the Strand, James Almond is due to face the media after triumphing in his privacy case against the *Sunday* newspaper,' she began.

Ten

In the corner of the hospital room, as the TV relayed pictures from outside the High Court, Julia could hear the most awful screaming she'd ever heard. She blinked and looked around, taking in the surroundings, struggling to work out where she was and where the ghastly sound was coming from. Nothing looked familiar. The simple white room was clearly some sort of hospital, but who on earth was making that dreadful racket?

Suddenly the door flew open and two nurses rushed towards her.

One said, 'Welcome back! You've certainly announced you're awake. The whole hospital can hear you!'

The other held her hand. 'Julia, I know you are in shock right now, but you need to try and get control of your voice. It's bound to feel strange because you've not spoken since you came in here, but just take it easy and do your best.'

Only then did Julia realize that the screaming was coming from her.

Eleven

James Almond walked from the court a free man. It definitely helped that he had recognized the judge straightaway and knew he had an ally. He might not have been wearing the Father Christmas costume he normally paraded around in at the kinky private members club they both frequented, but James would know that beard anywhere.

From the moment 'Santa' realized he'd been recognized, everything went James's way, but even he couldn't quite believe his luck when the judge awarded him £100,000 in damages.

'You leave here without a stain on your character. Every man is entitled to a private life,' the judge said.

As James came out on to the steps, he was swamped by reporters wanting his first words. Tabitha Tate stepped forward, and he made sure his gaze didn't drop to her impressive breasts – the last thing he needed now was a side-angle shot printed in *heat* magazine with some dodgy subtitle like 'Looking for milk' next to it. No, he'd have to be very careful now, he thought, as she loomed in.

'James, how do you feel to have been vindicated?' she asked, pushing a microphone into his face as cameras whizzed around him.

'Great,' he said with a big smile, hoping the microphone, which was a bit too close for his liking, was clean and not full of hundreds of sound bites' worth of bacteria. He battled to keep some distance, and keep his eyes away from her cleavage.

'Tabitha, I feel *just* great. I always had faith that the British justice system would see through this charade, and I'm pleased to have been proven right.'

He flashed a smile at the camera and tried to move past the crowd. Tabitha shouted as he strode by, 'What will you do now?'

James turned and a hush seemed to fall as the furry sound booms, cameras and hand-held Dictaphones loomed over him. 'You'll have to wait and see.'

With that, he strode down the steps and into a waiting car.

Breathing slowly in the back seat, he knew what he really had to do. Get even with those bitches from *Girl Talk* and get rid of them once and for all. His BlackBerry bleeped. James read the brief message from the new owner of Channel 6, Vladimir Vladislav. **Call me.** His lips twitched in a thin smile. Interesting.

Twelve

Karen felt awful. It was a week since James Almond had won his privacy case and she still wasn't sleeping properly. There were too many thoughts running riot in her head. She had no work, her weight was going up, and James Almond was far from ruined. In fact, he seemed to be back on the party pages of the gossip magazines, which was a very bad sign indeed.

She had been lying awake for hours, doing her best to keep still and not disturb Dave, who had to be up at five for an airport pick-up. Lara Durham, a showbiz reporter for one of the breakfast channels, was flying in from LA. Karen had felt a queasy sensation in her tummy when Dave said he would be ferrying the glamorous blonde around. Lara was an unashamed flirt both on and off camera, a woman who batted her eyelashes at any man she thought she might have the teeniest chance of nabbing – which was pretty much all of them. She had a fearsome reputation. Karen had seen her in action a couple of years earlier at a Channel 6 Christmas party before she landed the Hollywood gig, had watched her back the best-looking man into a corner and hold him captive until his wife saw what was happening and came to the rescue. The memory made Karen shudder.

Lara had white-blonde Marilyn Monroe hair and a penchant for clothing that showed off her amazing body. Rumour had it she had gone under the knife in LA and had a boob job. Not that she needed to. She already had magnificent breasts, which she showed off at every opportunity.

Karen lay flat on her back contemplating her own body. Her boobs were every bit as impressive as Lara Durham's. It was the rest of her that had gone to seed. She placed a hand on her stomach. Actually, it didn't feel too bad. She breathed in. It was really quite flat. For a fleeting moment she allowed herself to feel positive, until it dawned on her that everyone's stomach feels flat when they're lying down. It was a different story when she was upright, no doubt about that.

A vision of Lara Durham swanning around London with Dave at her beck and call, sun-kissed and California-tanned, and making everyone else look dull and pasty, induced a sense of panic in Karen. She gripped the side of the mattress and glanced at Dave, who had his back to her and seemed to be in a deep and peaceful sleep. There was no point in getting all worked up. She trusted him. Anyway, Lara Durham would never be interested in a humble driver. Would she? Karen tried to picture what Lara might make of Dave when she caught sight of him waiting for her in the arrivals hall. He was good-looking, with dark-blond hair and grey eyes that crinkled whenever he let loose that sexy smile. He was big and capable, with firm muscles honed by years of kick-boxing. It wouldn't take her long to work out that he was bright and funny and good company. Karen, distracted by her messy marriage break-up, had been a bit slow to register his considerable charms. A predator like Lara Durham would be on to him in seconds.

Karen turned on to her side and tried to make the thoughts go away. Another couple of hours and Dave would be getting up. She closed her eyes but it was no good. Now Lara Durham was inside her head, pouting, giving her a pitying smile, jockeying for position with James Almond to be her worst nightmare.

Later that morning, Karen stepped through the sliding doors of the private hospital. Facing her was a reception desk with a curved front covered in studded cream leather. Behind the desk a fresh-faced young woman in a crisp white shirt looked up and gave her a broad smile. Horribly conscious of the bags under her eyes after her sleepless night, Karen slid on her shades and strode across the shiny marble floor towards her. The receptionist handed her a pass. 'It's lovely to see you,' she said, keeping her voice low. 'Would you like me to get someone to take you up?'

'No, I'm fine, thanks. I know the way.'

She crossed to the lift. To her left was a mirrored wall. Everywhere she went these days she was faced with her own unpalatable reflection. She took a deep breath and stole a glance at herself. She looked fine. Dark glasses definitely helped, and it had been a smart move to wear black. It always lopped off a few pounds. A simple fitted shift dress, opaque tights and patent slingbacks created a flattering silhouette. So she had gained a bit of weight – so what? She smoothed the fabric of her dress as the lift doors opened and gave thanks for her beloved Spanx pants, which, unseen, were hard at work.

Thirteen

Julia picked up her compact from the bedside table and studied her face. Not up to her usual exacting standards, but not bad either, considering her beauty regime had gone to rack and ruin these last few months. That's what being in a coma did for you. Discovering she had not had so much as a Botox jab since careering into the side of the Strand underpass and writing off her Porsche had practically given her a seizure. Just wait until she got her hands on Joel Reynolds. Really, what was the point of having the best cosmetic surgeon in London on speed-dial if he couldn't be relied on to keep vital treatments going at moments of extreme stress? The man had zero initiative.

She shuddered at the thought of being exposed, utterly helpless, for months on end without a scrap of make-up. Heaven only knows how many people had seen her like that. Thank God she had woken up before things got completely out of hand. In the space of a few hours she had arranged for that fantastic girl, Louisa, from her favourite salon in Knightsbridge to come in and give her a facial, some strategic waxing and an eyebrow shape and to sort out her nails, which were tatty beyond belief. Luckily, Louisa had thought to bring in emergency supplies of beauty products and an enormous holdall stuffed full of make-up. The bag, a Mulberry Piccadilly in a fabulous leopard print, was a gift from the salon.

As for her so-called friends . . . Julia was a bit hazy on how things stood with the *Girl Talk* girls. It wasn't as if they'd been on good terms before her accident – far from it. She and Lesley had been at each other's throats. Yet there was a lovely card from them, and the nurses said the four of them had sent flowers every week without fail. They had been in to see her too. Strange. As far as she could remember, there was no love lost between her and Cheryl. As for Faye, well, she was a waste of space. As she struggled to think back, something odd happened. Her brow, under normal circumstances a line-free zone courtesy of Botox, seemed to move. She whipped out the compact again. Good God, she was frowning! The sooner Joel could sort her out the better. Unfortunately, her consultant had said absolutely not when she had asked about having some minor cosmetic procedures done prior to her discharge, which was ridiculous.

She thought back to the night she had almost killed herself, and a memory flooded into her mind of landing on Karen's doorstep in a drunken frenzy and shoving a gun in her face. Or was it her back? Both, she seemed to remember. Julia wondered if there were going to be any repercussions. Perhaps Karen had reported her. She closed her eyes. That could be awkward. Well, if it came to it, she would deny everything. At least she'd had the good sense to stop on Waterloo Bridge and chuck the gun into the Thames before putting her foot down and hurtling into the underpass. She had almost died. The truth was she had wanted to. And maybe it would have been better if she had.

There was a tap at the door. Julia frowned again and tugged at her hair, arranging it over her brow in an attempt to disguise the lines. She desperately needed a cut and some highlights. Her hair was an absolute mess – limp and much too long, with horrendous roots. Thankfully, Louisa had washed and styled it and at least made it presentable until she could get to a salon. There was another gentle tap at the door. She sat up straight. She wasn't expecting any visitors.

'Who is it?'

'Me – Karen.'

Julia felt a stab of panic. The fewer people who saw her in such a state the better. Then again, Karen had no doubt seen her bare-faced while she was out of things anyway. She considered putting on the massive pair of Gucci shades sitting on her bedside table but decided not to bother.

'It's OK, you can come in.'

The door eased open and Karen's face appeared. She gave Julia a wary smile.

'You're awake. It's so good to see you. I mean, it's not like I haven't seen you – I've been coming in every week, reading *heat* to you from cover to cover, keeping you up on the latest gossip—' She paused. Julia was giving her an odd look. 'I mean, it's fantastic to have you back in the land of the living and looking so amazing. I've been so worried – we all have.' Julia's face, devoid of expression-numbing jabs, was a vast improvement on the old, frozen version, as far as Karen could tell. Not that she would have dared say so.

'Just come in, will you – you're causing a draught,' Julia said.

Karen hesitated. She had thought there would be an emotional scene once Julia came round. From time to time she had pictured the two of them hugging, maybe shedding a few tears. Now she wasn't so sure. She took a tentative step towards the bed.

Julia looked her up and down. 'My God, what happened to you? I thought you'd gone all skinny. Or did I dream that?'

Karen flushed. Before she could answer, Julia said, 'You're not pregnant, are you?'

Karen went a deeper shade of pink and fiddled with her hair, twisting a shoulder-length ebony strand around her finger. Same old Julia. Even a near-death experience hadn't mellowed her. 'I've put a bit of weight on, you know, since the show came off and, well, I've been at a bit of a loose end . . .' Her voice trailed off.

Julia leaned forward. 'I could have told you that would happen. Diets are a total waste of time. You just end up piling it all back on the second you start eating again. I mean, look at that pop star – whatsername?' Karen shook her head. Julia gazed at the ceiling for a moment. 'No, can't for the life of me remember. My memory's shot to pieces. Must be all that time in a coma.' She gave Karen a sly look. 'In all honesty, I can't remember much about, well, you know, the night of the accident. I was hoping you might be able to fill me in.'

Karen dragged an armchair over to the side of the bed. The vibrant turquoise upholstery precisely matched Julia's eyes. Whether that was a coincidence or part of the five-star service private hospitals offered their celebrity patients it was impossible to say. Karen dropped into the chair, ending up a lot lower than she had imagined. She shifted in the seat, uncomfortable, as Julia gazed down at her, imperious.

'One thing I do remember,' Julia said, 'is confiding in you. I told you something I've kept quiet about all my life – my big secret.' She looked away and pulled at the edge of the bedspread, folding it, making sure it was nice and straight.

Karen stayed silent. She could still recall the anguish in

Julia's voice when she had admitted to having had a sex change operation.

'That night,' Julia said, 'I was sloshed, ranting – it was all about to come out in the papers. Or so I thought. I was sure that was it, my life was over.' She managed a brittle smile. 'That was the plan, actually. Jump in the car, drive like a maniac and end it all.'

Karen was shocked. 'Julia – don't talk like that.'

'It's not like me to mess up when I put my mind to something, but – ' She paused. 'Just goes to show. By rights, we shouldn't be having this conversation now, not if I'd hit that wall a bit faster and at more of an angle.'

'Julia, please—'

She shrugged. 'I know I said some terrible things, blamed you for leaking the story to the *Sunday*. Of course they never printed it, thanks to the heroic efforts of my wonderful publicist, Tom Steiner. I've really no idea what I'd do without him. He's quite the miracle worker, you know.' Karen opened her mouth to say something but Julia shook her head, silencing her. 'Anyway, all that business . . . I know it was nothing to do with you. That was me being paranoid and getting the wrong end of the stick. At least I can trust you to keep it to yourself.'

Karen gave her a weak smile.

Julia said, 'I *can* trust you, can't I?'

'Yes. Of course. I mean, I'd never tell a soul.'

Julia nodded, relieved.

'Just the other girls, that's all.'

Julia blinked. 'You've *blabbed*? To the *others*?'

'I had to. What was I meant to do? You'd threatened to kill me, then you went tearing off in the car. I was frantic. I didn't know what to do. Anyway, none of them would ever say anything.'

Julia sank her head into her hands. 'I don't believe this.'

'Seriously, we care about you. Me, the girls – we're on your side.' Karen leaned forward and put a hand on Julia's wrist. 'Look, I don't know how much you know about what's been going on while you've been out of it, but right now, if any of us want a career in TV we've got to stick together. Falling out among ourselves won't get us anywhere.'

Julia glanced at the TV in the corner of the room where *Good Morning Britain* was on. Helen England's replacement, an ex-model who'd done a couple of reality shows and was totally out of her depth coping with two hours of live telly every day, perched on the sofa hanging on to her cue cards as if her life depended on them. Julia nudged the volume up as the girl stumbled over a link into an item on families whose homes were about to be repossessed.

'Look at her,' Julia said in disgust. 'I'd be surprised if she can *spell* repossession, let alone explain what it means.'

Neither of them spoke for a minute.

'I don't know if I even want a career in television any more,' Julia said. She dipped the volume as Helen England's replacement appeared in close-up, eyes wide and full of fear. 'They could have picked anyone they wanted for that show, and they've gone for a complete airhead. It makes me wonder – what's the point?'

'You've heard about James winning his privacy case,' Karen said, her voice a whisper.

Julia gazed at the screen. 'Tom Steiner was in here last night. He reckons James is taking over again at Channel 6.'

'Oh God, it must be true then,' Karen said, her face grim. Tom Steiner was an impeccable source.

Julia lowered her head back on to her pillow. She yawned. 'Sorry, I'm done in.'

Karen scrambled to her feet. 'I didn't mean to wear you out. Shall I get a nurse?'

Julia closed her eyes. 'No, I'm feeling a bit wiped out. I need a little nap, that's all.'

'OK. Well, take it easy.' Julia's eyes opened a fraction. 'You know you really do look amazing, Julia. For someone who was at death's door for so long, you look fantastic. Absolutely radiant.'

Julia's glowing complexion was courtesy of a new break-through serum Louisa had brought in the day before. Beauty sleep in a bottle, she had called it. It was hardly a substitute for the trusty Botox, but it would do for now, until Joel could get to work on her.

'You know me,' she said. 'I'd rather die than let myself go.' She gave Karen an appraising look. 'About your weight problem – no one has to be fat these days, you know. There are things you can do. Like a gastric band. Or what about lipo? You know, get it all sucked out.' She made a loud slurping sound. Karen winced. Julia's eyelids fluttered and closed again. 'Just remember, I know a good surgeon if you need one, darling.'

Fourteen

Five months to the day after emerging victorious from his privacy hearing, James Almond was lounging on the sofa in his old office with one foot up on the coffee table, hands behind his head, watching the comings and goings of the porters as they removed Paula Grayson's belongings and installed his own. Promoted to Acting Controller of Entertainment in James's absence, she had not exactly been pleased when she had arrived for work this morning and found him with his feet under what had been her desk for the last few months. Nevertheless, as she took in the scene, Paula, in her sensible flat loafers and shapeless raincoat, had given little away. James had leered at her. Who wore calf-length skirts any more, he wondered? Her hair, a raggedy bob that was more grey than blonde, looked as if it hadn't had a comb through it for days. Really, she was hardly a shining example of an executive woman.

It was entirely thanks to James that she had been given no warning that he was coming back. The new owner, Vladimir Vladislav, prided himself on being a straight-talker, although his heavy Russian accent tended to get in the way of effective communication. He had wanted to get Paula in and explain what was going on. James, however, had argued that since Paula was a colleague he personally had nothing but respect and admiration for, he should be the one to handle things. It was a British thing, he said, a courtesy, and the least he could do under the circumstances. Vladislav, who had yet to get the full measure of his wily new appointment, was completely taken in.

James shook his head. After everything, he could still run rings round the lot of them. Deep down, he was hoping Paula might cause a scene, which would give him a chance to flex his muscle and make it clear he was not willing to stand for nonsense from anyone, no matter how senior. Word of a top-level sacking on his first morning would have gone round the building in no time at all and delivered precisely the right message. Irritatingly, despite his best efforts to goad her, she had reacted with impressive dignity.

'I'll arrange for the porters to pack up my things and have them moved,' she had said, unruffled, giving James a look of utter contempt.

'Thanks for holding the fort. Good to know there was a steady pair of hands on the tiller while I was, ah, otherwise engaged.'

Paula nodded. 'Indeed.' She had gazed round the room, sniffing the air and turning up her nose before moving away in a rather obvious manner, which made him wonder if he had stepped in something unpleasant on his way into the building. He hadn't, of course. It was just Paula Grayson's way of leaving him in no doubt as to what she thought of him. She might as well have gone the whole hog and called him a shit. Pity she hadn't, really, as that would have given him the excuse he wanted to go on the attack.

In a corner of the Channel 6 canteen, Paula Grayson sipped a cappuccino. She must have been mad not to have seen that little set-to coming. Hadn't James Almond bragged to Tabitha Tate about picking up the reins at the station again? So why on earth had she not taken him more seriously? She knew James was dangerous, a master manipulator, capable of pretty much anything. In fact, after the trial, she had prepared herself for a call from Vladimir Vladislav requesting an urgent meeting at which he would break the news that James was being re-instated. She went to work every morning grim-faced, ready to do battle. Days went by and she heard nothing. She chaired a commissioning meeting. Weeks went by. A hand-written note arrived from Vladislav congratulating her on the success of the *Best Ever Sex* show, the new vehicle for Lesley Gold. She began to relax. Meanwhile, the building continued to hum with specu-lation that her old boss was coming back, which was galling and unsettling, to say the least. Her stock reply to anyone who asked was an unequivocal *no*. James Almond was history. And now, just when she was sure she had seen the back of him, here he was. Bold as brass.

She typed an email into her BlackBerry and sent it to every-one she thought should know what was going on. The last thing she wanted was for anyone else to have the nasty surprise she had just had. Within seconds her mailbox was winking at her as emails expressing a mixture of shock, horror and fear streamed in.

The door to the canteen swung open and Bella appeared, ferreting about in her bag. She joined the queue at the counter, checked her BlackBerry and stood stock-still for a moment, her face troubled. Then she looked up and caught sight of Paula. She hurried over and took the seat facing her.

'Tell me it's not true.'

'He's up there right now. Settling in,' Paula said.

The colour drained from Bella's face. She took off her scarf, shoved it into her bag and ran a hand through her blonde curls. Bella had the kind of hair that seemed to require no maintenance. Although she was always complaining she couldn't do a thing with it, most women would have given anything for such an easy-care bouncy bob.

'What happened – how did you find out?'

Paula gave a slight shrug. 'I ran into him sitting at my desk.' She paused. '*His* desk now.'

'Oh God, that's awful. You're sure it's official? Maybe he smarmed his way into the building – you know what he's like. Perhaps it's all a mistake and they'll send him packing once word gets round.' Her face had a stricken look. 'Maybe we should call security.'

Paula picked up the empty sugar wrapper on the table and folded it into a tiny square. 'No point. You can't even get into my office without a keycard, so what does that tell you?'

'He broke in?' Bella sounded hopeful.

'It's all above board, unfortunately.' Paula stared into space for a moment. 'Hideous though it is, we're just going to have to get used to the idea.'

'The man's a perv!'

'That's none of our business, according to the legal system.'

Bella folded her arms. Her shoulders sagged. 'What will you do?'

'Well, I'm not going anywhere, if that's what he's hoping. We've got a hit show on our hands.'

'For how long, though? You know what he's like.'

They sat in silence for a moment. Paula had been the editor on *Girl Talk*, which James had managed to see off when it was at the height of its popularity.

The door swung open and Lesley stepped into the canteen. She was wearing a clingy black top – a cross between a jumper and a dress – that skimmed her shapely bum, opaque tights, and a pair of ludicrously high, clumpy tan slingbacks. Slung over her shoulder was an enormous red Chanel bag. Her blonde hair was backcombed into a beehive and her face was dwarfed by a pair of enormous diamanté-encrusted shades. Lesley teetered towards them, her face pale, her glossy red lips set in an anxious line.

'Tell me it's not true,' she said, echoing Bella.

Paula gave her a resigned look.

Lesley flopped into the seat beside her and covered her face with her hands. 'I feel sick,' she said, her voice a whisper.

Paula patted her arm. 'There, there. Bella – be a dear and get Lesley a coffee, would you? Get them to put a couple of extra shots in it.'

'Oh God,' Bella said. 'I need to tell Karen.'

'I've already emailed her.' Paula checked her mailbox. 'She hasn't replied. Probably in shock.'

Bella rallied. 'We can't let him waltz back in as if nothing's happened. It's – ' she struggled to find the words – 'plain *wrong*. We all know what he's like, how he snoops on his staff and compiles secret files. On top of that he's a pervert, for heaven's sake, and a sex pest.' She tried not to think of James in his nappy nuzzling Helen England in her sleazy nurse's outfit. 'Can't we complain to HR or something – say we don't feel safe? What if we compile a dossier on him? Maybe you could have a word with the new owner?'

'I don't see what good it would do. For reasons I cannot imagine, James Almond is obviously here with the blessing of the Board. I suspect he was chosen by our Russian friend, for

56

reasons only he knows. Our best bet is to keep our heads down and do our jobs.' She gave Bella a cryptic smile. 'You never know, he may not be around for very long.'

'I'm not so sure. He's like Captain Scarlet – indestructible.'

'He's also a marked man; a man with numerous enemies. Personally, I don't believe you can trample all over people the way he has and emerge unscathed. Not in the long term. Granted, he's slippery, but once the knives are out he may find it's all a bit trickier than he thinks.' She raised her hand and made a slashing motion. Bella shrank into her seat. 'Someone's bound to take him down. You mark my words.'

Fifteen

Once Julia was discharged from hospital, she vanished into thin air. No one seemed to know where she was until Karen received a cryptic email. **I need to see you. ASAP**. It turned out she had fled to a tucked-away hidey-hole far from prying eyes where she intended to convalesce. It was her refuge, she explained; the one place she could relax without fear of the paparazzi sniffing her out.

Karen was intrigued. She decided to give Julia a call. Expecting her voicemail, she was ready to leave a message questioning the wisdom of being cut off from civilization after a lengthy stint in intensive care, but, for once, Julia picked up.

'I'm not sure I like the idea of you living in the middle of nowhere all by yourself,' Karen said. 'What if something happens?'

'Something already did. I had a near-death experience, in case you've forgotten, so I think I can cope with a bit of solitude, don't you?'

'But this place you're at . . .'

'The Nook. I've had it for years. I bought it with my payoff from *Rise and Shine*, and, in all honesty, it's the only place I really feel at home. I've been coming here for years. It's where I spend the summer.'

'I thought you spent the summer at a bikini boot camp in Brazil.'

'I do, sort of. I go for a week. Then I come home, to Essex.'

Karen was astonished. Julia was full of surprises. 'How far is the nearest hospital – just in case?'

'Oh please, stop fussing. Don't you want to come – is that it?'

'No!'

'Fine, I'll send you directions, then. And Karen – this is my sanctuary. No one knows about it. Not a living soul.' That wasn't quite true. 'I need to know you can keep it to yourself.' There was silence for a moment. 'Although heaven only knows why I think I can trust *you*. You weren't much good at keeping my other secret, were you?'

'That was different,' Karen said, stung. 'Of course I won't tell anyone where you are, if that's what you want.'

'Hmmm. Well, I suppose I'm prepared to give you another chance, but no blabbing – not even to that bloke of yours. If word gets out, the paparazzi will be down here like a shot and I'll have to sell up, so make sure there's no one tailing you.'

Karen rolled her eyes. For heaven's sake.

'Just so you know, if you let me down this time, I'll have to kill you.'

Karen gasped.

Julia chuckled. 'I'm kidding, darling – where's your sense of humour? Instructions to follow. Memorize and destroy them.' There was a slight pause. 'Eat them if you like.' Another chuckle.

By the time Karen hung up she wasn't sure she wanted to visit after all. Julia could be such a cow, even when she was supposed to be recuperating. Still, she had been very poorly and now she was stuck on her own, so no wonder she was being a bit – Karen searched for an appropriate word – spiky? No. That wasn't quite right. Supremely bitchy? Yes. That was more like it. Still, it was probably a good sign. Clearly, she was on the mend.

Karen checked her rear-view mirror. A black Mercedes SUV with tinted windows that had been on her bumper for a long while aroused her suspicions. She had read somewhere about black cars being universally popular when it came to discreet surveillance. And the paparazzi loved a Sports Utility Vehicle. She braked, swung into a bus stop and put her hazards on. The driver of the Mercedes tooted and accelerated past. An irate woman at the wheel gave Karen a filthy look and a toddler strapped into a child seat in the back waved a feeding cup at her. Karen cursed. Julia was making her paranoid.

The driver of a double-decker, not quite able to squeeze into the bus stop, leaned on the horn. Karen gave an apologetic wave and eased back out into the traffic.

It seemed to take for ever to reach her destination. Talk about off the beaten track. She would never have found it without the screed of detailed instructions provided by Julia. Across the top in red, in big, bold type, were the words STRICTLY CONFIDENTIAL. At the foot of the page there was a vague threat about what would happen if Karen ever let slip that she knew about The Nook. It was off the map, Julia reminded her, and she wanted to keep it that way.

It wasn't easy driving and keeping an eye on Julia's complicated directions at the same time, and Karen went wrong more than once. It took her hours to get there. Even when she was practically on the doorstep she got a bit lost and sailed straight past the end of the lane that led to the cottage. Two miles on, at the edge of a village, sensing she had missed her turning, she pulled off the road next to a tumbledown farm building, consulted the directions again, and doubled back, swerving off the road at the last minute through a narrow gap in the hedge that had no signpost.

'For goodness' sake, Julia,' she said, exasperated, as she bumped along the rutted track, hoping she was going the right way. 'Could you find anywhere more remote?'

By the time she pulled up at a quaint little cottage, she was starving and dying for the loo. There was no house name visible, nothing to say it was actually The Nook. It had to be, though. According to Julia's directions, it was the right distance from the last crossroads.

Karen slipped her shoes back on, stepped out of the car and felt her stiletto heels sink into soft earth. She picked her way across uneven grass and up a path made from large stone slabs to the front door. There were trees all around and a neat front garden filled with tall flowers in vivid pinks and white. Hollyhocks, Karen thought. Or foxgloves, perhaps. She wasn't much good at plants. She stared up at the brickwork, which was painted yellow, and at the lavish purple climber clinging to the front wall and hanging over the porch. That was definitely wisteria.

The front door was open an inch or so and a faint smell of smoke drifted into the air from the back of the house. Karen knocked and stepped into a narrow, low-ceilinged hall. Her heels clicked against the stone floor.

'Only me,' she called.

The hall was chilly and she shivered.

'In here.' Julia's voice, sharp and impatient, rang out from the end of the corridor.

Julia was sitting in an armchair in the sitting room with her back to the window. The blinds were partially drawn, shutting out most of the daylight. She was wearing a long dress with a bold azure print and a slashed neckline. There was a heavy metal chain at her throat, and when she raised her hand to fluff up the spikes in her cropped blonde hair, several bangles chimed on her wrists. She looked every inch her old self. Well, almost every inch. Karen's gaze went straight to an enormous pair of fluffy white slippers she was wearing. Never in a million years would she have thought Julia was the type to wear slippers, not even in the privacy of her own home when there was no one else around. The coma really must have taken it out of her. Perhaps, Karen mused, it had given her a softer, more homely edge.

'For fuck's sake, stop staring at my feet,' Julia said. 'Haven't you ever seen a pair of slippers before?'

'Of course . . . I mean, I wasn't staring . . . not at all . . . I just . . .' She found herself stuttering under Julia's icy stare. 'They look very . . . comfy.'

'I didn't ask you here to make fun of me, you know. I've been in a frigging coma for months, at death's door, and all you can do – my so-called *friend* – is turn up and *laugh* at me.'

'No, Julia, I promise—'

'Oh, go on, have your fun. I *am* convalescing, you know, so pardon me if I don't get out the Louboutins.' Her voice rose and at the same time took on an unfamiliar deep tone. 'My feet were crushed in the crash, pinned under the brake pedal, practically smashed to smithereens. Did you know that?' Karen opened her mouth to protest, but Julia ignored her. 'As it happens, I'll need surgery to put them right. Some awful operation with pins, and bones being broken and reset, and God knows what.' She gave Karen a furious look. 'But never mind about that – feel free to take the piss, why don't you.' She ran her fingers through her hair, arranging the front into a series of jagged spikes aimed at Karen like a row of deadly missiles.

The bracelets on her wrists rattled ominously.

Karen swallowed, not sure what to do. She had been on the receiving end of plenty of Julia's tirades in the past, but there was something odd about this one. In full flow her voice had become a bit, well, rough. Not like Julia at all. She decided to bring out a peace offering.

'I've brought you something,' she said, searching in her bag and producing a small parcel wrapped in tissue paper. 'It's that new serum everyone's going on about – the one there's a waiting list for at Harvey Nics. I read somewhere that Kylie loves it.' She gave Julia an uncertain smile. 'Not that you need it. I mean, you look great.'

Julia rubbed her brow. 'Be a darling and get me some water, would you?' Her voice was back to being soft and silky. 'And a couple of painkillers – you'll find some in a white box next to the sink in the kitchen.' She nodded in the direction of an open door. 'I'm getting dreadful headaches and they're making me a bit, well, *off*, I suppose.'

That was an understatement. It took almost nothing these days to spark a furious outburst which, according to her consultant, was only to be expected after lying unconscious for months. There were, he had warned, not quite looking at her, unusual factors in her case that made things complicated. He didn't need to spell it out since it was obvious he was talking about the fact that she had been through a sex change.

Karen fetched the tablets. 'How many of these are you taking?' she said, concerned.

'Not enough.'

Karen sat down and gazed around the room. Set into bare brickwork on the wall facing her was an open fireplace. On one side of the stone hearth was a wicker basket filled with logs. Behind her was a bookcase crammed with rows of leather-bound volumes, their titles etched in gold on the spines. At the far end of the room was a china cabinet filled with coloured glassware and odd-shaped pottery in bold, splashy colours. The sofa she was sitting on was upholstered in the same sludgy beige fabric as Julia's chair, but in terms of style the two didn't quite match.

'How are you managing, stuck out here all by yourself, Julia? Wouldn't you be better off in London where at least people can look in on you every day?'

'I don't want to be in London,' Julia said. 'I don't want anyone seeing me like this.' She lowered her eyes. 'Once I'm better, properly on my feet again, I'll move back to town.'

'But you're miles away from everything, in the middle of nowhere. Don't you get lonely?' Outside, a crow let out a blood-curdling screech. Karen shivered again. The place was gloomy – creepy even. 'What if there's an emergency? You can't even drive.'

Julia gave her a withering look. The very notion of driving was still a sore subject. 'I *like* being in the middle of nowhere, as it happens. And anyway, I'm not completely abandoned. There's someone who comes in. A chap. Lives in the village. Bit of a drop-out, really, lives a simple life. Doesn't even have a television. He has no idea who I am. Perfect, really. '

Scott Walker was something of a loner. He had a brown and

white terrier called Jack Russell and a few Rhode Island Red hens for company. When Julia was away he kept an eye on The Nook. Not once had he overstepped the mark by trying to make friends or ask her anything about what she did, which made a refreshing change. It wasn't as if he was a cold fish, however, and when he saw she was convalescing, he had offered to bring in groceries and do a bit of cooking. To her surprise, she actually quite liked having him around. For one thing, he was quiet and unobtrusive. For another, he baked the most fantastic bread. As for his moussaka . . . well, it was to die for. The fact that he bore an uncanny resemblance to a singer that Julia once had a bit of a crush on was a bonus. And he was cheap. He seemed to have no idea what to charge for domestic help and seemed happy to accept the odd fiver. She sighed and gazed into space, a soppy smile on her face. 'So you see,' she said, 'there's absolutely nothing to worry about.'

Karen stared. All of a sudden Julia didn't look quite right. 'Have you had any thoughts about work? I mean, once you're better.'

Julia turned to her. 'I was thinking some kind of dramatic comeback.' Her eyes narrowed. 'While I'm stuck here with time on my hands, I'll be thinking of ways to get even with James Almond.'

'Seriously, Julia, forget it. You don't know what you're up against. He walked all over us in court.'

'Yes, well, I'd like to have seen that oily barrister of his take *me* on.'

Karen looked away. 'Really, we thought we had him and look what happened – he's king of the castle again and we're the court jesters.'

'I'm not quite ready for jingle hats, Karen. Look at me –

that man has put me in *What Ever Happened to Baby Jane*,'
Julia snarled.

Karen looked around her. The dreadful cottage could well
be the setting for a creepy film. She shivered. 'You've not got
someone locked away upstairs, have you?'

Julia gave her a poisonous look. 'I think you're getting the
story back to front,' she said. 'Blanche was the one . . . oh,
never mind.' Karen winced. 'Anyway, while I'm out of it I want
you to be my eyes and ears. So keep me in the loop. I want to
know exactly what he's up to, then once I'm up and about I'll
make it my mission to take him out.' Her arms flew up and
she sliced the air in a series of karate chops, making her bangles rattle. Karen inched further along the sofa.

'Just you wait,' she said, giving Karen an evil smile. 'He
won't know what's hit him.'

Karen dumped her bag on the passenger seat and started the
engine. Before she set off she craned her head to check her lippy
in the rear-view mirror and noticed a tall, good-looking guy
coming up the lane. He was wearing a fraying Guernsey sweater
and the kind of ripped jeans that suggested hard graft rather
than fashion statement. A small brown and white dog trotted
at his heels. Karen watched them go up the path to The Nook.
Well, well – if that was the local dropout popping in to see
how Julia was doing, she had well and truly fallen on her feet.
Karen cringed. So to speak. He was *hot*. She smiled. Lucky old
Julia.

Sixteen

'So, how was your day?' Dave asked Karen a few nights later, as he chopped up a yellow pepper.

Karen opened the fridge and took out a bottle of Sauvignon Blanc. 'I did a workout.' It was only a small lie.

Dave looked up. A lock of blond hair obscured one eye. He gave her a hopeful smile. 'You went to the gym?'

She undid the top on the wine and poured a large glass. 'Not the gym, exactly.' She poured half a glass for him and put it on the counter where he could reach it. He was in the throes of slicing up a red cabbage that was making quite a mess of the chopping board. Beside it, a mound of vegetables, brightly coloured, all sliced and diced, were ready to go into the healthy stir-fry he was making. She eyed them suspiciously. Given the choice, she would never eat courgettes.

'One of those fitness DVDs,' she said. She had chosen Tracy Anderson's *Mat Workout* because it was supposed to be easy to follow, promised amazing results, and, as far as she could tell, there was nothing too strenuous involved; no leaping about anyway. Also, hadn't Tracy Anderson been Madonna's personal trainer? That alone was good enough for Karen. Encouraged, she had pulled on a pair of baggy sweatpants and a vest, dug out her trainers and unfurled a yoga mat that hadn't seen the light of day for years. Then she had cleared a space in the living room and pressed the play button. It was more of a struggle to keep up than she had expected. Perhaps it was too ambitious to do the whole thing start to finish straightaway. Slightly out of breath, she had got comfy on the floor and watched Tracy complete the workout. Then she'd made a peanut butter sandwich, a reward for having taken the first step towards a proper exercise regime. Doing the first bit must have burned off a few calories, surely.

Dave tossed strips of chicken into the wok. 'So how was it, the workout – any good?'

Karen sipped at her wine as he stood with his back to her and stirred the contents of the pan. 'It was murder,' she said. 'I'm horribly unfit.'

He grinned at her. 'Yeah, well, bound to be hard the first time. You've just got to hang on in there.'

She pulled a face, taking in his toned, muscular arms, feeling bleak. 'I suppose.'

Dave nodded. He opened a cupboard and took out a couple of bowls. She could smell garlic and ginger. She wished they could have a quiet night in for once. 'Do you really have to work tonight?'

He turned the gas down and put a lid on the pan. 'All I'm doing is picking her up from the after-show party and dropping her at her hotel. I'll come straight home.'

Lara Durham was attending some premiere or other. Since the organizers had arranged a stretch limo to get her there, Karen didn't see why they couldn't take her home at the end of the night, but no, she was intent on dragging Dave out at a ridiculous hour. Just because she could. Who did she think she was?

'Can't she get a cab?'

'I'm being paid, remember.'

'What kind of a person makes someone come out in the middle of the night to drive them home from a party?'

'A famous one.'

'She's not even a proper celeb, just some showbiz reporter.'

'Doesn't bother me, as long as I get my money.' What he didn't say was that he was up for all the work he could get at the minute since he was the only one earning.

Karen was fed up of seeing pictures of Lara Durham, all bronzed legs and blonde hair, outside the best restaurants and clubs in the capital. The paparazzi certainly seemed to love her, no doubt about that. 'I bet you can't wait for her to go back to LA,' she said, sounding slightly more churlish than she intended.

'She might not go back. Depends on work.'

Karen felt a prickle of jealousy. 'She's not exactly bright.'

Dave shrugged. 'Give her a break.' He gave the pan a shake. He was happy for Lara to stay as long as she wanted. At least he was busy. Some of the guys he knew weren't doing much at all. 'She's OK. Once you get to know her.'

Karen bristled. What was that supposed to mean? Just how well *had* he got to know her?

She decided to change the subject. 'I'm meeting that agent first thing tomorrow. Suki Floyd. Cheryl went to see her and now she's asked me to go in. Faye as well.'

It all sounded a bit odd to Karen, who wasn't entirely sure she wanted to be looked after by the infamous Suki Floyd. There was something a bit disconcerting about her. She didn't exactly represent stars at the top of their game. Quite the opposite. She was known for breathing life back into the celebs no one else wanted to go near. Basically, if you were out in the cold, there was only one person to turn to and that was Suki.

Karen didn't much like the thought that she was in some kind of celebrity wasteland. If she was, it was entirely down to James Almond. But according to Cheryl, Suki was a miracle-worker, who was rumoured to have pulled off an amazing deal for O.J. Simpson. Karen couldn't decide if that was a good thing or a reason to steer well clear. If there was a chance of some work – and Cheryl seemed to think there was – she might as well see the woman. These were hard times and she needed to start earning again.

Dave began to dish up steaming portions of chicken and veg. He put a bowl in front of her. Karen's face fell. Hardly enough to feed a sparrow.

'Don't wait up for me if you've got an early start,' he said. 'I've no clue when I'll be in.'

She studied his face. 'I thought you were just dropping her off.'

'I am. I might end up hanging about, though.' He held her gaze, his grey eyes steely. Pride stopped him from saying that if there was a chance to earn a few more quid he'd take it. 'You know how it is.'

She did. That was the problem.

Seventeen

Tabitha cradled the phone against the side of her head as she filled the kettle. 'Three nights on the trot this week I've had the top story,' she said. She rinsed out the teapot and searched in the cupboard for a box of loose green tea.

'Your father and I are very proud of you, darling,' her mother said.

'The news editor's practically falling over himself to be nice to me.'

'That rough chap from Birmingham?'

'No more boring showbiz stuff for me – I'm his star reporter now.' She pinned a card for a cab firm on to the cork board on the kitchen wall and dropped a pizza delivery leaflet into the recycling box. 'I'm even getting a pay rise.'

'I should think so. You're a real asset to the team.' Her mother adjusted a cushion on the chair in the drawing room of her Cotswold house and sat down. 'I must say, it's nice to have someone on the news with proper diction for a change.'

Tabitha poured boiling water on to the tea leaves and left them to brew. 'Seriously, Mummy, he's so impressed. I really think he thought I'd never hack it, that I'd fall flat on my face. Not everyone can handle live TV, you know. Some people get in a right old stew.'

'In that case, he doesn't know you very well. You've always been good under pressure.'

Some of Tabitha's colleagues felt physically sick before they had to deliver a live piece to camera. She couldn't for the life of her understand why when it was such a blast. She loved the adrenalin that raced through her body, the director's voice in her earpiece, the PA telling her she had thirty seconds left before handing back to the studio. Strangely, other reporters tended to panic and speed up at that point. Not Tabitha. She remained steady and unruffled. It was everyone else who got tense. Going back a few months, the first couple of times they had cut to her live outside the High Court she could hear Charlie, the news editor, in the background, turning the air blue as the seconds ticked away, not that Tabitha took any notice. Even then, as a novice, she had had absolute confidence in her own ability to time her report to perfection. How hard could it be? When she heard the PA in her ear saying, 'Five seconds, four, three,' and Charlie cursing, sure she was about to mess up, she had almost smiled. Right on cue, she had wrapped. The handover was seamless. Quite why everyone made such a big deal out of it she had no idea. It was all about being cool-headed, thinking on your feet – things Tabitha had never struggled with. Predictably, the guys in the gallery loved her now because, unlike most of the Channel 6 reporters, they knew they could count on her. Literally.

'They're booking me on a load of courses at the BBC – law and boring stuff like that,' Tabitha said. She wasn't sure she needed any training since she was quick on the uptake and clearly had a knack for the job, but at the same time it might be useful, since she had no intention of spending the rest of her days at Channel 6. If she was to have a serious career as a news and investigative reporter, she would at some point be looking to move to the Beeb anyway.

'I do think you'd find more like-minded people at the BBC, darling,' said Tabitha's mother, who regarded Channel 6 as thoroughly downmarket and lived in hope that her daughter would one day land a job with the *Today* programme on Radio 4. 'I'd be amazed if anyone at Channel 6 went to Oxford.'

Tabitha had a think. 'James Almond was at Cambridge, apparently.'

Her mother shuddered. 'Dreadful man.'

Tabitha grinned. 'Don't be unkind, Mummy. It's thanks to him I got my big break.'

Eighteen

'I don't need to spell things out to you of all people, surely.'
James Almond stretched out his legs and placed the heel of one
shoe on the edge of the low glass table in front of him. 'I mean,
you've been around the block enough times to know the score.'

Lesley sat at the opposite end of the sofa in his office. It
was as if he had never been away. That hideous picture was
back on the wall, the one of the woman whose face seemed to
be made up of bits that didn't quite go together, and the desk
was devoid of paper. Not so much as a stray Post-it note. Bring
back Paula Grayson with her clutter and messy pinboard. Still,
one thing was different. Although James was as immaculate as
ever in a lightweight grey suit and open-neck white shirt, he
was also a fair bit bigger than he used to be. The weight had
been creeping on during his absence from Channel 6, and now
he was positively on the podgy side. Lesley gazed at the sur-
plus flesh threatening to spill over the waistband of his trousers.
In the bin next to the sofa was a crumpled bag from Patisserie
Valerie, and on the front of his shirt were telltale flakes of pastry
and a dusting of icing sugar. No question about it, he had let
himself go.

Lesley helped herself to coffee from the flask on the table.
James leaned forward and snatched up a couple of biscuits.

'I suppose what I'm trying to say is that there are limited

opportunities for broadcasters once they hit fifty,' he was saying. 'You're one of the lucky ones. For now, anyway.' He chomped on a custard cream, sweeping crumbs off his suit and into the bin.

'I'm nowhere near fifty,' Lesley said, indignant. 'And anyway, aren't you being a bit ageist? There are loads of good – ' she searched for the right word – '*experienced* people on telly.'

James clasped his hands behind his head and stared at the ceiling. He frowned.

'You see, age really is more than just a number in TV. You only have to look at the others.' He gave her a sly smile. 'It's not as if there's been a stampede to take them on since that unfortunate business with *Girl Talk*. I mean, obviously Julia Hill is indisposed – may never work again, poor thing – and the only work Faye could get is changing nappies.' He looked peculiar for a fleeting moment.

'Perhaps you should give her a call,' Lesley replied flippantly, then froze when she realized what she'd said.

James carried on, oblivious. 'Not a single offer for her baby diaries, you know. I did hear things are looking up for Cheryl West. She popped up on a training video for a friend of a friend who works in the brewery trade. We can look down our noses at corporate work, but I say there's nothing wrong with it – not when that's all there is, at any rate.' He tugged at the cuff of his shirt and Lesley caught a glint of gold. 'I had high hopes for Karen King at one stage, you know. The viewers loved her. She had that rare combination of sweetness and, well, integrity, I suppose, which is not a word you hear very often in TV these days. Not afraid to speak her mind. I rather liked that, even if she did have a tendency to cross the line into outright insub-ordination. Still, there's something to be said for a fighting spirit in these straitened times. It's rather fashionable to be feisty these days, don't you think?'

'Well, I—'

'I suspect we have Cheryl Cole to thank for that. Ah, well, dreadful shame about Karen King. In the right hands, with a decent producer and some professional styling, she could have gone far.'

Lesley could not contain herself. 'You're making it sound like she's gone into retirement!'

He gave her a meaningful look. 'We're in a fickle business, Lesley. Riding high one minute, mouldering in oblivion the next. Between you and me, if a high-profile show like *Girl Talk* that *seemed* to be doing well, pulling in the audience, couldn't be sustained, we all need to take note. Don't you agree?'

Lesley spluttered. 'It was doing fine until you axed it!'

James ignored her. 'All that in-fighting, no one speaking to anyone else, handbags at dawn, practically. Most unfortunate. Still, I do think it's asking for trouble, five women in the public eye working together.' He shuddered. 'All those rampaging hormones.' Lesley glared at him. 'It does seem to be a uniquely female thing, that horrible competitive edge. Almost as if it's programmed into the DNA. Don't you think?'

'No, actually, I don't.'

'Of course, an element of competition can be healthy, spur people on to great things.' He turned to look at her. 'Not when it's on a superficial level, however, and the only thing anyone's interested in is who's got the latest designer bag.'

Lesley placed a protective hand on her latest purchase, a large white Dolce & Gabbana Miss Sicily that took up slightly more of the sofa than she did. She reached inside for her lip gloss, an on-trend nude shade that was a perfect match for the dress she was wearing, and shovelled on a generous layer. James, once again staring at the ceiling, took no notice.

'I think we can all learn lessons from our national game, you know,' he said. 'Look at our top footballers. They know a thing or two about team spirit. I mean, you don't see the Premier League's finest getting all huffy about who has the best customized Bentley at the training ground, now, do you?'

Lesley thought that was, in fact, extremely likely.

'And why do you think that is?'

Lesley, aware that James was waiting for her to say something in order that he could interrupt, merely shrugged.

'Because they put the aspirations of the team above those of the individual, that's why.'

Lesley decided not to mention the recent and very public falling-out between two players over a reported extra-marital affair during which the best interests of the national team had seemingly come a very poor second. She made a mental note to look into the sexual peccadilloes of sporting idols on a future edition of *Best Ever Sex*. She had encountered her fair share of footballers, not to mention golfers, the occasional rugby player, and a tennis player who had made Wimbledon especially memorable one year, and had first-hand experience of the kind of unconventional pre-match preparation some favoured.

On the TV in the corner a pretty young redhead Lesley had not seen before was delivering the Channel 6 headlines. She then linked to a report from Tabitha Tate, something of a rising star these days, looking polished in a tailored lime-green jacket outside Downing Street. Someone must have told her to stop wearing that awful coat that looked like it had been made out of a sleeping bag. These days, almost everyone on screen, at

Channel 6 anyway, was considerably younger than Lesley – even the bloke who'd been reading the news for years and had just been bumped to the late-night headlines. Only recently had she discovered that he was a good five years her junior, which came as a bit of a shock, since she had always thought of him as old and boring and approaching retirement. A horrible thought dawned on her. Was that how other people saw her?

She studied her reflection in the glass wall that separated James's office from the rest of the executive corridor. No doubt about it, she was in fantastic shape, tall and lean with a narrow waist and pert boobs. Her legs were long and shapely with not so much as a hint of cellulite – good enough to go bare in bottom-skimming dresses. There weren't many women of her age – despite claiming to be a mere forty-three, she was in fact getting on for forty-nine – capable of carrying off such bold styles. She patted her hair, which hung in a loose plait over one shoulder, and tucked a stray tendril behind one ear. Maybe she should tone down the blonde, lose a few of the extensions and go for something a bit less brash. What if she couldn't get away with the big-hair sexpot look any more?

Much as she hated to think about it, for the first time in her life she was starting to feel her age – her *real* age – and it was quite a shock to the system. It wasn't as if she was losing her looks. At least she didn't think so. There were no awful saggy bits as far as she could tell, thanks to the extensive bed-time workouts with her gorgeous husband that kept her lean and supple. It was more a gnawing fear inside, a vague sense that time was suddenly against her. It had come out of nowhere and was keeping her awake at night. The fact that Dan wanted a baby was part of it. Lesley wanted a baby too – she loved the idea of being a mother – but rated her chances of getting pregnant as more than slim. She had been forced to face facts: she was way past her fertile best. It seemed cruel that having finally settled down after a lifetime of casual sex and one-night stands it might be too late to have a child. Not without the help of a fertility expert, anyway. If she and Dan were serious, they would probably have to go down the IVF route, and the very idea filled her with dread. Dan seemed to have little clue what it would involve. He was too excited to stop and think about the actual treatment and what it might be like having their hopes raised and dashed with no guarantee of a baby. Ever the optimist, he could barely contain himself.

'You never know, we might have twins – triplets even,' he'd said.

Lesley had given him a playful slap. 'Don't be greedy.' Secretly, she would be grateful to have just one healthy baby. Please God, just one. That would be perfect.

She was snapped out of her reverie by James getting to his feet. 'You see, Lesley, the truth of the matter is that there simply aren't the programmes available for – how shall I put it? – the more mature presenter. TV is really a game for young men.' He went over to his desk and peered at the screen of his laptop.

Lesley wasn't imagining things. He had definitely put the emphasis on *men*. She straightened her shoulders. It was obvious he was trying to intimidate her. Well, he had another think coming. Over the years she had eaten the likes of him for breakfast. On more occasions than she cared to remember, it so happened.

He sat down behind his desk and gave her a cool, appraising look. 'We all have a shelf life, don't you agree?' She opened her mouth to say something. What was he – some kind of mind reader? 'It's less critical in some sectors than others, of course. I mean, I don't suppose anyone would bat an eyelid at a barmaid, well past her sell-by, mutton dressed as lamb, if you get my drift, still pulling pints in a backstreet boozer. That's to be expected. However, we are in a very unforgiving industry, especially with the advent of high definition.' He glanced at the screen, where the fresh-faced newsreader was wrapping up the bulletin. Lesley winced. A shaft of sunlight spilled through the blinds. She was glad she had her back to the window.

James put an elbow on the desk and rested his chin in his hand. 'How old are you, Lesley?' Before she could protest he waved a hand at her. 'Rhetorical question. I know exactly how old you are, of course. I'm your boss. It's my job to know all about you.' He slid open a drawer and removed a file. 'You might be surprised at how much I do know, in fact.'

She stifled a yawn. 'Oh please – not *again*. No one *cares* any more. I'm a happily married woman.'

James gave her an amused look. He opened the file and flipped through the first couple of pages. 'Hmm,' he said, not looking up. 'That's right. So you are.' He scanned the page. 'Not only married – practically a newlywed. Ah, there's nothing like that first flush of love, is there – when you only have eyes for each other?'

Lesley shifted in her seat. Where on earth he was going with all this? It was lunchtime and she was dying for a drink. She gave him a bright smile. 'Will this take much longer? It's just that I've got another meeting.'

He closed the file. 'I'm so glad we've had this little chat. I think it's important that you and I understand each other. I like to think I'm a fair person; that when it comes to business I can put my personal feelings to one side.'

Lesley glanced at her watch. She wished he would get a move on. She could practically taste that first glass of chilled Sancerre.

'It's most fortunate that I have a fairly thick skin, otherwise I might have some difficulty keeping you on the payroll, bearing in mind you did your best to destroy me in court.' Lesley's smile slipped. 'Still, I'm not a vindictive man. As long as we understand each other and there's no doubt who's in charge, I see no reason why we shouldn't rub along. Make no mistake, Lesley, I'm not a loser. Never have been, never will be. I've taken on far tougher opponents than you and your menopausal cronies in my time. The fact that the others are all washed-up now should be a lesson to you. We're in a fickle business. It can all end – like that.' He clicked his fingers. 'Just because you've got a hit show doesn't mean you're safe.' He gave her a pointed look. 'You already know that, though, don't you? TV is all about having a face that fits.'

The more he droned on, the more thoroughly browbeaten Lesley felt. There was something about James Almond that sapped the fight out of even the most spirited opponent in no time at all. It was like having a general anaesthetic. Perhaps she should try counting backwards from ten and see how far she got. She sat on the edge of the sofa, hands in her lap, growing anxious. Perhaps, in that long-winded and convoluted way of his, he was getting round to sacking her. Her mouth felt dry.

James said, 'For reasons I could not begin to explain, I happen to like you. I even like your show. However, I am not in the least bit sentimental, and if there is even a *hint* of you ever crossing me again, you will be out of the door before you can say Kama Sutra.' He caressed the arm of his chair. 'Right – I think that covers it, don't you?'

Lesley nodded, grabbed her bag and got out of there before he thought of anything else.

Nineteen

By the time Karen went with Cheryl and Faye to see Suki Floyd, the meeting had already been rescheduled three times, which was hardly an encouraging sign. Keen to make a good impression, they had arrived early at the offices of Floyd Inc., which took up the ground floor of an imposing town house in Kensington. The door was answered by a young girl with jaunty plaits and black lipstick who showed them along a hall and into a poky room with views over a courtyard. She brought them coffee and told them to help themselves to magazines.

What she didn't tell them was that Suki wasn't there.

Every inch of wall space in the waiting room was plastered with photos of celebrities. Many of the shots featured a heavily made-up Suki, her chalky face framed by a mass of frothy peroxide hair, her arms around some celeb or other.

'She certainly moves in interesting circles,' Faye said, peering at the pictures. 'You don't suppose they're all her clients?'

'She's been in the game for ever,' Cheryl said, picking up a copy of *heat*. 'Suki knows everyone.'

'It makes you wonder why she's seeing us,' Faye said.

'What's that supposed to mean?' Cheryl bristled.

Faye tapped a photo of a beaming O.J. Simpson. Suki had her arm through his. 'I wouldn't have thought we were in her league, that's all.'

'I don't see why not. We had a hit show, after all.'

'*Had*, in the past tense.'

'If you're just going to be negative . . .'

Karen held up a hand. 'For heaven's sake, we're hardly going to persuade her the old *Girl Talk* chemistry's still there if we're squabbling before we even see her.'

Twenty minutes went by and Karen looked at her watch. 'She must be running late. Our appointment was ages ago.'

'That's probably a good sign,' Cheryl said.

Faye rolled her eyes.

After half an hour the girl with black lipstick popped her head round the door to ask if they wanted more coffee and to let them know Suki would be back any time.

Karen glanced at Cheryl. 'You mean she's not actually here?'

The girl shrugged. 'She had to run down to Beauchamp Place for something,' she said, before disappearing again.

Faye shot Cheryl a furious look. 'I don't believe it. She's doing her frigging shopping!'

Cheryl flung a copy of *OK!* on to the pile on the coffee table. 'Oh, give it a rest, will you. It wasn't exactly easy to set this meeting up, you know.'

Karen, wedged between them, wafted a magazine in front of her face. The room was stifling. She got up and rattled the handles of the French windows, which were locked. 'We don't *know* she's shopping,' she said. 'There might be an emergency or something, so let's not jump to conclusions.'

An hour later Suki Floyd finally showed up. Fifteen minutes after that, the girls were ushered into her office.

Suki, a wiry creature with a mass of wispy blonde hair back-combed to within an inch of its life, was on her feet behind her desk bawling into her phone. '*Anything* but lilies,' she shouted.

DENIAL

She examined her nails, which were long and dangerous and the same blood-red colour as her lips. 'She absolutely *loathes* them – that awful pong stinking the place out, pollen getting everywhere.' She glanced at her immaculate white trouser suit and plucked a speck of something from her cuff. On the floor beside her desk were several embossed carrier bags from high-end stores, at least two of them with Bruce Oldfield's name on. Faye shot Karen a desperate look as Suki waved them in the direction of a cream leather sofa. They perched in a line, facing the desk.

'Pick something cheerful. Orchids or lisianthus or something. Sunflowers, if you have to. Awful common things, I know, but she likes them.'

She hung up and gave the girls a long, hard stare.

'So, here you are – at last. And from where I'm standing, we need to get you back on the box *pronto* before you go entirely to rack and ruin.'

Twenty

Left to her own devices, Karen would have curled up in front of the television, snug in her pyjamas, with *Coronation Street* and a packet of giant chocolate buttons for company, but Bella, who suspected her friend was spending far too much of her time lolling about watching TV, wouldn't have it. The fact that Karen let slip when Bella phoned that she was hooked on *Neighbours* and something called *Burn Notice* brought things to a head.

'When was the last time we went out, just you and me?' she said.

Karen hesitated. *CSI: Miami* was on later and she had a bit of a thing for David Caruso. 'Why don't you come here? I'll order some food in and we can slob.'

'That's the problem.' Bella sounded stern. 'There's too much slobbing going on at the moment, and it's not good for you.'

Karen sighed. 'Now you sound like Dave. You know, I caught him throwing out a perfectly good packet of digestives the other day – or removing temptation, as he put it.' She sounded indignant.

Bella chuckled. 'I'm thinking of you, that's all. I hate the idea of you stuck indoors the whole time . . .' She paused. 'Festering.'

'I am *not* festering.'

'Jeremy Kyle is not suitable company day in, day out.'

Karen glanced at the TV in the corner of the bedroom where Jeremy, arms folded, squared up to a stroppy lad with bad skin. She skipped to a different channel. It was disturbing how well Bella knew her. 'OK,' she said, defeated. 'You win.'

Now she was wishing she hadn't caved in, because she had absolutely nothing to wear. She stared at the contents of her wardrobe feeling miserable. On the bed was a heap of clothes she had already discarded, among them a skirt with kick-pleats front and back that she had worn to death only a few months ago. Now it did nothing for her. There was no point even looking at trousers. Somewhere in the pile was a pair of black cigar pants. How she ever thought she looked good in those was beyond her.

She chewed her bottom lip. What was the point of having so many lovely clothes if she couldn't get into any of them? She rifled through the hangers and picked out a short-sleeved red shift dress with a deep V at the back. It had been expensive – set her back hundreds of pounds – but the cut alone had made it worth every penny. The first time she wore it Dave had practically gone into a trance. The memory made her smile. Now, as she stood in front of the mirrored doors of the wardrobe with the dress in front of her, she began to feel a bit more hopeful. The scarlet shot silk worked well against her pale skin, and even made her eyes seem a more intense shade of green. So far, so good. She yanked at her ponytail, letting her hair fall in soft ebony waves around her shoulders. She would work it into loose spirals, team the dress with a pair of killer heels and throw on a slouchy jacket. Inspired, she went to run a bath.

An hour later she was on the phone to Bella. 'It's no good, I can't come,' she said, stifling a sob.

'Why, what's happened?'

'I've got nothing to wear.'

'Nonsense,' Bella said, sounding brisk. 'You've got loads of clothes.'

Karen stared at the jumble of things on the bed. The red shift dress lay on top of the pile. 'Nothing looks right.'

'We all have days like that.'

'Nothing fits. I look hideous. I can't get my favourite dress over my hips. I just tried something on and got it stuck over my arms. It's hopeless.' She sank on to the end of the bed.

'Right,' Bella said. 'You've put on weight so none of your favourite things are any good *at the moment*. It's a temporary blip, that's all.'

'I look like a whale!'

'You must have something. 'What about that lovely top – the one with the swirly print? You could wear it with leggings.'

'It makes me feel fat.'

Bella took a deep breath. 'I know what you're doing, trying to wriggle out of our dinner date, and I'm not going to let you. You managed to find something to wear when you went to meet that Suki whatsername, didn't you?'

'Well, I—'

'So there's no excuse.' Bella let a few seconds of silence hang between them. 'Unless you don't want to see me and this is your none-too-subtle way of telling me . . .'

'No! Of course I do. You're my best friend.'

'Do you ever stop to think that *I* might be going through a crappy time right now, what with James Almond back on the scene – and that *I* might need a bit of a shoulder to cry on?'

'God, Bella, I'm sorry – I'm being such a selfish cow.'

'Actually, everything's fine, but that's not the point.' Her voice lost its brisk edge. 'Look, you're still gorgeous, even if you can't see it right now. You've got to stop moping around feeling sorry for yourself.'

Karen's cheeks grew pink. As usual, Bella was absolutely right. She thought about Julia, who until recently would never have been seen in anything less than six-inch heels, now forced to wear slippers and stuck in that dreary little cottage. All things considered, Karen had nothing to complain about.

Her spirits soared. She'd fix her hair and wear the swirly print top. At least the slashed neckline showed off her boobs, and there was nothing wrong with them.

She made a silent vow to start her diet in the morning.

Twenty-One

Bella put down her menu. 'Come on, then, spill the beans – how did it go with Suki? Is she as ferocious as she sounds?'

Karen pulled a face. 'She gave me the number of a clinic in Chelsea somewhere, said they specialize in weight loss by kinetics.'

'What's that when it's at home?'

'You hold out your arm and they tap it or something to test your resistance and . . .' She gave Bella a blank look. 'It might not be kinetics. It might be –' she closed her eyes for a second – 'kinesiology? I'm a bit hazy, to be honest. Anyway, it costs three hundred pounds and Suki can get me a discount. Thirty quid off. Well, fifty, but she takes a cut. You see a proper doctor, and once you've had your session thingy he tells you exactly what you can and can't eat. As long as you stick to the plan, it's guaranteed to work.'

'A diet, in other words.' Bella shook her head. 'I'd save your money if I were you.'

They were in a pricey Italian restaurant in Mayfair, in a booth set well back from the entrance. The room was narrow and went back a long way. A tea light flickered in a glass dish on the table. The walls were hung with plush velvet the colour of black grapes and the lighting came from a series of elaborate chandeliers that ran the length of the room. The decor matched Karen's swirly print top and the lighting was perfect. She looked radiant.

'I don't know why you made such a song and dance about coming out,' Bella said. 'You look pretty damned gorgeous to me.'

Karen gave her an uncertain smile. 'You know what it's like when you can't get into anything – ' She stopped. Bella, in a cream stretchy top that revealed bare, toned arms, was as slim as ever. She had probably never struggled to do up a zip in her life.

'Before you say anything, I've got a pair of amazing figure-hugging trousers at home that I bought in the Channel 6 Wardrobe sale last year,' Bella said. 'As worn by Marsha Caine in that detective series, the one about the serial killer who kept body parts as souvenirs.' She gave Karen a dreamy look. 'Marsha wore them in a scene where she got off with the hunky reporter. God, those pants are gorgeous, and I only paid a tenner for them. Anyway, as soon as I saw they were in the sale I had to have them, no matter what. Getting them on was a bit of a performance, mind. I had to lie flat on the floor, and once I'd got them fastened it took two of the Wardrobe people to heave me upright, but I bought them anyway because they are *hot*. Needless to say, I've never worn them, since they're a good two sizes too small and cut off the blood supply to several major organs. The fact is I am not and never will be waiflike à la Marsha, skinny bitch that she is. She's probably got an eating disorder. So, trust me, I am no stranger to the ever-expanding waistline. Now, dish the dirt on Suki.'

Karen picked up her Kir Royale and said in a low voice. 'Don't say anything, but she wants to bring back *Girl Talk*.'

'Some people might think bringing back the old show is a bit of a backward step,' Bella said cautiously.

'It's not like I'm swamped with offers, is it? And Suki seems to think she can get us a good deal. I don't suppose she'd bother if it wasn't worth her while.'

'So, the infamous comeback queen is now officially your agent?' Bella blinked. 'I hope she's not the old dragon everyone seems to think she is. I always got the impression she was a bit of a . . . well, Julia, really.'

'No, really, she's all right. She just shouts a lot. Even when she's not shouting, if you see what I mean. Her heart's in the right place, though.' Karen frowned. 'At least I think so.' She decided not to tell Bella that Suki had pronounced her too fat for TV and had got straight on the phone to the slimming clinic to fix up an emergency appointment.

'Well, you have to go with what's right for you. I only know Suki Floyd by reputation. As long as you got a good feeling about her, that's all that matters.'

Karen nodded. The truth was she had found Suki Floyd totally overwhelming and left the meeting with her head spinning. Several sleepless nights had followed. In an ideal world, Suki might not be the kind of agent she would want, but things being what they were, Karen could hardly afford to turn her nose up. And the others were keen and needed her on-board for the *Girl Talk* plan to come off.

Basically, she hadn't got much choice.

Karen glanced around the restaurant, which was busy. There were several people at the bar in the far corner, presumably waiting for tables. A girl with her back to them in a tiny backless minidress gazed up at a bloke in a football shirt. Karen assumed he must actually be a player to have come to a posh restaurant dressed like that. She imagined them being ushered into the VIP area of a club later, predatory women slipping him their phone number right under his girlfriend's nose. Celebrity was definitely a double-edged sword.

Bella tore off a piece of bread roll and buttered it. 'I'll get a bottle of bubbly, shall I, since we're celebrating your imminent comeback?'

'Maybe we should hold off until it actually happens.' Two vertical frown lines had appeared in the centre of Karen's brow.

'Come on, you should be happy – it's all looking good.'

'I know. It's just . . . I felt such a fraud when we were in with Suki, going on about how I can't wait to get back to work, when the truth is I'm a bit scared. *Terrified*, really.' She fiddled with the pepper mill. 'I keep thinking I won't be able to do it any more – that we'll go on air and I'll sit like a dummy and not manage to think of a single thing to say.'

'You're bound to be a bit anxious. That's normal.'

'Is it? What if I've lost my nerve?'

Bella looked thoughtful. 'I'd say it would be worse if you were super-confident. All the best performers get nervous. Nerves are what let you know you haven't turned into an arrogant whatnot.'

'I suppose.' She sighed. 'I can't imagine I'll ever be best friends with Suki.'

'I should hope not.'

'But she's probably just what I need at the moment – someone to give me a shake. You know, put the brakes on before I go all the way down the slippery slope.'

'I thought Dave was pretty good in that department. Isn't he doing his bit?'

Karen shrugged. In fact, Dave was being brilliant: filling the fridge with healthy food, cooking low-calorie meals, coming up with exercise plans. Thanks to him, there was a running machine – still unused – in the garage. That had appeared after Karen said she was too self-conscious to run round the common with him. He had even offered to go to a fit camp with her, a place run by an ex-Marine friend of his, and put in a couple of weeks of hardcore training to get her back on track. Karen was horrified. The thought of her collapsing five minutes into a workout, red-faced and out of breath, while Dave watched was too much to contemplate. She had been adamant: not in a million years. No, it wasn't Dave that was the problem – it was her.

'He's a bit busy at the moment, running all over the place with Lara Croft,' she said, sounding slightly more peeved than she had intended.

'Who?'

'I'm talking about Lara Durham. The queen of showbiz.'

'Oh *her*. The Beeb are after her for some new Saturday night entertainment show. They want her to co-host with Graham Norton according to what I've heard.'

Karen's heart sank. She had secretly hoped Lara would be on a flight back to LA any day now, not putting down roots in London. 'That's all I need – Dave ferrying her about for ever.'

'Karen, he *adores* you.'

'He adores the *thin* woman he used to know, the successful one that was on the telly every night, you mean.' Maybe that wasn't fair. Dave was as loving as ever. It was just her, feeling insecure. 'He didn't get in until six o'clock in the morning the other day.'

'She *is* a bit of a party animal, Lara.'

'What if she's got her claws into him?'

Bella gave her a bemused smile. 'We're not talking about Jason here. You know where you are with Dave.'

'I know, and once I'm working again I'll feel better. Too much time on my hands, that's the problem.' Her face brightened. 'From now on I'm going to count my blessings. I've got the legendary Suki Floyd on my case, a fantastic series in the offing – and I'm seeing the kinetics man tomorrow.' She grinned. 'Things are definitely looking up.'

Bella hoped she was right.

'Enough about me, anyway,' Karen said. 'How's the world of X-rated telly?'

'Fine, although Paula's gone a bit peculiar since you-know-who came back. Wearing suits and ranting about women having no power. I'm pretty sure she was reading *The Female Eunuch* the other day.'

'Poor Paula. It can't be much fun having to answer to James again.'

'She hasn't said much, but she doesn't need to. She's had this murderous look about her – think Glenn Close in *Fatal Attraction* – ever since he made his triumphant return. I keep fantasizing about her attacking him with an ice pick.' She screwed up her face. 'Wrong film – that was Sharon Stone in *Basic Instinct*, wasn't it?'

'Has she said anything?'

'Not really. It's just the way she stomps about and bangs doors. I get the distinct feeling she's up to something.'

'You can't blame her. It must be sickening taking orders from a prick like him after everything that's happened.'

'She has these weekly catch-up meetings in his office and she dragged me along to the last one. You could have cut the atmosphere with a knife – James on one side pretending to be civil, the whole time needling her about ratings and going off at a tangent like he does, and Paula tripping him up, bringing up stuff he doesn't know about from when she was running things. And the whole time she's got this strained, deranged look on her face. It was like she was possessed.' Bella shuddered. 'Seriously, you wouldn't want to meet her in a dark alley when she's in that mood.'

'Stop,' Karen said, laughing. 'You're making it up.'

'Brownie's honour,' Bella said. She paused. 'As for Lesley, you know I wasn't sure about working with her. I did think she might be a bit of a handful, but she's so into the subject it makes life super-easy. She's completely in her element. When it comes to sex, there's nothing she doesn't know – and I mean nothing. Some of the production meetings would make your hair stand on end.'

Karen giggled. 'Just as well you're broad-minded.'

'She was telling me a story about a bloke, some American she bumped into, literally, on the moving walkway at Heathrow, and how she ended up going straight from the airport to his hotel – the Landmark, no less – and having wild sex for two days. They didn't bother getting dressed – just stayed in bed and kept ordering room service. In the end she sloped off while he was having a shower. She never even asked his name or what he did for a living.'

'That's Lesley for you. She was pretty wild before she met Dan. Even then, it was ages before she calmed down. I don't think she understood the concept of monogamy.'

'Well, if I could only have one man in this life and it happened to be Dan Kincaid, I know what I'd do,' Bella said. 'He was in the other day. The pair of them were locked up in her dressing room, giggling and doing God-knows-what. When they finally appeared, Lesley was her usual immaculate self, slick of bright-pink lip gloss in place, and Dan looked like he'd been dragged through a hedge backwards, hair all over, shirt undone.' She sighed. 'Sexy beyond belief.'

'It sounds like they're still head over heels, anyway.'

'Crazy in love, if you ask me. They sit in the canteen holding hands, gazing at each other like a pair of teenagers. Incredibly sweet. I even overheard them talking about having a baby.'

Karen's mouth went dry. A few months ago she had been all loved-up, planning for the future with Jason – even talking about having a baby. They had also vowed to find the daughter they had given up for adoption when Karen was seventeen. Amy would be nearly twenty-four now. Thinking about it brought her mood crashing down.

'Are you OK?' Bella was peering at her. 'You've gone a bit pale.'

'I'm fine,' Karen said, grabbing her bag and sliding out of the booth. 'I'm just going to the loo. Order the linguine with crab for me if the waiter comes back, will you?'

Inside the Ladies, the girl from the bar in the backless minidress was touching up her make-up. A miniature can of hairspray poked out of her bag. Close up, she looked young, not even old enough to be drinking, but there was a glass of champagne on the marble surface next to the basin. As Karen wondered if her mother knew where she was and who she was with, something tugged at her. Her own daughter was out there somewhere doing heaven knows what, and Karen had no way of knowing, no means of finding out. Her efforts to track Amy down had come to nothing. Perhaps it was time to face facts: she wanted nothing to do with the woman who had abandoned her.

Karen blinked back tears and slipped into the loo furthest from the girl. She wanted a baby, she thought, putting down the toilet seat and sitting on it. Did she want a baby with Dave, though? She loved him, but . . . She studied her reflection in the gold-mirrored walls. Whoever was responsible for the lighting had done an amazing job. She looked fresh-faced, even though she felt like bursting into tears. She dug out her compact and blotted her nose with powder. Everywhere she looked her friends were having babies. First it was Faye. Now it was Lesley's turn. She felt as if time was rushing by, that if she didn't get her skates on it would be too late, yet she was only forty-one, still younger than Lesley.

Outside, a voice said, 'Karen?' Bella had come looking for her.

Karen took a deep breath. 'Just a second.' She gave herself a long, hard look. Get a grip, she told her reflection. She waved her hand at a button set into the wall and the toilet flushed.

'Did you think I'd got lost?' she said, giving Bella a bright smile as she washed her hands. The girl in the minidress had gone.

'You did that thing when you jump up and bolt. That means you're upset. What did I say?'

Karen kept her smile in place. 'Nothing. Don't be silly. I was dying for a wee, that's all.'

Bella narrowed her eyes. 'You'll have to do better than that.'

Karen picked up a towel from a basket beside the sink. There was no fooling Bella. She could see straight through her. Dropping the towel in a bin, Karen helped herself to a dollop of honey and vanilla handcream. 'You should do one of those investigative shows where you never give up, no matter how many times the person tells you to bugger off and slams the door in your face.'

'Funny you should say that . . .'

Karen fished out her lipstick and applied a fresh coat of Pink Lust. 'Seriously, I'm fine.'

'Nonsense. I know you, and when you get that weird frantic look and do a runner it always means you're in a state about something.'

'I told you, I feel like a walrus,' Karen said.

Bella studied her in the mirror. 'From where I'm standing, you look pretty good. Actually, so do I in this light.' She turned and examined her rear view. The combination of skinny black jeans and strappy wooden platforms created a long, willowy silhouette. 'Let's stay here,' she said, 'and admire ourselves in the trick mirrors and fabulous lighting.'

She slipped her arm through Karen's and gave her a squeeze. 'OK, I'll lay off my Spanish Inquisition routine, but if you want to tell me what's really on your mind, I'm all ears. You know that whatever it is, I won't breathe a word.'

Karen gave her a weak smile. 'I was thinking about Amy . . .'

Bella gave her a searching look. 'Don't tell me – you're pregnant?'

'Not even close.'

'But you're trying.'

Karen shook her head. 'I've wanted a baby for ages. Me and Jason were planning . . . Oh well, no point going on about that now.'

'Dave would make a brilliant dad.'

'I know. It's just that we haven't got round to the subject of starting a family.'

'In that case you need to talk to him.'

'Maybe once I'm working again and back to my old self. I'm not much fun to come home to at the moment. Plus we're not exactly rolling in money.'

Bella looked serious. 'Listen, I know you want everything to be perfect. You want to lose weight, you want to be working, back at the top of your game – I understand. But don't let life pass you by while you're waiting for everything to fall into place. Sometimes we have to make do with things the way they are now, as opposed to the way we'd like them to be. So get jiggy with Dave. Make a baby, if that's what you want. In the end, that's going to be a lot more important than whether you can get into a size 12 or bag the cover of *Closer*.'

She paused to make sure Karen was paying attention.

'Just don't put your life on hold – that's all I'm saying.'

Twenty-Two

Strictly speaking, the news and current affairs department at Channel 6 was nothing to do with James Almond. He made it his business, though, to keep an eye on everything that was going on at the station, and in his view, Tabitha Tate was definitely one to watch. She was young, bright and a pretty little thing, which always helped. Another news outfit would snatch her from under their noses if they weren't careful. There was a limit to how far she could go at Channel 6. They didn't do much in the way of current affairs or news features, and all their international news came from Sky. Still, there was no reason why a talent like Tabitha Tate should be confined to news. In his experience, anyone who could handle live reports and inject wit and colour into even the dreariest of political stories was capable of just about anything. After all, Helen England had come from a news background, and it was James who had recognized her potential. His decision to make her the face of *Good Morning Britain* had been a gamble, and some people had thought he was crazy, but he had been proved right. In a matter of weeks she had become the undisputed queen of daytime TV.

James sat back in his custom-made executive chair and toyed with the controls in the arm, reclining until he was practically horizontal, easing himself back into a semi-upright position, rocking back and forth. It was immensely soothing, and it pained him to think of Paula Grayson doing the same thing in his absence. The tension in his neck and shoulders melted away as he sank into the memory foam beneath the soft leather upholstery and miniature vibrating rollers caressed his spine. At the touch of a button a plump footrest glided into position and the chair turned through ninety degrees so that he was facing the Picasso on the wall of his office. It took a certain eye to appreciate the finer things in life. Take the Picasso, for instance, *Nude in an Armchair*. Not everyone liked it – he had seen the way Lesley Gold looked at it. Next time she was in for a little chat he would put her on the spot, ask for her opinion. He smiled. It wouldn't surprise him in the least if she thought a Picasso was a mass-produced car.

There was a tap on the door. 'Come,' he said, performing another ninety-degree turn to find Tabitha Tate facing him.

James, still semi-prone, gestured at the sofa. 'Take a seat,' he said.

Tabitha Tate sat on the end furthest from James and dumped her bag, which happened to be her old school satchel and was ideal for carting tapes around, beside her. She was wearing ripped jeans and biker boots and a baggy jumper that was starting to unravel at the hem.

'Have you been doing some kind of undercover work?' James said, thrown by her casual appearance.

'It's my day off,' Tabitha said, crossing her legs, the mucky heel of a boot threatening to graze the edge of the sofa. It had come from Milan, from a firm that specialized in one-offs in the softest leather. Not a patch on the albino heifers sacrificed in the name of his beloved office chair, but all the same. It had cost thousands. He pressed a button and jerked upright as a trace of mud was deposited on the edge of the sofa. 'I'm just going to go through some rushes,' Tabitha said, oblivious, patting the satchel. 'Get ahead a bit. I'm cutting a piece on urban foxes in a couple of days.'

James got up and went to sit next to her. Her phone rang and she dug around in her bag, removing tapes and piling them up on the sofa until she finally located her BlackBerry, by which time it had stopped ringing. James waited for her to apologize and switch it to silent, but instead, to his amazement, she fiddled with it and pressed it to her ear. 'Won't be a minute,' she told him.

He watched her, incredulous.

'I'm in a meeting, babe,' she said. 'No. No. I don't think so. They're on the hook on the back of the kitchen door. No? In the drawer, then, next to the sink. Yes, the Shane Lynch key ring.' She giggled. 'You couldn't stick a stamp on that letter on the kitchen table for me, could you? You're an angel. Later.' She hung up and turned to James, whose expression was like stone. Tabitha didn't seem to notice. 'Is this about the court case?'

'I beg your pardon?'

'Did you want me to do a compilation of all the reports or something? I don't mind, only it might be a while before I can get round to it.'

James frowned. 'No, I mean—'

'It must be strange seeing yourself on telly like that when you're not used to it.'

James cleared his throat. 'It's nothing to do with that. I wanted to talk to you – in confidence – about whether we might get you to branch out and add a bit of entertainment to your repertoire.'

Tabitha nodded. 'Oh, right, I'm with you.'

James studied her. She didn't seem the least bit impressed. What was wrong with the girl? He said, 'Have you thought about how you see your career developing?'

'Oh, absolutely. I'm very driven. The news editor didn't want me reporting on camera, you know – said I wouldn't be taken seriously – but I kept pushing. Then Penny James was rushed into hospital with appendicitis just as she was due to go to Downing Street for a press briefing, so I got to go instead.' She gave James a killer smile. 'There's always an element of luck in this business, isn't there?'

'Indeed.' James laced his hands behind his head. 'You do seem at home on camera, I must say.'

'I am – a natural, so I'm told.' She was brimming with confidence. 'I'm not being big-headed or anything, but I know my worth.'

James gazed at her. She really was a cool customer. A proper little minx.

'I'm thinking of arranging a little screen test for you – putting you in a studio, something informal, see how you adapt to a style of presenting that's more *intimate*, shall we say, than the cut and thrust of news.' He held her gaze.

Tabitha's bare knee poked through a rip in her jeans. The biker boot brushed against the sofa again. She looked right at James. Several seconds went by before she spoke. Finally, she said, 'What would I have to do?'

'I'm not sure I follow.'

'I'm ambitious,' she said, 'but I'm not the type to do absolutely anything to get on, if you know what I mean.'

James suppressed a smirk. Helen England had said almost the same thing the first time he met her. 'I should hope not.'

He lowered his gaze. It was impossible to get any sense of what was under that awful baggy sweater. Why such a well-proportioned young woman would want to hide her best assets was anyone's guess. 'You seem to forget I'm recently bereaved.'

Tabitha went a tiny bit pink. Aha, James thought, a chink in the armour.

'I'm sorry,' she said, flustered. 'I wasn't trying to say—'

He cut her off. 'As long as we understand each other.'

'Of course.'

'Strictly between the two of us, I'm thinking of you in terms of *Best Ever Sex*,' he said, lolling against the back of the sofa. A look of alarm flickered across Tabitha's features. James registered her panic and resisted the urge to smile. Not nearly so sure of herself any more, was she? He examined a perfectly manicured nail. 'I'm referring to our surprise late-night hit, currently presented by one of our veteran presenters, Lesley Gold. I'll be honest with you – she's very good and the show is practically tailor-made for her. She is positively unflinching, in fact, when it comes to tackling the most challenging topics head-on.' He extended his long legs and admired his immaculate dove-grey suede brogues. 'Now, the last thing I would ever do is tinker with a winning formula, and Lesley Gold *is* popular. She speaks to a certain kind of woman – ' he paused again – 'to the detriment, perhaps, of the kind of younger audience Channel 6 is constantly seeking to attract. We need to stay on our toes, be vigilant at all times, build on our audiences. I'm sure it's the same in news.' He gave Tabitha a penetrating look.

'Well, yes, we—'

'It's all about timing,' he went on, talking over her. 'You have to know when to change it up. Recently, I commissioned some research on *Best Ever Sex*.' He shook his head. 'The audience figures were disappointing, to say the least.'

Tabitha's brow furrowed. 'But I thought you said it was a hit.'

'I specifically sought the views of a focus group of under-thirty-fives and, frankly, the show barely registered on their radar.' That wasn't entirely true, but James had learned that he could make audience feedback say whatever he wanted it to. It was all a question of emphasis.

'Well, I'm surprised,' Tabitha said.

'When you're in my position, you learn not to be surprised by anything,' James said, aiming another penetrating look at her. 'In fact, the role of a good controller is to be prescient. It's something of a gift with me. I can identify trends before they happen, and when it comes to audiences I know exactly who's watching what.' He gave her an icy smile. 'Research merely confirms what I already know. How well do you know your audience, Tabitha?'

'Well . . .'

'It's probably something you don't concern yourself with, and yet – if you do have ambitions to succeed – you really ought to. Trust me, a sound knowledge of your audience is ammunition. It's a foolish presenter who fails to understand that.' He was thinking of Lesley. 'Right, I think we're through here now,' he said, glancing at his watch and getting up. 'I've enjoyed our chat and I'll set up that audition. Perhaps we need another little session first, though – a mini-brainstorm over lunch somewhere nice. I don't suppose you newshounds have much opportunity for civilized lunches when you're out on the road.' He smiled. 'My PA will be in touch.'

Tabitha stuffed her tapes back into her satchel and scrambled to her feet. 'Right – and thanks.'

'And remember – what we have just discussed is highly confidential.' He slid a finger across his throat. 'Careless talk costs lives.' Tabitha stared at him. James kept a straight face for several seconds before bursting into raucous laughter. 'No need to look so serious – I'm only joking!'

Tabitha grabbed her stuff and scarpered.

James strolled after her. Outside his office, Anne, his PA, was at the computer, straight-backed, dealing with a relentless flood of emails and calls. Anne, with her hair in a neat little ponytail, a modest string of pearls at the neck of her plain navy frock, represented, in James's view, the perfect PA. It had taken no time at all for her to grasp which messages required his attention and which were of no interest. She had learned her lesson on her first day when she had made a detailed log of each call that came in and presented it to James, only to be told to bin almost everything. 'Why would I have any desire to meet someone putting on a dreary play in a theatre no one's ever heard of in the middle of nowhere?' he had said. 'And this one – a marathon-running octogenarian who also plays the spoons. I think that's one for *Britain's Got Talent*, don't you?' Anne had stood in front of his desk, her cheeks flushed. 'Discretion,' James had said. 'I like a neat, orderly world. There is no place on my desk for pages of messages from time-wasters, however persuasive they might be.'

Sensing him behind her, Anne stopped typing and turned to face him. 'You've ten minutes before your next appointment,' she said. 'Can I get you a coffee or something?'

'You can get a cleaner up here,' he said. 'The delightful

Tabitha Tate seems to have left a trail of devastation in her wake.' He grimaced. 'Muddy boots all over the sofa.'

Anne jumped up and went to take a look. As far as she could tell, the sofa was fine.

'There,' he said, indicating a small speck of dirt.

She moved closer for a better look. Really and truly, he was insufferable. 'Oh, *that*,' she said, a note of sarcasm creeping into her voice. She fetched a pack of baby wipes from her desk drawer, dabbed at the leather, and pressed a clean tissue to the spot. 'I think that's it.'

James made a minuscule adjustment to the position of a gleaming statuette on a shelf groaning with awards. 'A tidy office is a tidy mind,' he said. 'Chaos is the enemy of creativity. Cleanliness . . .' he paused. 'Well, you get the picture.'

Anne returned to her desk grim-faced. She wished Paula Grayson was still in charge.

Twenty-Three

Lesley was sitting up in bed tucking into a smoked salmon bagel, dropping crumbs all over the sheets. On the TV in the corner, the drippy presenter of *Good Morning Britain*, Matt Preston, was asking whether sending explicit text messages to someone other than your partner constituted cheating. According to him, so-called 'sexting' was rapidly becoming the scourge of the modern relationship.

'Oh, for goodness' sake,' Lesley said. 'It's hardly new, is it? It's just another type of phone sex.'

The media had become obsessed, though, following a rash of high-profile cases in the press, one after another. Lesley knew only too well how it felt to have the press salivating over your private life. A particularly gory kiss-and-tell story in one of the tabloids had plunged her into total obscurity before *Girl Talk* came along and saved her skin.

Matt's equally drippy co-presenter was saying that a whopping 63 per cent of people had sent sexy texts to someone other than their regular partner at some point, usually after a night out and far too much to drink. Drippy Matt raised an eyebrow. 'Can we – would *you*? – write off sexy texts – *sexts* – as harmless fun? Or are they just another way of cheating on your other half?' Lesley guessed the reason he was being so po-faced was that his girlfriend had recently left him for a cage fighter.

It had been in all the papers. No doubt a bit of sexting had gone on there. Matt gazed into the camera. 'And by the way, sending obscene material via your mobile is against the law.'

'Thanks for pointing that out,' Lesley said. 'I'll get straight on to Special Branch and ask them what they're doing to stamp it out. As if the police don't have enough to do trying to catch proper criminals.'

She reckoned Matt Preston was just the type to dial 999 if he found a filthy text on his other half's phone.

Although Lesley still liked to think of herself as a bit on the wild side, the truth was that marriage had tamed her. It had revealed a morally correct and faithful side to her character she never knew she had. No sexting for her. Not these days. No, her crazy days were behind her. She loved Dan too much to mess about, and there was way too much at stake. She felt a stab of guilt. There had been only one transgression, a stupid mistake she blamed on pre-wedding nerves. Never again. Thankfully she had managed to keep it to herself.

A young girl, slathered in fake tan and wearing the kind of indecent dress that made Lesley think she had come straight from a club, was telling Matt Preston about meeting a married footballer in Chinawhite and how he had bombarded her with suggestive texts.

'*Sexts*,' Matt corrected.

Lesley rolled her eyes. 'Loser,' she said, sliding her plate on to the cabinet on Dan's side of the bed and depositing more crumbs on the sheets in the process.

'I thought he really liked me,' the girl was saying in a whiney voice, 'but since it all came out he's just blanked me.' She seemed utterly perplexed.

'This is priceless,' Lesley said. 'Where did they find her?' She wondered how many celebs were now having second thoughts about sending that half-naked shot taken during a bored moment in a hotel room far from home to some girl they'd only just met.

Dan padded in from the bathroom, hair dripping wet, a tiny towel wrapped around his waist. A peculiar little flutter caught at Lesley's insides as he whipped the towel off and stood with his back to her rubbing at his hair. If her phone was handy she would definitely have taken a snap of that perfect butt, purely for her own private use. She gazed at him, going all gooey. That taut muscular body and gleaming olive skin was irresistible. Mind you, he worked at it. All those egg-white omelettes and beetroot smoothies. Ugh. In the run-up to a modelling assignment, all he'd have for breakfast was a shot of wheatgrass. She could never be that disciplined. No wonder he was in such demand. Ten years ago, when his career took off and he landed a series of lucrative coffee commercials, Lesley hadn't thought he was all that hot: too skinny and a haircut that made her think of Rick Astley. Not any more. No question, the years had been kind to him, turned him into an all-round cool dude. A ripple of satisfaction went through her. She had married a sex god. She whipped a tangerine lip gloss from the bedside table and sloshed some on.

Dan turned to face her, towel in hand. 'Oh-oh,' he said. 'Lippy alert. That can only mean one thing.' Dropping the towel on the floor, he swaggered towards her. Lesley threw back the duvet to reveal a short peach chiffon teddy. 'Get in,' she said, her voice husky.

He slid in beside her. She lay on her side and stroked his chest, ran a hand through his damp chestnut hair. It was a bit longer than usual, practically touching his shoulders, but it suited him. She gazed into eyes that were tawny like hers and flecked with amber. Dan shifted towards her. Her heart began to race. He bent and his tongue traced patterns on her breasts. She shuddered.

'You're in big, big trouble,' he said, tilting his face towards hers, his eyes narrowing.

'What for – seducing my husband? There's no law against that.'

'Maybe not.' He flipped her on to her front and gave her bottom a slap.

'Ouch,' Lesley said, secretly thrilled.

'That's for eating your breakfast in bed – *again*,' he said, administering another slap. 'You're a very naughty girl. There are crumbs everywhere.' He grabbed her wrist and snapped on a fluffy pink handcuff, securing her to the headboard. Lesley wriggled with pleasure. 'You've run out of verbal warnings, Mrs Kincaid,' he said, running his hand over her pert behind. 'You leave me no option but to take things to the next level.'

'The whip's in my top drawer,' she said, sounding hopeful.

Twenty-Four

'You're hurting me,' Julia said, swiping at Joel Reynolds with the palm of her hand and connecting with the side of his head. Joel, who was one of the most sought-after cosmetic surgeons in London and was known for his light touch, flinched and backed away.

'Julia, please. I'm trying to examine you and you're not exactly making it easy.'

'Yes, well, I hate having my feet touched,' she said.

He gave her a stern look. 'Do you want to wear heels again or not?'

'Of course I do!'

'Fine. Keep still, then.'

Julia shifted in her chair. Her feet were propped up on a padded velvet stool while Joel, in a charcoal Savile Row suit, kneeled on the floor. She could see a few white flecks in his short dark hair. He was going grey at the temples too, in a George Clooney kind of way. It was so unfair the way some men looked better as they got older.

Joel glanced up at her and gave her a reassuring smile. Laughter lines appeared at the corners of his blue eyes. Julia graced him with a smile in return. No wonder he had celebrity clients queuing round the block. He was better looking than when Julia had first got to know him twenty-odd years ago.

Gripping the toes of her left foot with one hand, he put the other on her ankle, gently manipulating it. Julia leapt as if she had been scalded. Her other foot kicked out. Joel shuffled backwards out of range and shot her a warning look. She glared back, turquoise eyes flashing.

'That's my ticklish spot,' she said, yanking her foot free.

He grabbed it again. 'If you carry on like this, I'm going to give you a jab. Now keep *still*.'

'I meant to ask about those vitamin injections, the ones that give you the skin of a teenager. Meso-something or other. One of the beauty editors was going on about them. The effects are instant, you know, and they last months.'

Joel peered up at her, exasperated. 'You already have the skin of a teenager, and anyway I meant an anaesthetic to calm you down.'

'I am perfectly calm!'

Joel winced. 'No need to shout.'

'I am *not* shouting!'

It was the second time Joel had been to see her at the cottage in Essex. Each visit meant a day away from his busy practice in Harley Street and thousands of pounds of lost business. Not that Julia, as self-absorbed and single-minded as ever despite her recent brush with death, would have cared about that, and not that Joel really minded. Appointments could be rescheduled, and after everything Julia had been through, he wanted to do whatever he could to help her. Added to which he felt bad. After all, he was the one who'd tipped off the press about Julia's sex-change surgery – an operation he had performed. It was the prospect of being exposed that had prompted her to drink herself stupid and crash her car, and he felt dreadful now about betraying her. Of course, he had been driven to it by Julia, who had threatened and bullied him for years, but still. She had always been a tricky and demanding client, breezing into his consulting rooms, reducing his nurses to tears, shouting and stamping her feet. The very feet he was now examining.

'It's really not my field,' he said, tilting her foot up and examining the sole. 'I mean, we're really talking about specialist surgery. I don't know if it's ever going to be possible to make them as good as new.' He ran his hand along her instep and ducked as she lashed out again. 'In my professional opinion, for what it's worth, skyscraper heels may be a thing of the past. It might be better to lower your expectations. What about aiming for something a bit more manageable—'

Julia cut him off. 'I do *not* want to hear your professional opinion if all you're going to do is try to put me off. Do I look like the kind of woman who would wear flat shoes?' Her voice rose. 'What I *want* is surgery that will get me back into my favourite Louboutins. Am. I. Making. Myself. Clear?'

Her hospital consultant had told her high heels were out of the question, that her feet were so badly damaged there was a chance she would be in specially adapted support shoes for the rest of her life. All being well, and with lots of physio, in time she should be able to walk unaided. And, if she was really lucky, she might progress from support shoes to flatties. When she had protested, he had said she should be grateful to be alive. Julia, however, was not in the least bit grateful. She wouldn't be seen dead in the kind of footwear he seemed to think appropriate. Some of the so-called designs – a misuse of the term in her view – had stretchy panels and Velcro fastenings.

Joel scrambled to his feet. 'It may not be possible, that's all I'm saying. It's best to be realistic rather than get all hopeful and then—'

Julia put her hands over her ears. 'Will you stop being so frigging *negative*!' She waved a hand in the direction of the dining table where her laptop was set up. 'I've been on the Internet, done some research, and as far as I can tell nothing's impossible these days. If you can think of it, some clever so-and-so somewhere can do it.' Her eyes were blazing. 'What about cutting-edge surgery – stem cells?'

Joel looked puzzled. 'I don't see how stem cells can—'

'No – because you haven't even *bothered* looking into it.' Julia was breathing hard and her hands were clenched in tight little fists. 'I've printed off some stuff – there on the table. I came across a very similar procedure to the one I need, carried out by a surgeon in Brazil – or was it Mexico? – I can't remember. It's all there anyway.'

Joel picked up the papers and leafed through them. He glanced at Julia, who was staring into space. He could see her breath going in and out in sharp, violent bursts. Quite what she was thinking he had no idea. It was completely mad.

'This is all a bit sketchy and, well, experimental,' he said eventually, summoning as much tact as he could.

'Joel,' she said, her expression glacial, 'I am not asking you – I am *telling* you. You're my surgeon, the one person I trust to do this, so find a way.' The turquoise eyes pleaded with him. 'You're my only hope.'

He put down the papers and went to sit on the sofa. A spring poked him in the back and he grabbed a cushion, something big and velvety piped with gold braid, and stuffed it behind him. The sofa, like everything else in the place, belonged to another era and was slightly past its best. If someone had told him Julia owned a holiday home, he would have pictured a modern, airy property in a gated development in Cape Town, or a smart villa overlooking the marina in Barbados, not a cottage stuck in a time warp in Essex.

The rhythmic tick-tock of the grandfather clock in the hall reached him. He sighed. Julia, determined to have her own way, as usual, was fiddling with her hair. On the mantelpiece above the fireplace among several framed pictures, all sepia-toned, was one of a young man in uniform which Joel guessed dated from the Great War. Although he had known Julia for years, he knew virtually nothing about her family.

'All these people – who are they?'

She gazed at the row of pictures. 'I've no idea. They came with the house.' Joel gave her a curious look. 'I know what you're thinking – it's not very *me*, is it? She gazed around the room at the dowdy mahogany furniture. 'It just feels right somehow. My mum had old pictures of her dad and her uncles in uniform. At the seaside, on the beach in their best suits, shirts and ties, the whole lot.' She gave Joel an awkward smile. 'I don't suppose that makes sense to you.'

'Isn't it a bit creepy being here on your own with all these echoes of the past around you? I mean – ' he glanced at the mantelpiece – 'dead people everywhere you turn.'

Julia laughed. 'What – you think they somehow come alive at night and haunt the place?'

Joel shivered. No way would he stay here by himself. It was bad enough downstairs, especially as Julia insisted on keeping the blinds drawn, which created an air of perpetual gloom, but upstairs was even worse. The bathroom was freezing, even with the radiator on, which definitely wasn't normal. As for Julia's bedroom, it reminded him of that Stephen King film, the one where Kathy Bates played a psychopath. He gave Julia a sideways look. It probably wasn't ideal for her mental state being locked away like this, so cut off. No wonder she was on such a short fuse.

'How are you?' he asked. 'I mean, in yourself?'

Julia snorted. 'In my*self*? What's that supposed to mean? You're here as my personal surgeon to examine my feet. When I need a shrink I'll ask for one, thank you.'

'It's just that it's bound to have taken its toll on your mood – the crash, the coma . . .' He glanced at her feet, once again encased in the furry slippers she had been wearing when he arrived. His gaze slid to the side of the hearth and an ugly pair of orthopaedic bootees. 'All this uncertainty about getting back into your heels.'

'For your information, I'm fine, thanks. *In myself.* Never felt better.'

'You might consider some kind of relaxing complementary therapy – reiki, perhaps, or reflexology. I can recommend some good people. Very calming.'

'I suppose you saw the exclusive in the *Sunday*, all the stuff about me being in a private clinic undergoing an intensive programme of physiotherapy?' Julia said, changing the subject.

Not only had Joel seen the piece, he knew exactly how it had come about since it was his other half, Laura Lloyd, who had written it. Joel still hoped he would never have to break the news to Julia that he was actually seeing the woman who had been poised to out her as a sex-swap celeb before she wrote off her Porsche in the Strand underpass. It would definitely send her off the deep end. Best to keep it to himself, at least for the time being.

'It was the same writer who was supposed to do a profile piece on me a few months ago,' Julia said. I met her for lunch at The Ivy – you know, took her into my confidence, poured my heart out, and all the time the bitch was planning to stitch me up. *Ruin* me.' She closed her eyes. 'Two-faced little cow with her horrid scraped-back hair and . . . Still, no sense holding a grudge. It's all in the past now. Tom had a word. Got her back onside.'

Joel knew all about that too. He had been there when Tom Steiner, one of the most powerful publicists in the business, called and told Laura to concoct a sympathetic story about Julia's battle to walk again. 'You owe her,' he had said. Tom had instructed her to dream up a few appropriate quotes and run the copy past him for approval. 'Just make it up,' he said. 'I don't suppose that will pose too much of a challenge for a reporter of your calibre. And make sure Julia comes out of it well.'

Laura had done an amazing job. Anyone reading the piece would think she had spent several hours with Julia, who came across as brave and self-deprecating. According to Laura, she was managing to remain cheerful in the face of 'gruelling' physiotherapy sessions. Joel was worried it was going too far to quote an entirely fictitious director of surgery, but Laura said it rounded off the piece well and anyway no one would ever find out. The clinic was not identified 'for security reasons'. Tom had been more than happy.

'Actually, she's quite good, that girl from the *Sunday*,' Julia said. 'Frumpy beyond belief, mind you. I don't think she's heard of lipstick.' Joel felt his cheeks burn. 'Still, I don't suppose it matters when you spend most of your time in front of a computer. The main thing is the rest of the hacks will leave me alone now until I'm ready to step back into the public eye again.' She paused. 'In a pair of killer heels.' She gave him a steely look. 'That's *killer* – not *kitten*.'

'It said in the paper you're confined to a wheelchair,' Joel said.

'So?'

'Well, it's not strictly true, is it? I mean, you can get about to some extent.'

Julia shot a withering look at the bootees next to the hearth. 'Only if I'm prepared to wear those monstrosities. Which, by the way, I am *not*. So for the time being I can just about haul myself out of a wheelchair and into bed, and that's it. But, it's not for long. I'll be up and about in no time once you work out how to do that stem cell thingy.'

'Look, let's not get our hopes up quite yet,' Joel warned, beginning to feel desperate.

'Too late,' Julia said, gleeful. 'I've already found the perfect pair of comeback shoes. Louboutins, naturally.' She leafed through a copy of *Grazia*. 'They're in here somewhere and my name is on them.'

Joel's heart sank. No pressure, then.

Twenty-Five

Cheryl tiptoed across the landing and into the bathroom with her clothes bundled under her arm. Once inside, she snapped on the light, locked the door and flopped into the over-sized, zebra-print armchair positioned at the foot of the giant claw-foot tub. She was facing a rack of towels in an identical print to the chair, and the wall was covered in onyx tiles with some kind of ornate gold trim. The taps on the bath and sink were also gold and fancy-looking. The place was hideous – not to her taste at all. When it came to interior design, Cheryl was a modern, minimalist kind of girl. She liked clean lines, simple and understated pieces, not all this . . . fuss. She put her head in her hands. What on earth was she doing?

She started to get dressed, pulling on a short beaded chiffon shift that was just on the decent side of see-through and slipping on her shoes, a pair of caramel-coloured studded heels that zipped up the front. Oh God, where were her knickers? She must have left them in the bedroom. She groaned. Shit. Well she wasn't going back for them. Getting to her feet, she checked her hair, which showed no signs of a night spent in a strange bed. It fell in its usual sharp shoulder-length curtain, jet black shot through with purple highlights. She swept the fringe over to one side and examined her mascara, which was still intact. Well, that was something. Fishing about in her bag she found a plum lip gloss and slapped some on. Right, that was it. She was out of here.

As she shivered in the dark on the main road outside Hampstead tube looking for a cab, Cheryl cursed herself for getting involved with Felicity Prince. She was definitely not her type. There was no way she could have stayed the night. The thought of waking up beside that . . . urgh. Felicity, with her wet-look short back and sides and her liking for tailored trouser suits was way too masculine for Cheryl. She wouldn't normally have given her a second look. Suki Floyd had been adamant, though. 'She's your best chance,' she had said. 'I mean, she makes no secret of the fact that she's *one of them*.' She had given Cheryl a curious look. 'One of *you*, I suppose. Luckily, she likes to put it about. So if you want to work again, I suggest you get over there and bat those lashes.'

Cheryl had stared at her, open-mouthed. 'You *are* joking,' she said. 'You want me to get off with the controller at WBC?' She was thoroughly indignant.

'I can assure you I'm perfectly serious. And since I've given you quite a build-up, you might show a bit of enthusiasm when you get in there.'

'You've already spoken to her?'

'My dear girl, while you're out shopping and – ' she glanced at Cheryl's impressive gold talons – 'having your nails done, I'm doing what I do best – hustling for work. I make things happen. For the likes of you. Presenters who are, shall we say, in-between jobs. They don't call me the comeback queen for nothing, you know.'

'If you're seriously expecting me to get off with Felicity Prince—'

'Got it in one. She's very keen to meet you. In fact, I got

the distinct feeling she's got a bit of a thing for you already, so you're already halfway there.' Suki frowned. 'She said you always looked hot in your vest and running shorts. I suppose that was when you were doing your marathons.'

Cheryl spluttered. 'I was a world-class *sprinter*!'

Suki, her froth of blonde hair like a halo, gave her a blank look. 'Well, anyway, I'm sure the two of you will get on like a house on fire. You just need to convince her *Girl Talk* would be a brilliant coup. Maybe hint there are other interested parties.'

'I am *not* sleeping with her.'

Suki folded her arms. 'I suggest you do what you have to. It's not only your future at stake here, you know. There are other people counting on you. I can definitely get your career back on track, but only if you're willing to take my advice.'

'You can hardly expect me to shag my way back into telly!'

'There's no need to put it quite so crudely. The end justifies the means, you know.' Her face was stern. 'And please don't tell me you have never done questionable things in order to further your career. We all have.' Suki's gaze drifted. 'I once endured a three-month affair with an actor, simply to poach him from another agency.'

Cheryl gasped.

'Three months of the most uninspiring sex you could ever imagine, and with a man who was, frankly, morbidly obese.' Both Suki and Cheryl shuddered. 'It was the only way. He fancied me rotten. And it was a small sacrifice in the end because he signed to me and I got a mega-bucks deal for his memoirs.' She flashed Cheryl an alarming smile. 'A triumph! It proved a turning point for me and I've never looked back.' Cheryl opened her mouth to say something, but Suki ignored her. 'I know

Felicity Prince is what some might rather unkindly describe as a bit of a plain Jane, but I don't think that need concern us. It's what she stands for that matters. And right now what she stands for is your best chance.'

Cheryl was apoplectic. 'It's easy for you to say. It's not you that's got to get sweaty with her.'

Suki had given her a patronizing look. 'I'm trying to help you, dear,' she'd said. 'If only you'd let me.'

Cheryl hailed a cab and slumped into the back seat, the events of the evening going round and round in her head. There was a bite mark at the top of one of her long legs. She yanked at her dress and covered it up.

Felicity Prince had suggested dinner at a Greek place in Primrose Hill, a part of town Cheryl rarely visited. At least she was unlikely to bump into anyone she knew. Wrong! Within seconds of her arriving, an actor, who looked vaguely familiar but whose name she could not for the life of her remember, rushed up to say hello. She must have met him on one of those shoots she used to do for *Girl Talk*. He had held on to her hand and scribbled his number on to the back of the specials menu and said to call him and they would 'do' lunch. Cheryl suspected he was sloshed.

'Well,' Felicity said once he'd left, 'who's the popular one?'

Cheryl shrugged. 'Actually, I'm not even sure who he is.'

Felicity burst out laughing. 'He was up for sexiest newcomer at the soap awards.'

Cheryl checked her reflection in a mirror at the back of the restaurant. 'I'm not a huge soap fan,' she said.

Felicity laughed again. 'I had no idea you were such a joker,' she said. 'Weren't you the resident soap expert on *Girl Talk*?' Cheryl gave her a bewildered look. 'It's just that I seem to remember you getting out and about doing cast interviews on location. You were famous for them.'

'Oh, those.' It was her researcher, Natalie, who was behind all that. Cheryl had simply read the briefing notes and done as she was told. 'I was hardly an expert.'

Felicity placed a meaty hand on Cheryl's slender wrist. 'You're being modest. You were very good. Quite brilliant.' Cheryl wanted to slide her hand away but remembered what Suki had said about sacrifice and the end justifying the means.

'The thing is, Felicity,' she said, giving her the kind of look that suggested she was about to share an intimate secret, 'I really think there's still life in the *Girl Talk* format. The show was popular. There was a bidding war between the sponsors, you know. Those energy drink people paid a fortune. And, of course, it was a show *by* women and *for* women. I'm sure you can appreciate that. Going out live and late at night meant we could really go to town on stuff – no tiptoeing round sensitive subjects in case someone wrote a snotty letter to the *Daily Mail*. We told it like it was.' Cheryl had no idea where all this stuff was coming from.

Felicity Prince leaned towards her. The table was small and she was much too close for comfort. Cheryl had to work hard to keep her smile in place. She spotted a hair sprouting from a mole on Felicity's chin. For crying out loud, hadn't the woman heard of electrolysis? She soldiered on.

'There's still nothing else like it on TV.'

Felicity said, 'And what was the single most important ingredient that made it a success, do you think?'

'Well, the chemistry between the five of us was probably what gave it its edge. On paper we probably looked an unlikely bunch, but I guess that's what kept the sparks flying.'

Felicity looked thoughtful. 'I think you're absolutely spot on. I mean, whoever did the casting in the first place did a brilliant job.'

'If you ask me, all *Girl Talk* needs is someone brave and forward-thinking to come up with a way of reinventing it.' She took a deep breath. 'Someone like you, really.'

'Well, that's what we're here to talk about,' Felicity said, giving her wrist a squeeze. 'And you can call me Flick, by the way.'

Cheryl, hating herself, managed a grateful smile.

Twenty-Six

'I've had very encouraging feedback from our mutual friend at WBC,' Suki Floyd said, getting up from her desk and coming to sit on the sofa next to Cheryl. She kicked off her shoes, a pair of clogs with monstrous heels which clattered on to the wooden floor. The light spilling through the blind made her hair look even more like candy floss than usual. Cheryl had an urge to touch it. She had never seen hair like it. 'I'm so glad you took my advice and made an effort to be nice.'

That was one way of putting it. 'I've done my bit,' Cheryl said. 'I'm sure you can deal with her now.'

She had no desire to see Felicity – *Flick* – Prince again. Not socially, at any rate. *Flick*, however, had other ideas, and her PA had already been in touch to arrange lunch – The Ivy this time – where there would be more than some actor she couldn't put a name to seeing them and puting two and two together. Before she knew it they'd be all over *heat*. It was too humiliating to bear. Cheryl gave Suki a cold stare. She wouldn't put it past her to tip off the paparazzi herself. She was beginning to appreciate just how ruthless Suki Floyd was, and beginning to wonder if it had actually been a good idea to come to her in the first place. But it was a bit late to worry about that now.

'I rather get the feeling she likes dealing with *you*. Best to keep her onside, at least until we can get something signed.'

'Sleep with her again, you mean.' Cheryl closed her eyes

briefly. 'Look, I'm going to be straight with you.' Suki smirked.
'She's not my type. I can't just, you know, do it with someone
I don't fancy.'

'I do completely understand, of course.'

Cheryl breathed a sigh of relief. 'So you'll deal with her?'

'Of course.' Suki examined her nails. They were practically
as long as Cheryl's and painted blood-red. 'But we'll have to
tread carefully. No sense in blowing the deal when we're so
close.'

Cheryl nodded. 'I appreciate it's tricky, but I have every confidence in you.'

'I'm glad to hear that. The relationship between agent and
artiste can only work if it's based on trust.'

'Definitely. And I do trust you.' Cheryl would trust her with
her life, provided she got that ugly old dyke off her back.

'Excellent. Because I need you to do one more thing.'

Cheryl nodded again, eager to please.

'Keep this little thing with Felicity going for the time being.
Nothing heavy, just drinks, the odd lunch. And when it comes
to the other stuff, well, pretend she's someone you *do* fancy.'

Cheryl clutched the side of the sofa. It was a nightmare, the
whole thing, and she couldn't wake up. 'I can't,' she said, her
voice small.

'Of course you can, dear,' Suki said, sounding brisk. 'It's only
sex, after all. And it could be worse. Felicity has dropped several hints about getting together with you and Faye, if you get
my meaning. It's only a matter of time before she comes right
out with it and suggests a threesome.'

Cheryl's head began to spin. 'My God, the woman's a total
predator.'

Suki clapped her hands in delight. 'Just joking,' she said.
'You are *so* easy to wind up.'

Twenty-Seven

Lesley was the first to arrive. Before she got out of the car she rummaged in her bag for her lip gloss and slathered on a sticky pink layer of Dream Girl. Her driver caught her eye in the rearview mirror and grinned.

'What do you think, Ian? Will I do?'

He twisted round in his seat and gave her a long, appreciative look. 'You look like the bee's knees,' he said.

Lesley preened and fiddled with her hair. She had gone for a slightly mussed-up look, not wanting to look like she'd tried too hard. Her blonde locks, enhanced with extensions, snaked in loose curls around her shoulders. She stepped out of the car and tugged at the hem of her dress, an ivory figure-hugging number with a hemline that ended mid-thigh. The dress accentuated her curves and slender waist and showed off her fabulous legs, which gleamed, thanks to a layer of wash-off bronzer. The dress was almost identical to one she'd seen in *Grazia* but a fraction of the price. Lesley was sure anyone in the know would assume it was the real thing. She had teamed it with an eye-catching necklace made from chunky pearls and chainmail that had cost ten times as much as the dress. She had always been clever at styling. She slipped on a pair of huge black shades and struck out for the restaurant in a pair of wooden platforms that added a good six inches to her five-foot-ten frame.

When she was still several paces away, the door swung open and the maitre d' performed an exaggerated bow before hurrying towards her, clasping her hands and smothering them in kisses. 'Ah, Signora Lesley, my favourite customer,' he said, hanging on to her elbow and steering her inside.

Lesley giggled. 'Honestly, Nico, all that bowing – you'll put your back out.'

Nico straightened up and gazed at her. 'For you, *bellissima*, it is worth it,' he said, his face serious.

As always, Al Dente, tucked away in an unfashionable street not far from Victoria Station, was deserted.

Lesley took a seat facing the door at a round table in the furthest corner. Nico placed a Kir Royale in front of her, which she downed in one before he had even made it back to the bar.

The door opened and Karen appeared in leggings, a billowing flowery top and ballerina pumps. Lesley frowned. Was it her imagination or had she got even bigger? It was hard to tell with that frumpy tent-thing she was wearing flapping about.

'You look great,' she lied, getting up and giving Karen a kiss on both cheeks.

'I feel like a whale.'

'Nonsense. You'll soon shift it. Willpower, that's all you need.'

'I'm on a diet. It's to do with kinetics.'

Nico placed a basket of warm olive bread in front of them. The smell was tantalizing. Karen unfolded her napkin. Perhaps one tiny piece . . .

Lesley whipped it away. 'Sorry, you can't have bread. It's the worst thing.' She tore the corner off a roll and popped it in her mouth. 'Oh my God, that's so good.' She gave Karen a stern look. 'Lethal, though – you know, in your condition. Really, you should knock cheese on the head as well.'

Karen's face fell. 'I love cheese.'

'Yes, and look where it's got you.' Lesley patted her hand. 'I'm only saying this for your own good.'

Cheryl swept into the restaurant in an ankle-skimming purple dress and biker jacket. A large cross studded with amethysts swung from a long silver chain round her neck. Karen caught a glimpse of grey suede peep-toe boots with lots of buckles. At the table she greeted the others with a hug before flopping into the seat next to Lesley and dropping her mock-croc satchel on to the floor. Slipping off her jacket, she revealed toned arms the colour of dark chocolate. Karen felt a pang of envy. Cheryl had a will of iron when it came to keeping in shape. It was obvious she had been hitting the gym, not the biscuit tin. Then again, she did have a head start. She was a former Olympic sprinter, after all. For one mad moment Karen considered asking her to be her personal trainer. It would never work, though. Cheryl had an aversion to fat people.

'I can't believe that bastard is back at Channel 6,' Cheryl said, green eyes blazing as she shifted her chair a fraction further away from Karen. 'Will someone please tell me where the justice is in that? He should be locked up, the sleazeball.' She made a fist and thumped it into the palm of her hand with such violence that Karen jumped. Cheryl pushed a strand of gleaming black hair behind one ear. 'Someone should shoot him.' A sudden loud pop, like a gun going off, made Karen duck. Cheryl gave her a hard look. 'For goodness' sake, get a grip.'

Nico bustled over with a bottle of champagne. 'Bubbly, ladies?' He filled their glasses with the frothy liquid.

Somehow, without anyone noticing, Faye had managed to

slip into the restaurant. She hovered behind Nico, waiting for someone to spot her. When no one did she stepped forward and touched Lesley's shoulder.

'Sorry I'm a bit late,' she said. 'It takes me ages to get ready these days. It's like I'm moving in slow motion.' She had leopard-print leggings on and a tight T-shirt emblazoned with a grinning Cheshire cat that accentuated her tiny frame and impressively flat stomach. Her blonde hair was scraped back off her face and secured in a thick plait.

Lesley patted the seat between her and Karen. 'You're not late and no wonder it takes you for ever to get going. You've got a demanding little person to take care of now.'

Cheryl rolled her eyes.

Lesley said, 'She's gorgeous.'

Faye managed a weak smile. Cheryl threw her a hostile look across the table. 'We were just in the middle of something,' she said huffily, 'until you interrupted.'

'Oh, I *am* sorry,' Faye said sarcastically.

'Never mind. I've lost my thread now anyway.'

Lesley gave Faye a nudge and nodded towards the window. 'Oh my God,' she said. 'Julia's in a wheelchair!'

They scrambled to their feet as Nico held open the door and Julia, in a cobalt-blue shift dress, her hair teased into in a spiky elfin crop, glided into the room.

Lesley put a hand over her mouth to stifle a giggle.

Faye grabbed her wrist. 'Stop it, it's not funny.'

Lesley's mouth twitched. Julia had stopped just inside the doorway, her way barred by Nico, who was fussing over her. As he went to take the throw draped over her knees, she waved him away.

'It *is* funny, in a way,' Lesley said. 'I thought she'd have a good few years in her before she got to that stage.' She paused. 'Mind you, I bet they're queuing up to push her around. Can you imagine? I never thought I'd see the day.'

Faye sniggered.

Karen gave the pair of them a warning look. 'For heaven's sake – she nearly died.'

Lesley pulled a face. 'Yes, well, she didn't in the end. And anyway, she only has herself to blame.'

Julia's carer, a hefty bloke with a shaved head and a square diamond glinting in one ear, steered his precious cargo towards them with enormous care. Karen glanced at Lesley, bemused. 'I didn't know she couldn't walk.' She lowered her voice. 'No one said anything about that when I was at the hospital.' She remembered that Julia hadn't moved from her seat when Karen had visited her at The Nook.

'She'll be milking it,' Lesley said. 'She always was a drama queen. Anyway, would you walk if you had some burly bloke on hand to get you around without ever having to get off your fat backside?' Karen stared at her. 'Sorry, no offence. Actually, he's not bad looking.'

As Julia came to a rest at the table, they clustered around to greet her with hugs.

'You look lovely, Julia – really well,' Karen said.

Julia gave a tiny nod. 'It's nice of you to say so, but I'm still not a hundred per cent.' No harm in playing the invalid card a bit longer, she thought. The truth was she had undergone a marathon session with Joel Reynolds at his Harley Street surgery a couple of days earlier, having Botox and filler and some kind of innovative light-therapy facial. Joel had said it would take years off and he had been spot on. She had emerged from his treatment room firm and plumped-up and dewy. A bumper dose of hyaluronic acid had restored her famous pout and she had also managed to fit in a tooth-whitening session. She might be in a wheelchair, but she looked a million dollars and she knew it. Her feet were on the mend too. Bullying Joel into organizing risky reconstructive surgery had been a good move; she would be up and about, out of her hideous orthopaedic boots and back in heels in no time. She turned to her carer. 'I'll be fine now, Terence. I'll give you a call when I'm ready for you.'

'Blimey, Julia, you look like you've been in a spa, not a coma,' Lesley said, impressed, digging out her lippy and slapping on another bubblegum-pink layer.

Julia gave her a brilliant smile. 'I think just being at home and sleeping in my own bed has made a difference,' she lied.

'Well, it hasn't done you any harm, by the look of things,' Lesley said.

Karen picked up her glass. 'Let's have a toast,' she said, handing a glass of bubbly to Julia. 'To us, back together again.'

They raised their glasses. Cheryl added, 'And to the downfall of that slimy little prick, James Almond.'

'We've got to do something about him,' Faye said. 'It's not fair.'

Cheryl bristled. 'Come on, then – what do you suggest?'

Faye shrugged.

'Well, we did get our own back, kind of, didn't we? I don't see what more we can do,' Lesley reached for the champagne and emptied what was left into her glass. 'More alcohol, Nico,' she said, holding up the empty bottle.

'No wonder you want to stay out of it,' Cheryl said. 'He's still your boss.'

Lesley shuddered. 'As far as I'm concerned, I work for Paula.'

She paused. 'Who still has the most appalling dress sense, by the way. She was wearing culottes the other day – awful baggy ones – and something she called deck shoes. I couldn't look.' She grinned at Julia, who seemed to wince.

'There might be a very good reason why she can't wear heels,' Julia said. 'Maybe she's got bunions.'

'No excuse,' Lesley said. 'Look at Victoria Beckham – you don't see her giving up her heels, do you?'

'It's nice to wear flatties sometimes,' Karen said.

Lesley grimaced. 'I was meaning to say something about that. Let's just say there are certain things that should stay behind closed doors, and flat shoes are right up there at the top of the list. Take note.'

Julia looked away and adjusted her blanket.

'Are your legs useless, then?' Lesley said, lifting the corner of Julia's blanket. Julia slapped her hand. 'Ouch, that hurt.'

Julia glared at her. 'I can't really stand on them, not yet, anyhow,' she said. 'There was some spinal damage and I need physio. Don't you read the papers? For the time being, at least, I'm stuck in this thing.' She patted the side of the chair. 'I can heave myself in and out, but that's about all.'

Karen glanced across the table at Faye, who looked teary. 'So you can't walk at all?' Karen said.

Julia shook her head and dropped her gaze. She was enjoying this. 'They've told me I will, God willing, in time.'

A tear slid down Faye's cheek. 'Oh no – you poor thing. We didn't know. If there's anything we can do, you only have to say.'

Julia nodded. 'I'll manage. Terence is very good. He's a private nurse, so he knows what he's doing.' Actually, he was a tour manager in-between gigs, but no one needed to know that.

She managed a brave smile. 'I'm lucky, really. I mean, I'm still here, aren't I?'

Cheryl said, 'Do you think you'd be up to a spot of live TV?'

Julia stared at her.

'Because I just might have a plan . . .'

There was expectant silence around the table.

'I've had some good meetings with the controller of entertainment at WBC,' Cheryl continued, sounding as casual as she could. She'd die if the others found out her 'meetings' with Felicity Prince had so far consisted of two dinners and a lunch that had gone on all afternoon. Each time she had ended up at Felicity's tasteless pad in Hampstead with its knick-knacks and paintings of religious scenes, being mauled and . . . well, she could hardly bear to think about it. The woman was a sheer nightmare, phoning and texting all the time. She had even returned her knickers by courier after their first encounter. Cheryl had protested to Suki, but it made no difference. Suki was adamant: it was vital to keep in with her until a deal was done.

'It turns out Felicity Prince was a huge fan of *Girl Talk* – absolutely loved it,' Cheryl continued. 'She reckons it was one of the best things on the box and that there's been a gap in the schedules ever since it came off.'

'Well, she's right there,' Lesley said. 'It was a runaway success. Look at the ratings. The audience loved us.'

Cheryl beamed at the others. 'Well . . . she loves the format so much she wants to commission it.'

Lesley said, 'Hang on – she can't just nick it. I mean, it's our show. And it's not like there *is* a format, not really. It was always about the chemistry between the five of us.'

'Exactly.' Cheryl was triumphant. 'It's *our* show and she wants *us* to host it. Same show, same women, different channel. Genius. They're willing to put a massive campaign behind it, posters on the tube and all that, do a proper launch. Rub James Almond's nose in it, basically – show him what he's missing.'

'Oh my God, it's definitely happening then,' Faye said.

Lesley turned to her. 'You knew about this?'

'No, not exactly.' Faye looked flustered. 'I mean, I knew Cheryl was seeing Felicity Prince—'

'I am *not* seeing her,' Cheryl said, cutting her short. 'I've had a few *meetings*, and that's all. I don't know what you've heard, but you're way off the mark.'

Faye was bemused. She had been about to ask if Felicity Prince was the mystery woman the *Sun* had spotted Cheryl lunching with at The Ivy, but decided not to bother. 'I'm pretty much in the dark, really,' Faye said. 'I only know what Suki's said, and that's not much.'

Lesley looked from Cheryl to Faye. 'Suki?'

'Suki Floyd's representing us,' Karen said. 'It was her idea to bring back *Girl Talk*.'

Julia snorted. 'I should have guessed. You'd never have dreamed it up on your own.' She gave Cheryl a curious look. 'No wonder there's interest from Felicity Prince. I mean, she likes girls, doesn't she? Are you sure it's the show she wants and not you?'

Cheryl mustered a look of contempt. 'Think what you like. It seems I'm the only one here actually doing anything. If you'd all rather fade into obscurity and never work again, feel free.'

'Just a second – I've still got a job,' Lesley said, indignant. 'I'm doing a hit show, in case nobody's noticed.'

'Ah yes, only concerned about number one, as usual,' Julia

replied, moving her napkin to cover a darn in the threadbare tablecloth. 'Don't worry about the rest of us.'

'Can we please stop all this bickering,' Karen pleaded, 'or we're not going to get anywhere.'

Lesley gulped down some champagne, leaving a gooey layer of frosted pink lip gloss on the edge of her glass.

'Well, well, well,' Julia was saying. 'Suki Floyd. The original comeback queen.' She gave Cheryl a pointed look. 'She always did know how to get some other poor soul to do her dirty work. I can't imagine delicate negotiations with Felicity are much fun. Does she still Brylcreem her hair?' Cheryl glared at her. 'Still, if there's the prospect of a new series, it's probably worth putting yourself out . . . or *about*, even.'

'Now just a minute—'

'*Please*,' Karen said. 'So what do you think, Julia – seriously? Don't you think it could be fun, the five of us back together again?'

Julia's mouth twitched. '*Fun* might be putting it a bit strongly. We were ready to kill each other by the time *Girl Talk* came off the air.'

'Some more ready than others, if I remember rightly.' Lesley had her compact out and was dabbing powder on her nose.

Julia ignored her. 'I suppose we *could* make it work, and it would definitely be one in the eye for James Almond. I'm sure he thought we were all dead and buried.' She glanced at Lesley. 'I'm curious to know how you've managed to stay in his good books, by the way. Not up to your old tricks again, are you?'

Lesley bristled. 'It may just be that he recognizes talent when he sees it. I don't suppose you thought of that.'

'No, actually, it never crossed my mind,' Julia said.

Faye shot Karen a desperate look. 'I'm going to have to go

soon. Mike's got Daisy, but he has to go into work to put together a showreel for some award he's up for, so I promised I wouldn't be long.'

Lesley knocked back her champagne and waved the empty glass at Nico. 'Well, I think you should go for it. Why not?' Deep down, she wasn't so sure it was a good idea to breathe new life into an old show. She had always thought it was a mistake to go back. Once or twice she had tried that with ex-boyfriends and it had never worked. Still, she might feel differently if she was the one without a job. She gave Karen a warm smile. 'The old chemistry's still there. I mean, look at the sparks flying round the table. It's just like old times. Plus it might be a novelty – you know, Jeremy Clarkson on wheels here whizzing round the studio in a wheelchair.' She gave Julia a wicked grin. 'You could even have it customized – get *Pimp My Ride* to bling it up a bit.'

'I'm not planning to be stuck in this thing for ever, you know,' Julia said.

'The thing is,' Karen responded, 'Lesley hit the nail on the head when she said it's the chemistry between the five of us that makes the show what it is. It needs *all* of us to say yes if it's going to work.' She took a deep breath. 'So it's really down to you, Lesley. If you say no, we're pretty much stuck.'

Lesley gazed round the table. Four pairs of eager eyes were trained on her. 'What about *Best Ever Sex*? It's the perfect show for me and I don't want to just give it up.'

'You wouldn't have to,' Karen said. 'It's not as if you're on an exclusive contract with Channel 6, so there's nothing to stop you taking on other projects.'

'I know, in theory . . .' She gave Karen an awkward smile. Lesley was happier than she'd been for ages. She enjoyed having more time on her hands and putting it to good use trying for a baby with Dan. Then again, *Girl Talk* would mean more exposure. And it had been fun. Sometimes. When they weren't bitching and fighting and plotting to kill each other, that is. And the girls were counting on her. If she said no, there would be four other people – her friends – out in the cold. Then again, it wasn't fair to make her responsible for their careers.

'I need to think about it,' she said eventually. 'It's a lot to take in.'

'Oh, come on,' Karen said. 'It would be a laugh.'

'Don't pretend you don't miss live TV – that rush of adrenalin, no script, flying by the seat of your pants, knowing anything can happen,' Julia said. 'There's nothing like it.'

That was true. One thing Lesley hated about *Best Ever Sex* was the fact that it was recorded, and that meant umpteen takes to get things absolutely perfect. There was definitely something to be said for the spontaneity of live telly in front of an audience. Lesley missed all that: the regulars who queued up to get a seat on the front row night after night. There was a mother and daughter who'd been coming to *Girl Talk* once or twice a week since day one. Lesley wondered what had become of them now.

'Look, you're putting me on the spot. You can't expect me to say yes just like that.'

Cheryl, desperate to bring negotiations with Felicity Prince to a conclusion sooner rather than later, said, 'Why not? Seize the moment and all that. It's a fantastic opportunity, you know it is.'

'Well . . .'

Faye gave Lesley a wan smile. 'I'm going to have to get off in a minute. Please say yes – you won't regret it.'

'Imagine the look on James Almond's face when WBC makes the announcement,' Karen said.

Lesley put up a hand to shut them up. 'All right, all right, you've made your point.'

Julia allowed herself a superior smile. 'So, it's agreed – you'll do it?'

'No! Yes! I don't know.' Lesley's head was spinning.

'Oh, for heaven's sake.' Julia was running out of patience. 'Make up your mind.'

'Look, I'm not saying no,' said Lesley. 'But I'm not saying yes, either. Not yet.'

Twenty-Eight

Lesley lay on the sofa with her feet in Dan's lap. For once, at his insistence, the TV was off, and instead the soothing strains of Groove Armada filled the room as he rubbed her feet.

'OK,' Dan said. 'What you need to do is work out how you feel about the idea of doing *Girl Talk*.'

'That's the problem – I don't know. I keep thinking it might be fun, then I panic about what a nightmare it could all be.' Dan pressed his thumb into the ball of her foot. Lesley groaned. 'Yes, right there. That's where it's tender,' she said.

Dan glanced at the skyscraper heels in the corner. 'No wonder,' he said. 'It's your shoes. You're ruining your feet.'

'It's nothing to do with my shoes,' she said, sounding huffy. 'It's stress.'

He looked sceptical. 'In the balls of your feet?'

'I saw something about it on TV. That's the bit of your foot that relates to the adrenal gland.'

He shook his head. 'You're making it up.'

'Well, it's something like that. It can hardly be a coincidence that my feet are hurting when I'm stressed to the eyeballs.'

'It's not a coincidence,' Dan said, exasperated. 'I've told you – it's your frigging shoes!'

Lesley pressed a button on the remote and Groove Armada faded away. She rescued another remote from under a cushion and the TV came to life. Dan frowned. She gave him a pleading smile. 'Let me watch *Loose Women*,' she said. 'Take my mind off things a bit.'

Her BlackBerry beeped. 'Oh, for heaven's sake,' she said. 'Yet *another* text from Cheryl asking if I've had any more thoughts. How am I supposed to think with that lot harping on the whole time?'

Dan massaged her toes. 'They're bound to want to know. You'd be the same.'

Lesley stuffed the BlackBerry down the side of the sofa. 'There's no point going on at me. It's just making things worse.'

'It's actually very simple,' Dan said. 'Never mind all the pros and cons of doing *Girl Talk*. It's really a question of how it makes you feel.' He placed a hand on her stomach. 'I mean here, inside. That's the only thing you can trust. If it's right for you, you'll have a good feeling about it.'

Lesley felt a familiar fluttering sensation inside. She wriggled on the sofa and her chiffon teddy rode up to reveal a pair of exquisite peach polka-dot knickers, tied at the sides with satin ribbon. 'I know how *that* makes me feel inside,' she said, giving him a wicked look and lacing her fingers through his.

Dan grinned, defeated. 'I give up,' he said, pulling her towards him.

Karen had started the day with a cup of green tea and half an hour on the treadmill. She had lost another two pounds – the kinetics man was a miracle worker. She sat in the kitchen with a mug of miso soup. Still no word from Lesley. It was tempting to call again, but there was no point in piling on the pressure.

At the sink, Dave, barefoot and sleepy-eyed, was filling the kettle. He padded over to the breakfast bar and sat facing her.

Karen held her soup in both hands and sipped at it. Neither of them said anything. On the TV in the corner, Matthew Wright marvelled as an attractive female guest claimed she never wore deodorant.

Eventually Karen said, 'You must have been late last night.' In fact, she knew he had come in shortly after three because she was still awake and had only just put off the telly. She had lain on her side in the dark with her back to the door, eyes wide open, listening as he crept upstairs and went into the bathroom. When he had slid into bed smelling of eucalyptus and snuggled into her, she had shut her eyes and pretended to be asleep. Undeterred, he had put an arm round her waist and pressed his body into hers while she kept still and deepened her breathing, emitting one or two sleepy snuffles designed to let him know she was dead to the world. He had held her tight for a minute or two before turning on to his side away from her. For several minutes she had lain completely still, eyes open again, wrestling with the idea of rolling over and wrapping her arms round him. When she heard his breathing change, she knew it was too late: he was asleep.

Dave yawned. Behind him steam belched out of the kettle. 'Fancy coffee?' he said.

According to Karen's diet, she wasn't supposed to have coffee. Certainly not the way she liked it, with frothy milk and brown sugar. Since she didn't want to keep saying no to him, though, she nodded. 'I'll do it.'

She was hopeless at making proper coffee. How many spoonfuls did you need? Two should do it, surely. She poured water into the pot and stood over a pan of milk heating up on the stove.

'It must have been gone three when I got in,' Dave said.

Karen was dying to know what had kept him out so late, but was too stubborn to ask. She was fed up of hearing about Lara Durham.

The milk boiled and she whipped it off the stove and whisked it into a froth. The coffee smelt fantastic but looked a bit on the weak side. She put a cup in front of him and sat down again.

'Not that you didn't already know.' He kept his voice light. Karen stared at him. 'I mean, seeing as how you were awake and there's a clock with an LED display right next to you.' She opened her mouth to deny it. The wry smile that appeared on his face stopped her. He gazed at her with cool grey eyes. 'Look, if you don't want to do it, you only have to say.'

Karen went pink.

A lock of blond hair flopped on to his brow. 'Just be straight.' He picked up his coffee. 'I don't know – it's like I've done something wrong, but Christ knows what. Want to tell me?'

Karen looked away. It wasn't anything to do with him; it was more about her feeling crap about herself. Once she lost a bit more weight and started working again, things would be fine. Dave's last girlfriend had been in her twenties and he was a decade younger than her. Add Lara hovering in the background and Karen felt old and past it. For the first time in her life she could understand the appeal of cosmetic surgery.

Dave was leaning on the breakfast bar drinking his coffee, his forehead a mass of frown lines. She wished she was better at hiding whatever it was she happened to be thinking. He could probably see right into her soul. She glanced at the TV.

Dave got up. 'Fair enough – please yourself,' he said, losing patience. He poured the rest of his coffee down the sink. 'Four heaped spoonfuls, minimum,' he said. 'Five, really, to get a hit.'

She flushed. She couldn't even manage to make a decent cup of coffee.

'I'm going down the gym,' he said. 'Catch you later.'

Julia was sitting on the small terrace in the garden of her cottage shaded by a parasol. The rickety metal table was set for one, and inside the kitchen Scott bustled about getting lunch ready. There were yellow tulips from the garden in a jug in the centre of the table, and a basket of homemade bread and a small earthenware bowl of olive tapenade beside them. A bottle of Muscadet was standing in a terracotta cooler.

Julia stretched and allowed herself a contented smile. She drank some wine, which was dry and lemony. If there was such a thing as bliss, this was pretty close. Bumble bees buzzed around the flowers in the border a few feet away. Perhaps she should just forget about work. From where she was sitting, there was a lot to be said for the notion of obscurity. She could ditch TV and all the celebrity hoo-ha that went with it and settle into a simple way of life. She glanced at the kitchen window. With someone like Scott waiting on her hand and foot, perhaps. He looked up and gave her a little wave. 'Won't be a minute,' he said.

Julia gave him a gracious smile. 'No rush. It's not like I'm going anywhere.' She popped her white, jewel-encrusted shades on top of her head and watched a tiny violet butterfly settle on the edge of the table, its papery wings fluttering.

Scott appeared with a platter of grilled prawns. The smell was delicious. 'You're spoiling me,' Julia said. 'At this rate I may find it a struggle returning to the rat race.'

He sat down and began peeling the prawns while she watched, imperious. 'Maybe you've reached that point in your life when it's time to change direction, slow down a bit.'

Julia gave him a sharp look. It was one thing for her to think about fading into obscurity, quite another for the hired hand to suggest it. 'Actually, I'm at the top of my game right now. It would be commercial suicide to slow down, as you put it.'

Scott snapped the head off a prawn. 'There's more to life than money, and there's nothing like getting on a bit to make you consider your options, that's all. It's that thing of hitting forty, I suppose.' He stopped what he was doing and looked right at her. Julia glowered back. 'I'm not jumping the gun, am I? Perhaps you're not there yet. I'm not very good at judging a person's age.'

Her eyes narrowed. Was he trying to be funny?

'Anyway, it's your life, your choice,' he said.

What Julia didn't know was that Scott – far from the yokel she took him for – was speaking from experience. At one point, he had been a high-flyer in the City, earning a fortune, pocketing bumper bonuses and generally living the high life – until his wife suffered a deep-vein thrombosis after a trip to the Far East and dropped dead at forty-two. He had quit the trading floor, bought a smallholding, started growing vegetables, and from then on kept himself pretty much to himself. The millions he had amassed in the City meant he would never have to worry about money again.

He placed the plate of peeled prawns in front of her and got to his feet. 'You know, you remind me of someone I knew,' he said. 'Worked her fingers to the bone, put her dreams on hold, and then . . . well, let's just say events overtook her.' He was thinking of his wife.

'Really,' Julia said, sounding huffy. 'How fascinating.' She was still bristling from that remark about getting on a bit. 'You can get off now. I've left a fiver on the table in the living room for you.'

Scott affected a grateful smile. 'That's extremely generous. Really, I don't know how I'd manage if you didn't pay so well.'

Julia gave him a sharp look. She could have sworn he was being sarcastic, but his face gave nothing away. It was obvious he was clueless when it came to money.

She was about to tell him to leave her in peace to have her lunch when his face changed.

'Keep absolutely still,' he said.

Julia froze. He moved forward, taking small, careful steps, and leaned over her, so close that his hair grazed her cheek. She caught a whiff of sandalwood.

'Scott, I—'

'Sssh, don't move,' he said, his voice low, his breath warm on her neck.

Julia, utterly bewildered, felt her heart begin to hammer as Scott's fingers teased her hair.

'There,' he said, after what seemed like an age. He straightened up and showed her the magnificent butterfly on the back of his hand.

Julia blinked.

Scott's eyes were bright. 'It's a Purple Admiral. Very rare.' He grinned. 'It landed right in your hair on one of those spiky bits. I reckon that's a good omen, don't you?'

Julia's eyes widened.

The butterfly's wings rose and fell. It took off and fluttered away towards the woods at the back of the cottage.

'It's only the second one I've seen,' Scott said, watching it go. He turned to Julia, who was clutching the napkin in her lap. 'That was something, wasn't it?'

Julia, shaken, managed a tiny nod. It had made her feel very odd to have Scott invade her space like that. Her tummy did a little flip. Very odd indeed.

Twenty-Nine

'No,' Cheryl said, 'absolutely not.'

Suki Floyd hoisted her hard little rear on to her desk and crossed her legs. 'Just dinner,' she said. 'How hard can that be?'

'There's no such thing as "just" anything with her. It always ends the same way, with me having to go back to her place and . . .' She closed her eyes. 'I've done as much as I'm prepared to. Send Faye next time.'

Suki's scarlet lips twitched in amusement. As it happened, Felicity Prince was already on board so long as the original line-up was back together. Money had been discussed. A figure had been agreed. All that was holding things up was a firm yes from Lesley.

'You didn't let me finish,' Suki said, tugging at the jacket of her pinstriped trouser suit. 'What I had in mind was a nice dinner – you and me and *Lesley*. See if we can't use our powers of persuasion to stop her dithering.'

Cheryl, balanced on the edge of the sofa with her bag on her knee, appeared unconvinced. 'Right, so I turn up at the restaurant and discover you've cried off, there's no sign of Lesley, and – oh, what a surprise! – there's Felicity Prince, lying in wait.' She gave Suki a dirty look. 'I'm not a hooker, you know.'

'Of course you're not, dear. No one's suggesting you are.'

She shook her head. The frizzy halo didn't move. 'Shame on you. We do need to get Lesley on-board, however, or the whole thing will fall through and all your, er, hard work, will have been in vain.'

'Don't worry about Lesley. She's up for it.'

Suki uncrossed her legs. Her tiny feet were dwarfed by a pair of clumpy red patent platforms that would have looked at home in a sex shop.

'Let's hope you're right, dear,' she said.

Faye had sent texts to all the other girls, but no one had replied. She dialled Lesley's number, which went straight to voicemail. 'Hi,' she said, trying to sound less desperate than she felt. 'Just called to say hello and – ' she paused – 'well, to see if you've decided yet. About the show, you know. And . . .' She gazed at the kitchen, at the dirty dishes piled up on the draining board, the miniature vests and cute little all-in-ones clogging up the clothes horse in the corner. 'I just fancied a chat, so if you get a minute I'd love to hear from you.'

She hung up and ran a hand through her hair, which should really have been washed at least three days ago. There was only so much dry shampoo could do, and she was out of that now. She dropped her phone into her dressing-gown pocket. A few seconds later she retrieved it and rang Karen. 'Just me,' she said when the call went to voicemail 'Any news? Let me know if you hear anything.'

She stood, hands on hips, staring at the mess around her. It was nearly four in the afternoon. She should really clear up and get dressed. She opened the fridge and got out a bottle of wine that was already two-thirds empty. Sod it. She would have a drink instead.

Thirty

Tabitha Tate was at home working on the script for her series on troublesome urban foxes. It was hard to concentrate and she went into the kitchen to make some tea. Her tiny flat was on the top floor of a house just round the corner from the Portobello Road in Notting Hill. She could hear classical music coming from the flat below.

As the kettle boiled and she spooned tea leaves into the pot, she gazed out across the rooftops towards Ladbroke Grove and mulled over her meeting with James Almond. There was something odd about him; sinister, almost. Or was she letting her imagination run away with her? She opened the fridge, took out a slab of white chocolate and snapped off a few squares. The idea of the Controller of Entertainment showing an interest in her was definitely flattering – exactly the break she was looking for, perhaps – but she had a funny feeling about the whole business. She couldn't help thinking James might be using her to get at Lesley Gold, who, as far as she could tell, was terrific on *Best Ever Sex*. Tabitha had warmed to Lesley when she gave evidence during James's trial. The judge had allowed her to wear her gigantic Gucci shades on the grounds that she had conjunctivitis, a ruse, Tabitha was sure, since the paparazzi snapped her with Dan Kincaid coming out of a bar in Soho later that day minus the shades and looking fantastic. Tabitha couldn't help but admire her cheek.

She undid her ponytail and let her hair fall in dark waves on to her shoulders. She broke off another few squares of chocolate and put the rest back in the fridge. If James was plotting against Lesley, she wasn't sure she wanted anything to do with it. Then again, she had her own career to think about, and if she was serious about getting on, there was no room for sentimentality. Her parents had drummed that into her from an early age. It had been a definite advantage coming from a privileged background. Having well-heeled folks meant she had been to a brilliant school where all the girls emerged, like her, brimming with self-belief and a sense of entitlement.

She took her tea into the sitting room, which was also her office and served as a spare room when anyone came to stay, and sat at the desk, which was old and solid and made from walnut. It had been her father's until he had splashed out on something modern made from beech and frosted glass.

Tabitha knew fate had been kind to her, that things could all too easily have been different. She opened the bottom drawer of her desk, which was where she kept her mother's letters, held together with an elastic band. She was lucky, really. She didn't know anyone else who got letters any more. It was all phone calls and texts and emails these days. She took the latest one from the bundle and read it again. The stiff watermarked paper and the familiar handwriting in black ink felt reassuring. Each letter ended with the same words: *I'm thinking of you, my darling. Love always.* She smiled, put it back into the envelope, and returned it to the drawer. She really wanted to see her. Soon. It had been on her mind for ages, but her life was so hectic she just kept putting it off. Well, it was about time she did something about that.

Thirty-One

James stretched out on the sofa at home and thought back to his lunch date with Desmond Hart, the celebrity booker on *Good Morning Britain*. He had got to know Desmond during his brief stint at the breakfast show *Rise and Shine* in the days when Julia Hill was the star presenter. James was still finding his feet when a run-in with Julia got him the boot. Desmond had actually bothered to call to tell him not to take it personally, and they had continued to meet for coffee once in a while. Desmond, with his liking for bow ties in bright colours and clashing velvet jackets, had seemed old to James even then. Over twenty-odd years he didn't seem to have changed much, other than filling out a bit. 'Life's too short to skip dessert,' he would say, ordering something likely to give him a heart attack. Desmond Hart knew everyone and – amazingly, in celebrity-land – was almost universally well liked. James had never heard anyone say a bad word about him. If he wasn't organizing a do, he was invariably on the guest list. James had no idea how he did it at his age. He had to be in his sixties at least. Non-stop socializing was utterly exhausting, but old Desmond seemed to revel in it.

Desmond was a man with his ear very much to the ground when it came to showbiz gossip. Over lunch in Mayfair, Desmond had said he had spent a very pleasant five minutes chatting to Lara Durham at a charity do. 'You missed the boat there, James,' he said, tucking into his saffron risotto starter. 'That girl is going places.'

'Yes, well, the Beeb snapped her up while I was otherwise engaged doing my bit to ensure the wheels of justice turn as they should.'

Desmond raised an eyebrow. 'Ah, yes, most unfortunate. Timing is everything.'

'Indeed.' James ate a small piece of his halibut. 'I have my eye on another star in the making,' he said. 'A very exciting prospect, actually. I'm working on her at the moment.'

'Well, I can see why you'd want to poach Tabitha Tate.' James stared at him. 'I mean, she's wasted on news. She's very brainy, you know, as well as being immensely pretty.'

James did his best to remain composed. If there was a leak in his department, he would find it. 'Who told you I was talking to Tabitha Tate?'

Desmond gave a slight shrug. 'It's obvious. The girl has talent. I wouldn't expect you to overlook potential when it's right under your nose.' Desmond paused. 'No need to look so put out. I've been in this game a long time. Star-spotting is second nature to me.'

'I'd hate to think someone on the inside's blabbing.'

'Well, relax – they're not. It just so happens I have a sixth sense for these things. You know you could trust your delightful PA with your life – and I'm sure you've already put the fear of God into poor little Tabitha not to breathe a word. Not so?'

James laughed. 'You're very good, Desmond.'

He looked pleased. 'I know. That's why you pay me so much.' He put his fork down. 'How are you, James? I don't suppose it's been easy going back, taking the reins at Channel 6 again.'

'On the contrary, it's like I've never been away.'

Desmond gave him a searching look. 'Come on, it's me you're talking to. You've been through a lot these last few months, not least the business with Stephanie.' James looked away. 'You're bound to feel something. I can't imagine it's much fun going back to that mansion of yours, for a start. What do you do locked away behind those impressive gates?'

James managed a thin smile. 'Watch TV, work on ideas for new formats. Really, Desmond, I appreciate your concern, but I'm fine, so stop fussing.' He sighed. 'Seriously, it just makes things worse to dwell too much on things. I'm not one of those types to put a depressing album on and sit there feeling sorry for myself. I have a rule about wallowing, you know. There's no room for self-indulgence.'

The truth was, he had been doing a fair amount of wallowing, to a soundtrack of Morrissey and Joy Division, not that he was willing to own up. He had a rule about disclosing weakness.

'It's far better if I concentrate on getting my teeth into my work,' he said.

'You're made of stern stuff, I'll give you that. I wish I had half your fighting spirit. However, if at any point you find you really are not fine, give me a call – any time.'

James waved a hand in the air. 'If my life is all we can find to talk about, this is going to be a most unedifying lunch.'

'To be honest, I thought the reason you wanted to see me was to nail down all this business about *Girl Talk* coming back.'

James frowned. 'That's wishful thinking, I'm afraid. I have

no plans to bring it back. I spent long enough getting rid of it.' He picked up his wine. 'That's between you and me, obviously.'

Desmond fiddled with his bow tie, a purple confection splashed with gold and red. 'I'm not talking about you bringing it back. It's the bods at WBC who've got it in their sights.'

James looked amused. 'You mean they're planning some sort of *Girl Talk* rip-off, complete with idle chit-chat? How very original.'

'No, James – as far as I can tell, they're *relaunching* the show. Complete with the original line-up.' Desmond waited for this to sink in. 'Julia and the rest of them.'

'Julia's out of action.'

'Don't be fooled. She's well and truly on the mend, and from what I hear she's looking fantastic.'

James's smile had vanished. 'Where did you hear this?'

'My sources are impeccable. I got a hint that something was going on when I saw Cheryl West at The Ivy with Felicity Prince. That led me to do some digging, not that anyone seemed to know anything. Then I struck lucky, ran into the delicious Suki Floyd at a launch bash—'

'That old bat.'

'And over a glass or three of bubbly she happened to let slip she now has the *Girl Talk* gals on her books.'

James spluttered.

'I know, who'd have thought it? They've done well for themselves to get Suki on-board. I mean, she has the most extraordinary track record when it comes to rehabilitating celebs.'

'Suki Floyd. Unbelievable.'

'I think perhaps Cheryl was the driving force there. Now, there's another bright girl for you. Ambitious, focused and most striking. You must have seen the poster campaign she's done for London 2012 – no airbrushing. I spoke to the photographer. She actually does look that good.'

'So let me get this straight. Suki Floyd's taken them on and they're doing a deal to bring *Girl Talk* back on a rival channel.'

'That's about the size of it, yes.'

James drummed his fingers on the table. 'No, I don't think so. That is just not happening. Not while I'm running things at Channel 6. That's my show.'

'In fairness, you didn't actually want it.'

'That's immaterial. *Girl Talk* belongs to me. It's Channel 6 property.'

'They could always call it something else.'

James snorted. 'If it's coming back with the same five old hags, it doesn't matter what they call it – it'll still be the same show.' He shook his head. 'Do they really think they can get away with this?'

'Well, clearly—'

'Lesley Gold is already employed by me on one of our key late-night shows, and she has the gall to go behind my back doing deals with other channels. I can understand the others playing silly games, but Lesley . . .'

He decided not to mention that he would have sacked her the instant he regained control of Channel 6 if he could have got away with it. It was a non-starter, though. Paula Grayson would have been up in arms, as would the press, who'd have said it was pure malice. They had all enjoyed Lesley's witty little cameo in court. Still, there was more than one way to skin a cat. He would find a means of insinuating Tabitha Tate into the entertainment department and dispensing with Lesley if it killed him.

'I'm not sure there's much you can do about it,' Desmond said.

'Well, we'll see about that. If they seriously think I'm going to sit back and allow them to humiliate me, they've got another think coming.'

Desmond sipped at his wine. 'You could always do something nobody would ever expect, of course.' He gave James a crafty smile.

'Like what?'

'Like pull the rug out from under WBC and bring *Girl Talk* back to its original home at Channel 6.' James began to shake his head. 'Think about it,' Desmond said. 'It was always a strong show for you – no reason why it shouldn't still be. And imagine the publicity! It would be phenomenal. You could have the most fantastic launch – obviously I could make sure it's the hottest ticket in town – and it would do wonders for your reputation to be seen as the one holding out an olive branch.'

There were a few things James would like to do with an olive branch where those *Girl Talk* bitches were concerned, but offering it as some kind of symbol of peace wasn't one of them. He shook his head. 'No. Never.'

'The mark of a truly great man is his ability to forgive.'

'Who said that?'

'I did. Just now. Look, think about it.' He chuckled. 'Handled in the right way, this could be the most extraordinary TV comeback ever. And Suki Floyd wouldn't even be able to take the credit, because it would be *your* idea.'

It was tempting to get one over on Suki Floyd. He had endured contract negotiations with her in the past in which he had practically lost the will to live. She was like one of those attack dogs whose jaws lock, vice-like, on to their prey. As for that awful hair – it put him in mind of a pan scrub. He gave another sigh.

'Granted, it's an inspired idea, Desmond, but . . .' He made a helpless gesture. The idea of Julia Hill prowling the corridors again as if she owned the place was too much, really it was. Then again, he wouldn't mind the pleasure of Karen King's company. He had unfinished business there. 'In all honesty, I really don't have it in me. Perhaps I'm not the great man you seem to think I am.'

'With all due respect, James,' said Desmond, 'I think you underestimate yourself.'

'Perhaps I do,' James replied, looking thoughtful.

Thirty-Two

At The Nook, Julia's thoughts drifted to *Girl Talk*. Every so often she told herself she'd had enough of the shallow world of TV, but she knew how she'd feel if she switched on the telly and saw the others back in the limelight while she shuffled about in the back of beyond in her awful slippers. Felicity Prince had said she was only interested if all five girls agreed to do it, but what if Julia said no and they went ahead without her anyway? She would never be able to bear it. She glanced at Scott. It was the second time she'd invited him to stay for lunch, at which point she had found out a bit more about him. Now she knew he'd once been something in the City it mortified her to think she'd been treating him like a dimwit, not to mention paying him a pittance.

'Don't you mind being stuck out here on your own?' She searched his clear blue eyes and realized, to her amazement, that she actually wanted to hear what he had to say. It was the first time in ages that had happened. For as long as she could remember, the only opinion that had mattered to her was her own.

Scott pushed up the sleeves of his tatty old jumper. He appeared thoughtful and there were lines on his brow and at the corners of his eyes. For once, Julia didn't think about how much better he'd look if he had Botox. Somehow, he looked right just as he was.

'I have never once regretted moving here,' he said finally. 'There's no substitute for peace.' He tapped his chest. 'On the inside.'

'You make it all seem so simple.'

'Only if you know what you want.' The blue eyes locked on to hers. 'It so happens I do.'

Julia felt something begin to give way inside.

'Before I came here,' she said, 'I was in a bit of a mess. I suppose you know all about it?' She looked away. 'It was in all the papers and the celebrity mags.'

He shook his head. His hair was dark and shiny and looked like it hadn't had a brush through it for a long time.

'I only know what you've told me,' he said. 'I don't read the papers any more.' He gave her a smile. One of his front teeth was chipped. Julia, who would normally have been thinking about passing on the details of a cosmetic dentist in Harley Street, decided it suited him. 'I've never even picked up what you call a celebrity mag.'

She gazed at him. 'Not even *heat*?'

He laughed. 'Nope.'

She had probably encountered the only man in the country who knew virtually nothing about her. Her spirits soared. Moments later, they sank. He was bound to find out, though, and then he wouldn't be coming round, peeling prawns for her and picking butterflies out of her hair. Just thinking about that sent a shiver up her spine.

'The thing is, I've got a bit of a reputation,' she said.

He shrugged again.

'I can be a bit of a bitch.' She held her breath. It was quite

an admission for her, and was at the same time the understatement of the year.

'You should have seen me in my day on the trading floor,
bawling and losing my temper,' he said. 'I don't think you'd
have liked me very much.' He gave her a solemn look. 'People
can change, you know. It's all a matter of choice.'

'I know, it's just—'

He held up a hand. 'It doesn't matter. Now – I slaved over
this duck for hours, so relax and eat your lunch. Deal?'

She nodded. The funny thing was, she wasn't at all hungry
any more.

He leaned back, picked up his wine, and gave her an awkward smile. 'Sorry, am I being a bit bossy?'

For once Julia was utterly lost for words. No one ever shut
her up. Nobody told her what to do. Ever. Nobody dared. She
felt a surge of joy. Being bossed about felt absolutely wonderful.

Thirty-Three

Karen felt dreadful, thoroughly ashamed. Never, not even when things were at their lowest ebb with Jason and she was sure he was playing around, had she stooped so low.

She opened the wardrobe and put Dave's jacket on a hanger. Then she emptied the contents of the laundry basket on to the floor and sorted out a load of whites for the machine. The shower was still running. She glanced at herself in the mirror. Her cheeks were flushed and she had the distinct look of someone who had been up to no good. She faced the mirror, hugging his dirty smalls, and wondered if the best thing to do was tell him what she'd done. He'd be cross, furious probably, but he might just understand. Dave was nothing if not reasonable, and he knew what she'd been through with Jason, which went a long way to explain why she was prone to paranoia.

The shower stopped and she hurried downstairs. She wanted a bit more time before she decided what to do. Perhaps she wouldn't have to tell him. Perhaps he would just know. Maybe there was some kind of clever gizmo on his phone that sent an alert to say someone had been snooping. Now she really was being paranoid.

He was partly to blame. All these odd hours he was keeping driving Lara Durham around, coming home when it was getting light, were causing havoc. Karen went to bed on her own practically every night. By the time Dave got in, she was nearly ready to get up. She was grumpy, too, since she couldn't sleep properly when he wasn't there. Still, it was no excuse to dig around in his phone looking for signs of infidelity.

She shoved the laundry into the machine. Much as she hated to admit it, that's exactly what she had been doing. As it happened, she hadn't found anything suspicious, just the odd text from Lara to say she would be another hour and sorry – *soz* – for keeping him hanging about. There was usually a solitary X on the end, but Karen didn't read anything into that. It was second nature for celebs to sign messages with an X. She had actually put an X on the end of a text confirming an appointment with her dental hygienist the other day and pressed the send button before she realized. No, she would have been more surprised if there wasn't an X on the end of Lara Durham's messages. X was normal.

If she was honest, she wasn't so worried about Lara any more, since she seemed to be involved with Daniel Faith, the star of a smash-hit US cop show and now in London doing a play. They were all over the magazines and, from what Karen could gather, it was a proper romance, not just something dreamed up by an astute publicist. No, Dave was not having a fling with Lara Durham. The very idea was ridiculous. But if that was the case, where had he been the night before and why had her calls gone straight to voicemail? If he had been working, there was no way he would have switched his phone off. He had finally turned up looking the worse for wear just as *This Morning* was starting, made some coffee and gone for a shower, shrugging off Karen's questions.

'You know where I've been. Working,' he'd said, not looking at her.

'Until this time? Why didn't you call?'

'I didn't know I had to.'

'Your phone was off.'

'Probably going through an underpass or something.'

'I tried a few times.'

'Or parked up under the arches near that club on the way to Tower Bridge, waiting for them to come out. It's a dodgy signal there.'

'Them?'

He gave her a blank look.

'You said *them*?'

'Oh yeah, you know – she had her friend with her.' The way he said *friend* made it clear it was Lara's new squeeze, Daniel, he was talking about.

It all sounded completely reasonable, yet alarm bells were going off in her head, getting louder and more insistent. The last time they'd made such a racket was when Jason was sneaking off to see Hannah Blake and lying through his teeth about it. She put her hand on her brow. *Clang-clang.* She could hardly hear herself think.

Dave breezed into the kitchen in sweatpants and an old T-shirt he'd ripped the sleeves off. It was his workout gear.

Karen stared at the phone in his hand and waited for him to accuse her of checking his messages. Instead he went to the fridge and glugged some orange juice straight from the carton. She wished he wouldn't do that. It drove her mad. He glanced at the white roses on the counter, still in their cellophane. Jason.

His voice was sharp. 'Not more sodding flowers.'

'It's not like I ask him to send them.'

'It's not like you don't, either.'

'I've told him to stop!'

'Maybe I need to tell him.'

'I'll deal with it.'

'Yeah, right.' He dumped the flowers head first in the bin and let the lid clang shut on them.

Karen took a step towards him. 'I'll tell him again – I will.'

Dave shook his head.

'Shall I do you some breakfast?'

'I'm not stopping.'

'Don't tell me you're going out.' It came out as less of a question than she had meant.

'Said I'd meet a mate down the gym, do a bit of boxing or something, clear my head.'

'You've had no sleep!'

'Yeah, well, I don't feel like getting my head down now. I'll do half an hour in the ring, lift a few weights, see if I fancy a bit of shut-eye after.'

'But—'

He gave her a mock salute and backed away.

'I could cook dinner, if you like . . .' Her voice trailed off as she heard the front door close. A minute or two later the car started up and he was gone. She tipped the rest of the orange juice down the sink and tossed the carton into the bin with the flowers.

Thirty-Four

Dave drove all the way to Chingford and parked at the back of his old gym, Dooley's Fight Club. It was a run-down building with fly-posters on the walls and grills on the windows. Run by a red-faced retired welterweight called Pat Dooley, it was the one place Dave knew would be a blokes-only zone, guaranteed. He wanted to give women a bit of a swerve for the next few hours, get his head straight.

He pushed open the door. In front of him a bald bloke with huge biceps was on the bench press, lifting an impressive amount of weight. The veins in his neck stood out. It wasn't as if women were banned from Dooley's or anything. It was just that the facilities were pretty basic. It definitely wasn't one of those gyms where you paid through the nose to join and relaxed in the sauna after a session on the Power Plate.

Pat was at the side of the ring, saying something to a young lad with sweat running down his face. Dave felt the need to push himself to the limit, get in the ring with someone capable of knocking him senseless; anything to stop him thinking about what had happened the night before.

He felt bad about running out on Karen like that. He could see she was completely baffled. First he had come home hours after he was due, then he had legged it again without so much as a by-your-leave. She had been waiting for him to come downstairs so she could talk to him, he knew that. That was the trouble, though. The last thing he felt like doing was talking. He wasn't actually sure what he would say. He hadn't been lying when he said there was a dodgy signal outside that club south of the river. It was always a bit iffy round there. And Lara did have her friend with her, except it wasn't her boyfriend, as he'd implied. It was, in fact, a girl she'd been at school with. Dave had ended up taking the friend home after dropping Lara off. He had done his usual thing of waiting for her to go inside before pulling away, but she seemed to be struggling with the lock. She stood on the path fiddling with the key for ages and eventually turned and gave him an embarrassed shrug. Dave got out of the car and went to see what the problem was. She giggled.

'I'm like one of those drunks, can't get my key in the lock,' she said, her eyes bright.

'Want me to have a go?'

She handed him a heavy bunch of keys. He gazed at them. 'Don't tell me you really need this lot?'

'Three for the front door, three for the door to my flat, a cupboard I lock important stuff in, and . . .' Her voice tailed off and a look of intense concentration crossed her face. 'And . . . oh yeah, I always lock my bedroom door from the inside.'

He shook his head and began working his way through the keys. She sat on the wall next to the front door in her sparkly minidress and took off her shoes, a pair of black suede high heels with ankle straps. She had a tattoo at the top of one of her legs. After several minutes he managed to get the front door open.

She clapped her hands. 'Don't suppose you could do the same upstairs, could you?' Only I'm not sure I can see straight any more. One mojito too many.' She wasn't exactly drunk, just a bit merry.

He followed her to a bright yellow door and wrestled again with the keys. It was slightly quicker this time – at least he knew which ones not to bother with. That was when he should have left. He didn't, though. For some crazy reason he went in with her and sat at a tiny fold-up table in the kitchen while she got out a bottle of white rum and insisted on making him a drink. A proper mojito, as she put it.

Dave never had a drink when he was working, not even one, so the fact that he sat there while she chopped lime and searched for brown sugar meant he had already crossed some kind of line. He took his jacket off, stuffed his tie in the pocket and loosened a couple of buttons on his shirt. The drink tasted good. Too good, probably. He sank it way too fast. She disappeared into the bedroom and came out with a baggy jumper on over her dress. The funny thing was that it made her look even better. She emptied a bag of thick hand-cooked crisps into a bowl and poured him another drink. She was funny, showing him some daft dance move Lara had picked up in LA. He sank another mojito. And another. And then all of a sudden he was tired. Probably all the late nights catching up. He had never been much good at sleeping during the day.

Dave took himself off into a corner of the gym and pounded away at the punch ball, dodging and jabbing. Pat Dooley came up behind him.

'You look like you mean that, son,' he said in his soft Irish brogue.

Dave took a step back and caught his breath. 'Too right.'

Pat nodded at the ball as it bobbed on its spring support. 'Got someone in mind?'

Dave got ready to go on the attack again. 'Some complete dickhead,' he said.

'Go on then, you give him what for.'

Dave struck out and sent the bag flying. He didn't bother telling Pat the dickhead he was thinking of was himself. He didn't even know what had happened. When he came round he was in a strange bed, and a girl he didn't know with big eyes, dark, tousled hair and a huge grin was peeping round the bedroom door. 'I've made some tea,' she said. 'You look like you could do with some.'

She disappeared and he sat up. His head had that odd, spacey feeling from drinking too much. He was still wearing his boxers, which was something, but the rest of his clothes were on a chair in the corner. The bed took up most of the room. There was a wardrobe made from canvas and pale wooden slats against the wall facing him, and next to it a round art deco mirror above a small chest of drawers. The surface of the chest was covered in pots and make-up. At one end was an ornate bottle of perfume just like the one Karen liked. Christ, Karen! He flung back the duvet as the door opened and the girl, in a man's shirt – Oh fuck, not his? No, it was there, on the chair, thank God – came in with his tea. He got another glimpse of her tattoo as he pulled the duvet up again and she put the tea down on a table at the side of the bed. From the look on her face she was finding something extremely funny. She rummaged in the wardrobe for a pair of jeans. 'I'm out of milk,' she said. 'Won't be a minute. Have a shower or something, there's no rush.'

As soon as he heard the front door close, he jumped up, put his clothes on, checked his pockets to make sure he had his phone – damn, no signal – and his wallet and keys, and got out of there. He could hear Jeremy Kyle's voice coming from the other room. Shit, that must make it – what? Half nine? His hands felt clammy on the steering wheel as he drove away. Christ almighty, what had he done?

Thirty-Five

Faye had the afternoon to herself. Mike had taken little Daisy out, which meant she could do anything she wanted: hit the shops, get her hair done, have a late lunch at the Bluebird Café on the King's Road. The trouble was, she was so worn out that all she wanted to do was have a bath and go for a lie down. She had still been in her dressing gown when Mike arrived to collect Daisy. It was midday and she hadn't even had a wash or put a brush through her hair. When he'd asked if she was ill, she had practically bitten his head off.

'In case you hadn't noticed, I'm looking after a baby. And I got no sleep last night. *Again*,' she had said, tears welling up.

She was being unfair. It was hardly his fault she was on her own. After all, she was the one who'd been having an affair. And with another woman, at that. Mike had viewed his wife getting it on with Cheryl as a personal attack on his masculinity and had taken it very badly, to put it mildly.

Once she had the house to herself, Faye poured scented salts into the bath and watched the water turn a brilliant shade of blue. It made her think of St-Tropez and the holiday she and Mike had been on when they first got together. They had lazed on the beach, made love in the sea. She had been sure she would love him for ever, and in fact she still did, even though things were so strained they were hardly speaking. She had tried to

173

explain why she had got involved with Cheryl, but he wouldn't listen, said the very idea of it made him want to throw up. Faye was desperate for him to see things from her point of view. If he had been at home she would never have strayed, she said, but the fact that he was off reporting from war zones for months at a time meant she was lonely and vulnerable.

'So it's my fault?' he had said, incredulous.

'I'm just trying to explain. What do you expect me to do when I'm stuck at home for months on end?'

'You make it sound like I was off on a jolly, not risking my life on the front line in Afghanistan.'

'Oh, come on, you love it – Mr Hero War Reporter. So did you expect me to stay in night after night and have no life?'

'Stay *in*? You were on telly every night, in case you'd forgotten, living the high life. And it *still* wasn't enough to keep the boredom at bay. You want to try living like the rest of the army wives, see what that's like.'

'That's the whole point – I'm not a frigging army wife!'

It had been a dreadful row. If she could turn back the clock, Faye would have handled things differently. Then again, it hadn't all been her fault. Mike's love affair with war reporting had made her feel abandoned. He needed to understand that, really, if there was any chance of them patching things up. In the meantime, she needed to make more of an effort, not be so snappy. She would do her hair and put on some make-up, see if he fancied staying for dinner when he came back with Daisy.

He was a natural with his daughter, absolutely fantastic. Faye practically melted at the sight of the two of them together, Daisy gurgling, Mike all gooey, calling her his little princess. Maybe, once he'd had a bit more time to cool off, there was still a way out of this mess, a chance he might look at her again the way he looked at his baby girl. In the meantime, she just had to hope the house wouldn't sell. After four months, there had been plenty of viewers but no serious offer. Thank God for the recession. Or perhaps it was her inability to keep the place looking tidy.

Mike pushed Daisy round the common in her pram. He sat in the sunshine on a bench and watched a squirrel run head first down a tree, check for dogs, sprint across open ground and shoot up another tree. A woman with long dark hair and skinny jeans tucked into green wellies was trying to teach a scruffy dog to fetch a ball. She flung it across the common. The dog wagged its tail and jumped up at her. She shouted, 'Go on, boy,' and pointed in the direction the ball had gone, but the dog just dodged about, delighted, tongue lolling. He looked as if he was laughing. Mike smiled. The woman gave up and retrieved the ball herself.

Mike caught her eye. 'He's having you on,' he said.

The woman gave him a frosty look. Mike gave her his winning smile and was rewarded with a glimmer of recognition in her eyes. 'I think you're right,' she said, no longer cool, bending to give the dog a pat.

'He's not going to fetch it if he knows you will.'

She laughed. 'I hope you don't think I'm being nosey, but aren't you Mike Parry?'

He gave a modest nod. 'That's right – enjoying a bit of home leave.'

'Your eyes are amazing, really blue. They're not contacts, are they?'

Mike laughed in a way that made it clear there was nothing fake about him; his eyes really were that fabulous inky blue.

She was giving him the soppy look all women did after a few brief moments in his company. Any minute now she would be asking for his autograph and giving him her number.

'I'm not being funny, but your wife must want her head examining,' she said. Mike's smile slipped. 'None of my business, I know, but you're a bit of a pin-up at home. Even my husband likes you.' She put a hand over her mouth. 'Oh God, I don't mean like that. It's not like he's a closet gay or anything.' Her eyes widened. 'I'm *so* sorry. I didn't mean to put my foot in it.'

Mike gave her a disparaging look. Close-up, she was like a heifer with her ruddy cheeks and fat backside. At least Faye was hot – well, until little Daisy came along and wrecked her beauty routine – even if she was part gay, if there was such a thing. He got up. The woman hovered, looking hopeful, probably about to ask for an autograph. Well, she could forget that. He wished he hadn't bothered speaking to her in the first place. It was all too depressing. His last series of reports had seen him in the thick of a major battle with the Taliban, bullets flying past his head, one nicking his sleeve, his cameraman killed a few yards from where he lay flattened on the ground, and all anyone ever bloody did these days was go on about his marriage. Funny how they always managed to get some kind of gay jibe in as well. It was driving him mad. You'd think *his* sexuality was up for debate, just because Faye had been having it off with a woman. For pity's sake. *She* was the queer one, not him.

'Well, nice to meet you,' he said, releasing the brake on the pram and moving off. 'Good luck with Fido.'

Faye's lesbian fling splashed all over the tabloids had done untold damage to his ego. It had been like being ambushed:

176

utterly shocking, wholly unexpected. The fact that he had a reputation as a fearless and rugged war reporter just made things worse. One or two columnists had hinted that there must be something wrong with him, dropped veiled hints about his performance in bed and wondered if he was in any way responsible for driving his wife into the arms of another woman. It was so unfair. He was a brilliant lover. He had no doubts whatsoever about that. At least he never used to. No one had ever complained. Not to his face, at any rate. Even so, despite numerous glowing testimonials from various lovers over the years, he wasn't so sure of himself any more. Perhaps there *was* something wrong with him.

A seed of doubt had planted itself in his head and was growing, making him more paranoid by the day. At least he had managed to get his cheating wife pregnant, which was something Cheryl West would never manage, whatever else she was good at, and that made him feel slightly better. If nothing else, he was fertile. His tackle was in perfect working order, no blanks being fired there, that was for sure. The fan mail that poured in from women offering to cheer him up in the wake of his marriage break-up also helped bolster his ego. Some of them weren't bad, if their pictures could be trusted. And the gossip mags had waded in with pictures of him bare-chested in his combat pants and Faye hiding behind her sunglasses under headlines like *Is She Mad?*

He gazed down at his daughter, who was fast asleep, her hands raised above her head. She was perfect, as good as gold. Not that he had to get up to her when she cried the place down in the night. According to Faye, she only slept for an hour or two at a time, which explained why his wife always looked so bedraggled and wild-eyed these days. It couldn't be easy being a single mum. Then again, that was hardly his fault. And he was helping out as much as he could – he still had to work. There wasn't much chance of Faye finding another job after James Almond had done such a good job of shafting her. Come to think of it, James was to blame for the fix Mike was in right now – living in a miserable flat, the home he loved up for sale, his marriage in tatters. He shook his head. All that business about compiling secret files on his star presenters. Slimy bastard had left a trail of destruction in his wake and still managed to come up smelling of roses. One of these days someone would see to it that he got what he deserved.

He strolled through the sunshine thinking about different ways of taking revenge. The idea of unarmed combat, creeping up from behind and catching the Controller of Entertainment off-guard, telling him his time was up before expertly snapping his neck, was appealing. Mike knew plenty of hard men capable of such a thing. Tough, highly trained members of the special forces units. Unfortunately, he wasn't one of them. Still, no harm in dreaming. The smile was back on his face.

Thirty-Six

Faye put on a pair of grey skinny jeans and a stretchy print top that emphasized her slim waist. The jeans were a bit tight but looked good nonetheless. It was amazing how the weight had dropped off once she had given birth. Within a few weeks she was getting away with wearing jeans again. She was definitely less toned than she would have liked – by her strict standards her tummy was positively flabby – but she could work on that. Her face was tired-looking, though, and no wonder after so many nights of broken sleep with Daisy. A friend had urged her to adopt the Gina Ford method, claimed her baby had slept through the night from day one, but Faye was determined to do things her own way. Now she was beginning to think that had been a mistake. She would give anything for a proper night's sleep. Almost anything: she still had doubts about what her friend called controlled crying.

She studied her weary face in the mirror, dabbed concealer under each eye, curled her lashes and swept on a couple of coats of mascara. It was a miracle. The dark circles had vanished and she looked wide awake. Her skin looked less pasty against her cocoa-coloured top. Even her eyes seemed a brighter shade of blue. She ran her fingers through her hair, which settled on her shoulders in loose honey-blonde curls, and applied clear lip gloss. She didn't want to look as if she was trying too hard.

When Mike arrived back with Daisy, she was in the kitchen, at the stove stirring a pan, the scent of onions and garlic in the air. She heard him let himself in, checked her reflection in the back of a gleaming spoon, and quickly slapped on a fresh layer of lip gloss.

Mike parked up the pram in the hall, leaving Daisy asleep, and tiptoed into the kitchen to let Faye know he was going. She turned and gave him a warm smile, flicking a coil of hair over her shoulder. He took in the skin-tight jeans, the strappy heels, the fact that she had done her hair. The table, which had been covered in papers and baby paraphernalia earlier, was now clear. There were flowers, bright yellow marigolds from the garden, in a vase, and two place settings. Proper napkins folded into triangles. He stopped in his tracks. No wonder she was all done up; she was expecting company.

'I won't hang round,' he said, offhand. 'She's in the pram, asleep. She went off an hour ago.'

Faye put a lid on the saucepan and turned round. She looked jaw-dropping. Mike, who had got used to her being bad-tempered and slobbing around in pyjamas in recent weeks, felt a ripple of jealousy go through him.

'You're obviously expecting company,' he said, glancing at the table, 'so I won't keep you.'

Faye gave him an uncertain smile. 'Actually, I'm not. Well . . . only you.' She looked away and a strand of hair fell over one eye. 'I wondered if you felt like having a bite to eat. Nothing fancy, just some pasta . . . only if you're not rushing off somewhere, I mean.' She looked up at him and bit her bottom lip.

Mike wavered. 'I don't know. I was planning to—' He looked at his watch, unnecessarily, as he had nowhere to go but back to that flat which felt about as welcoming as a budget hotel room at a motorway service station.

Faye nodded. 'It's OK, I know you're busy. I thought it would be nice for us to have a bit of time to ourselves, while Daisy's sleeping.' She smiled. 'It's not often that happens.'

'Well—'

Her face was serious. 'I don't want us to be at each other's throats. We've got a beautiful baby and we were together a long time. Most of it was pretty good, if I remember rightly. If we can get along together – for Daisy's sake – I don't see any harm.'

He gazed at her. Despite everything, she could still do strange things to his insides.

'Thanks,' he said, taking off his jacket and sitting down. 'I'm not in a hurry. Dinner would be great.'

Faye opened a bottle of wine and poured them both a glass. She tipped fat green olives into a bowl and sat at the table facing him. On the stove the pasta sauce bubbled away. Mike was in a plain grey T-shirt that showed off his toned arms, and black jeans; what he would call his civvies. His hair was cut close and his face was stubbly. He looked fit and well, the kind of man who worked out and went for long runs in the open air. There was something about his eyes, though; a wariness. Faye knew he had messed around, had flings in the past, and so had she. As far as she knew there had been nothing serious on either side, not until she had fallen head over heels for Cheryl. That's what had wrecked their marriage. And for what? It wasn't as if she had ever wanted to leave him, not really.

They touched glasses. 'Cheers,' Faye said. She took a deep breath. 'I miss you, you know.'

Mike held her gaze. He was about to say she should have thought about that before she went off with her best mate, but stopped himself. He waited a couple of seconds and said, 'It's an almighty mess, isn't it?'

Faye bowed her head. 'And it's all my fault.' She didn't actually believe that. It was as much down to Mike going off and playing soldiers for months on end. No wonder she got fed up and lonely. All the same, swallowing her pride was a small price to pay if it meant getting her marriage back on track again. She wasn't sure how long she could carry on with practically no sleep, especially if *Girl Talk* really did take off. Her parents had offered to move in and give her a hand for a month or two, but that would never work. Her mother was way too bossy and her father liked his routine too much. She gave Mike a wistful look.

'I would do anything to change things, but I know I can't, so I just want to make things right from now on. I want to make it up, if I can.' She pressed her knee against his under the table.

Mike felt as if he had received an electric shock. He hung on to his wine. Faye pushed her chair back and went to check the pan.

'Won't be long,' she said, giving him a radiant smile. She stood with her back to him while she grated parmesan into a bowl.

'I don't want to be your enemy,' he said. 'You're the mother of my child. We should get along, do things as a family, never mind what's going on between us. It's Daisy that counts.'

Faye sashayed over to the table and topped up his wine. She was sick of everything revolving around Daisy. Daisy this, Daisy that. She felt a stab of guilt. How could she feel like that about

182

her own child? It was just that she hated feeling as if she no longer existed. No one cared any more how *she* felt.

She managed a conciliatory smile. 'Agreed.' She bent and planted a feather-light kiss on his cheek. 'Thank you,' she said, 'for being so understanding.' She played with a lock of hair, turning it into a perfect ringlet. When she spoke again she sounded a bit breathless. 'I want you to know – I'll always love you.' Blimey, she hadn't meant to go that far. What had got into her? The large glass of Chardonnay she had downed while she was soaking in the bath, probably.

Mike was rigid in his chair. Faye gave a tiny shrug. 'There, I've said it now. Me and my big mouth. Take no notice. I didn't mean to make things awkward.' She got up. 'Dinner's ready anyway. Give me a minute to serve up.'

Mike swallowed the rest of his wine and emptied what was left in the bottle into his glass. He needed a drink. Several. Had Faye just said what he thought she had?

'Anyway, enough about me,' she said, all innocent, as she placed a bowl of pasta with a bolognese sauce in front of him. 'What's going on with you?'

Mike cleared his throat. 'There's talk of me doing a new weekly current affairs programme. Studio guests, thirty minutes of live comment, you know the kind of thing.'

'That's brilliant,' Faye said.

'They're putting me up for a BAFTA – in the news coverage category – for that series of special reports I did with 45 Commando in Afghanistan. I think I told you about that already.'

Faye couldn't remember anything about it. 'You're bound to get it,' she said. 'No one else has done anything nearly as good as you.'

He smiled. 'I'm not sure it works like that, but thanks.'

She twirled pasta around her fork. 'Who are you taking?'

'Where?'

'To the BAFTAs.'

'Oh.' He shrugged. 'I haven't thought about it. It's not for ages. There'll probably be a crowd of us from ITN.'

Faye sipped at her wine. 'I wasn't going to say anything, but I've got a new agent. Suki Floyd.'

Mike stared at her. 'Not the one who worked with O.J. Simpson?' Faye nodded. 'I thought she was supposed to be a complete witch.'

'She's a bit eccentric, I suppose, but she knows her way round TV.'

Mike shook his head. Eccentric wasn't the word he'd have used. He'd seen Suki Floyd and her enormous hair holding court at an awards do a couple of years earlier, and even at a distance she had struck him as brash and overbearing – the sort of woman to be avoided at all costs. And that was being kind. 'I can't picture the two of you working together somehow,' he said.

Faye giggled. The wine was definitely loosening her tongue. 'I'm not supposed to say anything, so not a word to anyone, but she's working on getting *Girl Talk* recommissioned.' She gave him a triumphant smile. 'So, fingers crossed, I'll be on the box again before you know it.'

'You don't mean you'll be working for that prick at Channel 6 again?'

'God, no. Suki's negotiating with the head of entertainment at a rival station. It's a massive two fingers up to James Almond.' She giggled again. 'I'd love to be a fly on the wall when he finds out the show he axed without so much as a backward glance

is back on the air and stealing his late-night audience. Ha –
priceless!'

'So, Suki Floyd's putting together a new line-up then?'

'Oh no. The deal is it has to be the original famous five.
Same chemistry and all that.'

The colour drained from Mike's face. He put down his fork.
'Hang on – you mean the others are up for it?'

'We're waiting for Lesley to agree but we think she will. She
always loved *Girl Talk*. Well, until Julia turned a bit weird.'
Faye considered telling him about Julia's sex change. She might
never be able to compete with him on the work front, but when
it came to gossip she was always miles ahead. 'Julia's in the
back of beyond somewhere convalescing, poor thing – she can't
walk, you know – but she's up for it. I don't suppose she's
exactly spoiled for choice when it comes to offers of work.'
Faye paused. 'Mind you, imagine if everyone knew why she'd
really crashed her car . . .'

'I thought she was pissed.'

'She was. Pissed *off* because she thought Karen had tipped
the press off that she used to be a bloke.'

Mike stared at her.

'That is absolutely top secret,' Faye said, sounding a teeny
bit slurred. She was definitely feeling sloshed. 'Strictly between
us. You can't tell a soul.' She got up and pulled another bottle
of wine from the rack and handed it to Mike, who filled their
glasses again.

'So Cheryl's up for doing the show?' Mike kept his voice
light.

'That's the funny thing. Suki's using her as bait.' She gulped
down some more wine. 'The woman in charge at WBC, Felicity
Prince, is gay, so Suki thought it wouldn't hurt for Cheryl to

get in with her, if you know what I mean. Cheryl is fuming, apparently. Felicity Prince is no oil painting, trust me.'

Mike was still staring. 'Just as well this Felicity woman doesn't prefer blondes, or it might be you on your back instead of your pal trying to clinch the deal.'

'I hardly think—'

'Why? Because you're not gay? Well, you had me fooled.' He drained his glass and jumped up, sending his chair flying. 'You know, I wish you could hear yourself going on about your so-called friends, giving away their secrets – even the woman you were supposed to be in love with five minutes ago. It's obvious you've got no qualms about working with her again, never mind what it does to us.'

Faye's fork clattered on to the table. 'I thought you'd be pleased I'd got a job. Of course I don't want to work with Cheryl – I've got nothing to say to her – but I don't have much choice. It's got to be all of us or the show won't happen.' Her voice wobbled. 'And I never loved her—'

Mike bent and picked up his jacket from the floor. 'No, probably not. Just using her, I suppose, same as everyone else in your life.' He threw her a look of disgust. 'And by the way, you've got tomato sauce down your front.'

Thirty-Seven

Lesley emerged from her dressing room with her sunglasses on and her phone in her hand, checking for messages as she clip-clopped along the corridor in a pair of sandals with wooden soles that were murder to walk in – worse than any stilettos she'd ever had. Whoever thought it was a good idea to bring back clogs had a lot to answer for.

A text message from Faye popped up saying she was thinking about having Daisy christened and would Lesley and Dan consider being godparents? Lesley tapped out a reply straight away. **OMG – YES! XXX**. There was a saucy picture message from Dan – a sext, really – that made her smile. He had been bombarding her with rude texts ever since she complained she was the only person she knew who wasn't getting sexts on a regular basis. She rattled off a reply: **I could have you locked up X**. Seconds later Dan responded with: **Yes pleeeease! X**

She was still scrolling through the messages on her phone as she gave the door to the conference room a shove with her bottom and tumbled in backwards, going over on her ankle. Cursing her shoes, she waved in the direction of Paula Grayson, who was sitting in her customary spot at the head of the table, laptop in front of her, Bella at her side. Paula aimed a withering look at Lesley and peered at her watch. Bella managed an odd, awkward smile. For heaven's sake, Lesley thought, so she was a few minutes late – well, twenty, actually. So what? There was no reason to be so po-faced.

It struck her that maybe the cool reception was down to the email she had sent about what goes on in the weird Internet world of chat-room roulette. It had been a bit on the explicit side. Perhaps it had been an error to copy Paula in. Lesley had been a bit tipsy when she sent it, and Channel 6 had strict rules about their electronic communications meeting certain standards of taste and decency. It wouldn't be the first time Lesley had landed in hot water, her wholly innocent emails intercepted by the company firewall, whatever that was.

'Sorry I'm late,' she said, flopping into a chair and dropping her bag on the table. She reached for the coffee flask and poured herself a drink. Someone had already been at the biscuits. There were crumbs on the table and one measly Rich Tea left on the plate. She shot an accusing look at her editor and producer. 'OK, who ate all the pies?' she said, gesturing at the plate with a well-manicured hand.

A voice from the far end of the room said, 'Good afternoon, Lesley.'

She swung round to see James Almond, with his arms folded, leaning against the back wall. 'I thought I'd sit in on the conference today, get a feel for what you girls are doing. Paula seems to have a bit of a knack for churning out hit shows, so I thought I'd find out what her secret is.'

'No secret,' Paula said, sounding chilly. 'I just happen to know what I'm doing. It comes from years of programme-making and hands-on experience.' She gave James a long, hard stare.

A smile played on his lips. 'Quite. Well, you must have been in the business for what – getting on for thirty years?'

Paula snorted. 'Very funny, James. Actually, I joined the BBC on a graduate trainee scheme the year after you.'

Lesley caught Bella's eye. It was obvious they were both doing some quick mental arithmetic. Clearly Paula Grayson was a lot younger than she looked. In fact, she was a good few years younger than Lesley. Proof, if ever she needed it, of Lesley's philosophy that you are what you wear. All those dreadful twin sets and blouses that tied in a bow at the neck put years on Paula. Not to mention her hair. A decent cut and a few highlights instead of something that looked like a perm gone wrong would have done wonders.

James took a seat at the other end of the table, opposite Paula. 'I'm only teasing. Not everyone wants to be a high-flier, do they? The cut and thrust of the boardroom isn't for everyone, and just as well. A company needs its foot soldiers. Each to their own, I say.'

Paula patted her wiry hair. 'There's a saying: those that *can* make programmes – and those that *can't* go into management.'

James turned to Lesley, who glanced from one end of the table to the other, her hair, piled up in a perilous beehive, wobbling with every turn of her head. 'Do you have any thoughts, Lesley?'

She gave him a blank look and fumbled for her lip gloss. 'I'm sorry, I'm not with you.'

James rested his elbows on the table and laced his fingers together. 'I'm talking about the nature of success. What's better, do you think – to be front of house, like yourself, or a back-room girl, like Paula here?'

Lesley glanced at Paula, whose face was impassive. 'Well, I—'

'My own view is that a well-oiled machine needs all its parts to be in good working order. Don't you agree?'

Lesley frowned. Bella doodled in her notebook. She drew a flower and wrote a single word – *nutter* – in the margin. Paula kept her eyes on James.

'We are all vital to the smooth running of Channel 6. Every one of us. From the humble producer' – Bella looked up from her doodling – 'to the star presenter and the dynamic management team. Actually, Paula, I include you in that last category. You are that rare creature with a flair for programme-making *and* a business brain. Much the same as myself. You and I – cut from the same cloth.'

Paula flinched.

Lesley said, 'Are we having our programme meeting?'

'Now, I like to think I'm as progressive as the next person,' James said, ignoring her. 'And *Best Ever Sex* is certainly one of the most radical and edgy shows on TV. There's nothing else that claims to be mainstream yet also falls into the risqué category. It treads a fine line, no doubt about it, and somehow succeeds in being informative and entertaining without being offensive.' He looked thoughtful. 'Although the episode that tackled unusual sexual practices came close, but we shan't dwell on that. Anyway, it's a major hit. It has a far bigger audience than a show in such a late-night slot would normally command. It even has a sponsor.' He leaned back in his chair. 'You should all be congratulated.'

Paula Grayson placed her hands flat on the table. 'I'm sure we all appreciate you coming here to deliver such a positive message. Now, please don't let us keep you from your busy schedule.'

James leaned back and placed his heels on the table. Bella underlined *nutter* on her pad and wrote the word *rude* above it.

'I have watched every episode of *Best Ever Sex*, and I like the way you girls think,' James said. 'It's sharp and funny and fearless. You're at the top of your game.'

Lesley's phone bleeped. Another picture message from Dan. She peered at it. How on earth had he managed to take a photo from that angle? He was definitely getting the hang of sexting. She gazed at James Almond from behind her massive shades, wishing he would stop droning on and clear off. He was giving her a headache. If he didn't shut up, she would have to excuse herself and go back to her dressing room for a lie-down. In desperation, she poured more coffee and ate the Rich Tea biscuit. Maybe there was something to be said for bringing back *Girl Talk* on a rival channel. It might provide an escape route from Channel 6. Not that she especially wanted to leave. She loved her job and had struck lucky with Paula and Bella. The three of them worked well together. There was every chance they would pick up a nomination – if not wipe the floor in the late-night entertainment category – when it came to the Domes, TV's most prestigious awards. All the same, she wasn't sure how much more she could stand of James Almond sticking his oar in.

'I was just mulling over an idea,' he was saying. 'It's not fully formed, so bear with me.'

He rocked in his chair and stared at the ceiling.

'There's always a temptation with a successful format to keep it exactly as it is, which of course makes complete sense.' He seemed to be talking to the striplight directly above him. 'I wonder if that's the best way to go, though.' He swung his legs off the table and sat up straight, locking eyes with Paula and then Lesley. 'You're the star, Lesley – what do you think?'

'Yes, I mean, the show works, so why change it?'

'Why indeed?'

Paula glared at him over the lid of her laptop. 'Is there a point to this?'

'I was wondering if we need to, well, change it up . . .'

'Absolutely not,' Paula said. 'If and when we do, that will be up to me as editor.'

James nodded. 'You don't see Simon Cowell trotting out the same old tired-looking stuff just because he's got a winning formula.'

Lesley's head was starting to thump and she hadn't even been drinking. She touched up her lippy again. What did he mean – tired-looking?

'We really should get on,' Paula said.

'He constantly reinvents his shows, keeps them fresh. Look at what he did with *The X Factor* auditions.'

'I hated that. I preferred the way they did it before,' Lesley said.

'It never hurts to change it up, that's all I'm saying.' He got to his feet. 'Right, with that thought hanging in the air, I shall leave you three lovelies to it.'

Bella wrote *creep* on her pad.

As the door swung shut behind him, Lesley shot a frantic look at Paula. 'What does "change it up" mean when it's at home? He's going to axe the show, just like before, isn't he, the slimy bastard!'

'Don't get so worked up,' Paula said. 'That's what he wants – to unsettle us.'

'Well, it's working,' said Lesley.

'I'm not sure what he's playing at, but one thing's certain –

if he thinks I'm going to roll over and let him wreck things all over again, he has another think coming.'

Paula's mouth was set in a thin hard line.

'If he wants to get his hands on this show, it'll be over my dead body,' she said through gritted teeth.

Thirty-Eight

'I've got a feeling,' Lesley said. 'One of those horrible knotty ones – here.' She placed a hand on her stomach, and her lips, covered in a thick layer of frosted peach gloss, trembled.

Dan reached across the table and caught hold of her free hand. Her nails were painted a brilliant shade of orange. His face was serious. 'Is it, you know, *women's stuff*?'

Lesley snatched her hand away. 'No it's bloody not! It's James frigging Almond, spoiling everything. *Again*.'

Dan leaned back in his chair. 'I wish you'd take your sunglasses off. How am I meant to talk to you when I can't see your eyes?'

She shoved the gigantic specs on top of her head and gave him a huffy look. 'It's very bright,' she said, blinking.

'We're in the shade, under a parasol.'

They were at a corner table on the terrace of a restaurant in the heart of the West End. When the cab turned down Portland Place and dropped them a few doors down from the Chinese Embassy, Lesley had wondered where on earth they were going. Dan refused to say, insisting it was a surprise. 'You need cheering up,' he had said, leading her into a magnificent building and up a staircase. She puffed up the stairs, hanging on to Dan's arm, muttering about how it would have been a lot easier to go to The Ivy where the car dropped you right outside the door, and wanting to know why he was taking her to a place that looked more like a library than a restaurant anyway. Dan said it would be worth it, and he was right. They walked through a high-ceilinged dining room on to a terrace that was utterly peaceful despite the throb and bustle of Oxford Circus just minutes away.

Lesley gazed around her. White painted walls enclosed them and lush green ferns and shrubs hinted at somewhere more remote than central London. Ivy tumbled out of a zinc planter filled with bright pink flowers. 'What *is* this place and how come we've never been here before?'

Dan stroked the tips of her fingers. 'Don't you like it?'

'It's amazing.' She glanced up. Beyond the enclosed court-yard a jumble of buildings towered above them. 'I feel like I'm in a little oasis; almost like I'm not in London at all.'

'I thought you needed a treat.' He poured her more cham-pagne. 'All this stress over work's really getting to you.'

Lesley gripped his hand. 'I'm going to tell the others I'll do *Girl Talk*,' she said.

'Babe, you're already stressed without taking something else on.'

'It's insurance.' Her amber eyes widened. 'For when James sacks me. At least I'll have something else up my sleeve.' She tugged at her dress, a confection of palest pink ruffles with a slashed neck and a hemline several inches longer than she was used to. Positively demure. Her blonde tresses were arranged in a loose up-do with a soft fringe. It was the closest she would ever get to Jackie O elegance.

'Paula won't let that happen.' Dan frowned. 'I'm worried about this *Girl Talk* thing. It's a bit of a red rag to a bull, taking it to a rival station. Almond's never going to stand for it, and

I don't want you in the middle of it all when things turn nasty. Which they will.'

Lesley gave him a huffy look. 'At least I won't be on my own, like I am now. I'll have the other girls.'

Dan gave a hollow laugh. 'Oh right, and you can count on them when things get ugly, can you?'

Lesley reached for the champagne. 'Let's get another bottle,' she said.

Dan nudged her ankle under the table. 'It's hardly all for one and one for all with you lot, is it? I mean, the idea of Julia rallying round . . . oh well, never mind. Just promise me you'll give it a bit more thought before you tell them.'

Lesley sighed. She looked tired and fragile. It wasn't only work that was keeping her awake at night, it was the whole baby business and knowing, deep down, that the chances of her getting pregnant at her age were practically zero. She had missed a period a few months ago and, filled with hope, rushed to the chemist for a pregnancy test. It was negative. Since then, her periods had become a bit erratic. It terrified her to think she might be hurtling towards what her mother called the Change. Still, they could work miracles these days. Even women in their sixties were having babies. Not that Lesley much liked the idea of that. It struck her as going just a bit too far. If she was honest, she couldn't bear the thought of IVF and all it entailed. At the same time, she was worried Dan would get fed up and leave if they couldn't have a child of their own.

'And don't look so worried,' he said. 'Never mind what happens with the girls and James and all that – you've still got me.'

'Have I?' Her voice was small. She blinked and put her sunglasses back on. It took hardly anything for her to get teary these days. A dancing dog on *Britain's Got Talent* had made her cry. 'I'm just worried . . .' She gave a little shrug and knocked back the rest of her champagne.

Dan gazed at her. 'Tell me.'

Sometimes Lesley struggled to say what was really on her mind. It was all there in her head, going round and round, but when it came to saying it out loud she somehow couldn't find the words. Dan wouldn't let her sink into silence, though. He seemed to think it didn't matter what you said, as long as you said something. A few words, even the wrong ones, were a start. 'You know,' she said, 'I'm worried you might get fed up.' She rooted round in her bag for her lip gloss, and when she couldn't find the peach one she was wearing she settled for a glossy tangerine that matched her nails. She shot Dan a desperate look. 'If I can't have a baby.'

He kept his eyes on her. 'Take off your glasses,' he said. Her eyes were shiny. He was looking at her in that unflinching way he had that always made her stomach do a little flip. Lust meets love times ten. His voice was husky. 'What did we say? For better, for worse.' He caressed the platinum band and diamond engagement ring on her wedding finger. 'And I meant it.'

Thirty-Nine

Karen was expecting the others for lunch for a *Girl Talk* powwow. Julia claimed to have heard something extremely interesting from a source she described as impeccable. That usually meant her publicist, Tom Steiner.

Karen had whizzed round Waitrose first thing and stocked up on the kind of food that required no effort on her part. Now, looking at the spread on the kitchen table, she wondered if she had perhaps gone a bit over the top. Cold meats from the deli, one of those barbecued chickens, a platter of shrimp and smoked salmon and a delicious nutty bread that had cost a small fortune. Not to mention a cheeseboard. Anyone would think she was feeding a small army, yet none of the others were big eaters. And they certainly weren't into desserts. She should never have bought a chocolate sponge pudding, especially not one that claimed to be 'seriously chocolatey'. Why she had also bought clotted cream to go with it, she really didn't know. None of the girls would want it and she would be left with the chocolate equivalent of an explosive device ticking away in the fridge, threatening to blow her diet out of the water. She was doing so well, too. To her delight she had managed to get into a pair of black jeans and the kind of bottom-skimming top Lesley would wear as a dress. Thanks to an industrial-strength control garment that restricted her breathing and made sitting down a bit tricky, she now had a lovely smooth silhouette. With a pair of cream suede high-heeled court shoes and her black hair over one shoulder in a loose ponytail, she felt a surge of optimism for the first time in ages when she looked in the mirror. As for the pudding, the thing to do was leave it in its box, and if no one fancied any she could palm it off on the people next door. They might not want it either, but that was their problem.

Julia turned up first, hoisted into the hallway in her wheelchair by her carer, Terence. The candy-pink cashmere throw over her knees went with her dress, a simple sleeveless shift. Her hair framed her face in creamy-blonde spikes, and when she removed her shades her eyes shone. She looked radiant and relaxed. One of these days Karen would summon the courage to ask where she went for her cosmetic procedures.

Terence wheeled her to the head of the table, where Karen had removed one of the chairs.

'God, Julia, I wish I knew your secret. You look phenomenal.'

Julia's turquoise eyes sparkled. For once, her beauty was more than skin deep; she was in love.

'Actually, you're looking well too,' she said, giving Karen the once-over. 'Not nearly as chubby as the last time I saw you. It's a good trick to wear your jeans a bit long with heels. Mind you, if you really want to see results, get yourself some of those ski pants, the ones with stirrups. They work wonders.'

Karen gave her an uncertain smile. She was never sure whether Julia was being nice or if everything she said was veiled in sarcasm. She couldn't help remembering it was Julia who'd paid the Wardrobe chap at Channel 6 to ensure her wardrobe malfunctioned at every opportunity last year.

'I've finally found a diet that works,' she said. Actually, that was only part of it. Ever since the night Dave had stayed out she had been off her food, and as a consequence the weight was coming off at an astonishing rate.

Terence bent and whispered in Julia's ear. She gave him a coy little smile. 'Of course I'll be fine. You get off and I'll call you later.'

As Terence lumbered off, Karen poured Julia a glass of wine. 'Come on, then,' she said. 'What have you heard?'

Julia gave her a smug smile. 'Let's just say we're in a very strong negotiating position.'

Lesley turned up next. She was wearing a sleeveless black jumpsuit with a deep V at the front, her usual enormous shades and bright-red, high-gloss lipstick. She pointed at the planks of timber forming a makeshift ramp from the path to the front door. 'I take it Julia's already here, milking her disability for all it's worth?'

Karen put a finger to her lips. 'Keep your voice down, she'll hear you.'

Lesley teetered up the ramp. Her shoes comprised a complicated web of fine strips of black and tan leather and cone-shaped wooden heels. Behind her, a black saloon with tinted windows pulled up and Cheryl, in a stretchy purple minidress and cropped leather jacket, got out. She heaved what looked like a bright green Bottega Veneta crocodile tote onto her shoulder. Lesley was transfixed. That was a cool fifteen-grand's worth of handbag. It had to be a fake.

Cheryl strode up the path and stopped at the ramp. 'What's going on? Have you got the builders in?' she said, puzzled.

'Sshh, it's for *Julia*,' Karen said, her voice barely a whisper.

'Just because I can't walk doesn't mean I'm deaf,' Julia shouted from the kitchen.

'Bloody hell, talk about bat ears,' Lesley said, giggling.

'Maybe when you lose one of your faculties the rest go into overdrive,' Cheryl said.

'I have *not* lost *any* of my faculties, I'll have you know,' Julia boomed.

Lesley clapped a hand over her mouth. Karen tried not to laugh. 'Stop it,' she mouthed.

Faye appeared at the end of the drive in a yellow-print maxi-dress and denim jacket. She fumbled with the latch on the gate, rattling it and tugging at the wrought iron frame. Her bag slid off her shoulder in the process, and a set of keys ended up on the ground. She scrabbled about on her hands and knees, groping about under the privet hedge.

Cheryl's face was the picture of irritation. 'What on earth is she doing?'

Faye gave a defeated shrug. 'Help – I'm locked out!'

Karen hurried down the drive to help her. There was nothing tricky about the gate as far as she could see. It was a simple case of undoing the latch and giving it a push. Faye brushed a twig from the front of her dress and flung her arms round her friend. 'Lifesaver!' she said.

'Oh, for God's sake, stop making such a song and dance,' Cheryl said, going inside.

Faye linked arms with Karen. 'I feel like I'm out on remand or something,' she said, a bit breathless. 'You've no idea what it's like stuck in that house, imprisoned with Daisy. I mean, don't get me wrong, I love her—' She stopped and gave Karen a soppy look. 'I really, really do love her. It's just . . . she doesn't have much to say.' She chuckled. 'In fact, the conversation can get very one-sided.' She chortled. 'Joke! I mean, she *is* a baby!'

Karen gave her a curious look. She could have sworn she could smell alcohol.

Forty

Karen put a second bottle of wine on the table. 'Help yourselves to food,' she said.

Faye reached for the bottle and filled her glass.

Karen said, 'Shall I put a few things on a plate for you, Julia?'

'I'm not entirely useless, you know.' Julia's voice was glacial. She grabbed the wine and filled her glass to the brim.

Lesley dipped a shrimp in mayonnaise. 'Come on, then – the suspense is killing us. What've you heard?'

Julia ignored her and reached for a slice of smoked salmon. She piled watercress on to the side of her plate. 'I don't suppose you have capers,' she said, giving Karen a sweet smile.

'Oh, I'll have a look,' Karen said, getting up.

Lesley said, 'In your own time, Julia. Deal with the important things first, right? Like *capers*.'

Karen placed a jar on the table. 'Well,' Julia said, 'brace yourselves – the word is Channel 6 want to bring back *Girl Talk*.'

Karen stared at her open-mouthed.

Lesley shook her head. 'No way. James Almond would never agree.'

Julia smirked. 'Well, that's where you're wrong, because it just so happens to be his idea.'

Lesley had gone pale. 'No. I don't care where you heard it, it can't be true.' She thought back to James crashing the *Best Ever Sex* meeting, smarming on, coming out with all that stuff about changing things. It was his way of telling her he wanted her out, she was sure of it. He hated her. He hated all of them.

'Look, I've seen him strolling about, full of himself, making veiled threats about changing this and that, and I can promise you he hasn't mellowed one bit. He's still the same self-satisfied, smug, double-crossing creep he ever was.'

'Well, I can promise *you* that, as we speak, he is drawing up plans to bring back the show. With us fronting it,' Julia said.

Faye reached for the wine, trailing the sleeve of her jacket in a bowl of potato salad. Cheryl gave her a look of disgust.

'Who told you?'

'I can't say, obviously, but it's not idle gossip, if that's what you're thinking.' In fact, it had come from Tom Steiner, who had bumped into Desmond Hart at Shoreditch House a couple of days after his lunch with James. Desmond had been adamant that he had talked James round and that he was serious about reviving the show.

'Actually,' Cheryl said, 'Julia might be on to something.'

'There's no *might* about it,' Julia said, indignant. 'This is one hundred per cent kosher.'

'It's just that I spoke to Suki this morning and she said James has requested a meeting. He wants to see the four of us.'

Lesley looked alarmed. 'What about me?'

'I suppose he can see you any time he wants,' Cheryl said, spearing a piece of chicken.

Karen frowned. It sounded like a trap. It was absurd to think that James would welcome them back to Channel 6. He had to be up to something. Then again, Julia sounded confident and Suki Floyd was no fool. James would know better than to mess with her, surely.

'What exactly did Suki say?'

'She's setting something up for next week. She'll come with us.' Cheryl smiled. 'I can't wait to see him try his know-it-all routine with her. She'll have him for breakfast.'

'Maybe I should be there too,' Lesley said, not liking the way the discussion was going.

Cheryl shrugged. 'I don't know. I mean, it's come through Suki and she doesn't look after you. Maybe we should see what he has to say first. It might not even be about *Girl Talk*. It could be something else entirely.'

Karen chewed her lip. There was something very odd about all this.

'Oh, it's about *Girl Talk*, all right,' Julia said. 'He must have got wind that WBC wants it. You know what he's like. He'd take it as a personal affront if the show rose from the ashes on another station. He might well hate us, but at the end of the day he's a businessman and we gave him a hit show. Just imagine if a rival channel snatched it from under his nose and sucked up all that advertising revenue. He would have some explaining to do at the next Board meeting.'

Lesley drained her glass. 'Something's not right,' she said.

'Why? Because you're not invited to the meeting?' Julia said.

Lesley turned on her. 'Oh, don't be so childish. I couldn't care less about your precious meeting. Can't you see what he's doing? He's heard a whisper of what's going on, and now he's doing his level best to screw things up.'

'Actually, I think we're in a strong position,' Julia said. According to Tom Steiner, there was every chance of a bidding war if two channels had *Girl Talk* in their sights. 'We can play him off against whatsername at WBC – see who makes the best offer.'

'I think Lesley's got a point,' Karen said. 'Isn't it weird that James suddenly wants to meet us?' She got up and went to the fridge for another bottle of wine. The idea of coming face to face with James again was making her feel sick. 'He's already got us in a spin. At this rate, we'll have fallen out before we even get in to see him.'

'It seems to me she's the only one objecting,' Julia said, aiming a hostile look at Lesley. 'Not jealous because you've been left out, are you?'

'Get lost, Julia.'

Faye picked up the wine as soon as Karen put it on the table. Her cheeks were flushed. She smiled. 'This is all delish, by the way.'

Cheryl said, 'How much have you had to drink?'

'You'll have to give me notice,' Faye said. 'About this meeting. I'll need a babysitter.' She gave Lesley a bright little smile. 'Don't suppose you could take Daisy? I mean, if you're not coming.'

Lesley gasped. 'I should *be* there, not babysitting while you lot make decisions that affect my career just as much as yours. There were five of us on *Girl Talk*, you know.'

'No worries. I'll get my mum to take her.'

'As I recall, Lesley, you haven't even said you're definitely up for doing the show anyway,' Julia said.

'That's true.' Cheryl gave Lesley a cool look. 'So what are you saying? You're definitely in.'

Lesley looked away. 'I'm still thinking it over.'

Julia snorted. 'In that case, what gives you the right to tell the rest of us what we should and shouldn't do? I'm not even sure what you're doing here.'

'You seem to have a very short memory,' Lesley said. 'It's not five minutes since James Almond had it in for you – all of us, actually. Doesn't that make you the teeniest bit wary of his motives?'

'Not in the least. As I said before, he's a businessman. Remember all those stupid rules of his? I seem to recall one of them was something to do with never letting sentimentality get in the way of a good deal. He won't care it's us. We're a commodity, that's all. None of this is personal – it's about making the right decision for Channel 6.'

'He cared it was us before,' Lesley said. 'In fact, I'd say it was very personal.'

'What goes around comes around,' Faye said.

The others looked at her.

Julia said, 'What's that got to do with anything?'

Faye looked blank.

Cheryl said, 'She's drunk.'

'I think if we're seeing James we should have Lesley there, put on a united front,' Karen said.

'It's not our call,' Cheryl said. 'It's down to Suki.'

'Oh, for fuck's sake,' Lesley said, losing her temper. 'I wouldn't trust her as far as I could throw her any more than him.'

'Just as well you don't have to,' Julia said. 'It's us she's representing, not you.'

Lesley didn't reply.

Forty-One

'Of course, I would never allow my personal feelings to get in the way of a business decision,' James Almond said, sounding matter of fact. 'It's the first rule of commerce.'

Suki Floyd gave him a searing look. 'Really, James, you must know by now that all that high and mighty business-school bullshit is totally wasted on me. I've been around long enough to know how the industry really works, and I'd be amazed if you were the cool-headed captain of industry you like to think you are.'

'Well . . . I suppose there has been the odd occasion when I've been influenced by the smallest flicker of emotion.'

Suki threw her head back and guffawed. 'That's very dry – hilarious,' she said when she finally stopped laughing. 'I tell you, James, I always had you down as a bit of a bore – sense of humour bypass, you know.' James worked hard at keeping his smile in place. 'Actually, behind that stern face, you're very funny. I just never saw it.'

'Well, contract negotiations are hardly the ideal showcase for one's comedic talent,' he said, doing his best to sound less put out than he felt. Suki Floyd grinned. James wasn't sure what was worse – Suki in dragon mode or Suki on a charm offensive. Either way, the woman was utterly insufferable. Something about her bony face made him think of a death mask he had seen while filming a circumcision ritual in a remote part of West Africa.

It had been his idea to meet for lunch. He hadn't climbed the dizzy heights of light-entertainment TV without knowing how to get into bed with the enemy, in a manner of speaking. The thought of *actually* getting into bed with her . . . well, it was too gross to contemplate. He pushed his seafood salad around his plate, not feeling very hungry any more, then raised his glass and breathed in the faint honey aroma of the Chablis. When lunching with someone disagreeable, he made it a rule to ensure that the wine, at least, was sublime.

'I must say, I was rather surprised when you got in touch,' Suki said. 'I mean, there could only be one reason – clearly, I had something you wanted – although I couldn't for the life of me think what that might be.' She sipped at her wine. She had barely touched her scallops, which were arranged on the plate like a work of modern art. 'Perish the thought that you might actually be interested in those girls you had so little time for when they were going down a storm at Channel 6.' She gave him a superior smile. Her lips bore their usual blood-red stain. James wondered if it was a tattoo. It certainly showed no sign of slippage and she wasn't in the habit of slapping on lipstick every five minutes like most of the women he knew. Imagine waking up to that in the morning. The image of the death mask returned, making him shudder.

Suki cut into a scallop and dipped it in some of the brackish liquid drizzled with such care on the plate. 'Yet, lo and behold,' she said, 'it *is* those very same girls who seem to have caught your eye. Well, well, well. How utterly extraordinary.' She narrowed her eyes. Her lashes were unusually long, thick and curled. James had seen an item on *Good Morning Britain* about women paying hundreds of pounds to have eyelash extensions and some sort of perm that gave them a lasting curl. Was anything natural any more?

'Well – would you care to explain your sudden interest?' Suki examined the diamond-encrusted Rolex Oyster that dwarfed her slender wrist. 'And by the way, I have meetings this afternoon, so I can't hang around.'

James cleared his throat. 'A little bird told me you have plans to resurrect *Girl Talk*.'

Suki gazed at him, her face giving nothing away. As James waited for her to speak, she consumed another sliver of scallop.

'Perhaps I've been misinformed,' he said.

Suki sipped at her wine. A waiter bustled over, hoisted the bottle from the cooler hooked over the side of the table, and topped up their glasses.

'Of course, if I'm wide of the mark, you only have to say.' James gave her what he hoped was a disarming smile.

Suki continued to gaze at him. Her expression remained utterly impassive.

James fiddled with the stem of his glass, memories of difficult and protracted negotiations over contracts coming back. Suki was the absolute master at playing her hand close to her chest. The back of his neck felt damp. His face ached from smiling. Before he gave anything away, he wanted to be sure that what Desmond Hart had told him was correct. Otherwise he could end up looking very foolish. 'I suppose what I'm trying to say is I'd hate you to do anything without the two of us having first had a full and frank discussion.'

Suki placed her cutlery on the side of her plate. She had eaten half a scallop. 'It may surprise you to know that I like you, James.' Her foot brushed his ankle under the table. Good

God, don't say she was making a pass. A rush of nausea put him right off his food. He put down his fork.

'Sorry, was that your foot?' Suki pulled a face and gave one of her ghastly laughs. 'I'd hate you to think I was coming on to you. I'm not that desperate.' She laughed again. 'No offence.'

'None taken.' Seriously, she was impossible.

'I just mean that my casting-couch days are well and truly behind me. Now, as I was saying, what I like about you is the fact that you're clearly on the ball. Not afraid to swallow your pride, either, if you think someone's about to get one over on you.' The red lips parted in a broad smile. 'Some might think that's a weakness, but not me. It takes a big man to eat humble pie. I happen to think the two of us are on precisely the same wavelength, James.' She tilted her head on one side. 'I see no reason why we shouldn't do business.'

Forty-Two

James stood at the window of his office and gazed at the traffic streaming over Tower Bridge. On the street below, a *Big Issue* seller leaned against the railings with his back to the river. A police motor launch chugged past. The sun burned bright in the clear midday sky.

James adjusted the slats at the window to cut out some of the glare. He raised his hands above his head and stretched, then turned to examine his reflection in the glass doors of his wall unit. He had shed most of the weight gained during his trial when he had developed an unexpected taste for junk, and was almost back to his former lean self. He removed his tie, put it in the top drawer of his desk and undid the top button of his shirt. Instantly, he appeared softer and less formal. He put his suit jacket on, took it off, put it back on again, and did up the buttons. Looking good. He would never have thought to buy a purple suit, let alone team it with a lime-green shirt, but he was glad the shop assistant had talked him into it. The effect was remarkable. It was the second time he had worn the ensemble and it turned heads wherever he went. He felt like a rock star. That Ozwald Boateng chap was a genius.

He flipped a switch on the console on his desk. 'Give me ten minutes, Anne, then show them up,' he said.

*

In the reception area of Channel 6, Cheryl was pacing up and down, phone pressed to her ear, suede platforms echoing on the tiled floor. The chiffon skirt of her emerald-green maxi-dress billowed as she stomped around. 'Still no answer,' she said, exasperated, sinking into an armchair next to Karen.

'She's probably on her way.' Karen smoothed the front of her little black dress and checked her make-up in her compact.

Julia said, 'I don't think she's coming.'

Cheryl sat forward. 'Of course she's coming. She knows we can't do this without her.'

Julia shrugged and turned her attention to the bank of televisions ranged along the wall facing them. Each screen showed a different image, everything fast-cut and jumping about. They had done something with the colours too, made them deeper, more saturated. The jerky pictures and the super-bright colours were making her feel dizzy.

In front of the building, Faye, in paint-spattered jeans, a vest and cowboy boots, swigged from a bottle of water as she soaked up the sun.

Julia watched her through her new Marc Jacobs shades. 'You'd think she might have made an effort,' she said, 'for such an important meeting.'

Karen glanced at Julia, flawless in a teal chiffon and jersey asymmetric dress, a cluster of pale-pink pearls at her throat. A feather-light cream angora throw obscured her bottom half.

Cheryl's phone beeped. 'It's a text from Suki,' she said, perplexed. 'She can't make it.' She took off her sunglasses and stared at the phone.

Karen said, 'How come – has her car broken down or something?'

'She doesn't say.'

Julia gripped the sides of her wheelchair. 'Get on the phone now and tell her she had fucking better be here *or else.*'

'I've already called her about twenty times and she's not answering.'

'Well call her a-fucking-gain!'

'Who do you think you're talking to? Call her yourself – and stop causing a scene!'

The receptionist peered at them over the top of her desk and a solid-looking man with epaulettes on his shirt and a radio on his hip shuffled a step or two closer. Faye breezed through the revolving doors, a sheen of sweat on her brow. 'It's gorgeous out there,' she said. 'Have we been summoned by His Highness yet?' She edged past Julia, bashing her on the side of the head with her Kelly bag.

Julia ducked as the bag swung her way again. 'For fuck's sake, watch where you're going!'

Faye waved a hand at her. 'Sorry, sorry, sorry,' she said, climbing over Cheryl and flopping on to the sofa beside Karen. She took another swig of water. Her lippy, in a fashionable tawny shade, was a bit wonkily put on.

Karen shot an anxious look at the others.

Cheryl leaned forward and hissed at Faye. 'Have you been drinking?'

Faye began emptying the contents of her bag on to the low table in front of her. Out came a print scarf, a set of keys, a copy of *Look*, fish-oil capsules, a pair of Havaianas and an Evian spray. After scrabbling about for several more seconds, she held up a lip gloss. 'Ta-da!' she said.

Julia closed her eyes. 'Perfect,' she growled.

*

Suki Floyd was sitting at her desk in her Knightsbridge office. She crossed her legs and jiggled a bare foot up and down, turning her ankle from side to side, admiring her pedicure. There was a ponyskin mule on the floor. She stopped jiggling and slipped it back on. 'Trust me,' she said into the phone, 'it's a very bad idea, that's all. Sorry, Flick, I can't go into details right now, but you'll thank me in the end.' She definitely owed James Almond one. If they hadn't had that lunch, things could have got awfully messy. She flipped through her desk diary. 'Now, what about a bite to eat the week after next? There's someone else on my books I wanted to talk to you about. I really think she could be perfect for WBC.' Suki glanced over at the figure on her sofa poring over a story about Charlotte Church in *heat* magazine. Helen England looked up and gave her a grateful smile. Suki winked. 'You're casting for the survival show? Well, I think she would be ideal. Ciao for now.'

The lift doors opened on to the executive floor and Anne stepped out, followed by Cheryl, Karen, and Faye. Last but not least was Julia. James, waiting at the far end of the corridor, smiled at the sight of her, chin up, shades on, managing to look regal and haughty even though a burly bloke with an earring and a visitor's badge stuck on his chest was pushing her in a wheelchair. Whatever anyone said about Julia Hill, she was a cool customer all right. He turned and went into his office as the little party processed along the executive corridor, turning heads as it went.

'Come on in, ladies,' James boomed, rubbing his hands and nodding in the direction of the conference table at the far end of his enormous office. 'I don't bite, you know.'

Karen hesitated at the entrance to the inner sanctum.

Horrible memories flooded back of James putting her on the spot, droning on about his rules, stringing her along with the promise of a job that was never going to be hers. She took a deep breath. She had to put all that behind her now if they were going to work together again. It wasn't going to be easy, though. She glanced around the office with its gleaming, paper-free desk, oversized sofa and arty pictures. The fancy executive chair was missing. Knowing James, she thought, he was probably in the throes of upgrading to something even swankier.

Once they had all sat down and Julia's carer had gone, James indicated the empty seat beside him. 'We're still waiting for one more,' he said, checking his watch.

Cheryl exchanged a look with Karen. 'Suki can't make it. Car trouble or something,' she said.

James rested his elbows on the table and laced his fingers together. He frowned. 'Strange, I got the impression she was double-booked. When she phoned to cancel. Earlier.'

'I think you're mistaken,' Julia said. 'She's stuck on the North Circular.'

James nodded. 'If you say so.' He reached for a glass-and-chrome flask in the centre of the table. 'Can I pour you ladies some coffee? Finest arabica beans from the Sidamo region of Ethiopia. It's the birthplace of coffee, you know.' Julia gave him a pitying look. 'I won't tell you what a pound of this little beauty costs, but suffice to say it's money well spent.' He gave Julia a pleasant smile. 'Do you need a special cup or something?'

Her lip curled. 'Is that meant to be funny?'

Karen nudged her. 'I'm sure James was trying to be polite.'

'Absolutely. You must bear with me. I'm not *au fait* with – what's the correct expression these days? – special needs?' His brow crinkled. 'Do forgive me if I've just committed the most dreadful faux pas. Anyway, shout if I can get you anything, you know – ' he lowered his voice – '*unusual*. And if you feel we've slipped up anywhere – any improvements we should be making to the disabled loos, perhaps – you must let us know. Here at Channel 6 we pride ourselves on being accessible to all. There's no reason why you shouldn't work in TV just because you're in a wheelchair.'

Julia bristled.

Karen cut in. 'Thanks. I'm sure Julia will let you know if she needs anything,' she said, her voice firm. Julia gave her a filthy look.

'I must say,' James went on, nudging a plate of biscuits towards Julia, 'it's lovely to see you all.' Julia pushed the plate away. 'And all looking so utterly ravishing. Clearly, unemployment suits you.' He clapped his hands together in mock horror. 'There I go again, putting my foot in it all over the place.'

Faye, oblivious, dropped a couple of sugar lumps into her coffee. She had managed to slop half her drink into the saucer. As she bent to rummage for a tissue in her bag, a strand of hair trailed in her cup.

James looked at his watch again. 'Well, thank you for coming anyway,' he said. 'It's good to know there's no ill-feeling after all that's gone on.'

Julia snorted.

There was a tap on the door. 'Ah, excellent, we can get started now,' he said. 'Come!'

A thickset man with sallow skin, thinning hair and a bulging file in his hand stepped into the room. The lapels of his pin-striped suit were shiny. 'Hope I've not kept you,' he said, sitting down beside James, revealing a glimpse of red braces.

'Not at all.' James beamed at the women. 'Ladies, this is

Roderick Charles, our Head of Contracts. I thought it would be useful to have him here to clarify one or two key points.'

Julia looked him up and down. What an absolute drip.

Karen had a peculiar feeling in the pit of her stomach. Something was definitely not right. She wished Suki was there.

'Now, I understand there are moves afoot to relaunch *Girl Talk* on a rival channel,' James said.

No one said anything.

'No need to be shy,' he said. 'After all, that's what we're here to talk about.' He beamed and spread his hands flat on the table. 'I can see why you'd want to bring it back, naturally. It's an excellent show.'

Julia was unable to contain herself. 'Perhaps you'd like to tell us why you went out of your way to wreck it, in that case.'

James gave her an indulgent look. 'Good to see you've lost none of your legendary acid wit, Julia, after being out of it all that time. You really are something of a miracle of modern science, I must say.' Julia glowered at him. 'Now, where were we? Ah yes, *Girl Talk*. Well, my view is that it belongs here, at Channel 6, obviously,' he said. 'I'm sure you can see that. The very idea of it springing up somewhere else – well, frankly, it's not something I could tolerate.'

Julia resisted the temptation to smirk. Despite being such a clever dick, the smarmy bastard was going to have to admit it had been a mistake to axe the show. Well, if he didn't want them to sign to WBC he could do some serious grovelling first. She exchanged a tiny triumphant smile with Cheryl.

James turned to the Head of Contracts, who had opened his file at a page of small, smudgy print marked with a bright-yellow sticker.

'I'm sure you're all familiar with your contracts,' Roderick

Charles said, taking a pair of spectacles from the top pocket of his jacket. 'Specifically item thirty-three, clause two, on page six, which stipulates that you are excluded from working together in any capacity for five years pending the cessation of said contracts.' He looked at them over the rim of his specs.

There was a moment of silence, then Cheryl said, 'Just hang on a minute.'

'It has come to our attention that you are in talks to recreate a Channel 6 show on a rival network,' Roderick Charles went on. 'According to the terms of the contract you all signed, that is expressly forbidden. If there is any breach, we will sue.' He took off his glasses. His expression was steely. Julia's mouth fell open; not nearly as drippy as he looked, after all.

James sat back, arms folded, grinning. 'Well, that seems pretty straightforward to me.'

Faye said, 'I don't understand. Does that mean we can still work for Channel 6?'

James gave her a baffled look.

'I mean, isn't that why you wanted to see us? So we can bring back *Girl Talk* – same line-up and everything – just like it was before, in the old days?'

'The *old days*?' James burst out laughing. It was obvious Faye Cole had completely lost the plot. She had slopped coffee all over the table – a pile of sodden tissues lay in her saucer.

James said, 'Correct me if I'm wrong, but weren't there *five* of you in the *old days*?'

'Just because Lesley's not here doesn't mean she's not on-board,' Cheryl said. Karen kicked her under the table. 'We've been talking about it for ages. The five of us. And we're *all* agreed.'

'I very much doubt it,' James said. 'In case there's any misunderstanding, there will be *no* revival of *Girl Talk*, not at WBC, not here – not anywhere. Once a show's gone, that's it as far as I'm concerned. I make it a rule to never go back. *Girl Talk* had its moment, but that was in the past, so I suggest you mourn its passing once and for all and move on. Think of something else, why don't you, instead of boring everyone half to death with the same old stuff.' He turned again to the Head of Contracts.'Roderick, old chap, I know it's tedious, but would you mind having another go at putting these lovely ladies in the picture? Despite your best efforts, there still appears to be some confusion.'

Roderick Charles adjusted his glasses. 'You are all – including Lesley Gold – bound by the contracts you signed with us. The exclusion clause is perfectly clear. Continue with this plan to work together again on a format owned by Channel 6, and to which you have no rights, and we *will* see you in court.'

'No rights?' Julia said. 'Fuck you! Who do you think turned a half-baked idea into a hit show? *We* did.' She glared at James. 'There *was* no format, not in the beginning. It was only ever supposed to be a stop-gap, a six-week run, to get Channel 6 out of a hole. It was *us* who moulded it into an award-winning formula. And by the way, it was up and running way before Mr Special Needs here turned up and started decimating the entertainment department.'

Roderick Charles snapped shut his file. 'I assume we've covered everything, so unless you need me for anything else, James, I'll leave you to it.' He got up and cast a wary glance at Julia, whose hands were clenched. 'Would you like me to call security?'

'No need, they're already on alert, standing by to see our friends off the premises in the event of an outburst of hormonal rage.' He gave a helpless shrug. 'I'm no good when it comes to dealing with *women's stuff*, I'm afraid.' He got to his feet. 'Well, I think we're all done here, and just in case anyone is still in any doubt, let me spell things out for you once and for all. There is *no* place on this channel for clapped-out, past-their-sell-by-date has-beens. Not now, not *ever*. I mean, why employ old witches – ' his gaze went from Julia to Cheryl to Faye – 'not to mention dykes, when I can have my pick of nubile telly totty? I make it a rule to stick to younger models whenever I can.'

Cheryl gasped. 'Hang on a second . . .'

Julia glared at him. For a split second she was almost lost for words. 'You nasty little—'

James cut in. 'Oh, do spare me the histrionics.'

'You'll be sorry you took that tone with us, you vicious bastard!'

'I hope that's not a threat, Julia. Now, how about I escort you from the premises?'

'Fuck off!' Shaking with fury, Julia fumbled for her phone to summon Terence as James skirted the table and released the brake on her wheelchair.

'Allow me,' he said, executing a swift three-point turn and propelling her towards the door.

'Get your fucking hands off me!' Julia shrieked as James jogged past his PA into the corridor and headed for the lift.

Picking up speed, jacket flapping, James loped along, grinning like a madman. 'Weeeeeeeeeeeeee!' he said.

Karen and Cheryl stared at each other for a moment before scrambling to their feet.

'It's a shame Suki wasn't here,' Faye said, unconcerned, taking a swig from her water bottle.

'Yes, well, I don't suppose that was an accident,' Cheryl said under her breath. She yanked at Faye's arm. 'Come on, will you – we're going.'

James gathered speed as he hurtled past the secretarial pool, Julia clutching at the rug over her legs, terrified her awful shoes would be exposed. They came to an abrupt stop in front of the lift and James jabbed at the call button. As Julia struggled to regain her composure, James tilted her back in her chair. Upside-down, rug dislodged, orthopaedic shoes on display, she scowled at his leering face.

'Put me down!' she screamed.

'Oh, give it a rest, Julia.' He rocked her back and forth. 'What's up – did you lose your sense of humour as well as the use of your legs when you smashed up your car?'

She wrestled with the rug. 'Bastard – I'll have you for this!'

James let go of the chair and the wheels thudded down on to the tiled floor. Karen, hurrying towards them, winced. Behind her, Cheryl tugged at an unsteady Faye, who was doing her best to bat her away. 'Off *me*,' Faye slurred. 'I'm *absholutely* fine.'

'Do let me know if you'd like a private meeting sometime,' James told Karen's breasts as the lift raced up from the ground floor. 'You're still an outstanding talent in my eyes. I can always be persuaded to squeeze you in for a little *tête-à-tête* if required.'

There was a ping and the smoked-glass doors of the lift opened. James gave Julia a push, sending her careering into the mirrored wall at the back of the carriage. She gave his reflection her most poisonous stare. He raised a hand and offered her a mocking wave. Furious, Julia stuck two fingers up as he chuckled, turned on his heel, and strode back to his office, almost knocking Faye off her unsteady feet on the way.

Forty-Three

The four of them sat huddled in a booth in a private members' club in Soho. At a nearby table Max Beesley was sharing a pot of tea with a stocky chap in a denim shirt who looked familiar. Karen thought she might have seen him in *Prime Suspect*.

It was a long time before anyone spoke.

'Maybe one of us should phone Suki,' Karen said eventually.

'Actually, I don't think you can use your mobile in here,' Faye said to no one in particular.

Julia spluttered, her face white with fury. She glared at Karen. 'You want to phone that double-crossing bitch? Are you out of your tiny mind? Why do you think she wasn't at the meeting?'

Karen shifted in her seat. 'Car trouble, I suppose. For all we know, she's still stuck on the North Circular waiting for the breakdown truck. Maybe we should see if she needs any help.'

'Oh, for fuck's sake! She's probably having a late lunch somewhere or getting her nails done.' Julia's raised voice had caused Max Beesley's companion to swivel round in his chair to see who was making such a racket.

'Keep your voice down, will you? You'll get us chucked out,' Cheryl said. She glanced at Faye. 'And will you put that bloody bottle of water away. If you want water, just order some for goodness' sake.'

'Suki frigging Floyd,' Julia said. 'The only thing we can be sure of is she's not having her hair done.'

'What makes you say that?'

'Isn't it obvious? No decent stylist would go near that awful frizz in a million years. Imagine her walking out of your salon, scaring away all the other clients. Not much of an advert, is she? She doesn't need a hairdresser, she needs a frigging magician.' Julia twiddled with her own immaculate blonde spikes. 'She's probably on Nicky Clarke's blacklist – no appointments under any circumstances.'

Faye's eyes widened. 'I didn't know he had a blacklist.'

'Oh, for fuck's sake,' Julia snapped, exasperated. 'I'm just saying that if he *did*, she'd be on it. Anyway, the point is, she *knew* what was going to happen in there and *that's* why she didn't come. That fucking creep James Almond probably tipped her off. They're two of a kind.'

Karen frowned. 'I don't think we should jump to conclusions quite yet.'

Julia stared at her. 'Get real, will you! She has *dumped* us.' She clicked her fingers. 'Just like that, devious cow.'

Karen chewed her bottom lip and shot a desperate look at Cheryl.

'Julia's right,' Cheryl said. 'I reckon she got wind of that contracts business and that's why she's done a bunk.'

'And how do you think that happened?' Julia gazed at the others. 'Who tipped him off about the WBC deal? I'm telling you, the two of them are in cahoots – it's obvious.'

'Maybe she's sleeping with him,' Faye said, giggling.

Cheryl snatched at her bottle of water and took a sip. 'I thought so – she's been knocking back vodka all day!'

Faye shrugged. 'It's water with a teeny hint of vodka, that's all, to take the edge off.'

'Oh, pull the other one! It's neat vodka.'

Faye shoved the bottle into her bag. 'Yeah, well, I need something to get through an afternoon with you lot.'

Karen gasped. 'Faye!'

'No one listens to a thing I say.' She held Karen's gaze. 'And don't look so shocked – you're just as bad. I might as well not exist. So excuse me if I get blotto.'

'Well, when you actually say something useful we'll be all ears, darling, I promise,' Julia replied.

'We might take you more seriously if you managed to stay sober,' Cheryl said.

Faye frowned. 'Sober schmober,' she said.

Julia rolled her eyes. 'Well, don't let us keep you if there's some kind of meeting for desperate drink-addled housewives you need to be at. Now, can we *please* get back to the matter in hand? What's happened is we've been well and truly screwed. We might as well get used to the idea that none of us are going to be working again any time soon.'

The colour drained from Karen's face. 'So what do we do now?'

'Forget about Suki Floyd, for a start,' Julia snapped. 'She's a bit-player here. It's *him* at the bottom of all this. That bastard, Almond. I could kill him.'

'Not if I get there first,' Cheryl said. 'Did you see his face? He had it all planned. He got us in there just so he could rub our noses in it.'

'He acted like I'm some kind of imbecile,' Julia said, smarting at the memory. 'Who the fuck does he think he is? Do I *look* like I'm incapable of drinking coffee from a normal cup like everyone else?' Her turquoise eyes flashed.

'He thinks he's such a smart-arse,' Cheryl said. 'Well, he's not getting away with it. No way. I'm going to wipe that stupid smile off his face once and for all.'

'I'll give you a hand,' Karen said as the awful truth finally sank in. They had no agent and no prospect of work any more. She could feel tears welling up.

Faye looked puzzled. 'I still don't understand. I mean, why doesn't he want us to work together anyway? It's not like he wants us at Channel 6, so why should he care?'

Julia stared at her, incredulous. 'Shall I spell it out for you? James Almond *hates* us. His mission is to bury us and he will do anything – and I mean *anything* – in his power to destroy us.'

'But why?'

'Are you on a different planet? It doesn't matter *why*. For the fun of it, probably. He thinks we're just going to crawl away. Well, he can fuck right off. There's no way I'm letting a jumped-up little creep like him ruin my life.'

'Me neither,' Cheryl said.

Karen's stomach was in knots. The memory of two Channel 6 security guards waiting in reception to escort them from the building as they emerged from the lift was still scorching her. She had never felt so humiliated. Even Julia's carer, Terence, minding his own business in the corner of the lobby, flicking through a copy of *Metro*, was flanked by a couple of stout blokes with telltale epaulettes and radios. James Almond really was a complete shit.

'I wish I'd chucked his precious Ethiopian coffee in his face,' she said, trying not to cry. 'Stupid prick.'

'It tasted like mud anyway,' Julia said. 'Did you hear him – all that crap about the birthplace of coffee? Blah-frigging-blah. I've never heard such drivel.'

'He's full of shit, no doubt about that,' Cheryl agreed.

'The man is pure evil,' Karen said, choking back tears.

'I could kick him in the goolies,' Faye replied, finally catching on.

'Well, if he thinks that's the end of the matter, he doesn't know anything,' Julia said.

'I don't see what we can do,' Karen said. 'I mean, you heard the contracts bloke – we're stuffed.'

'I wasn't thinking of a legal challenge,' Julia said, radiating menace. 'I'm more inclined to catch him off-guard, give him a good kicking, so to speak, and leave him in no doubt that making enemies of us was a very bad idea indeed. Once I'm back on my feet, obviously.'

Karen said, 'I just hope we haven't dropped Lesley in it.'

Cheryl frowned. 'I wouldn't worry about her. She's the only one with a job right now.'

'I know. But . . . she hadn't actually agreed to do *Girl Talk*, had she?'

'So?' Cheryl was glaring at her.

'Well, maybe you shouldn't have told James she was on-board. I mean, you know what he's like.'

'I don't know what you're getting at.'

'I just thought it might be worth giving her a call – you know, to put her in the picture. Just in case.'

Cheryl tossed her head. 'Lesley's a big girl. She can look after herself,' she said. 'And so can we.'

Forty-Four

James Almond reclined in his temporary office chair, a large Manila folder on the desk in front of him. On the cover was a white sticker printed with the words *Highly Confidential* in bold. Inside were a brief report, interview transcripts, a log of text messages sent and received and a sworn affidavit. Although the contents comprised only a few pages, they were nonetheless explosive. He finished his coffee and scanned the first sheet.

A few feet away, on the oversized leather sofa, Lesley sat straight-backed. She had been with Paula Grayson, discussing the running order for *Best Ever Sex,* when she had got a call to say James wanted to see her. *At once.* Lesley was nervous. She knew the others had been due in to see James with that awful Suki Floyd woman to discuss *Girl Talk*, although she wasn't entirely sure what time. Since she had been excluded, she had been in a huff, not speaking to anyone. The girls had claimed they wanted her to join forces with them and yet had left her out of discussions that could well affect her future. It wasn't on. So although Cheryl had called umpteen times and left messages, Lesley had decided to let her stew. See how she liked being cold-shouldered. Now, however, she was thinking it might have been an idea to pick up the phone after all. She had tried to call Cheryl on her way to see James, but she wasn't answering. Nor were the others. Maybe they were paying her back for the silent treatment.

Actually, it seemed to be catching. James Almond didn't seem to have anything to say either. He had barely looked up from whatever it was he was reading for the last few minutes. Goodness knows what was so urgent.

'I had your chums in here today,' James said at last. 'It was a most illuminating meeting.'

Lesley felt at a distinct disadvantage. She wished she had arranged to meet them afterwards, find out what had been said, instead of being so stubborn.

'Really, Julia Hill is remarkably spirited for someone who is' – he paused and frowned – 'confined to a wheelchair. It must be dreadful to be so impaired, especially when one only has oneself to blame.' He rested his elbows on the desk, clasped his hands and closed his eyes, as if he was deep in prayer.

Lesley shifted position and tugged at the hem of her skirt, which was riding up her thighs. At least she had opaque tights on. As she moved, the leather sofa squeaked. James remained in his reverie. She whipped out her compact, checked her make-up and applied a fresh coat of Sheer Sparkle lippy.

A minute or so went by before he opened his eyes and aimed a lascivious smile at her. 'So, how are you finding married life?'

Lesley flicked a coil of blonde hair over her shoulder. Her marriage was none of his business. 'I can't complain,' she said.

James nodded. 'Excellent. And what about Mr Gold?'

She stiffened. 'Kincaid.'

'Sorry?'

'His name is Kincaid.'

'Ah yes, of course, you each have a different surname. How very modern,' James said. He gave her a probing look. 'I do hope that if you ever had anything on your mind – anything at all – you would come to me.' He leaned across the desk. 'Contrary to what you may think, I'm a good listener.'

Lesley had an urge to laugh – he really was a pompous arse. As if she would ever confide in him. It would end up in one of his secret files. She eyed the folder now open on his desk and managed a thin smile. 'I'll bear that in mind.'

James nodded again. 'I don't know about you, but I'm not very good at surprises. They throw me and put me off my stride, make me feel uncomfortable. Does that make sense?'

Lesley was about to respond, but James pressed on. 'I actually have a secret deep-seated fear that one day someone will throw a surprise party for me.' He shuddered. 'The very idea gives me nightmares.' Lesley thought the chances of anyone ever arranging a 'Surprise, Surprise!' moment for him were extremely slim, but didn't say so. 'That's why I have made it crystal clear that there are to be no surprises at the Channel 6 party next month,' he said. 'Perish the thought.'

It occurred to Lesley that he was bored. Lonely, too. Perhaps he had no one to talk to and that was why he called people in for impromptu and completely unnecessary meetings. She was actually starting to feel sorry for him. Mind you, he didn't half go on. She stifled a yawn.

'Anyway, I thought a little background might be useful,' he said. His face became serious. 'My own dislike of surprises means I am always well prepared. However, I was thrown off balance somewhat this afternoon, albeit briefly. By your little party, as it happens.' He paused. 'See what I did there – linked *surprise* with *party*.' He seemed pleased with himself. 'The subconscious is quite an extraordinary thing.'

Lesley wished she'd gone to the loo before seeing him –

she'd had no idea he'd keep her there so long. She crossed her legs. A canvas peep-toe dangled from her foot.

'Imagine my dismay to learn that you – a valued member of the Channel 6 team – are involved in a plot to take one of our formats to a rival station.'

Lesley swallowed. What on earth was that supposed to mean? 'I'm not with you.'

'Quite,' he said. 'You most certainly are *not* with me. Not with me at all. You are merely biding your time, all the while scheming to desert me. Not so?'

Lesley blinked. He had completely lost her. 'I don't—'

James held up a hand. 'I am not in the least surprised to discover that your erstwhile colleagues are engaged in talks with WBC about bringing back *Girl Talk*. No – no surprises there. However, the fact that you are secretly engaged in this plan . . .' He waited a moment. 'Well, that did come as a bolt from the blue.'

Lesley gasped. 'But I'm not.'

'You may as well save your breath. It emerged during the meeting that you're part of this madcap scheme.' He shook his head. 'In all honesty, *surprise* is hardly a strong enough word to describe my feelings: shock, betrayal and disappointment come closer.'

'I don't understand,' Lesley said. She hadn't agreed to be part of the *Girl Talk* revival. True, she was on the brink of doing so, but she hadn't actually got round to telling the others.

James made a tut-tut sound. 'Cheryl West made it perfectly clear this afternoon that the *Girl Talk* plan involved all five of you, which is why I thought we should have this little chat.'

'But—'

'By the way, in case word hasn't yet filtered through, the

only version of *Girl Talk* anyone will be watching anytime soon is the back catalogue we've just sold to the Far East.'

Lesley blinked. The meeting hadn't gone well, then.

'Now, I pride myself on being a fair-minded person. And despite what you and your girly clique might think, I'm nobody's fool.' He took a page from the folder in front of him. 'I'm so glad to hear married life is working out for you. I did think that perhaps you were having second thoughts. After all, just hours before saying *I do* you were having sex with someone else.' He gave her a pleasant smile. 'I must say, Mr *Kincaid* must be a very understanding chap.'

Lesley had gone pale. She felt nauseous.

James turned another page. 'Ah yes, text messages. They can be so revealing, can't they?'

Lesley gripped the edge of the sofa.

'Personally, I can't stand all the abbreviations. Still, what can you expect when you're dealing with a nineteen-year-old?' He gave her a knowing look.

'How . . . ?' Lesley's head was swimming.

'You're curious as to how I found out? Well, that would be telling. Let's just say I make it a rule to ensure not much gets past me. I take it from the look on your face that you chose not to let your new husband know you'd had a fling on the eve of your nuptials.' He gave her a reassuring smile. 'Oh, I'm not judging. I mean, I'm in no position to, am I? The fact of the matter is that I'm actually extremely well placed to understand how corrosive infidelity can be to a marriage.'

'Look, it was a bit of innocent flirting, that's all,' Lesley said, desperate. 'He got the wrong end of the stick. It's not like we actually did anything.'

James turned another page. 'That's not what he says. Not according to the affidavit he gave us.'

Lesley put a hand to her brow. She was burning up. The boy must have been a set-up. They had snogged in the club and he had followed her when she went outside for air, sneaked up and put a hand up her skirt. She should have told him where to go, but she had been feeling tipsy and horny, and what was the harm in one final fling before she got married, she had thought at the time. It was practically compulsory. However, if Dan was no angel, nor was he a cheat where she was concerned. He hadn't even bothered with a stag do. How he would react to news that she'd done the dirty the night before they tied the knot was anybody's guess. Actually, since she had got off with that bloke in the early hours, technically speaking she had cheated on their wedding day. It could hardly be worse. If it had happened the other way round and he'd been with some bimbo, what would she do? Shout and cry and carry on – and boot him out, probably.

Lesley's mouth went dry. What had she done? She loved Dan. She had loved him on their wedding day *and* the night before. So why, oh why had she let one stupid drunken act put everything in jeopardy? The fact that they were trying for a baby made it all seem much worse. She wasn't fit to be a mother. Her stomach contracted. She threw an uneasy look at James who, unconcerned, was busy lining up his computer keyboard with the edge of his desk. He was such a spiteful, scheming bastard.

Eventually she said, 'What are you going to do?'

'*Do?*' He affected a look of confusion. 'I'm not going to *do* anything.' He picked up the file. 'This is strictly between us.'

Lesley held her breath.

'Then again . . . I would hate to think you're plotting while my back's turned. Frankly, Lesley, that's not something I am willing to put up with.' His voice was cold. 'If there's any hint that you and the others are conspiring to undermine me *or* Channel 6, then I shall take swift action.' He dropped the file into the top drawer of his desk. 'So really, it's up to you. I assume you do like working here?' Lesley nodded. 'You're happy with *Best Ever Sex*?' Another nod. 'Well, then, I see no reason to make your little faux pas public at this present time.' He tapped the side of his nose. 'Let's just call this an informal warning, shall we?'

She nodded again, relieved.

'I'm so pleased we're able to talk so openly with one another. Run along, then.'

Lesley picked up her bag and fled.

Forty-Five

Dan was cooking when Lesley got in. She hovered in the doorway to the kitchen watching him chop onions and toss them into a pan. The air was garlicky and it made her stomach turn. On the wall at the far end of the room the TV was on too loud and Dan, who hadn't heard her come in, was singing along to Billy Joel's 'She's Always A Woman'. Lesley had a lump in her throat. She wanted to cry.

'Honey, I'm home!' she said, doing her best to sound cheerful.

Dan turned to face her. He was wearing an old James Dean T-shirt and snug jeans that showed off his long legs and fabulous behind. His face was flushed from the heat of the kitchen. He gave her one of his thousand-watt smiles and his tawny eyes crinkled at the corners. Lesley's stomach lurched. She had bagged herself a god among men and she still couldn't behave.

'Come and give your man some love,' he said, wiping his hands on a tea towel and moving towards her.

Lesley held up her bag like a shield. 'I don't want your greasy hands all over my new Joseph top.'

Dan grinned. 'Fair enough. Take it off, then.'

'I thought you were cooking?'

'I can always turn the heat down. Under the pan, anyway.'

He put his arms round her and held her tight.' Lesley wriggled. 'Can you tell I'm pleased to see you?' he said.

'I'm pleased to see you too.' She gave him a half-hearted peck on the cheek.

'What's that when it's at home?'

'Sorry, I've just got a banging head, that's all.'

Dan took a step back and gazed at her. 'Actually, you are a bit pale.'

'I think I'll take a couple of codeine and have a soak in the bath.'

Dan steered her towards a chair. 'You sit down and I'll run a bath for you.'

'No, it's fine . . .'

'Do as you're told.' He pulled open a kitchen drawer and rummaged about for painkillers. 'Right, here you go,' he said, handing them to her. 'You get these down you.'

Lesley swallowed the tablets. She had been sick when she got back to her dressing room after her meeting with James and had been battling waves of nausea ever since. On the counter, next to the chopping board, was a mound of odd-looking mushrooms. Something about them made her feel sick again. She dashed to the bathroom, where Dan was pouring scented oil into the water.

'I'm going to be sick,' she said, pushing him out, locking the door and retching into the toilet.

Outside, Dan said, 'Babes, are you OK?'

Lesley knelt on the tiled floor, sweat running down the back of her neck. Her heart was racing. 'I'm fine,' she managed to say. She pulled the precious Joseph top over her head. She was red hot.

He jiggled the handle. 'Let me in, babe.'

'No!' The idea of him seeing her in such a state made her feel worse. She flushed the loo and a vision of her marriage going down the pan came to her. 'Give me a second, will you?' She got up and perched on the edge of the bath. She knew she couldn't trust James, that the day would come when he would expose her wedding-day fling and destroy her marriage. She felt the tears threaten again.

She had to find a way to stop him.

Karen was right off her food. Things were strained with Dave, who had taken to creeping into the spare room in the early hours rather than disturb her. They were barely talking, just tiptoeing around each other and having the odd stilted conversation. It was lunchtime now and Dave had only just surfaced. She should show willing, make him breakfast. Since he was working all hours, the least she could do was be the perfect housewife. If only *Girl Talk* had been recommissioned, Dave would be driving her round, not Lara Durham, and everything would be fine again. She could kill James Almond. It was all so unfair.

All she wanted was for things to go back to normal, the way they were in the beginning.

Dave appeared in the kitchen in sweatpants and a Brazil football shirt. He stifled a yawn and his dark-blond hair flopped over his face. He padded over to Karen and put his arms round her. 'I'll do some eggs if you like,' she said, resting her hands on his shoulders.

He stepped back and gave her an awkward smile. His grey eyes made her think of the sea in mid-winter when she was growing up in Blackpool.

'You're all right. I'll pick up something when I'm out.'

She was about to object but decided against it. He was already picking up his car keys.

'What are you up to today?' he asked.

'I'm not sure. I might meet Bella for lunch.' She didn't want to say the chances were she would snuggle up in bed and watch TV, maybe tuck into a bar of organic dark chocolate, get some of those health-giving antioxidants into her system. She wished he would stay in for once and keep her company. It was as if he always had something else to do these days. 'How about you?'

He looked away. 'I thought I might go over to Chingford, check the flat.'

'I could come with you if you like.'

'Nah, no worries,' he said, turning away and opening the fridge. 'I won't be long. You enjoy yourself.'

Karen stared at his back, her heart starting to race. He seemed to be spending an awful lot of time back on his old stomping ground these days – at the gym, calling in at the flat. He never used to. She should say something, ask what was going on. Then again, she didn't want him thinking she didn't trust him. So he was going to Chingford – so what? Why shouldn't he want to check on his old flat now and then? It was perfectly normal, nothing to get worked up about.

As long as that was all he was doing.

Cheryl was all in black: skinny jeans, ribbed sweater, fitted leather jacket zipped right up. Her hair was loose, a gleaming black curtain that skimmed her shoulders as she walked. She was wearing her favourite biker boots with shiny straps, peep-toes and cone heels. The only splash of colour was a slick of deep purple lip gloss that matched her nails. She slung her D&G

bag over her shoulder and put on a pair of enormous round sunnies. As she strode through the square behind Kensington High Street, she checked her reflection in a gallery window and smiled. Storm trooper meets Catwoman. Perfect.

It had taken her ages to get hold of Suki Floyd following the debacle with James Almond. Even though it was pretty obvious Suki had abandoned them, a tiny shred of hope remained that some genuine mix-up – or indeed a genuine breakdown on the North Circular – had kept her from the meeting. Suki soon put her right.

'You do see why I couldn't be there,' she said when Cheryl finally got through. 'I mean, there was no point. Of course, if you girls had been straight with me regarding the contracts position at the outset, it's most unlikely I'd have taken you on in the first place.'

For a full twenty seconds Cheryl was speechless. 'You don't think we misled you?'

'Oh, not *intentionally*, I'm sure. These things happen. Anyway, no hard feelings, I trust?'

'You mean that's it? You're dumping us!'

'There's no need to be so melodramatic. It hasn't worked out, that's all.' Cheryl heard her tell someone she'd be with them in a minute. 'Sorry, my four o' clock's just walked in,' she said.

Cheryl kept quiet.

'Look, I know it's a letdown and it's not what you hoped for, but you're strong. You'll get over it. We all will. It just wasn't meant to be.' Suki paused. 'And you really are a very good presenter, so I'm sure something else will turn up.'

As quick as a flash, Cheryl said, 'You'll still want to look after me, then – since I'm so good.'

'Ah, sadly not, darling,' Suki replied. 'Anyway, must dash – I wish you well.'

Before Cheryl had a chance to say another word, the line went dead.

Now, a week later, she was still fuming. She felt used, violated, thanks to that hard-faced bitch. She was responsible for her having to endure a humiliating fling with Felicity Prince – the kind of woman she wouldn't normally look at twice – and all for nothing. The chances were she would be emotionally scarred for life: the mere thought of that ugly lump pawing her triggered horrible flashbacks. As she had tossed and turned, unable to sleep at night since her call to Suki, she had considered marching round to her office and lobbing a brick through the window, until she remembered there were anti-burglar bars on the ground floor.

She turned left out of the square, cut along a narrow street and arrived in front of Suki's office. She walked up and down until she located her black Audi R8. It was impossible to miss with its private plate – 5LOY0 1 – which, from a distance, appeared to read FLOYD 1. Cheryl grimaced. The plate was about as tacky as its owner. Shame about the car, though, she thought, rummaging in her bag and bringing out a chisel. Still, needs must. She got to work scratching *bitch* on the boot of the car. Just for the hell of it she knelt down and used the chisel to dig into the paintwork on the driver's door, scoring *slag* in big letters. She smiled. See how she liked that. Straightening up, she walked back along the street to Suki's front door, took an aerosol from her bag and sprayed *bitch* across the glossy red paintwork. Enjoying herself, she added a smiley face on the brickwork. Then she strolled back down the road, not caring if anyone had seen her, dropped her tools in a skip, hailed a cab and went home.

Faye had persuaded her mum to take Daisy. Anyone would think she'd jump at the chance of babysitting her grandchild, but no, she had complained, pointed out that it was the third time she'd asked in as many days, said Faye was taking advantage and that, while she didn't mind helping out, she really felt a child's place was with its mother. In the end, Faye had put the phone down while she was still in full flow. She felt bad afterwards, but all that nagging was giving her a headache. Just as she was wondering who else she could call, the doorbell went. It was her mum, most put out that her daughter had hung up on her.

'Really, Faye, I don't know what's got into you,' she said, sweeping in. She dropped her gloves on the hall table and shrugged her bouclé jacket on to her daughter. Faye put it on a hanger and popped it on the coat stand as her mother headed for the kitchen, the heels of her patent leather slingbacks tapping on the tiled floor.

Faye went after her. 'I didn't hang up,' she lied. 'It's the phone. It needs new batteries or something. It keeps cutting out.'

'Well, you need to do something about it. A reliable phone is an absolute must with a baby in the house.' Her mother adjusted her Hermès scarf.

'There's always my mobile if I need it. Anyway, I was just looking for batteries when you turned up.'

Her mother gazed at the kitchen table, which was strewn with clutter. 'Perhaps I'll give you a hand to tidy up before I take Daisy.'

'No!' Faye said. The last thing she wanted was her mum hanging round. She didn't have time for that. 'I mean, there's no need. I'll do it.'

'You said you're off to see a new agent?'

'It's a guy who used to be with one of the big agencies who's setting up on his own, so he's building a client list,' Faye said, surprising herself. As it happened, there was no new agent, no meeting. She was simply desperate for some time to herself. 'He's got some good people on his books already – actors mainly – and he got in touch with me, so that's got to be good, don't you think?' Amazing how the lies flowed so easily. Even more amazing that her mother fell for them. What agent in his right mind would be interested in her?

'I'm very pleased for you, darling.' Her mother, immaculate as ever in a cashmere sweater and wide-legged trousers might have been on her way to lunch in Knightsbridge instead of pre-paring to spend the afternoon babysitting. Faye felt a pang of guilt. Only last week Daisy had been sick on her mother's new Burberry coat.

'You don't mind having her again, do you? I know I keep asking you, but the thing is – ' she gave her a grateful smile – 'I don't know what I'd do without you.'

'Nonsense, she's no trouble.'

Faye bustled about and handed over a bag of baby things, put a foldaway buggy into the boot of her mother's car and settled Daisy into her carrycot on the back seat.

Once the car was out of sight, she went inside, opened some wine and poured herself a large glass.

Julia was in the mood for champagne. She had every reason to celebrate. At last, after all the crushing setbacks of late, things were looking up. She shook her head in disbelief. It was almost too good to be true.

She slipped out of bed, hobbled over to the dressing table, whipped a sheer black Stella McCartney slip out of the top drawer and pulled it over her head, pausing to look at herself in the mirror. Her reflection prompted her to do a double-take. Not a scrap of make-up and yet she looked . . . well, amazing really. Her eyes shone, her skin glowed, and her hair looked as if it had been expertly mussed-up by a top stylist. Tempting though it was to slap on some lip gloss – maybe a natural nude shade – she decided not to bother. For once, she didn't need it. It was just fine to be herself.

She climbed back into bed, plumped up her pillows and dabbed some Chanel No. 5 behind her ears, fighting the urge to let out a whoop of joy. It was mad, but she could barely contain herself. Now she knew what people meant when they talked about bursting with happiness. She put a hand on her heart, convinced it had a different, more upbeat rhythm, and laughed. That was just being silly. Or was it? She definitely felt different – as if some kind of supercharged energy was surging through her system. It had to be the endorphins, up and about doing their thing. Nothing imaginary about those.

It wasn't only the news that her feet were on the mend and she'd be back in her beloved heels in no time that had made her so ecstatic – although that had definitely put a spring in her step, so to speak. No, it was the sudden blossoming of her love life that had sparked her delirium. She sank back into the pillows, tingling from head to toe. It had actually happened. Scott had stayed the night. Not only that, but he had been in no rush to leave. They had spent the whole day in bed. To say she was in heaven was putting it mildly; she was practically in a trance.

'Budge up,' Scott said, appearing with champagne and glasses and climbing back into bed with her. His bare skin brushed against hers, making her tremble. Julia hooked her leg over his and admired his muscular body. He was in impressive shape, no doubt thanks to all that manual work, chopping wood and tending the land and whatnot. And he was strong. The night before, he had picked her up as if she weighed nothing and carried her up the stairs.

He handed her a glass of bubbly and gave her a long, lingering look. Julia gazed into his eyes, feeling her heart rate quicken. Damn, those endorphins were off again. His skin was tanned from being outside so much and there were lines around his eyes and frown lines on his brow. She ran a hand along his shoulder blade, over taut, smooth skin, tracing the mole on his shoulder.

'If you keep looking at me like that, you know what's going to happen,' he said, sounding husky.

Julia shivered, feeling goosebumps spring up on her arms. 'I don't mind,' she said, giving him a shy smile.

'You know, you've got the most amazing eyes.'

'Turquoise is my birthstone. December,' she said. Oh no, why did she tell him that? He'd probably want to know how old she was now!

'I know what to get you for your birthday then.' He cupped her chin in his hand. 'That blue-green . . . it makes me think of a perfect little bay in Sardinia.'

Julia summoned all her courage. 'I'd like to see it.'

He stroked her cheek. 'You will.'

She really had died and gone to heaven.

He took her glass, put it on the table next to the bed and leaned in to kiss her. His lips barely brushed hers, triggering an odd, light-headed sensation. His tongue was in her mouth, moving slowly, making her ache with longing. She closed her eyes as he slid the strap off her shoulder and stroked her breast, all the while taking his time. She heard him exhale as her hand went round his neck and she dug her nails into his skin.

'Tell me what you like,' Scott said, his hand moving over her stomach, caressing the top of her thigh. He nibbled at her ear. 'Tell me.'

Julia was breathing fast. 'I like it when you . . .' her voice faltered.

'When I what?' Scott nuzzled her neck. His hand slid between her legs.

'You know, what you did before,' Julia said, unexpectedly paralysed with shyness.

He raised himself up on his elbow and gazed into her eyes. Julia trembled. Scott bent and kissed her pale, smooth skin, sliding his tongue over her navel. She squirmed.

'Yes,' she whispered, her hands gripping his shoulders. 'Like that.'

Forty-Six

James Almond stood in the middle of Studio 1, which now looked just like the interior of a Moroccan-themed club he'd once been to for a launch party in Soho. There were jewel-coloured drapes against the walls, squares of silk suspended from the ceiling, soft amber lamps strung here and there, a roped-off VIP area and plenty of nooks and crannies created by the clever use of booths and enormous low sofas strewn with cushions. At one end of the room a bar was being set up, and right in the middle of the floor a plinth for the DJ had been put in place. Once the party was under way, girls in harem pants and cropped tops were going to do the rounds with canapés and champagne.

The corridor that led to the smaller Studio 6 had been decked out with swathes of diaphanous fabric in ruby and gold, and metal lamps designed to throw soft shadows along the walls had been hung from the ceiling. Studio 6 was what the designer called a chill-out zone, which, as far as James could see, meant lots of day beds and clever lighting effects that made it look as if the guests were sitting under a starry night sky. In this room, the girls serving drinks would be in short leather dresses and bondage shoes. On a gantry behind a transparent screen at one end of the room there would be exotic dancers.

James smiled. It really would be a party no one would ever forget.

Officially, the Channel 6 bash was intended to welcome the new owner, Vladimir Vladislav, but as far as James was concerned, its real purpose was to make it crystal clear to anyone who still hadn't got the message that he was back in charge. He had planned the whole thing himself – drawn up the guest list, briefed the designer and even chosen the caterers. He had devoted an afternoon to auditioning the girls who would mingle with his guests, handing out nibbles and topping up their drinks. Every single hostess, as he called them, was stunning and in possession of a pair of magnificent breasts. It was attention to detail that would ensure the whole event was perfect from start to finish. He was determined to make it the party of the year, an event that would be talked about for weeks afterwards.

Tom Steiner, Julia's publicist, had tipped her off about the party. She answered his call in a foul mood, having just opened a letter from the legal department at Channel 6 reiterating her contractual obligations and setting out what steps the station would take if she sought to work with any of her old *Girl Talk* colleagues. She was livid.

'Who the fuck do they think they are?' she wanted to know.

Tom Steiner sighed. He had hoped to find her in a better frame of mind. These days she was up one minute, down the next, and generally all over the place. As for her temper . . . well, to say she had sudden explosive episodes didn't even come close. When Tom had hinted – with as much tact as he could muster – that it might be worth having another scan, on the off-chance that a lingering and hitherto undiagnosed head injury was causing her outbursts, Julia had gone ballistic. He had kept his views to himself after that.

Adopting a soothing tone, he said, 'Now, now, let's not get ourselves all worked up. I expect they're just covering their backs.'

'Well, they can fuck right off. There's no need for written fucking warnings. We already *know* what the contracts say. It's not like we're stupid.' Tom held the phone away from his ear as Julia's voice rose. 'It's James frigging Almond again, turning the screw every chance he gets, the bastard. I'm telling you, Tom, I've just about had it with him. I've a good mind to send him a warning letter of my own accusing him of harassment. I'm at a crucial stage in my convalescence. Any more stress and I could have a relapse.' Tom thought that was highly unlikely. 'Any fool can see there's no fucking chance of us ever finding work now – thanks to him – so why the fuck won't he let it drop? Well? What is that tit-sucking pervert's problem?'

Tom closed his eyes and pinched the bridge of his nose. She really was exhausting, and as for her language . . . utterly shameful. 'If you'd let me get a word in edgeways, I was *actually* calling to say he's throwing an almighty bash at the studios and it might be a good opportunity for me to have a word, clear the air a bit.'

'Don't bother on my account,' Julia said, immediately wondering how she could get herself on the guest list. At the other end of the line she heard Tom sigh. 'There is something you could do for me, though,' she said.

'Go on.'

'Take me as your plus one.'

'Julia, you know that's out of the question.'

Her mind went into overdrive. She had to be at that party.

She *would* be there one way or another. This was her chance to get even with that slimy snake-in-the-grass once and for all.

'Fine, if you won't help me, I'll find someone who will.'

'Julia, I—'

It was too late. She had hung up.

Forty-Seven

Karen was nervous about gate-crashing the Channel 6 party. She was sure she would be stopped and frog-marched off the premises before she even made it as far as Studio 1, but no one batted an eye as she swept through the main entrance. The security chap barely bothered to look at her invite, which had come courtesy of Bella, who had managed to intercept a batch of invitations intended for a hot new burlesque troupe due to appear on *Best Ever Sex* and forwarded them to the *Girl Talk* girls instead.

Karen headed straight for the loos on the ground floor and sent a text to Cheryl: **I'm in!** Seconds later a reply popped up: **Meet us at bar in Studio 1.** Karen checked her make-up and slicked on a fresh layer of soft pink lip gloss. She had managed to squeeze into a red off-the-shoulder dress in a flattering draped design. Underneath, she had on a pair of control pants that started under her boobs and went almost to her knees and made it hard to breathe. Worth it, though, for the sculpting effect. She would have to be careful her dress didn't ride up and give the game away. Her hair fell in loose ebony curls around her shoulders, and a gleaming clip studded with emerald glass, which matched her eyes, held her fringe off her face. She lifted a curl, sprayed Annick Goutal scent on the back of her neck and took a couple of deep breaths. She was ready for anything.

Lesley stood in a corner of Studio 1 knocking back champagne, keeping a wary eye out for James Almond. As a girl in harem pants approached with a tray of drinks, Lesley drained her glass and swapped it for a full one.

'Steady on, babe,' Dan said, slipping a hand round her waist. 'Don't want to get slaughtered, do we?'

Lesley swallowed another hefty slug of bubbly. 'Don't see why not,' she said, catching sight of James on the other side of the room with the new owner of Channel 6, Vladimir Vladislav. The Russian said something and James threw back his head and roared with laughter. Phoney bastard, Lesley thought.

Dan's hand caressed her bottom. 'Bet we could slip behind one of those drapes and get our own little party started,' he said.

Lesley, in a clingy little black dress that showed off her amazing legs and a pair of shiny blue peep-toe Louboutins that had a tropical flower sprouting from the ankle strap, gave him a playful slap. 'Hands off,' she said, still watching James.

'How am I supposed to keep my hands off when you look good enough to eat?' He said, nuzzling her neck and giving her rear a squeeze. 'Are you actually wearing anything under that dress? What about if we disappear behind that curtain and find out?'

Lesley wriggled free. 'Stop it! You can bet Mr Party Animal over there has hidden cameras in every corner, dirty pervert that he is.'

She had done her best to stop Dan from coming to the do, afraid that James might decide to drop her in it over her hen-night fling, but it didn't matter what she said; he'd refused to be put off.

Eventually, he'd given her a cheeky grin. 'What's up? Not ashamed of me, are you?'

'As if! It's a work thing, that's all, and James Almond – possibly the least entertaining controller of entertainment ever to walk this earth – will probably make one of his mind-numbing speeches. You know what he's like.'

Dan had shrugged. 'If he does, that's our cue to sneak into your dressing room and make our own entertainment.'

Lesley was nervous. She hadn't mentioned that her *Girl Talk* chums were planning to publicly humiliate their old boss at the do. Cheryl had secretly taped that last fraught meeting when he'd had the four of them thrown out of Channel 6. She hadn't been sure what to do with the recording, since rules governing privacy would no doubt mean it was off-limits to the newspapers, but then she'd had a brainwave. It so happened that a gay chum of hers, Minxie Minx, was dee-jaying at the bash. Minxie adored Cheryl and was more than happy to cut together a wicked mix featuring James at his pompous worst. The plan was to let rip with what she and Cheryl had dubbed 'The Full-of-Crap Rap' as soon as the speeches were out of the way and the party was in full swing.

Lesley knew James would go ape, but at least it would take his mind off her and Dan. It was just a case of steering well clear until the speeches were over. The Russian had his back to her now, blocking her view. As he turned to shake hands with a woman in a skimpy playsuit who was tanned to the nines, Lesley realized that James was no longer there. Damn, where had he got to?

She felt a tap on her behind and gave Dan another slap.

'Ouch – what was that for?'

She felt another dig and swung round to see Julia in her wheelchair flanked by Karen, Cheryl and Faye.

Despite her lack of mobility, Julia seemed remarkably well. Somehow she gave off the air of a superior being attended by willing minions. She waved an imperious hand that sent Karen scurrying to her side. 'Bag!' Julia said, and Karen held out a fuchsia Chanel quilted clutch. Julia got out her compact, touched up her lippy and thrust the bag back into Karen's eager hands. Lesley shot Dan an amused look. It was quite a performance.

'You made it, then,' Lesley said. 'How did you get in – dig a tunnel?'

Julia gave her a sniffy look. 'I'm a bona fide guest,' she said. 'I have an invite and everything.'

Karen gave a nervous giggle. 'We're on the guest list as the Cupcakes.'

Lesley gave her a quizzical look. '*The* Cupcakes? The burlesque troupe?'

Karen giggled again. 'Bella hijacked their invites.'

Lesley gazed down at Julia. 'Burlesque in a *wheel*chair. There's a novelty.'

Julia shot her a filthy look.

Dan bent and kissed Julia's hand. 'Can I get you a drink, princess – how about a Kir Royale?'

Lesley rolled her eyes. Not him as well!

Julia gave him a dazzling smile. 'That would be lovely, thank you.'

Dan patted Lesley on the backside and trotted off to the bar. Lesley had to admit Julia was looking good, even if she was in a wheelchair with a rug over her legs. A rug that was shedding. She picked fluff off her dress. No doubt about it, Julia had a real glow about her, an aura almost. She was wearing a sheer ivory top embellished with crystals and, by the look of things, barely any make-up. Her eyes seemed a more intense shade of greenish-blue than usual – contacts, perhaps – and her skin was luminous. That surgeon of hers was a miracle worker.

Lesley gave Karen a hug. 'Does James know you're here?'

'No. We want to catch him off-guard.'

'Preferably in a dark alley at the back of the building,' Cheryl said. She was in a skin-tight black leather one-sleeved jumpsuit with plenty of gleaming chocolatey flesh on show, gigantic platforms and an expression that oozed attitude.

'Who've you come as?' Lesley chuckled, thinking she looked like a cross between Rihanna and Lady Gaga.

Cheryl, busy adjusting her conical fascinator, ignored her.

Faye, in a low-cut blue and white floral full-skirted dress, her blonde hair in a loose up-do, hung back, one hand on Julia's wheelchair. 'When I see him he's getting my drink in his face,' she said.

'If there's any left,' Cheryl muttered, frowning at her empty glass.

'Just like Anna Ford and Jonathan Aitken,' Faye went on. 'Remember her chucking red wine at him after she got the push from TV-am?'

Lesley shook her head. 'Bit before my time,' she said, horrified, even though she knew exactly what Faye was talking about. The Anna Ford episode was nearly thirty years ago, for crying out loud – talk about giving away your age!

Paula Grayson, in a low-cut black lace dress, came over. Lesley blinked. She had no idea Paula had a decent pair of boobs, or such good legs, for that matter. Her hair had been styled as well, cut into a shaggy bob, and the grey was cleverly masked by creamy blonde highlights.

Paula registered Lesley's expression and smiled to herself. Just because she had no interest in dressing up for the office didn't mean she wasn't prepared to make an effort when it was a special occasion. She kissed each of them. 'You might want to know that Suki Floyd's here.'

Cheryl's eyes narrowed. 'She'd better keep out of my way.'

Karen caught sight of Bella, who waved and headed over. They hugged. 'You look amazing,' Bella said. 'I take it all back – the kinetics man knows what he's doing.'

'I don't think it's much to do with him,' Karen said. 'I'm off my food at the moment.'

'Me too. Maple syrup, lemon juice and cayenne pepper for three days.' She pulled a face. 'I'm ready to keel over. Worth it, though, since I managed to get into Marsha Caine's trousers. Ta-da!' She did a twirl.

Karen laughed. 'They look fantastic.'

'As soon as I get in tonight, these are coming off and I'm hitting the pizza.' She lowered her voice. 'You'll never guess who I've just seen?' Karen shook her head. 'Only Helen England! Swanning about with her tits falling out of some awful vomit-coloured frock. You can't miss her.'

'I don't believe it! Do you think James knows?'

'He knows all right. I saw them air-kissing. I'm not sure if it was that or the dress that made me want to throw up.' She looked thoughtful. 'Or it might have been the fact that I'm awash with maple frigging syrup.'

Karen scanned the room for Helen.

'Another thing,' Bella said. 'She's with Suki Floyd.' Karen's mouth fell open. 'The pair of them and James . . . all very cosy, if you ask me.'

Karen stared at her. 'Suki? Are you sure?'

'I'd know that dreadful barnet anywhere.'

Karen's face darkened. 'He's such a pig. I could kill him. And her.'

Bella nodded. 'Join the queue,' she said, sashaying off in her fabulous trousers.

Karen scanned the room for James, who seemed to have disappeared. 'I think we should split up,' she said to the others, starting to feel nervous. 'It's a bit obvious, the five of us in a huddle like this. He'll spot us a mile off. We don't want to get chucked out before Minxie does her thing.'

'Knowing that bastard, there's probably something in our contracts about not socializing as a group for the next twenty years,' Julia said. 'I'd love him to come over and have a go. I'd—'

'Yes, well,' Lesley said, interrupting. 'Karen's right. If he spots us together, the game's well and truly up.'

Cheryl nudged Karen. 'Isn't that Dave?'

Karen followed her gaze. Sure enough, there was Dave, standing on his own at the far end of the bar. Karen's heart leapt. He must have got off early. But how come he was at the party? He couldn't be looking for her since she'd kept quiet about going, knowing he'd have told her she was kidding herself if she thought she could take revenge on James Almond. Then she caught sight of Lara Durham, in a micro-skirt and plunging silver top, dragging James on to the dance floor. There was a ripple of applause as Lara began to fling herself about and James jerked out of time, his stilted dance moves accompanied by a series of disturbing facial expressions.

'Oh gawd, I think I'm going to be sick,' Lesley said.

'Me too,' Karen said, still watching Dave, whose eyes were on Lara. It was obvious – he was with her.

Karen pushed her way through the crowd towards him, finding her way barred by a couple doing a very uncoordinated dirty dance routine. As she tried to sidestep them, she caught sight of Tabitha Tate, who was wearing a short white dress that showed off a tattoo encircling one of her thighs, creeping up on Dave from behind. Karen stopped dead as Tabitha reached up on tiptoes and put her hands over his eyes. He stiffened as she leaned close, his expression uncertain as she whispered in his ear then took her hands away and flung her arms round his neck. Then he shook his head, looking pleased, and scooped her up in a bear hug. Karen's heart thumped and her breath came in short, painful gasps. Never mind about getting even with James Almond – now she just wanted to go home. A hand touched her arm and she swung round to find her ex-husband facing her.

Jason spread his arms. 'Wow, babe, looking good,' he said.

'Who let you in?' She looked him up and down, taking in the ripped jeans and Blondie T-shirt. Was he ever going to grow up?

'Who let *you* in, you mean? I'd have thought you'd be on some kind of blacklist after turning Jimbo over in court.'

'Yes, well, no hard feelings.' She didn't want to let on she hadn't actually been invited. As a girl in voluminous harem pants glided past, Karen plucked a glass of champagne from the tray and tipped half of it down her throat.

Jason took a step closer. 'In the party mood, eh? How about a dance – for old times?' He began swaying from side to side.

She glanced over her shoulder. Dave was now deep in

conversation with Tabitha Tate. The pair of them appeared to be finding something hilarious: their heads were practically touching. What on earth was going on?

She shook her head. 'No. Bad idea.'

'Ah, don't be like that,' Jason said, putting an arm round her shoulder.

'Oh, get lost,' she said, shaking him off. 'Shouldn't you be over there with the Page Three girls? Isn't that more your style?' She finished her drink, shoved the empty glass into his hand, gave him a furious look and stomped off towards Dave.

Dan handed Julia her Kir Royale. 'What happened to Lesley?' he said.

Julia shrugged. 'Oh, she won't be far away, I don't suppose.'

The room was crowded now. One of the Sugababes floated past, wearing some kind of jumpsuit that seemed to have a leg missing. Out of habit, Dan checked her rear view. 'I can't believe they've all gone and left you sitting here,' he told Julia.

'Oh, I'm fine. Be a darling and wheel me over to Tom Steiner, would you? He's over there. In the vermilion checked jacket.' She would have to have a word about his appalling fashion sense.

Faye had found a quiet spot to sit down and was adjusting the strap on her new shoes when Mike loomed over her.

'Where's Daisy?' he said, his expression stony.

'Good to see you too,' Faye said. 'She's at the bar, getting us both a drink.'

Mike's brow furrowed. 'Oh, for heaven's sake, where do you think she is? Tucked up at home with my mother. It's not a crime for me to have a night off, you know.'

He folded his arms. 'No, I suppose not.'

Faye wondered if he had anything in his wardrobe these days apart from khaki T-shirts and battle fatigues. Fancy coming to a party in camouflage gear. She was sure her invitation said smart casual. She slipped her shoe back on and gazed up at him, but he wasn't looking at her. He seemed thoroughly preoccupied, one leg juddering, his highly polished army boot going tap-tap in a frantic jerky motion. By the look of him, he definitely needed a drink.

'At ease, soldier,' Faye said, and at once he spread his legs and clasped his hands behind his back. She watched him, amused.

'Atten-*shun*!' Mike's shoulders went back and his heels clicked together. Faye giggled. 'Mike – are you all right?' She motioned to a waitress and took a couple of drinks from her tray. 'Here, have a glass of fizz.'

He snapped out of his reverie and his blue eyes bored into hers. 'I can't drink,' he said. 'I'm on a mission. Seek and destroy.' His right eye twitched.

She giggled again, not sure if he was being funny. It was one thing playing up to his hard-man reputation, but all this army malarkey was starting to get a bit weird. If he wasn't careful, people would start to think he was losing the plot. He'd gone a bit far with his crew cut, as well. Even proper soldiers had more hair.

'I don't suppose you're allowed to tell me what your *mission* is?'

Mike tapped the side of his nose. 'It's a surprise.'

Dave was too engrossed with Tabitha to see Karen coming. She yanked at his arm and the sight of her made his smile vanish.

'Having a good time?' she said.

'What's going on?' he said, surprised. 'I didn't know you were going to be here.'

'Obviously not.'

Tabitha leaned forward. 'Hey, can I get you a drink?' she said to Karen, flashing a smile that showed off perfect white teeth.

Karen stared at her. The flaming cheek of it!

Dave said, 'Look, Kaz, let's get out of here.' He gripped her elbow, but she hung on to the bar. She wasn't going anywhere.

'What about you, babe?' Tabitha said to Dave, putting a hand on his arm. 'Fancy another?'

Babe! Without warning, Karen raised her hand and slapped his face. Tabitha's eyes widened, and for a second or two Dave was completely still. A couple at the bar looked the other way and a red-faced man next to them asked if they'd mind shifting along a bit before, as he put it, things really kicked off.

'Kaz,' Dave said, catching hold of her wrist, 'you've got the wrong end of the stick.'

She fought back tears. 'I'm not blind, you know.'

'Oops, domestic alert!' Tabitha clasped a hand over her mouth in mock horror.

'You know what – you're welcome to him,' Karen said, sounding a lot more composed than she felt. She glared at Tabitha. Then she turned on her Jimmy Choo heels and plunged back into the crowd.

Forty-Eight

Dan bumped into Lesley as she came out of Studio 6. 'I've been looking everywhere for you,' he said. 'You just disappeared. James Almond's making his speech any minute now.'

Lesley gave him an awkward look. 'I nipped into the other studio to check out the chill-out zone and got a bit lost. It's like a cave in there – pitch-black.' She looked away and tugged at the hem of her dress.

Dan put an arm round her waist and they headed off along the corridor. As they went through a set of double doors, fetchingly draped with embroidered tulle, a fire door to their right creaked open and Cheryl stepped into the corridor. For a split second she appeared startled before managing a smile.

'Just nipped out for some air,' she said, wafting a hand in front of her face.

Lesley's gaze went to a scratch on her bare shoulder. 'Is everything OK?'

Cheryl put a hand over the mark. 'The fire door swung back and caught me,' she said, not looking at either of them. 'Bloody thing, weighs a ton.'

Inside Studio 1, Vladimir Vladislav was coming to the end of a speech that had gone on too long. It was to be hoped that

261

James Almond would be more succinct. If they didn't get the music going again soon, the party would die on its feet.

Tom Steiner checked his watch and looked around for Julia. He had delivered her to the disabled loo and left her to it, since she was insistent that she could manage perfectly well and find her own way back. Not that she'd put it quite like that. 'Stop fussing, for fuck's sake,' had been her exact words. That was a while ago, getting on for half an hour. How long did it take to have a pee and re-do her lippy? If she was in there snorting coke through a rolled-up twenty pound note he would have something to say. Just as he was thinking the worst, a vision of her helpless on the floor and unable to reach the emergency cord came to him. Flooded with guilt, he hurried out of the studio to go and find her.

Faye slipped back into the party from behind one of the drapes as Vladimir Vladislav was saying that if they could be patient for just a little longer, James Almond was going to have a few words, and then everyone could get back to having fun.

She grabbed a glass of bubbly and took a long drink. In the DJ booth, Minxie leaned against the rail, arms folded. Faye took a deep breath. She had cut through Studio 6, which was pretty dead apart from Lara Durham making a spectacle of herself, writhing about on one of the day beds with her other half while Massive Attack blared out. Just as well there were no press – not as far as anyone knew, anyway – or she'd be all over the papers tomorrow. Faye had searched high and low for the other girls, but there was no sign. They must be in the main party somewhere. Mike seemed to have vanished too. She hoped he had aborted his so-called mission and gone home. If he carried on like this, he'd end up in an institution, and it wouldn't be the army.

The disabled toilet was vacant. No sign of Julia. Tom called her mobile, which went straight to voicemail. He wandered away from the party towards the dressing rooms, cursing her, about to give up, when he heard a sound coming from the scene dock at the end of the corridor. He stopped and listened. A heavy opaque curtain barred his way. There it was again: a grunting sound. He paused, not sure whether to investigate further. It would be just his luck to stumble on James Almond having a quickie behind the scenes with some busty glamour model. Bracing himself, he pushed the flap aside and ventured in. There, struggling to heave her wheelchair over a thick knot of cables, was Julia, a film of sweat on her brow.

'Julia! What's going on?'

'Don't just stand there, give me a hand,' she snapped.

Tom manoeuvred her over the obstacle and back into the corridor, picking up speed as he hurried towards Studio 1.

'Slow down, will you, it's not *Wacky Races*,' she said, holding on to the sides of the chair as he screeched round a corner.

'What have you been up to? You know very well I don't want to miss the main event – James Almond's speech,' Tom said, sounding frosty. 'He may well have something to say about the shape of things to come.'

'I wouldn't worry about that if I were you,' she said, turning to give him a malevolent look. 'I don't think he'll be around long enough to make any difference to Channel 6.'

'What's that supposed to mean?'

Julia gave an enigmatic shrug.

*

Tabitha Tate finished her drink and waved her empty glass at the barman. Before she could get a refill, someone tapped her on the shoulder. She turned to find Vladimir Vladislav behind her.

'I would like for you to do me a favour, Tabitha,' he said in that formal, quirky way of his. 'I would like for you to go and find James Almond and bring him here so that he can make his speech and we can all resume our party time.'

Tabitha was about to suggest he ask a runner but thought better of it. It was quite a compliment that the owner knew her name. 'Of course – but I've no idea where he is.'

'Ah, that's simple,' Vladislav said, giving her a broad, toothy grin. 'Where else would a workaholic be but at his desk?'

Tabitha left the studio and took the lift to the dimly-lit executive corridor. As she approached James's office she could see light filtering through the blinds. The door was shut. She tapped on it. 'Hello?'

No reply.

She knocked again, louder, and bent to peer through a narrow gap in the blinds. He was in there, she was sure. Someone was, anyway. She could see the glow of a TV screen and the outline of a figure at the desk. Bracing herself, she opened the door. 'Hello?'

James was at his desk, his chair angled away from her, facing the house monitor in the corner that fed live pictures of whatever was going on in the studios. A small desk lamp threw a narrow beam of light against the wall behind him. Tabitha hesitated in the doorway. On the screen she could see a wide shot of Studio 1 crowded with partygoers. She picked out Vladimir Vladislav deep in conversation with the blonde weather girl. To his left, Helen England was knocking back champagne, and –

hang on – was that *Lara* climbing the rope ladder to the DJ booth? Tabitha grinned. That girl made Paris Hilton look positively tame. She glanced at James. He really was an odd one, slipping away from the fun so he could sit in the gloom and watch it all at arm's length. The fact he was filming it was a worry. Archive for his infamous secret files, no doubt, although from what Tabitha could see it all looked pretty innocuous. Honestly, James's penchant for rigging the place with hidden cameras was making Channel 6 more like *Big Brother* every day.

She cleared her throat and knocked at the open door again. 'James?' No response. Irritated, she stalked into the room and stood in front of the desk. 'Mr Vladislav sent me. They're waiting for you to make your speech.'

He ignored her.

She frowned at him and leaned on the desk. The mouse pad next to his computer was at a funny angle, which set an alarm bell ringing in her head. James was way too anal to let anything sit even slightly out of place. She moved closer, her eyes darting to the shadowy corners of the vast office. What if he wasn't alone? She began to edge round the desk. James still kept his face turned away from her. She hesitated. In the gloom she could just make out something dark on the front of his suit, a wet patch glistening against the pale fabric.

What the—?

Her hand flew up to her mouth and she sprang back. No, she was imagining things. Something was definitely wrong, though. Maybe he'd drunk too much and passed out. Perhaps he'd sneaked a slapper upstairs for a quickie and had some kind of seizure, a heart attack.

Her own heart thumped inside her chest as she moved

around the desk for a proper look. As she stared at his vacant eyes, the mess on the front of his suit, the lurid bloodstain spreading to his groin, she could hardly breathe. It definitely wasn't a heart attack. She had to do something, get help. Her hand went for the phone on James's desk but something stopped her picking it up. Tabitha had seen enough episodes of *CSI* to know you should never touch anything at a crime scene. She cursed herself for leaning on the desk. Fumbling in her bag she grabbed her mobile and dialed 999.

'Police,' she said, her voice cracking. 'I think someone's been murdered.'

Forty-Nine

The operator told Tabitha to stay where she was and not touch anything. She felt jumpy and wanted to put the light on but didn't dare. She might – what did they say on *CSI*? – compromise the crime scene. Instead she used the torch on her mobile, which made things feel even more creepy. She had explained about the party at Channel 6, hundreds of people milling about, said the killer might very well still be in the building. The 999 operator had told her not to worry about that, said that the officers would determine the correct course of action, and that she should just stay where she was.

She stood at the window watching the police cars speed towards the building, sirens blaring, blue lights flashing. Six cars pulled up in front of reception, one after another, parking on the forecourt, which was strictly forbidden. Tabitha was shaking but at the same time she could feel a rush of adrenalin that made her feel alert and pumped up. It was the same buzz she got whenever she was on a big story. Her reporter's instincts kicked in. The police would be here any second and the first thing they'd do was chuck her out. She needed to memorize everything. She switched on the record device on her mobile and started to dictate her impressions of the room. 'In the darkness,' she began to say, 'James Almond lay slumped in his chair, blood pouring from a wound in his chest.' Was he slumped? Was the blood actually *pouring*? She nipped back to the desk and checked the floor. 'The blood loss was so severe a pool had formed at the base of his chair,' she said. That fancy imported Italian rug of his was ruined. She was starting to feel much better. There was a tiny piece of fluff on the sleeve of his jacket. She made a mental note. 'The state of the controller's desk indicated there may have been a struggle.' A wonky mouse pad might not seem much to anyone else – she'd better point that out or the police would no doubt miss it – but Tabitha understood its significance to a neat-fiend like James only too well. As for the lamp pointing at the wall, well, that definitely wasn't right.

She bent and looked under the desk. A BlackBerry lay on the floor, its red light flashing. It must be his. Perhaps it would explain why he had slipped away from the party. There might be a message, an indication that he had arranged to meet someone. She looked at the fluff on his jacket again. A woman, definitely, wearing a wrap of some description. Cashmere or angora, perhaps. She was getting carried away. Nothing was certain yet. 'In the struggle a mobile phone, thought to belong to the Controller of Entertainment, ended up on the floor.' Or perhaps the phone belonged to the killer? She felt another ripple of excitement. The light snapped on and she swung round.

'What do you think you're doing?' A young guy who was the spitting image of the current Dr Who was glaring at her. Behind him were two uniformed police officers, an older man and a chunky woman with blonde streaked hair tied in a severe ponytail. 'I'm DI Tim Ellis,' Dr Who said. 'I take it you called it in.'

Tabitha nodded.

The DI was wearing a pair of latex gloves. 'Did you touch anything?'

She shook her head. 'Just the desk.' She pointed. 'There, before I saw he was . . . you know.'

Tabitha watched him stride towards James and check the side of his neck for a pulse. He frowned at the male officer and shook his head. 'Make sure no one leaves, Tony,' he said, 'and tape off this whole corridor.' He turned to Tabitha. 'What were you doing up here?'

'The owner sent me. James – ' she pointed at the figure in the chair – 'was meant to make a speech. Everyone was waiting.'

'Why you?'

Tabitha shrugged. 'How should I know?'

'What was your relationship to . . . James?'

'He's my boss.' Tabitha gasped. 'Hang on! Am I a suspect?'

'If you could wait outside a minute, we'll need a statement.' He took her arm and steered her towards the door.

Tabitha wanted to say something smart to DI Ellis, put him in his place, but her reporter's instincts told her not to. If he was going to be running a murder inquiry, she wanted to keep him sweet. She glanced at her dress, which was short and white. It was spotless. If she was the killer she'd be covered in blood: it wouldn't take Dr Who long to eliminate her from his inquiries. For now, the main thing was to be cooperative and stay in his good books.

It would pay dividends in the end.

Fifty

Karen was standing outside the main entrance of Channel 6 waiting for a taxi to take her home when the first police car screeched to a halt in front of the building. Two officers jumped out and ushered her back into the lobby. More police cars arrived as one of the officers took her name and wrote it in a notebook he produced from a pocket on the front of his stab jacket. Karen wondered what on earth was going on. Perhaps there'd been a bomb scare, but if that was the case they'd be clearing the building, not keeping people there. Once her details had been taken, she took herself back to the party in Studio 1, which seemed to have come to a halt. There was no music and Vladimir Vladislav was rambling on about how proud he was to be at the helm of a broadcasting giant like Channel 6. From the bored looks on the faces of the partygoers, he'd been speaking for quite some time. Karen spotted Lesley, hand in hand with Dan.

'What's happening?'

'It's the new owner proving what an asset he'll be to the enter-tainment output of the channel,' Lesley said, pretending to stifle a yawn. 'James is supposed to be making a speech, but God knows where he's got to so the Russian's filling in. God help us.'

Karen looked around the room. Nothing seemed amiss. 'Has there been a fight or something?"

Lesley frowned. 'Don't think so. Mind you, if he doesn't shut up there'll be a frigging riot any minute now.' She helped herself to a glass of champagne from a passing waiter.

'It's just that the police are here.'

Dan raised an eyebrow. 'Maybe it's a drugs raid.'

'It's weird. I was outside waiting for a cab, but they wouldn't let me go home.'

A uniformed police officer had appeared at the side of Vladimir Vladislav. The Russian frowned and nodded and handed over the microphone.

'If you could bear with me, ladies and gentlemen,' the officer said, 'we have a major incident on our hands and it is imperative that you all remain where you are. For the time being, no one is to leave the building.'

A murmur went round the studio. Two uniformed officers barred the exit.

'Why do policemen always say things like *imperative*?' Lesley asked.

'Maybe someone's had a purse snatched or something,' Dan said.

Lesley sipped at her champagne. 'That's a lot of police presence for a bag thief.'

Karen felt uneasy. 'I think something's happened.'

'Obviously something's *happened*. That's why the boys in blue are here.'

'Something serious, I mean. I've got a bad feeling.'

In the conference room on the ground floor, just along the corridor from Studio 1, DI Ellis was leaning against the wall, facing a weeping Helen England. It seemed logical to question her first. Someone had gone to James Almond's office, followed him

271

perhaps, stabbed him and sloped off, taking the murder weapon – as yet unfound – with them. There was some history between Helen England and the Controller, and it hadn't ended well. Perhaps she blamed him for her fall from grace. That was motive.

Ellis folded his arms and studied Helen. Next to her was a woman with extraordinary hair and blood-red lips. When Helen England insisted on having her representative present, Ellis assumed she meant a legal brief, but the woman with the hair was actually a showbiz agent going by the name of Suki Floyd.

Helen dabbed at her eyes. 'Poor James,' she said. 'Who would want to hurt him?'

The woman with the hair drummed on the desk with her long nails. They were like claws, red and filed to a point. 'Who *wouldn't*? I mean, I hardly know where to start, darling. It's not like he was Mr Popularity.'

Helen snivelled into her hanky. 'I still loved him, you know.'

'Of course you didn't, dear. That's just the champagne talking.'

Suki Floyd fixed DI Ellis with her beady eyes. Something about her made him think of a bird of prey. 'Get a move on, Detective,' she said. 'As you can see, my client is distraught.'

'Where exactly were you earlier this evening?'

Suki snorted. 'She was at the party. Like we all were.'

Ellis ignored her. 'You know your way round the building. Did you go to James Almond's office?'

Suki's birdlike eyes narrowed. 'She was with me. All the time.'

He looked at Helen. 'You didn't slip away on your own at all? I know you and James Almond were close at one time.'

Suki cut in. 'He's not banging her, if that's what you're getting at. That's all in the past.'

Helen's shoulders shuddered. Suki gave her a perfunctory pat on the arm. Her mind was in overdrive. As soon as they were out of there she'd set up an exclusive interview with the *Sun*, maybe something with one of the magazines. This was Helen's moment. She could say what she liked now, since James was in no position to complain about his precious privacy any more.

'Will this take much longer?' Suki said. 'You can see she's upset.'

'It's not me you should be talking to,' Helen said. 'You need to question the *Girl Talk* lot. They hated James.'

'Heaven knows how they got in,' Suki said. 'Gate-crashed, bet you anything, so they could get even with him after all that business in court.' The birdlike eyes sparkled. 'If I were you I'd look no further, Detective.' She got up and gave DI Ellis a hideous smile. 'Now, is that all?'

'A few more questions.'

'It's just that she's diabetic and I think her blood sugar's dropping.' Suki placed a bony hand on Helen's brow. 'As I thought – burning up.' She yanked Helen to her feet. 'Is there a reward, by the way?'

DI Ellis frowned. 'I'm sorry?'

'You know, for tipping you off about the killers. My money's on Julia Hill. She might have lost the use of her legs, but don't let that fool you. She's as strong as an ox. Hell of a temper too. Just ask James – ' She clapped a hand over her mouth. Helen let out a wail. 'Oops, listen to me.' She chuckled. 'You can't, can you? Poor James. Oh well, everyone knows what a crazy bitch Julia is.' Her face darkened. 'I wouldn't mind, you know, but I spent ages chatting to James tonight, buttering him up, running through an idea for a new show. He liked it too.

I was on the brink of a deal.' The scrawny shoulders rose and fell. 'Complete waste of time. I mean, he's hardly going to commission anything now, is he?'

DI Ellis watched, speechless, as she stalked off, dragging Helen behind her.

Julia was not in the mood to be questioned by a detective who looked like he'd barely started shaving.

'Do I look like I'm capable of sneaking to the executive floor in my wheelchair and stabbing James Almond?' she said.

'Who said he was stabbed?'

Julia sneered. 'They did a newsflash. That Tabitha Tate girl, reporting live in her party frock.'

DI Ellis clenched his fists. He should have known she'd be on camera the second he'd finished questioning her. He suppressed a sigh of frustration. 'You didn't get on with James Almond.'

'You're right about that. I *hated* him. And do you know why?' Ellis held her gaze. 'That piece of shit went out of his way to destroy me.' She gave him a defiant look. 'He had it in for *Girl Talk*. Axed the show and ruined the lot of us.' Ellis raised an eyebrow. That wasn't quite true. At least one of them, Lesley Gold, was still employed by Channel 6 as far as he knew. Julia's expression hardened. 'Quite frankly, I couldn't be happier he's dead. I didn't kill him, though, if that's what you're thinking.'

'You're quite sure about that.'

Julia laughed. 'I may not be able to walk, but I assure you my short-term memory is in perfect working order.'

Ellis dropped his gaze to the throw covering Julia's knees. 'We found something on the sleeve of James's suit – a bit of fluff.'

'So?'

'It may have come from you – that thing on your knees. It's the same colour.'

Julia gave him a disparaging look. 'That *thing* happens to be the finest angora money can buy.' She gave the throw a loving caress. 'I had it imported.'

Ellis said, 'I might need to take it.'

Julia manoeuvred round the desk and glided over to the DI. 'Keep still,' she said, brushing against him and depositing specks of fluff on his black trousers. 'It went everywhere, I'm afraid.' Julia gave him a sly look. 'I hope an exquisite throw with a tendency to leave bits everywhere isn't the best you can do, Detective.'

Lesley crossed her long legs and flicked a strand of gleaming blonde hair over her shoulder. The detective was cute. She batted her eyelashes in an obvious way.

'You know, you remind me of someone,' she said, tilting her head on one side.

DI Ellis cut in before she could say he looked just like Matt Smith. 'I'll come straight to the point. Did you leave the party this evening to meet James Almond in his office?'

Lesley's amber eyes were huge. 'God, no! There's no way I'd spend time alone with that filthy pervert.' She shuddered. 'You *do* read the papers, right? I mean, you know he's got a weird nappy fetish.'

'What was the nature of your relationship?'

Lesley's mouth dropped open. 'I'm not sure . . .'

'I'm told he sacked all the *Girl Talk* presenters but you're still working at Channel 6.' He let that sink in. 'So I'm wondering if the two of you had what you might call a special relationship.'

Lesley pulled a face. 'Oh, please. Have you *seen* my husband? Drop-dead gorgeous. And just so you know, when Paula Grayson took over, *she* hired me – not James – to host *Best Ever Sex*.' She preened. 'For obvious reasons. Make no mistake, James would have got rid of me if he could, blackmailing bastard that he was. In fact, I think he was angling to do exactly that, even though the show's a massive hit.'

Ellis pounced. 'In that case, you wouldn't have been sorry to see him gone?'

'Course not. He was a pest. Couldn't keep his eyes off your tits. He had stuff on all of us, you know – secret files. That's how he kept everyone in line.' Lesley rummaged in her bag for her lip gloss and slathered on a layer of bright tangerine. 'I hope you're not suggesting I might be a suspect, Inspector.'

'You had a motive.'

'Oh, well – if you're going to accuse everyone who had a *motive*, you'll be here all night.'

'Who would want James Almond dead?'

Lesley frowned and picked at a speck of fluff on her dress. Ellis watched. Julia Hill's throw again. 'Me. All the other girls. Helen England, probably. Her husband, I'd have thought . . . oh God, *loads* of people.'

Ellis thrust his hands into his pockets. Helen England's husband wasn't in the building, so he was off the hook. 'Where were you when Mr Vladislav made his speech?' As far as anyone could tell, James had gone AWOL just before then.

'I was with my husband, clapping in all the right places.' She suppressed a yawn. 'Look, I didn't even speak to James tonight. I see enough of him at work without wanting to spend time in his company when I'm meant to be having fun. I don't see what more I can tell you.'

In the conference room, something about the way DI Ellis was looking at her made Karen feel guilty, which was ridiculous since it was hardly a crime to leave a party early.

'You didn't get on with James Almond, did you?'

'You could say the same thing for half the people who worked for him.'

'Yours was a major falling-out, though, wasn't it – high profile?'

Karen flushed. 'He promised us all the same job, led us on, then axed our show. So, no, we weren't exactly friends.'

'Why were you leaving the party?'

'I'd had enough, that's all.'

Ellis was blunt. 'Did you go to James Almond's office?'

'No!'

'You didn't come here to take revenge on him in some way?'

Karen's cheeks burned. 'No!'

'You're sure about that?'

'I'd have loved to see him brought down a peg or two.' Karen's eyes were shiny. 'That's all. I wouldn't have killed him.'

'You had good reason, from where I'm standing. Your career went down the pan, thanks to him.' A thought occurred to Ellis. 'Maybe there's a way back for you at Channel 6 now he's out of the way.'

Karen stared at him. 'You think I'd kill him to get my job back?'

'Would you?'

She gasped. 'That's absurd.'

'I've seen the guest list and you weren't on it, so what exactly were you doing here?'

'I just . . .'

'You were here on a mission, weren't you, you and your friends?'

DI Ellis waited for Faye to finish her coffee. She looked wasted. Not much chance of getting any sense out of her until she'd sobered up.

'How come you were at Channel 6 tonight?'

Faye held her mug in both hands. 'It was a party,' she said.

'You weren't on the guest list.'

She brightened. 'We were. We're the Cupcakes!'

Ellis frowned.

'The burlesque dancers. You know – fans and feathers and nipple tassels.'

Ellis was confused. 'I'm not with you.'

Faye giggled. 'They were supposed to come, but we got their invites.'

'Were you planning to confront your old boss?'

Faye's brow was furrowed. 'Not confront, exactly.'

Ellis waited for her to say something else. When her eyes started to close he said, 'Did you see James Almond tonight? Speak to him?'

Faye blinked. 'I hate him. *Hate* him. He axed our show!'

Ellis took a deep breath. Not again! 'So you came here to get your own back.'

Faye put her coffee down. 'I'm a single mum, no work, nothing.' Her dress was crumpled. Her caramel hair was no longer in its up-do. She wound it into a messy coil and arranged it over one shoulder. All of a sudden she brightened. 'Do you think we'll get our jobs back now?'

Ellis gritted his teeth. He was getting nowhere fast.

'You'd arranged for your DJ friend to play a prank on James Almond at the party,' Ellis said. He'd eventually managed to get this much out of Karen and Faye.

Cheryl gave him a frosty look. 'Only he went and got himself killed before she had a chance, inconsiderate prick.'

'You don't exactly seem upset.'

'I'm not.'

'Did you go to James Almond's office this evening?'

'Why would I?'

'You tell me. It's obvious you came here looking for revenge.'

'And I'd have been quite happy for Minxie to play the Full-of-Crap mix, so everyone could see what a shit he is. Was.'

'Maybe you decided to take things further. I mean, it can't be easy for you, him back in charge in his old job, while you and your friends are out in the cold.'

'You're right. That's why we were planning to wipe the smile off his smarmy face tonight.'

Ellis gave a hollow laugh. 'Someone did that all right.'

'If you ask me, whoever it was deserves a medal.' She moved her fascinator half an inch to the left. 'I just wish they'd waited until after Minxie had done her thing.'

He was losing patience. 'You don't seem to realize you could be in serious trouble.'

Cheryl stared right at him. It would take more than a Dr Who lookalike to ruffle her feathers. 'So, charge me with something.'

He held her gaze as the green eyes bored into him. 'Did you kill James Almond?'

A smile played on her lips. 'It's not my style. I'd rather have rubbed his nose in it in front of everyone, let the Russian know his Controller of Entertainment was a mean little tosser.' She gave a tiny shrug. 'Cruel, I know, but so much more satisfying. And now I won't be able to watch him squirm.'

Fifty-One

The day after the murder, DI Ellis sat at his desk and flipped through the witness statements. None of them told him very much. Any one of those women had a motive for killing James Almond. The trouble was he had no hard evidence – just the fluff from Julia Hill's throw, and that was about it.

He rubbed at his brow. Half the people at the party had bits of fluff from her damned throw on their clothing. He could hardly charge her with murder on the basis of that. And she was in a wheelchair. How would she have got close enough to James to catch him off-guard and stab him? There was also the question of how someone sitting down could have got their hands on the murder weapon. An inventory had revealed that one of the award statuettes on the shelf behind the Controller's desk was missing. The pathologist had examined an almost identical one and confirmed that the sculpted, solid metal statuette, tapered to a point at one end, could well have inflicted the fatal wound. So someone had reached up, grabbed the missing statuette and plunged it into his heart. Ellis had pulled up a chair and tried to reach something on the same shelf without getting up. It was impossible, which seemed to rule Julia Hill out. Unless for some reason the statuette was not in its usual place but on the desk. Ellis thought about that. Would there be any reason for James Almond to take the statuette down? None that sprang immediately to mind. He was obsessed with order and neatness, it seemed, not the type to have anything out of place. All the same, DI Ellis was reluctant to take Julia Hill off his list of suspects, mainly because the idea of her flying into a violent rage and killing someone seemed entirely possible. At the same time he was usually pretty good at picking up on small, almost imperceptible signs that gave the game away when he was quizzing a suspect – a tiny flicker of something in the eyes, subtle changes in the tone of voice – yet he had detected nothing in her response to support his hunch that she might be the killer. He let out a sigh.

He ran through his remaining suspects. Karen King had looked as guilty as sin when he questioned her, but according to the Channel 6 doorman she'd been in reception for a good half-hour waiting for a taxi by the time the first squad cars showed up. Surely if she'd just committed murder and wanted to flee the scene she'd have gone to the end of the road, jumped in a cab and been long gone? Ellis yawned. He'd had no sleep.

He wasn't sure what to make of Lesley Gold. He could have sworn she was flirting with him. As for Faye Cole, the word was she was a bit of a lush these days. She couldn't even walk straight when she came into the conference room. And she was tiny, fragile almost, like a little doll. Capable of murder? Unlikely, but at this stage he was keeping an open mind. Cheryl West wasn't so much cool as cold. She had made it clear that her agenda was about making James suffer rather than killing him, and Ellis was inclined to believe her. She brought to mind a cat playing with a mouse.

Two officers had gone through the CCTV tapes from the party. All the *Girl Talk* women went missing at some point before James Almond was due to make his speech. In theory, any one of them could have followed him to his office. Then again, lots of people were coming and going. Ellis still couldn't work out why James had gone back to his office in the first place. Why watch the party from a distance when he was meant to be in the thick of it? He was supposed to be the host, yet he was sitting in the dark spying on his guests. There were no clues on the mobile phone recovered from beneath the desk either, just two missed calls from Vladimir Vladislav and a curt message to say everyone was waiting for James to make his speech.

DI Ellis decided to go out and get a breath of fresh air and a decent cup of coffee. As he strode along the street, Tabitha Tate fell into step beside him. He gave her a hard look and walked faster. Tabitha picked up her pace.

'You've got a nerve,' he said. 'You do know you made it bloody hard for me to question the suspects when they already knew as much as I did?'

Tabitha gave him a winning smile. 'Sorry. I wasn't trying to make things tricky. It's just – well, it was a fantastic scoop. No way could I have sat on it.'

DI Ellis crossed the road. Tabitha stuck like glue.

'I'll buy you a coffee to make it up,' she said.

Ellis ignored her.

'We might as well work together on this.'

He looked at her as if she was mad.

'Seriously,' she said. 'Think about it. I can be your contact on the inside, make sure the story gets the coverage it deserves and all that.'

Ellis stopped dead and turned to face her. 'We're talking about the murder of a Channel 6 executive. I hardly need you to make sure it's on the news.'

She gave him a cheeky grin. 'Oh, you know what I mean.'

Ellis grunted. She had some front, he would give her that. 'I don't want you getting in the way.'

'I won't.'

'Doing stuff that's likely to compromise the investigation.'

She gave an airy wave. 'You don't have to worry – I'm up to speed on all that. I've seen how they do things on *CSI*.' Ellis cracked a smile. 'I don't know what's so funny. It's not as if I touched anything at the crime scene, did I?'

He gave her a long look. 'OK. As long as you play by my rules.'

'Does that mean I'm on the case?'

'It means you're buying me coffee. Then we'll see.'

Fifty-Two

Paula Grayson stood back and admired her new office. Once the police had removed the crime-scene tape, she had asked a production designer friend to come in and give the place a complete overhaul. Within a couple of days it had been transformed, removing every trace of its previous occupant. Now that several weeks had passed, she had really settled in. No chance of him making a comeback this time, Paula told herself.

Her designer friend had sourced a retro cream-coloured leather sofa piped in red, burgundy Persian rugs and a quirky coffee table crafted from ethically sourced hardwood. In place of the hi-tech spotlights favoured by James, Paula had gone for a chandelier crafted from coloured glass. The crowning glory was a daybed in the corner where the conference table used to be. She was the new Controller of *Entertainment*, after all. At the window, sheer muslin blinds billowed in the breeze. She had brought in an ancient walnut partners' desk from home and opted for a classic recliner in leather and rosewood, just like the one designed for the film director Billy Wilder in the 1950s. Old movie posters had been hung on the walls: *Some Like It Hot*, *Single White Female*, *Crash*, *Million Dollar Baby*, *My Life as a Dog*. James's things had been consigned to a cage in the props department.

There was a tap on the door and Anne appeared. 'Just to remind you, the production meeting's in fifteen minutes.'

Paula nodded. 'What do you think of the new look?'

'It's amazing. I'm struggling to picture what it was like before.'

Paula smiled. She slung her quilted bag over her shoulder and smoothed the front of her taupe shirt dress. 'Good. That was the idea.'

Bella Noble was going through the brief she had prepared for Paula when the door to the conference room swung open and Karen appeared, wearing a fitted grey dress with a slashed neck and three-quarter-length sleeves. She dropped a leather duffel bag dotted with studs on to the table.

'Like the bag,' Bella said. 'Is it a Mulberry?'

'M&S.' Karen dug around inside and brought out a lip gloss. She slicked on a fresh coat of Dusky Pink.

Bella poured her a coffee. 'How are things?'

'Still not speaking.' Karen gave her an awkward smile. 'Well, he is, I'm not.'

'So he's not driving you?'

'Oh yeah – he dropped me off just now.'

'That must be tricky.'

Karen sighed. 'He says nothing happened.'

'But you don't believe him?'

'He must think I was born yesterday. She was all over him at the party.' Karen thought back to Tabitha Tate sneaking up behind Dave and slipping her hands over her eyes. There had been something inappropriate and familiar – intimate, in fact – in the gesture.

'Have you talked – really talked?' Bella said. 'Or have you been giving him the cold shoulder?'

Karen shrugged. It was disconcerting how well Bella knew her – she could practically read her mind. The truth was, Dave had been well and truly in the dog house and Karen had refused to speak to him ever since the party. When she had got home that night, she had gone round the house gathering up his belongings like a whirlwind, intending to chuck them out on the street. Then she had remembered that the slag who'd run off with her husband had done exactly the same thing and, in the nick of time, managed to stop herself. The tabloids would have had a field day poking fun at Karen for taking a leaf out of her love rival's book. No, the last thing she wanted was for anyone to draw comparisons between her and a slutty glamour model, so she forced herself to count to ten and calm down.

Predictably, Dave had had an explanation ready about Tabitha, but Karen wasn't in the mood. She had seen the two of them with her own eyes making a fool of her at a party where practically everyone knew Dave was supposed to be with her. From the way he and Tabitha were canoodling, it had been obvious they were more than friends. Or had it? All that business with Jason had left her a shade oversensitive and liable to go into orbit at the slightest whiff of infidelity.

'It might be innocent, you know,' Bella said, reading her thoughts in that way of hers.

'Didn't you see them – laughing and hugging?' Karen closed her eyes as a vision of Tabitha whispering in Dave's ear came to mind yet again.

'I know. It's just, well – I can be like that with guys I like and it doesn't mean there's anything going on.' Bella gazed at her. 'Sometimes it's easy to get the wrong end of the stick. That's all I'm saying.'

'And sometimes people – blokes – can lie through their teeth.'

'Maybe you should hear him out. It's worth bearing in mind that you're not dealing with Jason. Dave's a different kettle of fish.'

'That's what I thought too – and look where it's got me.'

'Just talk to him.' The door opened and Lesley teetered in, her face obscured by a massive pair of shades. Bella lowered her voice. 'Give him a chance to explain,' she said.

Lesley dumped her beloved Miss Sicily bag on the table. She was wearing a biker jacket over a short, skin-tight tan dress, and red gingham peep-toes with cork heels. She bent and kissed Karen and waved a hand at Bella.

'Well,' she said, digging around in the bag for her lippy, 'does anyone else have a weird sense of déjà vu?'

Karen smiled. 'I know. I can't help feeling bad about James, though.'

Lesley took off her shades and peered at her. 'I don't see why – unless you stabbed him to death.'

'Of course I didn't!'

'Thought as much.' Lesley slathered a thick layer of Flirty Peach on her lips. 'Did anyone see those pictures of Amanda Holden coming out of The Ivy? What do you think – filler in her lips or not?' Lesley examined her own fabulous pout in her compact.

Karen and Bella exchanged a look.

The door flew open and Paula Grayson entered, in a tailored shirt dress and espadrilles, with Cheryl hot on her heels.

'So the police are no further forward?' Cheryl asked as Paula took a seat next to Bella at the top of the table. 'It's been weeks.'

'Search me,' Paula said. 'As far as I know, they haven't charged anyone.'

'I wish they'd get on with it,' Cheryl said, flopping into a seat next to Karen. She shrugged off a purple velvet jacket and tie-dye scarf to reveal a tiny black vest that showed off her toned arms. Around her neck a heavy crucifix swung from wooden rosary beads. Karen sneaked a look at her middle. Not so much as a hint of a muffin top.

Lesley gazed at Cheryl. 'What's up – worried they might come for you?'

Cheryl gave her a filthy look.

Faye, in a floral prom dress and denim jacket, slipped into the room and sat on the far side of the table next to Lesley. 'Sorry I'm late,' she said.

Lesley leafed through a copy of *heat* magazine. 'I feel sorry for the police. Just think – they must be overrun with suspects. I mean, who *wouldn't* want to kill James Almond? What did you make of that cute detective, DI Ellis? I told him he was welcome to take down my particulars any time.'

'He gave me his card,' Faye said.

'Babe, he gave everyone his card. He's a police officer investigating a violent and brutal murder and we're the number-one suspects. Giving out cards is what they do.'

Faye looked crestfallen.

Lesley checked her watch. 'Are we *still* waiting for Julia – pleasing herself as usual just because she happens to be in a wheelchair?'

Paula looked up from her laptop and gave her a withering

look. 'We'll give her another minute or two. It can't be easy getting around.'

'You're joking – she's in her element with everyone running round after her,' Lesley said. She looked at Karen. 'She's got *you* waiting on her hand and foot, for a start.'

Karen went pink. 'I'm only trying to be helpful.'

'After she tried to kill you, as well,' Lesley said, looking thoughtful. 'Do the police know there's a killer in our midst? I think they should be told.'

Karen spluttered. 'She's hardly a killer – I'm still here, aren't I?'

'Lesley's right,' Cheryl said. 'The fact that you had a lucky escape doesn't mean she wasn't serious. You don't go waving a gun around unless you mean business.'

'She wasn't well!'

'I don't think we should joke about it,' Faye said.

Cheryl glared at her. 'Who's joking?'

'Once you've got that bloodlust thing going on, I don't suppose you ever really lose it,' Lesley said, turning a page. She held the magazine up. 'Don't you think Robert Pattinson looks a lot better now he's had his hair cut?'

The door swung open and Julia glided in – upright. She was in a short, flesh-coloured chiffon dress and a thigh-skimming jacket. Her blonde hair was tousled and arranged into a soft fringe à la Carey Mulligan. Her turquoise eyes sparkled and her lips, with an on-trend nude finish, were parted in a huge smile.

The others gasped. Karen's jaw dropped and Lesley's gaze shot to Julia's feet and the sublime turquoise suede killer heels with the giveaway glimpse of red visible on the underside of the stiletto.

Julia did a mock bow. 'What's up? Don't tell me you're actually lost for words.' She gave Lesley a superior smile. 'That must be a first for you.'

'You're w-walking,' Lesley stuttered.

'Ten out of ten for observation.' Julia put her hands on her hips. 'Would it kill you to look a bit more pleased to see me?'

Karen jumped up. 'It's just that we had no idea you were back on your feet.' She took a step forward and did her best to hug Julia, who towered over her in her seven-inch heels. Julia pushed her off.

'Watch it, you'll crush my dress,' she said.

Faye looked tearful. 'Oh Julia, it's a miracle.'

Cheryl rolled her eyes. 'Get a grip, for goodness' sake. She's been having physio for heaven knows how long.' She turned to Julia. 'So, when did you take your first steps?'

'Oh, I've been on my feet for ages.' Julia gave an airy wave. 'I was hobbling about before James Almond threw his murder-mystery party, actually, but I wanted to wait until I could get back into my Louboutins before I went public.'

'So you didn't need to turn up in your wheelchair?'

Julia shrugged. 'You couldn't expect me to be seen out in pumps.' She shot a look at Paula Grayson. 'There are limits, you know.' She tottered the length of the room and settled into a chair facing Paula.

No one spoke.

'Well,' Julia said, 'let's hope you lot have more to say for yourselves when *Girl Talk* relaunches or we're in big trouble.'

'Well, Julia, of course we're all delighted to see you up and about again,' Paula said, at the same time making a mental note to cancel the work scheduled to improve wheelchair access to the dressing-room corridor.

Julia ran a hand through her hair. 'I should hope so. Let's face it – you need me firing on all cylinders to have any chance of making *Girl Talk* a success.'

'Well, you know what they say – there's no show without Punch.' Lesley shoved *heat* back into her bag and turned to a copy of *Grazia* with Jennifer Aniston on the cover.

'If that's your way of saying I'm crucial to the success of *Girl Talk*, I couldn't agree more,' Julia said.

'Actually, I was just thinking how much you remind me of Mr Punch – loud, bad-tempered, prone to violent outbursts . . . need I go on?'

'I thought Judy was the violent one,' Karen said.

'I always thought they were as bad as each other,' Faye said. 'They used to frighten the life out of me. I tell you what, there's no way I'll be taking Daisy to see Punch and Judy.'

'Oh, I wouldn't worry – I don't think it's as brutal as it used to be,' Karen said.

'For goodness' sake,' Cheryl said, exasperated. 'What is this – a production meeting or a frigging nursery?'

'Right,' Paula said, 'if we could make a start.'

'I hope you told the police your wheelchair was just for show,' Lesley said. 'Who knows what else you might be hiding.'

Julia bristled. 'What I choose to tell the police is nothing to do with you.'

'It is if you managed to hoodwink them into thinking you couldn't have murdered James. For all we know, you were probably wearing a pair of *killer heels* the night he was stabbed to death.' Lesley held Julia's gaze. 'They still haven't found the murder weapon. You could have smuggled it out under that throw you kept over your legs – you could have been *wearing* it.'

'You seriously think I'd waste a pair of my favourite shoes on him?'

'That's enough,' Paula said. 'You're all well aware the police seem to think the murder weapon was the statuette that went missing the night James was killed.'

'We don't know for sure, though, do we? It might have been something else.' Lesley glared at Julia.

Julia laughed. 'Oh, priceless.' She peered at Lesley. 'I don't suppose you had a liquid lunch? Because you don't seem to be making much sense.'

'I'm perfectly sober.'

'Amazing – some things do change, then.'

'Yeah, well, it's a pity your near-death experience didn't change *you*, make you a nicer person.'

'Lesley!' exclaimed Karen.

Lesley gave Karen a dirty look. 'I'm only saying what everyone else is thinking. She nearly died and she's *still* the bitch from hell.'

Julia preened. 'I'll take that as a compliment.'

'Oh, get lost.'

Paula Grayson thumped the table making Bella jump and slop her coffee on to the table.

'Will you all just *stop*! We have a terrific opportunity here to bring back a show that should never have been axed in the first place, so let's make the most of it. The only tragedy is that our former Controller of Entertainment had to die before *Girl Talk* could be revived . . .' She paused and suppressed what looked like a flicker of triumph. 'Now, we still need that old *GT* spark, of course we do, but we do *not* need you coming to blows before we even get back on air.'

Lesley folded her arms and pouted at Paula. 'Tell that to Mr Punch over there,' she repleid.

'That is quite enough,' Paula said. 'As you just pointed out, Julia has been through a dreadful ordeal and I think it's up to us to show some understanding.'

Lesley gasped. 'I can't believe—'

Paula cut her dead. 'I said that's *enough*. We're all on edge and no wonder.' She gazed around the room. 'There's a cold-blooded killer on the loose, someone with access to Channel 6 who knows their way round, who's capable of creeping about and carrying out a frenzied attack undetected.' She paused. 'We're dealing with a cool customer here. It's quite possible that having stabbed James Almond to death, the killer calmly rejoined the party. We may even have rubbed shoulders with them, engaged in some light party chit-chat.'

Karen felt the hairs stand up on her arms. Paula was scaring her.

'I suggest we all remain vigilant. Just in case.'

Karen shivered. 'The police didn't say anything about the killer striking again.'

'What would they know?' Julia said. 'There could be bodies all over the place before they work out who's responsible.'

'Can we give it a rest?' Cheryl said. 'So someone killed James. So what? Let's face it, he must have had more enemies than the rest of us have had hot dinners.' Karen was chewing her bottom lip. 'If you ask me, there is *nothing* to get worked up about, so let's all chill out, eh?'

Paula gave her a hard look. 'Let's hope you're right.'

She glanced at Karen, whose face was deathly white.

'I still think it wouldn't hurt for all of us to be on our guard. Just in case.'

Fifty-Three

Karen hurried along the dressing-room corridor in a mild state of panic. What on earth was Paula playing at, putting the fear of God into them like that? Perhaps she saw James's murder as a chance to get tough and lay down the law, make it clear who was calling the shots while everyone was still spooked and jumpy. Well, there was no need.

As Karen put her key in the lock, the door opened an inch. Damn, she'd left it open and her laptop was in there. There it was, on the low table next to the armchair, just as she'd left it. She shut the door and locked it, closing her eyes for a moment, feeling the stirrings of a headache.

Bella had been right about Paula. There was something decidedly odd about her behaviour. The look on her face when she was talking about James being killed – for a split second Karen had thought she was about to burst out laughing. Then again, she reasoned, James had been a complete shit, making no secret of the pleasure he took from booting Paula out of his office when he made his unexpected comeback. She had probably gone to hell and back in recent months and kept most of it to herself. Perhaps she had no one to confide in. Well, no wonder she was gloating now that James had more than got his comeuppance.

Karen rubbed at the bridge of her nose. Tension throbbed

behind her eyes. Better take a couple of painkillers, just in case. She sank into the armchair and fished about inside her bag.

Something caught her attention and made her sit up, alert. The air conditioning was unusually loud, hissing away. No, hang on, it wasn't the air con, it was . . . she got up and tip-toed towards the door in the far corner that led to the shower room. The hissing sound, whatever it was, was coming from inside. She put a hand on the door knob and for a few seconds stood frozen, craning to hear, aware of her heart thumping, a sharp pain stabbing her temples. Was someone in there? It was her own stupid fault, leaving the place wide open. Anyone could have wandered in while she was in the meeting.

For goodness' sake, she told herself – get a grip. Who'd be strolling along the dressing-room corridor trying doors to see if they were unlocked? An uncomfortable thought dawned. The door wasn't unlocked now, though, was it? She had locked herself in. Her throat felt dry and gritty. She clung on to the handle, taking deep breaths, waiting for her heart rate to return to normal. This was stupid. If someone *had* been in, an oppor-tunistic thief or whatever, they'd have nicked the laptop and legged it, not shut themselves away in the en suite. Karen swal-lowed. Unless they were waiting for her to come back. Her heart was doing its best to escape from her chest. She could go and find someone, get them to come with her and see what was what. What if they thought she'd lost it, though?

Come on, Karen, she thought, stop being such a wimp. You're letting your mind play tricks on you. *Just get in there.* She was dying for a pee anyway. How pathetic would it look if she didn't even dare use the loo in her dressing room? If anyone found out she'd never live it down. *Heat* would prob-ably run a double-page spread about what a baby she was. As for Julia – it didn't bear thinking about. Karen tried to imagine what Julia would do if she came into *her* dressing room and heard a strange sound coming from the shower. She'd march right in, that's what, and if there was an intruder in there, heaven help them. Karen crossed her legs. Perhaps she should fetch Julia . . . No!

She gripped the handle, turned it and flung the door open. The room was filled with steam and the hissing sound was coming from the shower. Karen's hand covered her mouth. Her soap, her lovely Jo Malone, was blocking the plughole and the tray was about to overflow. Karen stifled a scream as she stared at the water spewing from the shower head. It was bright red. Blood red.

Fifty-Four

Julia could barely contain herself. 'I'm sorry,' she said, laughing, 'but you've got to see the funny side.'

Karen stared at her. 'Funny! I almost had a heart attack.'

'There you were, thinking you'd walked into a scene from *Psycho*, and all the time it was red dye. I mean, you've got to laugh.'

'Someone broke into my dressing room and went out of their way to put the wind up me! It's no laughing matter.'

Karen was mortified that Channel 6 security had put the building on immediate high alert and refused to let anyone in or out while they waited for the police to arrive. A government minister had missed his slot on the lunchtime news thanks to her. It hadn't taken long for DI Ellis to work out it was dye, not blood, in the shower, but by then the reception lobby was full of people complaining about being held hostage. Once word got round that it was some kind of silly prank involving her, she would be a laughing stock.

That cow Tabitha Tate had even turned up with a news crew in tow and done a piece to camera at the end of the dressing-room corridor. She was becoming an almighty pain in the backside. DI Ellis had been polite enough, but Karen could tell he was irked to be called away from proper police business to deal with what now seemed like an extreme overreaction on her part.

Now she was sitting in the canteen with the others, all huddled over cappuccinos at a table tucked behind a pillar. On the wall above them was a shot of Boyzone. Someone had drawn a moustache on Ronan Keating.

'Look at the state of her,' said Lesley, nodding at Karen with a serious expression. 'She's shaking, and you think it's funny.'

'Oh, lighten up,' Julia said. 'It was probably one of the props boys messing about.'

Cheryl glowered. 'I don't suppose you'd find it quite so hilarious if it was your dressing room that had been violated.'

'I always lock mine.' Julia looked at Karen. 'That's a tip for you, darling – make sure you don't leave it open and then no one will be able to play practical jokes on you.'

'Whoever did it must have a pretty twisted sense of humour,' Faye said. 'And anyway, who'd be in the dressing-room corridor? It's not as if people wander up and down it.'

'Good point,' said Lesley.

Karen sipped at her cappuccino. Her heart was still going like the clappers.

'Come to think of it, you were the last to arrive at the meeting today,' Cheryl said, turning on Julia. 'It's just the kind of sick thing you'd do.'

'Are you accusing me?'

'Go on then, deny it.'

Lesley kept her eyes on Julia. 'It makes sense. She makes us all think she's stuck in a wheelchair when for all we know she's been on her feet ever since she came out of hospital—'

'I have not!'

'Then she turns up late for the first meeting, having given

299

herself time to break into Karen's dressing room and fiddle with the shower.'

'Do I look like I'm dressed for a spot of plumbing?'

'She comes flouncing in – in a pair of thousand-quid shoes by the look of them – and all we can think about is the fact that she's walking again, as opposed to what she's been up to while our backs were turned.' She clapped her hands. 'Classic distraction technique.'

Julia sneered. 'Who are you – the frigging Mentalist?'

'She makes sure to pick on the most vulnerable person—'

Panic clouded Karen's face. 'Faye's the most vulnerable person, not me!'

'And totally freaks her out.' Lesley sat back, pleased with herself.

'OK, Patrick bloody Jane,' Julia said. 'So what's my motive?' Lesley frowned.

'Come on, then – if you're so clever, tell us exactly why would I clamber about messing with the plumbing in my thousand-quid Louboutins?'

'Well, it's obvious,' Lesley said. 'Because . . .' She frowned again. She couldn't actually think of a good reason. It was true that Julia thought so much of her precious shoes it was unlikely – out of the question, in fact – she'd have risked getting them wet or, heaven forbid, flecked with dye.

'I still think you're the prime suspect,' Cheryl said.

'Don't tell me Jane Tennison's here as well,' Julia said, amused. She looked at Karen and Faye. 'Who are you two – Rosemary and Thyme? Cagney and Lacey? The Lone Ranger and Trigger?'

'Just wait until you're the one that's targeted,' Cheryl said.

Julia narrowed her eyes. 'Oh yes – would that be a threat?'

'I'm just saying.'

'And *I'm* just saying it was most likely one of the props boys having fun. And before anyone says anything, we all know they're famous for what you might call a black sense of humour.' Julia shuddered. 'Have you *seen* the way they dress? Horrid baggy shorts and flip-flops. In winter. They're a funny bunch, I'm telling you. Pretty harmless, though, on the whole. Let's face it, the building's awash with James Almond's murder so there's bound to be the odd practical joke.'

Karen opened her mouth to protest but Julia pressed on.

'I know you got a fright, but we're in the entertainment industry, for God's sake. You can't expect everyone to wear black and keep straight faces. Now that *would* be weird.'

'If it turns out you had anything to do with this,' Lesley began.

'I didn't, OK?'

'If you did, Julia, you'll be sorry,' Cheryl said.

Julia laughed. 'Oh yeah – says who? You? That's even funnier than someone putting dye in the shower.'

Karen butted in. 'Look, Julia's probably right. Chances are it was someone messing about. Let's just forget it.'

'Still, I'd ask for another dressing room if I were you,' Julia said. 'You won't fancy having a shower in that one now some psycho's been in there.' She raised her hand in a stabbing motion. 'Ee-ee-ee.'

Karen winced. 'I wish you wouldn't.'

'And I wish you'd get your sense of humour back.' She looked gleeful. 'I must say, I had no idea working with you girls again was going to be so much fun.'

Fifty-Five

Faye was walking through reception at Channel 6 when a voice said, 'There you are!'

She spun round to find Mike in dirty jeans and a khaki T-shirt.

'What are you doing here?'

'Can't I take my lovely wife for a drink?'

Faye gave him an odd look. Technically, she was still his wife, but it wasn't as if they were on the friendliest of terms any more, and she was sure they hadn't arranged to meet. Then again, it was just possible she had agreed to see him and forgotten all about it. She was getting lax about writing stuff down these days and her memory was shocking. It was the strain of everything, and the wine, of course. Relaxing over a couple of large glasses at the end of the day – sometimes in the middle of the day if her mum had Daisy – probably wasn't the best move. But Lesley did it all the time and she seemed to manage.

Faye had tripped when she was putting the rubbish out a few days back and ended up flat on her face on the path. She was wearing a pair of scruffy old pyjamas at the time and her hair needed a wash. Just as well there wasn't a stray paparazzo lurking or she'd have been all over the papers. Not that her tumble was anything to do with the bottle of rosé she'd polished off after lunch – although the tabloids would no doubt have

302

seen things differently. She would have to get the path seen to – it was dreadfully uneven.

She glanced at Mike who was waiting, ramrod straight, with a beatific smile on his face. Really, he didn't look all there. He actually looked like the kind of person Faye would usually cross the road to avoid. Still, he was offering to buy her a drink, and now she thought about it, she could murder one. Anything to delay going home for a little longer.

'OK, that would be nice,' she said. 'Just the one, mind.'

In the bar overlooking the Thames, Mike ordered a Peroni for himself and a bottle of South African Chenin Blanc for Faye. A whole bottle to herself! All of a sudden she was feeling a lot perkier and a whole lot more kindly disposed towards him.

'Isn't it great?' Mike said, beaming, while they waited for their drinks to arrive.

Faye gave him a bemused smile. 'Well, yes.' She hesitated. 'What is?'

'It's all different now – Channel 6, I mean,' Mike said. 'Lighter, you know – the energy – in a quantum sense. You can feel it as soon as you walk into the building.'

Faye had no idea what he was talking about.

'All that creativity set free.' His voice rose. 'Hallelujah!' The barman stopped polishing a glass and gave them a long look. Mike raised a fist in the air. 'Power to the people!' The barman picked up the phone on the end of the counter. 'Remember that?' Mike blinked rapidly. 'Wolfie. *Citizen Smith*. Freedom for Tooting!'

Faye glanced around. People were looking. 'Keep your voice down, will you?' she hissed.

Mike gave her a dazzling smile. 'When you've been out in

the field all day in Ganners, what you wouldn't do for a cold beer.'

He seemed to have lapsed back into a semi-normal state. Faye gave him a wary look. 'Yes, I'm sure.'

'We should raise our glasses to our dearly departed enemy, James Almond, prince of evil. Sent to the gates of hell courtesy of a stake through the heart.' Mike chuckled. 'I mean, isn't that just perfect? It almost has a cinematic ring to it, don't you think? Like something out of a horror film.'

Faye wished he would shut up.

'Channel 6 must be a much happier place. Relaxed. No one putting the fear of God into the staff any more.'

'Not exactly. Someone tampered with the shower in Karen's dressing room, put a pellet of red dye in it – totally freaked her out. She thought someone had been murdered in there.'

Mike looked amused. 'Dear-oh-dear.'

'Julia reckoned it was a prank, but it really shook her up, poor thing.'

His face became serious. 'You've got your show back, though?'

'Yep, *Girl Talk*'s back in the schedule.'

The waiter appeared and put their drinks in front of them. Faye picked up her wine. That first sip was always the best.

'All's well that end's well,' Mike said. 'That's what they say, isn't it? I'm not so sure about that, though. The thing is, it's not always obvious when you've reached the end. Is it? It seems there's always more work to be done.'

Faye wasn't sure she knew what he was going on about. Didn't really want to know. Her mind turned to the wine – delicious, icy cold, with a hint of apple.

'I mean, look at Afghanistan. No one can tell me it was

worth losing Billy boy, never mind what happens in the end there.'

Faye glanced at him. She knew how devastated Mike had been when the cameraman he'd worked with for most of his career in news had died during a gun battle with the Taliban on the last trip to Helmand, just days before they were due home.

'You are still seeing the therapist, aren't you?' she said.

He nodded. 'It's all talk. Blah-fucking-blah. Gets you no-where. Round in circles, that's where we go, on and on and on.' He slumped forward and put a hand over his eyes.

'Mike?'

He jerked upright again, the too-bright smile back in place. 'That's enough of that. We're celebrating!'

'Are we?'

'Power to the people!' His fist was in the air again.

A well-built bloke in a black suit, black shirt and black tie, was now standing at the end of the bar, summoned, no doubt, by the barman. Security. He took a step towards them. Faye yanked at Mike's arm.

'Right, OK, – shush, will you? Have another beer or some-thing, but shut *up* or they'll chuck us out.'

Fifty-Six

Dan was away on a modelling assignment, some new after-shave, which, for reasons Lesley didn't understand, involved a shoot in Spain. He had been on a diet of wheatgrass and rabbit food for days. The campaign shot would probably end up as a close-up of Dan, looking stubbly and impossibly sexy, against the kind of generic background that could have been created in any studio in London, but never mind.

Lesley wasn't used to being alone in the house she and Dan had bought together a few months earlier, and felt a little bereft as she let herself in and eased off her shoes.

There was a card on the mat, a note to say a courier had called and left a parcel tucked behind the hedge at the side of the door. Lesley opened up and scanned the street. All clear. It wouldn't be done to be snapped in her bare feet. She stooped and retrieved the parcel from its hiding place and went back inside. It would be Dan, sending a little something to cheer her up while he was away.

She wandered into the kitchen, put the box on the table and opened the fridge, taking out a bottle of white wine she'd opened the night before and hadn't felt like finishing. She smiled. It wasn't the same drinking on her own any more – it just made her pine for her gorgeous husband. Still, the saucy texts were arriving in her inbox thick and fast, and the night before he'd called last thing and they'd had a pretty wild long-distance sex session. A tingle went through her at the memory.

She poured a drink, had a sip and got to work opening the parcel. The stiff brown paper hid the most gorgeous black embossed gift wrap. Held in place by a black bow was a card in a little stiff envelope. Lesley opened it. The card said: *What do you get the woman who has everything?* She didn't recognize the writing, but Dan had probably ordered online and someone in the shop would have written it. She stuck it on the fridge, fixing it in place with a Britney Spears magnet, and had another drink. As she undid the wrapping paper, she took care not to tear it. It must have cost a fortune. Underneath, the box was cream and solid and there was a small gold heart on the lid. A pink note shaped like a pair of lips was stuck on one corner. It said: *Can you guess?*

Lesley grinned. 'No I flipping can't! Honestly, Dan, I hope all this cloak and dagger stuff's worth all the effort.'

She lifted the lid off the box and found another one in red and made from some kind of vinyl. Another note in the shape of a neon-pink pout said: *Keep going!* 'You are in such big trouble,' she said, giggling, holding the red box to her chest and unclipping the lid. As she lifted it up the smell hit her. She recoiled and dropped the lid. The contents of the box slopped down her front, soaking her. Something fat and slippery landed in her hands. She gazed at it. *What the—?*

She let go and jumped back as the thing landed on the floor and rolled under the table, leaving a smeary trail in its wake. The box was on the table on its side, blood spilling onto the surface. Lesley stood transfixed, holding her hands away from her body. They were covered in blood. She glanced at the front of her dress, now blood-stained. A minute or two went past.

She was unable to move. Finally, she forced herself to look at the thing on the floor. Even *she* knew it was a heart. A sob caught at her throat. She ran to the sink, threw up over the breakfast dishes and turned the cold tap on full so that water bounced off the crockery, giving her another soaking as she stood with her hands under the tap, tears running down her face, trembling from head to foot.

Fifty-Seven

DI Ellis was pretty sure the heart had come from an animal –
a pig, probably.

'Who would kill a pig just to scare the shit out of me?'
Lesley said.

'You can buy them easily – hearts, not pigs,' the detective
said. 'Most butchers would sell you a pig's heart.'

'Isn't it against the law or something?'

'No, afraid not.'

'What kind of sicko would buy a pig's heart anyway?'

'Well, some people do eat them, I think. Or they feed them
to their dogs.'

Lesley's eyes widened. 'You're joking?'

He shook his head. 'They're very nutritious. Dogs go mad
for them. A mate of mine had a Boxer, Tyson. He loved a pig's
heart.'

Lesley stared at him. She wished Dan was there instead of
hundreds of miles away in some snazzy Barcelona hotel.

'Can't you fingerprint the box or something?'

'We'll do our best. It was probably handled by a lot of
people, though, before it got to you, and you can bet that whoever's behind it probably wore gloves. I'd be amazed if it gets
us anywhere.'

'What about the gift wrap? It's expensive stuff. Can't you track it down?'

'As I said, we'll do our best.'

She stood, arms folded, in a corner of the kitchen in a pair of old Juicy Couture sweats and one of Dan's sloppy jumpers. Her ruined dress had been taken away by a uniformed PC. DI Ellis had rolled up his sleeves, put on a pair of Marigolds and cleaned up the kitchen once the evidence had been bagged and taken away.

Lesley dreaded him going.

'You can't think of anyone who'd do this to you?' he said. 'Usually it's an ex, someone who's been dumped and didn't take it well.'

'No. I've been married for ages. I didn't really have a boyfriend before I met my husband.' It was true. She'd had loads of men but none she'd have called a boyfriend. If James Almond hadn't already been dead, she'd have put him in the frame. A thought occurred to her. Perhaps he arranged it all before he was killed, just another nasty little episode in his campaign to turn her into a nervous wreck.

'Can you find out who sent the package? You know, trace the credit card or whatever you do.'

'That was the first thing we did,' he said, a note of impatience creeping into his voice. He flipped open his notebook. 'It was paid for by cash at a depot in Vauxhall.'

'Don't they have CCTV or something?'

He gave her a thin smile. 'We'll see what we can do.' He snapped shut the notebook. 'Look, I'm not making light of this, but at the end of the day it's a pig's heart so – being totally honest – I don't think my governor's going to want me spending a huge amount of time and resources on it.'

Lesley blinked. They didn't care.

'The other thing is, you're in the public eye. You might have put someone's back up without even knowing it – refused to sign an autograph or pose for a picture or something. Maybe it's a disgruntled fan. Then there's the press. I wouldn't put it past one of them to pull a trick like this just so they can write about it.' He frowned. 'I'm sure I read somewhere about a celebrity who used to send human excrement – her own, if I recall correctly – to people who got on her wrong side, gift-wrapped in some kind of fancy box too.' He gave her a wry smile. 'You do mix in odd circles when you think about it.'

Lesley shook her head. 'What if it's really serious? What if I've got a stalker? I mean, my boss was killed and the maniac responsible is still out there. What if I'm next on the list? You know, like in *Dressed to Kill*.'

'Ah, well, in *Dressed to Kill* the second victim actually witnessed the first murder,' he said. 'So as long as you didn't see whoever it was killing your boss, I think you're safe.'

'You *think*! What if you're wrong? What if he's out there now?' She shot a furtive look at the kitchen window.

He went over and pulled the blind shut. 'Maybe you can get someone to come round, keep you company. Or is there a friend you can go to?'

'Can't you stay?' Lesley's voice was a whimper.

'Really, there's no need.' For God's sake, he was in the middle of a murder investigation. He retrieved his jacket from the back of a chair. 'Now, how about if I drop you off somewhere?'

She didn't want some freak driving her out of her own home. No, fuck him. Even if he was out there, lurking in the undergrowth waiting for the police to leave, she didn't care. She was staying put. Then again, you had to be pretty disturbed to post a pig's heart. Assuming it *was* a pig's heart. That had yet to be determined. What if it turned out to be a *human* heart and old DI Ellis waltzed off, leaving her here without police protection? She was starting to feel sorry for herself. If anything happened it would be his fault. She glared at him, thinking he wasn't even all that good-looking – not a patch on Matt Smith. No more than a passing resemblance, in fact. When Dan got back from his trip she would tell him the police had abandoned her. She shuddered. Assuming she was still alive to tell the tale when he got home.

'Sure you don't want a lift anywhere?'

Lesley hesitated. Did she really want to stay in alone after being the victim of . . . she searched for the right words. What would be the correct term for what had just happened to her? If she told everyone she'd had a box of offal through the post it would sound like the act of a nutter rather than a fully-fledged psychotic killer. Some people – she was thinking of Julia here – would even find it funny. She smarted at the thought. Then it came to her in a blinding flash. Basically, she had just suffered a *heart attack*. Inside her ribcage her own heart went *douf-douf* in sympathy. Under normal circumstances a heart attack would bring paramedics and flashing lights and doctors – real ones too, not someone impersonating a TV Time Lord.

OK, she was getting a teeny bit carried away. She hadn't *actually* had a heart attack, not in the usual sense of the term, but she *had* been attacked with a heart and now she was in a bad way: panicky, nauseous, thumping head, clammy hands. Her blood pressure was probably through the roof. How could the police clear off and leave her in such a state? She glanced around the kitchen, now spotless thanks to the clean-up efforts of the detective she had until a few moments ago thought cute. The back door was locked and bolted and she could put the chain on the front. Even so. The chances of relaxing now were slim, to put it mildly. She was way too jumpy. It was no good.

'Give me a minute and I'll grab some stuff,' she said.

Fifty-Eight

'It's obvious,' Paula Grayson said. 'We have a practical joker in our midst.' She gazed around the conference room.

'I hope you're not saying it was one of us,' Julia said, giving Paula a filthy look.

'I was speaking more generally, inferring that it might well be someone working at Channel 6. Someone who would know all about the feud, for want of a better word, between you girls and James Almond.' She glanced at the screen of her laptop, tapped a couple of keys and looked up again. 'There may be people not a million miles from here who find the idea of picking you off one at a time – so to speak – most amusing.'

'I already told you,' Julia said. 'It's the props boys.'

Lesley, her pale face swamped by a gigantic pair of shades, gave a toss of her head, sending blonde curls cascading over one shoulder. 'Well, I'm not laughing.'

'Me neither,' Karen said. She had taken Lesley in the night before, not that she was able to offer much reassurance. They'd both been too scared to go to bed and had sat up, doors and windows locked, every light in the house blazing, until Dave got home from work just after midnight.

'Bella, dear,' Paula said. 'See if you can make some discreet enquiries, find out if there's a prankster at Channel 6.'

'What kind of a person sends a pig's heart?' Faye said.

'Perhaps we should make stalking the subject of tonight's show,' Julia put in.

'Actually, that's not a bad idea,' Paula said. 'Launch the new and improved *Girl Talk* with the kind of show everyone's going to be talking about. Stalking is a serious problem. Lots of women will relate to it. You can talk about your own experiences and in the process maybe put the brakes on the joker giving you the willies.'

Lesley looked panic-stricken. She clutched at the throat of her mesh sweater. 'What if it makes things worse? You know, gives more ammunition to the maniac who's frightening the life out of us?'

Julia took an elegant silver compact inlaid with tortoiseshell from her bag and checked her reflection. 'The point is we're supposed to be a gang of strong women, not meek little mice.' She gave Faye a pointed look. 'It's our duty to take on tricky subjects and stir things up. Who knows, maybe we'll even flush out the creep who's doing all this stuff.'

Lesley flinched. 'I don't *want* to flush him out. I want the police to find him and lock him up.'

Julia smirked. 'What for – sending a box of innards?'

'It's all right for you,' Lesley said. 'You've not been on the receiving end of any of this crap.'

'No,' Cheryl said. 'Funny, that.'

Julia swivelled round in her chair. 'What – you think *I've* got something to do with this? I'm barely out of a coma!'

'Yeah, well, good to see all that time on life support had no effect on your bitch gene,' Cheryl said.

'Now, now,' Paula said. 'It may be that our prankster is targeting those of us he – or indeed *she*' – she glanced at Julia – 'deems to have a sense of humour.'

315

Julia snapped her compact shut, her face thunderous. '*I've* got a sense of humour!'

'Of course you have, dear, but let's face it – you're not exactly famous for your sunny disposition.' Paula aimed a disarming smile at Julia and at the same time shrugged off her jacket, a navy blazer with gold buttons. She pushed up the cuffs of a striped Breton sweater. 'You should think yourself lucky.'

Julia glanced under the table at Paula's white calf-length skirt and navy flatties with their rope trim. She looked ready to skipper a yacht. If the so-called prankster was after victims with a sense of humour, he need look no further. Anyone who showed up at the office dressed for a trip on the high seas definitely saw the funny side of life.

'I think we should try and get Elen Rives to come on,' Faye said.

'Why – do you fancy her?' Cheryl said.

Faye flushed. 'She's a strong woman and, well, you know, she's getting on with life after . . .' She gave a helpless shrug. 'She'd just be a good guest.'

'Actually, you're right,' Cheryl said. 'She'd be a great guest.' Faye's face lit up. 'That's why she's already been on *Loose Women*. Keep up, will you?'

Faye shrank low in her seat.

'So,' Julia said, gazing at the others and then directing a penetrating stare at Faye, who pretended to look for something in her bag. 'Who's next on our friendly neighbourhood nutter's list?'

Faye shivered and clutched at her denim jacket. 'Why are you looking at me?'

Julia shrugged. 'Did you notice how he sent the package to Lesley when Dan wasn't there? And he made sure not to pick on Karen at home, presumably because he knew he might run into Dave.'

Faye was looking alarmed. 'What are you saying?'

'Well, *you're* on your own, and not just for the odd night here and there. You're *permanently* on your own.'

'So are you! So is Cheryl!'

'We're big girls, though, whereas you're – what's the word? – well, a bit of a wimp.'

Faye's face crumpled.

'See? The slightest bit of verbal sparring and you go straight to pieces. Heaven knows how you'll cope with a weirdo on the doorstep.'

Tears streamed down Faye's face.

Paula intervened. 'That's enough, Julia. You girls are back on air tonight for the first time in months, and I'm looking for smiles and harmony – not an atmosphere the viewers can cut with a knife.'

Lesley put an arm round Faye. 'For goodness' sake, it's not five minutes since she had a baby. Her hormones must be all over the place. Show a bit of sensitivity, will you?'

'Yes, well, it's not five minutes since my life was hanging by a thread—'

'Oh, change the record,' Cheryl said. 'You should have a show of your own – *Me and My Coma*. Then you could bore the rest of the world to death as well.'

'Oh, it's all coming out now,' Julia said, livid.

Karen waded in. 'Look, we're all on edge right now.'

Julia gave her a look of contempt. 'Speak for yourself. I'm perfectly calm, thank you.'

Paula ran a hand through her hair, which was in dire need of a professional blow-dry, and wrestled with a wiry curl that sprang repeatedly from its hiding place behind her ear. She closed the lid of her laptop. The old magic between the five women was still there, no doubt about it. Now all she needed to do was keep the adrenalin flowing until they went on air later, and, all being well, *Girl Talk* would be a smash hit all over again.

Fifty-Nine

Tabitha Tate ordered a large skinny cappuccino, a soya latte with a hazelnut shot and a cheese twist for Lesley.

In a corner of the canteen, Lesley, ghostly pale, was playing with her hair, coiling strands into corkscrews round her index finger. She felt worn out even though she had actually managed to sleep well. Hopefully a shot of caffeine would wake her up. Meanwhile, Faye was having a lie-down in her dressing room. Well, in Lesley's dressing room. She was too nervous to use her own after Julia's little performance. Karen was also in Lesley's dressing room, on the grounds that there was safety in numbers. Cheryl, who refused to be intimidated, had gone to the gym.

Lesley had been on her way out for a coffee when she ran into Tabitha Tate, loaded down with tapes and, it turned out, keen for a chat. She was following the James Almond story, she said, talking to the detectives on the case and desperate for a breakthrough.

Tabitha hadn't slept too well since the night of the party when she had found the Controller of Entertainment in his blood-stained suit at his desk. The shocking image had stayed with her, but she was a news reporter and knew it was vital to take grisly and unexpected events in her stride. If her career went to plan, she would encounter far worse things in life than a murdered TV executive. Right now, the main thing was to focus on the story and get the scoop when the police tracked down James's killer. That was what mattered. DI Ellis had tipped her off as soon as he got the call about 'blood' in Karen King's dressing-room shower. Then Tabitha got a tip-off about a box containing pig's intestines or sheep's entrails – she hadn't been able to get hold of Ellis to confirm that one – showing up at Lesley Gold's house. All very intriguing. As soon as she saw Lesley in the corridor she had braced herself and asked for a word.

'I heard about what happened in Karen King's dressing room. That it turned out to be just dye in the shower,' Tabitha said, sitting down and sliding the cappuccino and the cheese twist towards Lesley. Secretly, Tabitha, still smarting from that business at the Channel 6 bash, had been less sympathetic towards Karen than she might have been and had laughed along with the murder-squad boys at Karen's request for a forensics team to be dispatched.

'Did Dave tell you? I gather the two of you are *close*, shall we say.'

Tabitha went pink. 'There was a misunderstanding, that's all.'

'Is that what they call it these days?' Lesley broke off some of the cheese twist.

'Look, really—' Tabitha started to say.

Lesley put up a hand to stop her. 'It's OK – I've had a few *misunderstandings* in my time.' She ate some more of the pastry. 'Did you hear about my heart attack?' she said.

Tabitha's eyes widened. Blimey, that really *was* a story. 'No, I had no idea. I mean, are you OK?' She had thought Lesley looked on the peaky side, that she didn't seem to have the usual spring in her step, but she would never have known she'd suffered a heart attack. 'Shouldn't you be in hospital or something?' she said, peering at her.

'I don't mean *that* kind of heart attack,' Lesley said, looking distracted. She ripped open a couple of sachets of brown sugar and stirred the contents into her coffee.

Tabitha looked confused.

'Someone sent me a heart – gift-wrapped,' Lesley said.

Tabitha gasped. 'A human heart?' Ellis had kept that one quiet.

Lesley gave a tiny shrug. 'Probably. For all I know.' As she waited for Tabitha to take in what she'd said, Lesley whipped out a scarlet lip gloss and applied a fresh layer. 'The police said it was a pig's heart – if you can believe them. I mean, how come they're so sure without doing proper tests and whatnot?'

A crease had appeared in Tabitha's brow. She had heard plenty of stories about what drama queens the *Girl Talk* lot could be, and now she was experiencing it first-hand. A pig's heart. Not quite so bad, after all. Not quite as bad as finding a murder victim, in fact. All the same, it was clear someone in the know was behaving in a very odd way, and it might well be the same someone who, according to the police, had plunged the statuette for best comedy performance from the Dome Awards 2009 into the heart of James Almond. In which case she intended to take it very seriously indeed.

'Any idea who might have been behind it?' she said, injecting as much concern into her voice as she could.

Lesley hugged her coffee cup. 'Oh, I know *exactly* who was behind it,' she said.

Tabitha sat up, jolted by the sudden surge of adrenalin she felt whenever she was on the verge of a scoop.

Lesley lowered her voice. 'The same person that killed James Almond.' She gazed at Tabitha. 'I mean, you're a reporter – isn't it obvious?'

Tabitha, thinking about the black humour of the murder-squad lads, fought an urge to laugh. 'Actually, that's just what I was thinking,' she managed to say.

Lesley looked agitated. 'First Karen, now me. I mean, who's next?'

'Any ideas?'

Lesley snorted. 'I know who it won't be – Julia.'

'Why not?'

'No one, not even a crazy psycho-killer, would dare pull a stunt like that on her. Not if he valued his life.' Lesley took a sip of coffee. 'Or she.'

Tabitha gave her a curious look.

'Paula Grayson reckons it could be a she.'

'I suppose it could.'

'She also reckons that whoever's having a go at us is just mucking about, having a laugh.'

'But you don't.'

Lesley shook her head. 'That's what he – or she – wants us to think. Me, I think there's a killer out there, watching, playing games, making us all get twitchy and then . . .' She let her words hang in the air.

'And then?' Tabitha said.

'I don't know.' Lesley gave her a haunted look. 'That's what worries me.'

Sixty

Julia was rattled. What Lesley was calling her heart attack had landed her on the front of half a dozen magazines. It was ridiculous, completely over the top. So she'd got a pig's heart in the post – and it definitely *was* a pig's heart, according to the police. So what? It was hardly the crime of the century. It was a prank, that was all – nothing to get so worked up about. Even DI Ellis had managed to get his face all over the tabloids, coming out with stuff about how the police took such things seriously, blah blah blah. It made Julia sick.

She had got straight on the phone to Tom Steiner to demand that he come up with a way of bumping Lesley off the covers. Why were the police being so touchy-feely anyway, Julia wanted to know? She had never found the boys in blue the least bit helpful.

'You can hardly complain,' Tom had said. 'In fact, you should thank your lucky stars they didn't prosecute you for smashing up the Porsche.'

'What? I ended up in a coma!'

'So you keep saying. The fact is you should never have been behind the wheel in the first place. Not with all that vodka inside you. Honestly, Julia, I don't think you have the foggiest how much lobbying I did behind the scenes to keep you out of court while you were busy having your near-death experience.'

Julia hated it when Tom got all uppity with her. 'All right,' she said, sounding sulky. 'I know you saved my skin and I'm grateful.' She glanced at the copy of *heat* in front of her. A shot of Lesley, head down, shades on, as Dan guided her through the paparazzi, dominated the front cover. Anyone would think she'd *really* had a heart attack.

Julia hung up and shoved the magazines under the bed. She should never have brought the gossip mags to The Nook. The whole point of her cottage was that it was a bolt-hole, a place she could escape to at weekends, leaving behind the stresses and strains of celebrity life. At least the press had gone mad about the return of *Girl Talk*. There had been plenty of coverage, with one of the columnists saying what a joy it was to see Julia back on the box at her witty, bitchy best. She had made it into *heat*'s 'This Week's Best Dressed' feature, sandwiched in-between Sarah Jessica Parker and Kelly Brook. The fabulous turquoise Louboutins had got a special mention. Of course, Julia would have got a lot more coverage had it not been for Lesley.

She got up, pulled on a silk dressing gown and tiptoed downstairs. In the kitchen, she saw eggs and butter and one of Scott's spelt and rye loaves on the counter. He was making breakfast, humming to himself as he prepared a tray to take up to her. The back door was open and the sound of birdsong drifted in. Scott's brown and white terrier, Jack Russell, pottered around at the edge of the lawn, sniffing. Julia stood in the doorway breathing in the scent of Italian coffee as Scott took a gingham napkin from a drawer and tucked it between an oversized cup and saucer and a glass of fresh orange juice. She wasn't used to being looked after. Usually, she hated anyone making a fuss – it was guaranteed to send her off the deep end.

But not now. Scott Walker could make as much fuss as he wanted.

Julia's heart ached with love and joy and longing. She crept up and slid her arms round his waist, pressing her face into his back, smelling sleep and soap and sandalwood.

He turned round and kissed the top of her head. 'I thought I told you to stay in bed,' he said, doing his best to sound stern.

'I missed you,' Julia said, holding on tight.

He grinned. 'That's all right, then.'

She peered over his shoulder. 'What are you making?'

'Kedgeree.'

'Isn't that difficult?'

'It's easy. I'll show you one day. First, though, you might want to tell me what's bothering you.'

Julia went and sat at the kitchen table. 'Nothing,' she said, watching Jack Russell accelerate across the lawn in pursuit of a robin.

Scott took the lid off the pan on the stove and gave what was inside a stir, replaced the lid and turned the heat right down. He sat down next to Julia and put coffee in front of her.

'You don't have to tell me,' he said, giving her a concerned look. 'Maybe it's none of my business. Just say. But don't pretend.' He stroked Julia's wrist. 'I don't think we should pretend with each other – do you?'

Julia drank some coffee. It was as if his blue eyes could see right into her. 'It's work,' she said. 'The gossip mags. It's all about getting on the cover, keeping people interested.'

Scott frowned. His hair was a bit shorter than before. He had cut it himself and, strangely enough, it looked fine. There were a few stray grey hairs here and there. Julia reached up and stroked his cheek. It was rough and stubbly.

'You know I haven't got a clue about all that gossip stuff,' he said, 'but tell me anyway. If it's getting to you, I'll do my best to understand.'

Julia took a deep breath and told him about Lesley nabbing all the covers.

He didn't speak for a while. Then he said, 'OK, I get it. It's that whole competition thing.' He nodded. 'You can't let it get to you. That kind of stuff eats you up inside. Not good.'

Julia wished she had his easy-going nature. 'I know,' she said at last. 'It's just . . . it drives me mad.'

'You feel better now you've told me, though? Better than bottling it up?'

Julia nodded. Funnily enough, she did.

'I don't want you keeping things from me, OK?'

Julia swallowed. It was a bit late for that. She had been keeping something from him all along – the truth about who she really was. He still had no idea. She shuddered and fiddled with her dressing gown. Eventually he would find out. Faye would get drunk and blab to someone. Or Lesley would let it slip accidentally on purpose. Then what? She wouldn't see him for dust, that's what.

'Julia – is there something else?'

She managed a small smile. She should be the one to tell him. 'What's the matter?'

She shook her head. She would. Tell him. When she was ready. 'It's nothing,' she said.

He shrugged and turned back to the stove, stirred and scooped and then came back to the table and put her breakfast in front of her. Steam rose from the kedgeree. He put a basket of toasted bread in the centre of the table and topped up her coffee.

Julia gave him a tortured smile. She wouldn't be able to eat a thing. Once she told him the truth, he would get his things together and go and that would be the last she'd ever see of him. A voice in her head was telling her he didn't need to know everything, that she could keep the past buried, safe in the knowledge that Scott was not the kind of man to go digging around, finding things out. At the same time another voice interrupted to ask how she thought she would sleep at night if she chose to continue keeping such a massive thing from him. What he'd said before, about not pretending and how stuff eats away at you, came back to her. Scott was decent. Too decent to lie to. If she did, it wouldn't be long before her secret destroyed what they had anyway.

'Julia,' he said. 'What on earth's the matter? You look terrible.'

She closed her eyes, close to tears. It had all been too good to be true. She had just been kidding herself. The idea that a man like Scott would fall in love with a woman like her, with her past, that it would last and they'd have their happy-ever-after, was ludicrous. She was bound to be found out. Either something would happen or he would work it out anyway. Her eyes remained shut. A tear rolled down her cheek. The room started to spin.

She heard Scott's chair scrape back on the slate floor and his arms went round her. She felt his breath on her face. When she opened her eyes he was on his knees in front of her, his blue eyes searching hers.

He reached up and touched her cheek. 'What is it? Are you sick?'

She gulped. 'Not the way you think.'

He pulled her close and rocked her in his arms as her tears

fell, making his sleeve wet. He stroked her hair. 'It's OK,' he said, kissing her. 'Whatever it is, it's all OK. We'll sort it.'

Julia shook her head and hung on to him, sobbing and wiping her face on his T-shirt. It's not OK at all, she thought.

Sixty-One

'I always like to be straight with my clients,' Suki Floyd said. 'It's not my style to dismiss potentially lucrative offers without first giving them a good airing.' She tilted her head to one side. 'It pays to take a grown-up, open-minded view when there's a firm offer on the table, regardless of what it might be – especially after what we might call a dry spell.' She adjusted a floppy bow holding her infamous barnet in place. 'Even darling O.J. was willing to consider – how shall I put it? – proposals that were not quite worthy of him.'

Helen England was about to say something, but thought better of it. She glanced at the pile of DVDs on her agent's desk.

Suki's eyes bored into hers. 'What's wrong, dear – cat got your tongue?'

Helen took a deep breath. 'It's just that . . . *Porn?*'

'Adult entertainment,' Suki said, sounding brisk. 'It's a huge market – and growing.'

'But it's . . .' Helen's face was clouded with doubt. 'I mean, it's *porn*. What happened to the survival show? I thought they were supposed to be interested.'

Suki inspected her nail polish. It had been her manicurist's idea to experiment with black, but she wasn't convinced. 'I do hope you're not going to go all prudish on me,' she said, and waited a moment before adding, 'not with your history.'

'My history? I'm one of the most experienced broadcasters in the UK!'

'Indeed, but you know what they say? You're only as good as your last show.' Suki got up from her desk and perched on the sofa next to Helen. 'And your last show – indulging the fetishes of a man who, quite frankly, should have known better – was positively X-rated.'

Helen looked away.

Suki patted her hand. 'You can see why the more explicit channels are after you. They're practically fighting to sign you up.'

Part of Helen, the sensible part, felt like telling Suki where to stick the porno offers. It wasn't as if she needed the money, now that she'd inherited James's share of Stealth TV, the production company they'd set up illicitly together. She was raking it in, but it was best not to mention that to Suki – the less she knew about her personal circumstances the better. After all, Stealth had not been entirely above board, since James had formed the company specifically so that Channel 6 could commission programmes from it – a practice that broke all kinds of legal and ethical codes. The way he had managed to cover his tracks with offshore accounts and a couple of talented and wholly innocent producers at the helm was nothing short of genius. No one had the slightest idea that James and Helen were actually Stealth's sleeping partners.

Helen gave Suki an awkward smile. Heaven forbid that she should ever find out – it would be on the front page of *Broadcast* before you could say 'insider trading'. Perhaps she should tell Suki where to go and plump for a quiet life in the country. The only thing was that the very thought made her feel as if she was being buried alive, which was why the reckless part of her was telling her not to be so hasty about the notion of adult entertainment. If it was done right, there was no reason why it couldn't actually be tasteful. And it wasn't as if broadcasters were queuing up to offer her mainstream work.

'There's really no chance of getting me on WBC's survival show?'

Suki's bony shoulders rose and fell in a gesture of defeat. 'Darling, believe me, I tried, but for some reason Felicity went for Anthea Turner in the end. I could see if I can get you on the stand-by list . . .'

Helen smarted. It was obvious that the career she wanted in proper telly was over. She had two options: to fade into obscurity in the back of beyond in Wiltshire with that dead-beat of a husband of hers, or become the hottest thing in adult entertainment. Porn. Well, she wasn't ready to settle for a watered-down and less entertaining version of *The Good Life*. She wanted some fun. She missed the limelight, the whole star routine, and if the only way back in was by taking her clothes off – well, she had a good body. It wasn't just a matter of baring it all, though – she'd have to get it on with blokes she didn't know. She closed her eyes for a moment. Actually, when she'd looked at the sample DVDs Suki had sent her, she'd found it all a bit of a turn-on. She opened her eyes. There were worse things in life.

'OK, I'll do it.'

Suki gave her hand another reassuring pat. 'Good girl.'

Sixty-Two

Cheryl found the weekends long and tedious. She didn't like lazing around in bed, but once she was up she could never imagine how she was going to fill her day until it was time to go to bed again. Sometimes, when she was particularly desperate, she considered phoning Faye. Always, though, she managed to stop herself. The last thing she wanted was Faye finding out that she was as lonely and fed up as she was. Often, when there were two long, empty days stretching in front of her, Cheryl would take off to a spa or rent a cottage somewhere. It made a change, but she still ended up on her own, just in a different place. Almost everyone she encountered at the upmarket spas she favoured was there with a friend or their bloke. Pretty much always she ended up eating at a corner table on her tod, surrounded by couples and groups of friends. A sign of how low she had sunk came one Saturday afternoon when in a semi-psychotic moment she actually considered calling Felicity Prince – just to see if she fancied going out for dinner. *Just* dinner, mind you. She would have made that crystal clear. Not that she did phone in the end. Her pride wouldn't let her, thank goodness.

She put on a pair of huge gold hoop earrings and ran a hand through her glossy hair. She might get a couple of inches lopped off next time, go for a jaw-length bob and keep the front long. She was getting tired of the shoulder-length look. If she'd thought about that sooner, she could have made a hair appointment and idled away part of the day in the salon. Well, it was too late now. They'd be fully booked and she hated it when they squeezed her in as a favour. It seemed to make her stylist manic and harassed, which meant he didn't do a great job. No, she would stick to her original plan and have a mooch around Harvey Nics, buy some beauty products – totally pointless since her skin looked as dewy and line-free whether she used cold cream or something that cost a hundred quid – and treat herself to a glass of bubbly in the Fifth Floor Bar.

She put a studded denim cropped jacket on over her favourite purple maxi-dress, slipped into a pair of Stella McCartney nude wedges and slung her Bottega Veneta bag over her shoulder. An extra slick of damson lip gloss completed the look.

Just then the doorbell went. Cheryl's heart gave a hopeful leap. Perhaps it was Faye, also at a loose end, wanting to call a truce. They could hit the shops together and to hell with the paparazzi! She dropped her bag on the bed and hurried downstairs, hitching up the front of her dress, and undid the catch on the front door.

'Oh, it's you,' she said, making no attempt to conceal her disappointment. 'I hope you don't mind if I don't ask you in, but I have to be somewhere.' She frowned at her watch. '*Now*, as it happens, so if you'll excuse me . . .'

'I don't need long. A minute, two, max . . . Please,' said the figure in the doorway.

Cheryl turned on her heel. 'Two minutes and then I really have to go,' she said over her shoulder, keeping her voice as cool and unwelcoming as she could manage.

The door clicked shut and she headed along the hall towards the kitchen. The sudden blow to the back of her head sent her crashing to the floor. A searing pain robbed her of her breath. She lay utterly still looking at something odd: an animal's paw. No, it was the claw-foot of the hall table. She tried to focus as it blurred and distorted.

A face appeared in front of hers. She blinked, battling to keep her eyes open, struggling to work out what had happened. The ceiling must have fallen in – that chandelier in the hall that everyone said was too heavy. Her fingers twitched.

The figure kneeling at her side rolled her on to her back, unzipped a bag, took out a gleaming gold statuette and plunged it into her chest.

Sixty-Three

Faye was clutching a tissue. Her eyes were red and swollen.

'I can't believe she's dead,' Karen said, her voice a whisper. 'The police said there was no sign of forced entry, that she must have known her attacker.'

The girls were huddled over coffees in the canteen at Channel 6. As news had got round about Cheryl, Karen had invited everyone round to her place, but Lesley said she didn't feel safe. She would rather be out and about – somewhere where there was less chance of a killer creeping up and catching her unawares.

Lesley's face was the colour of wax. 'How can they be so sure? I open my door to people I don't know. Whoever it was might have tricked his way in.'

'I can't believe she would just open her door to a killer.' Faye's voice cracked with emotion.

'It's all very fishy,' Julia said. 'Makes you think nobody's safe.' She had been at The Nook over the weekend and returned to her London flat to find a uniformed PC on the doorstep.

'The police spent hours asking me what I did at the weekend,' Karen said. 'Wanting to know every last detail. It was like he was accusing me . . .' Her voice tailed off.

'Same here,' Lesley said. 'As if one of us could do something like that.'

Faye dabbed at her eyes. 'Poor Cheryl. I wonder how long she was lying there.'

Lesley gave her arm a squeeze. 'Don't upset yourself.'

'She might have been there all weekend.'

Lesley glanced at Karen. 'Nobody knew.'

'She might have survived if someone had gone round.' Faye sobbed.

'You can't think like that,' Lesley said.

DI Ellis had visited each of them to break the news about Cheryl. He had said it was likely, although not certain, that whoever killed James had also targeted Cheryl. There was no telling what the killer would do next. Potentially, they were all at risk.

They sat in silence for a minute or two. 'Shall I get us some more coffee?' Karen said. 'These have gone cold.'

Faye blew her nose. 'I'm frightened.'

Lesley gave her hand a squeeze. 'We're all frightened.'

The colour had drained from Faye's face. 'I know, but I'm on my own.'

Julia said, 'I think we should still go ahead with *Girl Talk*, show we're not intimidated. It's not as if Cheryl was a major contributor, after all.'

Lesley glared at her. 'I hadn't realized you'd had a feelings bypass while you were in that coma of yours.'

'I'm being practical, that's all.'

'Out of interest, where exactly were you the night James Almond was killed?'

'At the party, Miss Marple, same as you.'

'Tom Steiner was looking for you at one point. You'd gone missing.'

'I went to the loo. Is there a law against it? I happened to be in a wheelchair as well, in case you've forgotten.'

'Yes, and it wasn't long before you seemed to be perfectly capable of walking, in case *you've* forgotten,' Lesley said.

Julia gave her an icy stare. 'I seem to recall Dan looking for you too. Hunting high and low. Care to explain?'

'I don't have to explain myself to you.'

Julia smirked. 'No, course you don't.'

Karen appeared and put a tray on the table. Lesley helped herself to a cheese twist.

'The woman behind the counter was saying how sorry everyone is about Cheryl,' Karen said. 'Maybe we should think about taking *Girl Talk* off air, just for a bit, as a mark of respect.'

Julia ignored her. She turned to Faye, who was snivelling into a hanky. 'Actually, you were gone rather a long time too, I seem to recall. I remember looking for you and you'd completely disappeared.'

Faye gasped. 'What are you saying?'

'Let's face it – thanks to James Almond, you had no career, no marriage, your little gay love-in with Cheryl was over.' She paused and gave Faye a long look. 'Not to mention your drink problem. No wonder you'd want him dead.'

Karen butted in. 'Now hang on—'

'As for you,' Julia went on, 'all wound up over your boyfriend, stalking off in a murderous rage—'

'What?!'

'Any number of witnesses saw you slap Dave. It's obvious you've got a violent streak.'

'You can talk – it's not so long ago that you were waving a gun in my face!'

Julia gave an unconcerned shrug. 'Oh that. Well, I was hardly in my right mind, was I?'

'If anyone had a motive to murder James, it was you,' Lesley said. 'It's thanks to him you ended up in a wheelchair.'

Julia raised an elegant foot in the air and admired the black suede platform with its row of silver spikes running down the spine of the heel. 'As you pointed out a moment ago, I'm *not* in a wheelchair. And as it happens, my life's pretty good. In fact, I couldn't be happier.'

Karen banged the table the way Paula Grayson did when she wanted to restore order. Everyone looked at her. Her eyes were shiny with tears.

'Cheryl's dead and – ' she let out a sob – 'all we're doing is fighting and blaming each other. In case it's escaped your notice, there's a *real killer* out there, and one of us might just be next up.'

Lesley looked away and dug out her lippy. 'She's right,' she said. 'This won't solve anything. We need to stick together.'

Julia shrugged. 'Suits me.'

'Although, if you ask me, whoever's doing this is definitely an insider,' Lesley went on. 'They know us, where we live, when we're at home, that sort of thing. They know their way round the studios at Channel 6 too.' A thought occurred to her. 'It makes me think—' She broke off. 'No, that's mad.'

The others stared at her. 'What? Who?'

'I'm just being stupid.'

Julia shuffled her chair closer to the table. 'You can't stop now. Come on, spit it out.'

'We-e-e-e-ll,' Lesley said. She lowered her voice. 'What about Paula?'

Karen blinked. '*Paula?*'

'She hated James as much as we did.'

Julia started laughing. 'Quick, call the police, detective what-sisname, tell him there's been a vital breakthrough.' She clutched her sides. '*Paula*. Oh God, sorry.' She grabbed a tissue from Faye and dabbed at her eyes. 'Tell you what, don't let her hear you say that or – ' she raised a hand and made a stabbing motion – 'Ee-ee-ee.'

Karen shivered. 'Actually, she *has* been acting a bit odd.'

'And look at the size of her,' Lesley said. 'She's definitely strong enough to take on James *and* Cheryl.'

'Why would Paula want to hurt Cheryl?' Faye looked bewildered.

Lesley ignored her. She gave Julia a long, hard look. 'Is anyone else thinking what I'm thinking?'

Julia looked irritated. 'Sorry, darling, I left my mind-reading skills at home today. How the fuck are we supposed to know what you're thinking?'

Lesley took a deep breath. 'Well, I mean, *look* at her. Those awful shapeless clothes.'

Karen glanced at Faye.

'You must have noticed,' Lesley said.

'So she'll never grace the cover of *Vogue*,' Julia said, sounding smug. 'Unlike my good self.'

Lesley gave her a triumphant look. 'She may have more in common with you than you think.'

'Meaning?'

'*Meaning*, what if she's a bloke in drag? You know, like you!'

Julia looked ready to vault the table and throttle Lesley. 'I am *not* a bloke in drag!'

'Well, not now,' Lesley went on, unperturbed. 'Not any more, you're not. But it might be, you know, that Paula's going through the change, or whatever you call it.'

Julia gave her a nasty smile. 'Oh, the *change*. You mean, *menopausal* – like *you*, in fact.'

Lesley flushed. 'I mean she may be a tranny in transition. You know, still waiting for some of the ops.' She wafted a hand in Julia's direction. 'I don't know – it's more your area of expertise than mine.'

'Oh, fuck *off*,' Julia said, her voice rising to a bellow.

At the counter, the Head of Contracts, Roderick Charles, turned and gave them a disapproving look.

'What's he still doing here?' Julia said. 'Can't we get Paula to sack him?'

'Or bump him off,' Faye said, shooting him a spiteful look.

'Have you been on the vodka again?' Julia said.

Karen gave them a pleading look. 'All this arguing isn't getting us anywhere. We need to stick together, watch each others' backs.'

She glanced around.

'Literally,' she said in a whisper.

Sixty-Four

Karen found a table at the back of the coffee shop. She was nervous. Tabitha Tate had cornered her in the canteen the day before and said she needed to speak to her. In private. Away from the studios. All kinds of wild thoughts had raced through Karen's head, and now, twenty-four hours later, she had managed to convince herself that Tabitha was pregnant with Dave's child. Why else would she want to talk? *In private.*

The door opened and Tabitha, in a black vest, combats and dark glasses, hair tucked under a camouflage Mao cap, stepped into the room. Karen's stomach tied itself in knots as Tabitha weaved her way between the tables and sat down. She took off her glasses and hooked them over the front of her vest.

'Thanks for coming,' she said, her voice cool.

A girl wearing a white apron over black jeans came from behind the counter to take their order.

'I'll have a large cappuccino, cinnamon topping,' Tabitha said.

Karen nodded. 'Same for me.'

Once the girl had gone away, Tabitha glanced around and leaned forward. Her expression was serious. 'How are things?' she said. 'Any more weird stuff going on, you know, like the shower prank?'

Karen frowned. Surely she hadn't got her here to talk about

that? Hadn't events moved on since then with Cheryl's murder? 'I don't understand,' she said.

'Anything at all,' Tabitha said. 'Even if it seems insignificant, another prank maybe.'

'No . . . no, I – ' Karen bit her bottom lip and waited for Tabitha to dispense with the chit-chat and tell her why she really wanted to see her.

Tabitha sat back as the girl with the apron placed the cappuccinos on the table.

'There's some strange stuff going on,' she went on when she'd gone. 'Two murders involving high-profile figures at the same TV channel.' She gave Karen a sharp look. 'Thing is, I don't think that's the end of it, not by a long way.'

Karen's brow creased.

'The other night I came out of the building late, and when I got to my car it had been broken into. Someone had left a note on the passenger seat telling me to back off.' She stirred her coffee. 'Actually, not just me. It said something about "those other bitches", which I assume means you and the other *Girl Talk* girls.'

Karen swallowed. 'Why would someone threaten us?'

'Why would someone kill Cheryl West? And why stop there?'

Karen's eyes widened.

'Look, the police have got the note and they're working on it. Not that I expect them to get very far. Whoever's doing this seems to be pretty good at covering their tracks. Nothing on the CCTV tapes. No telltale DNA left at either murder scene. So far, it's a mystery.' She waited a moment. 'It could be me next. Or you. Or one of the others.'

Karen went pale.

'I'm not trying to scare you, but you need to know. Just because it's all gone quiet this last couple of weeks doesn't mean the killer's finished.'

'Oh my God.'

'If anyone's at risk, it's probably me because I keep digging and running stuff on the news every night, but you were the first one to be targeted after James Almond was killed with that shower business, so I wanted to put you in the picture.'

Karen now felt truly afraid. Her hands shook as she lifted the giant cup, slopping coffee into the saucer. Sunshine streamed into the café. Outside, Dean Street was busy. A delivery truck reversed down the road, its alarm bleeping. It was all completely normal. Yet somewhere out there, if Tabitha was right, a killer might have her – both of them – in his sights.

'I thought this was about Dave,' Karen blurted out. Her face flushed.

'That can wait. I wanted you to know you might be in danger.' Her tone softened. 'You need to be on the alert, that's all. Tim Ellis has got a couple of plain-clothes guys at the studios keeping an eye out.' She gave her an unconvincing smile. 'It may turn out to be nothing but, well . . . it may not. Best to be safe.'

Karen spent a moment taking it all in. 'Why are you telling *me*?'

Tabitha sighed. 'I don't want anything to happen to you.' She was silent for a few seconds. 'Look, there's something I need to tell you. I've known for a while, but it's never been the right time to say anything.'

Karen braced herself for the bombshell.

'The thing is . . .' Tabitha hesitated. 'I might as well come out with it . . . You're my mum.' Karen's jaw dropped. 'I know – I'm Amy. Weird or what?'

Faye had tried to ring Mike, but he wasn't picking up. She had left messages but he hadn't called back. It was just as his editor, Nick Green, had said when he rang Faye asking if she'd heard from her husband in the last week or so – Mike seemed to have gone AWOL. When Faye asked him if something had happened, there had been an uncomfortable silence. It emerged that one of the librarians had found Mike in the bulk-eraser room in the bowels of the news centre methodically wiping tapes containing his reports from Afghanistan. The librarian, who had booked the tapes out to him in the first place, had been about to ask what the hell he thought he was doing until he saw the look on Mike's face – weirdly serene, according to the editor – and decided instead to back off and call security.

Nick Green had suggested that Mike take some time off, maybe get away on holiday. Since then the editor had tried to call him several times and was now seriously concerned, as Mike was known for never switching his phone off, taking calls no matter what. He was right about that, Faye thought, remembering a ruined performance of *West Side Story* at Sadler's Wells when Mike took a call in the middle of 'America'.

'I don't mean to alarm you,' Nick Green said. 'I'm just being extra cautious. I'm sure there's nothing wrong.'

Faye suspected something was most definitely wrong. She hadn't seen Mike for days, hadn't even spoken to him. The last time he was meant to take Daisy he had failed to show and Faye, furious, had sounded off on his voicemail before dragging her mother away from her weekly Bridge club to cover. Mike hadn't called back, but then again, Faye's message had been a tad over the top, considering it was the first time he'd let her down over Daisy. She decided to be reasonable when he called to apologize.

That night, though, when she got home from doing *Girl Talk,* sank a couple of glasses of wine and still hadn't heard from him, she had rung and left another message. She couldn't really remember what she'd said, although she had a pretty good idea of the tone: drunken, incoherent and abusive were the words that came to mind. Ever since, she'd been lying low, hoping she could avoid Mike for a few days until things cooled down.

Now, since he still wouldn't answer her calls, she had taken a cab over to his rented place in Battersea and was standing on the front step. The windows were grubby and the front lawn was overdue a cut. She rang the bell. It didn't look like he was in. She tried peeking through the window at the front, but the curtains were drawn. She lifted the letterbox and peered inside, but there was a flap to stop anyone seeing into the hall. She tried the door knocker, then pressed the bell again and kept her finger on it. Just as she was about to give up, she heard bolts being drawn back and the lock turning. The door opened.

'Power to the people!' Mike threw his arms round her and gave her a hug that threatened to crush her ribs.

No sign that he was still angry about her messages, then. That was something.

'I've got time off for bad behaviour, you know,' he said, giving her that vague, dreamy smile he seemed to have culti-vated lately. 'They sent me home for doing something I wasn't supposed to.' He frowned. 'Can't remember what it was now. Nothing serious.'

'You were trying to destroy all your reports. Everything you sent back from – ' she hesitated – 'Ganners.'

Mike grinned. 'Shit and corruption! No wonder Nicky boy blew a gasket.' He pointed at the ground. 'Naughty step!'

Faye looked confused. 'Look, I just came—'

He flopped to the ground. His clothes were in a shocking state – shabby and grubby and, well, when he had hugged her she couldn't help noticing he was a bit smelly.

'Mike Parry,' he said, sounding solemn, 'you have been sentenced to a spell on the naughty step for . . . that thing, whatever it was I did.' He grinned, his blue eyes faraway. 'I do this all the time, you know, talk to myself. First sign of madness.' He threw his head back and roared with laughter.

Faye threw a furtive glance at the street. It would be just her luck if a paparazzo was getting all this. 'Can I come in?'

Mike got up. 'Naughty duties completed. Follow me, ma'am.'

Faye rolled her eyes and followed him into the hall.

He locked and bolted the door behind her. 'Security,' he said. 'Vital. Good habits – discipline and routine – save lives. Never leave anything to chance.' His face was solemn.

She shook her head. He was getting worse, no doubt about it.

The house smelled musty. Faye followed Mike down the hall and into the room he used as his study. There were piles of tapes everywhere, banked up in towers, lying around on the floor, some out of their boxes. On the laptop a show was playing: *Citizen Smith*. Mike pointed at the screen and laughed. Cereal bowls and mouldy mugs littered the desk. At the window there were blackout curtains. Faye gave him a bemused look. He swept a pile of magazines off the armchair in the corner.

'Sit down,' he said. 'What about a drink? I've got tea. I think.' He frowned. 'No, it's coffee I've got.'

Faye perched on the edge of the chair. The room smelled of overripe bananas. 'Coffee would be nice,' she said.

'No milk. I might have a bit of UHT.'

Faye shook her head. 'Black coffee is fine.'

'Something to eat?'

The room was making her gag. 'No, really.'

He was giving her his weird, brainwashed smile. What on earth was wrong with him? He climbed over a pile of tapes, knocking the top couple over, kicked them under the desk and went into the kitchen. Faye decided it had been a bad idea coming here alone. He needed help. Proper, professional help. The odd counselling session clearly wasn't enough. She would have a word with Nick Green and ask if the therapist who'd been helping Mike come to terms with seeing his cameraman shot to pieces could get him into The Priory for a bit, until he was more his old self again.

She got to her feet and started tiptoeing to the door, but managed to send a tower of tapes toppling noisily to the ground in the process. She froze.

Mike appeared in the doorway. 'Just leave them,' he said. 'I've found some evaporated milk. What do you think?'

Faye nodded. 'Great.'

'Sit down – put your feet up.'

He grabbed her, pushed her back into the chair and lugged over a footstool from the corner of the room. He leaned over her, one hand resting on each side of the chair she was in, his face almost touching hers. She could have sworn he hadn't had a shower for days.

'You look all strung up and stressed. Feet up! As your commanding officer I am ordering you to *relax*!' He grabbed her feet and shoved them on to the stool. Faye sank deeper into the chair. Mike straightened up. There was sweat on his brow. 'Now *keep still* until I get back. It's an order!'

She nodded, wondering what her chances were of making it to the front door and undoing all those bolts before he came back in with the coffee. She stared up at the bookshelves on the wall facing her, at the hardbacks held in place by sturdy wooden bookends they'd bought years ago at Camden Market. Next to one of the bookends were a couple of Mike's awards, one of which was a familiar-looking golden statuette. She got up and moved closer, putting her hand on the cluttered desk to steady herself. Her throat tightened and her mind started racing. She blinked several times. Surely she was getting carried away, imagining things – it must be the strain of recent events. Mike had won so many awards over the years – but what was he doing with this one on his shelf? She forced herself to look again, reached up and took the statuette down. It was heavier than she had expected and caked with what looked like dried blood. Good God. She couldn't believe what she was seeing. It didn't make sense.

She heard Mike in the kitchen stirring the coffee, dropping the spoon on to the metal draining board. It was too late to escape now.

She stood there ashen-faced, cold, with her legs trembling, clutching the statuette. Waiting for him to come back in and find her.

Sixty-Five

Tabitha took off her cap and coils of raven-black hair tumbled on to her bare shoulders. Karen gazed into eyes a shade of green that made her think of the ocean somewhere hot and exotic. Several seconds went by and neither of them said anything. Karen hung on to her cup with both hands. She was holding her breath, felt as if she might pass out. The girl in front of her no longer looked like an ambitious TV reporter. She looked young and fragile and – Karen forced a breath out and gulped in more air – very like *she* had twenty-something years ago.

Tabitha unbuckled her satchel, brought out a pile of letters held together with an elastic band and placed them on the table. Karen stared at the bundle. Those were her letters. Not all of them. A few. Tears blurred her vision.

'Just so you know,' Tabitha said. 'It really is me. Amy.'

Karen reached into her bag and found a tissue. There was a pain in her chest, as if something inside was smacking against her breastbone. She placed the hand holding the hanky on her heart and felt its beat. It was even, steady – nothing that gave away the peculiar sensations now taking hold. She felt dreadful – sick and dizzy – as if the booth they were in had started lurching from side to side. Under the table she pressed her feet hard against the floor, desperate to anchor herself. All the while Tabitha, a model of composure, watched and sipped her coffee, silent.

Mike appeared holding two mugs of coffee. 'I thought I told you to keep *still*,' he said, clearing a space on the desk with his elbow and putting the cups down.

Faye stood frozen to the spot, statuette in hand. 'Mike,' she said.

He pointed at the armchair. 'Sit.'

She shuffled over and sat down. 'Mike – where did this come from?'

He moved her mug to the footstool and frowned. 'Let me see.' He took the gleaming object from her and examined it. 'This one was for Iraq, I think. Can't remember.'

She stared at him. 'It's just . . . it's . . . I mean, look at it.'

'Needs a clean, that's all,' he said, tossing the award on to a heap of magazines at the side of the desk.

'Mike,' Faye said. 'Listen to me. Did you go to see Cheryl?'

He slurped his coffee. 'I saw you,' he said. 'That night, at the party.'

Faye stared at him. 'I know. I saw you.'

'No you didn't.'

What was he going on about? 'I spoke to you – remember?'

'I don't think so.'

Faye felt sick.

'I actually prefer evaporated milk to the normal stuff,' he said. 'In coffee, anyway. We had it in Ganners. Brought back memories of jelly with fruit cocktail out of a tin, all smothered in Carnation. Used to have it when I was little. Yum.'

'*Mike.*'

'Mum would make two holes in the lid and put it on the table so we could help ourselves. You'd have to put it in a proper milk jug these days.' His brow creased. 'Not that we'd have it. Us. It would be proper cream, fresh stuff.' Another slurp. 'I'd rather have this any day.'

'Did you . . .' Faye hesitated. 'Did you hurt Cheryl?'

He gave her a sharp look. 'You're happier now, aren't you?'

'I-I don't know. How do you mean?'

'No more James *I-am-the-man* Almond. Cheryl-*lezza*-West off the scene. I mean, between them they did a pretty good job of screwing things up for us, didn't they?'

Faye swallowed. 'Have you been going to your therapy sessions?'

'Work to be done. No time to sit around chit-chatting. Chop-chop. You know how it is.'

Faye looked around the squalid room in despair. 'I can help you straighten the place up if you like.'

He looked pleased with himself. 'No need. Clean-up complete. Enemy eliminated. Roger and out.' He leaned over, retrieved the statuette and polished it on his T-shirt.

'We make a great team, you and me,' he said, kissing it.

'Oh, Mike,' Faye said, her voice cracking. 'What have you done?'

'It's OK,' he said, giving a clenched-fist salute. 'Mission accomplished.'

Karen felt thoroughly confused. This wasn't anything like what she had imagined when she had dreamed about meeting her lost daughter. She had pictured the two of them throwing their arms round each other, hugging and laughing and crying, talking non-stop, catching up on all those lost years. Instead, she and Tabitha – she might as well get used to the idea that that was her name – faced each other in silence.

Karen kept thinking of things she wanted to stay and stopping herself. All her questions were to do with Dave. No wonder she felt sick – her long-lost daughter had slept with her bloke. She couldn't think of anything worse. Karen had thought that when she found Amy – Tabitha – her life would feel complete. Her little girl was the missing piece of the jigsaw, the only thing she needed to feel whole. But the image she had created in her head was nothing like the aloof beauty sitting across the table from her now. While Karen had blubbered and wiped her eyes, it was Tabitha who had signalled to the waitress to bring more drinks. It was Tabitha who had put three lumps of brown sugar into Karen's coffee without even asking if she took sugar, had just assumed that's what you did for someone in a state of shock. It struck Karen that Tabitha's job covering news probably meant she had dealt with many incidents more shocking than discovering her mother was also the partner of her lover.

Karen frowned. Good grief, it was complicated – complicated and sordid. Another thought hit her. It was Tabitha who'd found James Almond's body. Karen knew how bad she had felt when someone had put red dye in her shower, so heaven only knows what Tabitha had gone through when she had found James covered in blood. She should ask how she was, whether Channel 6 had arranged any kind of counselling for her. Stumbling on a dead body was traumatic – enough to give her nightmares at the very least. Tabitha was her daughter and it was her job now to protect her. Forget what had happened with Dave – this was more important. She formulated several questions in her head but still sat there in helpless silence.

Eventually, Tabitha leaned forward. 'One more thing. It's really important,' she said. 'I want you to listen to me – OK?'

Karen nodded, her stomach churning.

'That stuff at the party with Dave. You think we spent the night together, don't you?'

Karen managed a nod.

'You're right, we did.'

A blade went through Karen's heart.

'Kind of. He was driving Lara and I'd gone out on the lash with her, had a few. When I got home I couldn't get my key in the door and Dave helped me. I didn't even know he was *your* Dave then. I persuaded him to stay for a drink – a few drinks. I got the impression he wasn't in a hurry to go home, not that he said anything. He's too loyal to say a bad word about you.'

Karen's heart lurched.

'Anyway, he stayed over, slept in my bed. On his own. I dossed in the other room. I could tell he didn't know what had gone on when I woke him up the next day. I just thought it was funny, decided to tease him. Anyway, I didn't get the chance because he cleared off as soon as I nipped out to get milk. When I saw him at the party, I couldn't resist creeping up on him and pulling his leg a bit. He wasn't exactly happy to see me. If you were watching, you must have worked that out.'

Karen thought back to the look on Dave's face when Tabitha started whispering in his ear. She was right – he hadn't seemed all that happy, not to start with.

'It was only when I explained, told him he had nothing to worry about, that he managed to see the funny side,' Tabitha said.

Karen couldn't speak.

'I've got a bloke actually. He's a director. Away on a shoot in Norway at the moment.' Tabitha held Karen's gaze, those dazzling green eyes boring into her. 'Believe me, I get tons of offers, but I wouldn't cheat on him. No way. Not even when I've been caning it.' She waited a second or two. 'And you know what? I'd be amazed if Dave would cheat on you.'

Another tear escaped from Karen's eye. She dabbed at it with a fresh tissue.

'Now,' Tabitha said, sounding weary. 'Can we start again?'

Karen struggled to compose herself. 'It-it . . . it's just so much to take in.'

'You're telling me.' Tabitha made a face. 'I mean, it's bizarre, isn't it, you being my mum?'

That was one way of putting it. Karen took a deep breath. 'I suppose you want to meet your father.'

'I already have.'

Karen's face registered astonishment.

'I ran into him at an after-show party ages ago. He was a bit the worse for wear, trying to get off with some girl half his age, acting like a complete prat.' Tabitha rolled her eyes.

Karen's cheeks were burning. She could easily imagine Jason, plastered, showing himself up. It was mortifying.

'Anyway, we got chatting and I steered the conversation round to you – obviously he hadn't a clue who I was.' She looked thoughtful for a moment. 'Who I *really* was. I said I'd heard the two of you had patched things up, and he went on about how he'd blown it, came out with all this stuff about a love child – I actually thought he was talking about me, but he was on about another baby, some other bloke's. It all seemed a bit complicated.' Tabitha frowned. 'I twigged he was on about the glamour model he'd been knocking about with. I said what about the kid he'd had with you, and he said he'd messed up there as well because you'd wanted to keep the baby and he wouldn't let you.'

Karen was staring at her.

'I got the impression he was lonely, needed someone to talk to, you know? It was sad, really.' She gazed at Karen. 'And it was obvious he felt bad about the whole adoption thing.'

'I'm so sorry.' Karen's voice was small.

'The funny thing is, I liked him. He's got that little-boy-lost thing going on – do you know what I mean? – that makes you want to take care of him.' She gave a wry smile. 'I know it should be the other way round, but still.'

Karen sighed. 'If things went wrong between us, it doesn't mean he's a bad person. I mean, he can be a total pain in the neck, but . . .' She shrugged. 'You need to get to him when he's sober. His heart's pretty much in the right place. It's just that he never really grew up.'

Tabitha smiled. 'He was wearing a Take That T-shirt! Can you believe it?'

Karen nodded. She could.

'It's OK, I'm cool about it. The best bit is that my dad's called Jason King. Way back, when I googled him, up popped some bloke with monster sideburns and a cravat. I got the fright of my life.'

Karen managed a smile. 'He's a TV nut. He loves the fact that he's got the same name as a cult character. A few years back he actually went to a Seventies party as the fictional Jason King – cravat, sideburns, the lot. I've got the pictures some-where.'

Tabitha's eyes sparkled. 'Oh God, I'd love to see those.'

'I'd love to see what you were like growing up, too.'

'We'll have a session – bring out all the old photos.' She looked thoughtful. 'I was blonde for a bit.'

'No!'

'It looked shocking. I got out the peroxide and did it myself, ended up with orangey-yellow hair that felt like straw. Mum went mad.' She caught Karen's look. 'She's still my mum.'

Karen swallowed.

'It's just that you're in the picture now, so things are a bit different.'

She could say *that* again.

'How come things didn't work out? You know, with you and my dad.'

Karen gave a shrug. 'It's complicated.'

There was a second or two of silence, then Tabitha said, 'Was it really his idea to give me away?'

Karen winced. Whatever Jason's faults were, now was not the time to heap blame on him.

'We were so young. I was still at school, hadn't even done my exams, when I found out I was expecting you.'

'Oh well, wouldn't want to think you might have mucked up your education for me, would we?' A note of sarcasm had crept into Tabitha's voice.

Karen flushed. 'I would have kept you if I could have. Honest to God, if there was the slightest chance I could have given you a decent life. The thing is . . .' She gazed at Tabitha. 'We were just kids, and there's no way things would have turned out so well – for you – if we'd kept you. It would have been an almighty struggle.' She hesitated. 'From what I can see, the couple who got you did a really great job.'

'They did.'

Karen chewed her bottom lip. She felt like she had a headache coming on.

'I want to tell you what happened, all of it. But I need to get my head round all this first. Can we save the rest for another time?'

Tabitha's green eyes held hers. 'You mean, even though your daughter's turned out to be a hard-nosed hack and nothing like you imagined, you want to see her again?'

Karen began to protest. 'No, honestly—'

'It's OK. I can see it's all a bit of a shock. Same here, really. I never thought my real mum would turn out to be . . .' She shook her head. 'Well, someone like you.'

Karen's face fell.

'Hey, don't take it the wrong way,' Tabitha said. 'I know I can come across as a bit tactless, but I don't mean any harm. That's what working in news does for you – no room for tippy-toeing about, if you know what I mean.' She held Karen's gaze.

She had Jason's confidence all right.

Tabitha said, 'I nearly didn't come to Channel 6 because of you, you know.'

'I don't understand.'

'It was a toss-up between this job and a junior researcher on one of the soaps.' She looked away. 'I knew who you were by then. I didn't want you to think I was stalking you.'

Karen waited for her to say more.

'In the end, this was the better job, a chance to be on camera and all that, so I thought, oh, sod it.' She grinned. 'I think it was the right decision, all things considered.'

'I'm glad.'

Tabitha nodded. 'Yeah, me too.'

Sixty-Six

'I just don't feel right,' Lesley said. 'Off-colour, if you know what I mean, and I've got no energy. I'm worn out all the time.' She rubbed her ankle. 'And my feet hurt.'

Jean Jones, the Channel 6 nurse, gave her a stern look. 'My dear girl, I could show you X-rays that would give you a good idea how much damage you're doing to your feet with those shoes.' She clucked in disapproval. 'Clarks do a nice range these days. Modern, very smart, even a bit of a heel if that's what you want. They'd be a lot better for you than those things. You might as well be walking on stilts.'

Lesley peered at her shoes, a new pair of lizard peep-toes that had set her back more than a grand. Julia had practically passed out with envy. Jean Jones had to be insane if she was suggesting she should give up her heels. As it happened, she *liked* walking on stilts.

'You're awfully thin,' the nurse was saying. Before Lesley could reply, Jean had whipped out a thermometer and stuck it in her mouth. 'I don't suppose you eat red meat, do you?'

Lesley shook her head.

Jean extracted the thermometer. 'Hmm.'

'What? What is it?'

'Temperature's normal, I'm pleased to say. You might be a bit anaemic. Let me see your tongue.'

Lesley stuck it out.

'Hmm.'

'What?'

'Red meat once a week wouldn't hurt – get some iron inside you. Offal, liver. Anything like that's ideal.'

Lesley put a hand over her mouth. Didn't the woman know about her heart attack? 'I had a bad experience. I can't eat offal,' she said.

'Can't or won't?' Jean said, sounding brusque. She placed a finger on the inside of Lesley's wrist and tilted up the watch face pinned to her navy-blue nurse's uniform. 'Of course, it could be a hormonal problem. Are your periods regular?'

'Yes, like clockwork,' Lesley said. She wasn't about to admit that her periods were a bit hit and miss these days. She didn't want anyone thinking she was menopausal, even if the chances were she was. 'I'm probably just a bit run-down – working hard, trying to come to terms with what happened to Cheryl. There's a lot going on,' she said, gabbling. 'Tell you what – I'll get an iron tonic.' She hoisted her bag over her shoulder, desperate to get out before Jean started going on about hormone levels and suggesting she visited – horror of horrors – a menopause clinic.

'Where do you think you're going?' Jean said. 'I need to take some blood, see what that tells us.'

'There's no need,' Lesley said, panicking. They could tell from looking at your blood whether you were going through the Change, and she really didn't want to know. Nor did she want anyone else knowing.

Jean was in her element, though, and advanced on Lesley with a syringe before she had a chance to stand up. 'Don't look if you're squeamish,' she said, and plunged the needle into her arm.

'Bloody hell, that hurt.'

'That's it, brave girl,' Jean said. She removed the needle and handed Lesley a wad of cotton wool. 'Just hold that on your arm,' she said, as she labelled up the vial of blood. 'Now, nip into the toilet and do me a sample.'

Lesley stared at her. 'What for?'

'You'd be surprised how much a urine sample can tell you.'

As it happened, Lesley was desperate for a pee. She was always running to the loo these days. A weak bladder was another sign of the dreaded menopause. She took the bottle and hurried to the toilet.

'Mid-stream, now,' Jean called after her.

In the loo, Lesley did as she was told and peed into the bottle mid-stream. In the other room she could hear Jean Jones on the phone to someone, no doubt arranging the relevant blood tests that would confirm she was menopausal and therefore officially past it. Tears sprang to her eyes and she blinked them away. She took a paper towel from the holder on the wall and wrapped it round the sample bottle for modesty's sake before opening the door and handing it over.

'I want you to lie on the bed for a minute or two,' the nurse said, her voice soothing.

Feeling defeated, Lesley lay down.

'Someone's bringing a cup of tea for you. And some nice shortbread biscuits.' She put her hand on Lesley's brow. 'You do look peaky, dear. I don't want you leaving here until I see a bit more colour in those pretty cheeks.'

Lesley smiled. If she'd known, she'd have slapped on a bit more blusher while she was in the loo. Still, it was nice being fussed over. In a way, Jean reminded her of her mum, who had also been bossy, in a comforting way. She felt a lump in her throat. Why was she bursting into tears all the time? She never used to be such a softy. It had to be her hormones.

There was a tap at the door and Lesley glimpsed one of the girls from the canteen handing over a tray.

'Here we are,' Jean said. 'You tuck in and I'll be with you in a minute.'

Lesley bit into some shortbread. It was delicious, rich and buttery, just like the shortbread her mum used to make, except that she always did rounds dotted with golden caster sugar instead of fingers. A memory returned of sitting at the old Formica table in the kitchen, the two of them eating homemade biscuits that were still warm from the oven. Tears pricked her eyes. All these years on and she could still burst into tears just thinking about her.

Jean Jones came and sat in the chair next to the bed. 'You're a naughty girl, aren't you, pretending you're having your periods?'

Lesley nodded, miserable. Tears ran down her cheeks.

Jean passed her a box of tissues.

'I was going to tell you,' Lesley said. 'It's just . . .' She shrugged and blew her nose.

'Now, now. No need to get upset. It's perfectly natural, nothing to worry about.'

Lesley shook her head. She was finished

'Come on, it's not the end of the world.' Jean Jones stroked her hair. 'There's absolutely no reason you can't still work.'

Until word gets round, anyway, Lesley thought, feeling bereft already, and they sack me for being over the hill.

'You can keep going almost up to your due date, providing you're healthy. I'll keep a special eye on you, don't you worry.'

Lesley's jaw dropped. What was she saying? 'I don't understand.'

'You're pregnant, dear, it's official,' Jean said, holding up the test stick. 'Isn't it wonderful?'

Sixty-Seven

Lesley burst breathlessly into the conference room with her cheeks flushed and a radiant smile on her face. Paula, looking for any hint of inebriation, fixed a keen eye on her as she sashayed to the far end of the room and took a seat next to the window.

'Sorry, sorry,' Lesley said, fumbling about in her bag and pulling out a packet of Quavers. 'I got held up.'

'That second bottle of champagne does tend to slow one down,' Julia said, sneering.

'Not a drop has passed my lips,' Lesley said. She nibbled on a Quaver. 'Not that it's any business of yours.'

Julia gave her a look of disgust. 'Do you have to eat those things in here? You're driving me mad with all that rustling.'

Lesley ignored her.

'We were discussing topics for the show,' Paula said.

'I thought we could do something inspired by what happened to poor Cheryl,' Julia said. 'I mean, from the outside she had the perfect life – after a bit of a rough patch, admittedly.' She glanced at Faye. 'But behind closed doors it wasn't like that at all. Her life was *rubbish*. I bet when she went home and shut the front door she was completely miserable. All on her own, no one to share her life with.' Faye looked pale and ready to burst into tears. 'I mean, think about it – lying there, bleeding to death, head smashed in, for *days*, and no one noticed.'

Lesley put a hand on Faye's arm. 'Give it a rest, Julia – that's enough.'

'Not a single friend looking out for her.' She kept her eyes on Faye. 'I bet loads of our viewers can identify with that – long, tedious weekends alone, nothing to do except work your way through the boxed set of *Sex and the City*. Again. Your so-called chums too busy with their own lives to notice what's going on.'

Karen stared at her. 'Julia, do you have to be so insensitive?' She nodded at Faye, whose face was now covered by a curtain of thick blonde hair. 'You're really not helping.'

'Sorry. I just thought the kind of people who watch us would get all that.'

'It's not appropriate,' Lesley cut in.

Paula was looking thoughtful. 'You know, Julia might be on to something.'

Faye let out a noisy sob. Lesley patted her shoulder. 'If you ask me, no one wants all that depressing stuff at the end of the day,' she said. 'They want a bit of a laugh.'

Lesley had been on a high for days, ever since Jean Jones had confirmed her pregnancy. She had gone straight home and told Dan, who had swept her off her feet, carried her to the sofa, made her comfy and smothered her in kisses. A scan had revealed she was nine weeks pregnant. A few more weeks, just to be safe, and she would let everyone know. She thought about Dan bringing her muesli and hot buttered toast in bed that morning and let out a contented sigh.

Julia eyed her with suspicion. 'Are you sure you're all right?'

Lesley laughed. 'We should be doing happy stuff. Did anyone

see the story in the paper the other day about the woman who gave up her daughter for adoption twenty-odd years ago, gave up all hope of ever seeing her again, and it turned out they actually worked together? Can you believe that?'

Karen felt the blood drain from her face.

'It was in Milwaukee or somewhere. They'd been on the factory floor, practically the same production line, stuffing sausages or something, for a year before they realized they were mother and daughter.' Lesley cocked her head to one side. 'I can't remember how they found out. The weird thing is that when you see the pictures, it's obvious because they're so alike.' She placed a surreptitious hand on her tummy and let her thoughts drift to her own baby, which she was sure would be a girl, a pretty little thing, the spitting image of its mum, with blonde ringlets and tawny eyes. Dan, predictably, was equally sure she was having a boy who would look just like him.

'We could do something about losing touch with loved ones and finding them again,' Lesley said, all fired up. 'Happy reunions – you know.'

Karen, wishing someone would change the subject, pretended to rummage in her bag. The peculiar rocking sensation she seemed to experience whenever she was stressed started up.

Julia yawned. 'Sorry, you've lost me,' she said, looking at Lesley. 'I thought the idea was to get people watching, not switching over in their millions.'

Paula said, 'It's a nice thought, Lesley, dear, but it's a bit – what's the word?'

'Boring,' Julia replied.

'*Safe*,' Paula said, giving Julia a stern look.

'We could always look at sexuality,' Lesley said, feeling mischievous, glancing at Julia. 'People with terrible dark secrets they keep hidden for years – like blokes who cross-dress and their wives know nothing about it until they come home early one day and there's Grayson Perry swanning about the place.'

Faye swept a hank of honey-blonde hair out of her eyes. 'You mean like Alex Reid?'

'I don't think that's a secret,' Lesley said. Her eyes went from Paula to Julia and back to Paula. 'I was thinking of people with a secret *so big* no one else knows. They claim to be one thing, but it's all an act – a good one too, since almost nobody knows the truth.' She gave Julia a knowing smile. 'Imagine the strain of living like that.'

Karen had a pretty good idea where Lesley was going with this. 'I'm not sure it would work,' she said, casting a furtive glance at Julia, who looked ready to explode.

'Actually,' Paula said, 'I suspect you might have touched a nerve there.'

'I think you're right.' Lesley beamed at Julia.

'I'm thinking about couples who keep important stuff hidden from each other,' Paula said. 'I mean, it's there in the agony columns all the time. *My husband's gay. My man wears women's clothes—*'

'*My wife used to be a man,*' Lesley said.

Julia, looking like thunder, snatched up her bag. 'Would you excuse me, Paula, darling? I've got a check-up at the hospital this afternoon. Another CT scan. Shouldn't take long.'

'Of course. Do you want someone to go with you?'

'Actually, someone's already taking me,' she said. She gave Lesley a superior look. 'My boyfriend's coming.'

Lesley burst out laughing. 'Your *boy*friend! I've heard it all now. I suppose you're paying that carer of yours to do a bit of escort work now you're back on your feet.'

Julia glared at her for several long seconds, then turned on her heel. Let her think what she liked. She couldn't care less.

Coming clean and telling Scott about her past had been one of the hardest things she had ever done. He hadn't really taken it in at first. When the penny finally dropped, he was silent for a long time. For once, Julia kept quiet too and waited for his reaction. In the end he told her he was struggling to get his head round what she'd just said. Maybe she could go right back to the beginning and fill in all the blanks. Would that be OK? He was so reasonable she could have wept. In true Scott style there were no histrionics, no storming out and getting drunk and smashing things, which was once her favoured way of behaving in a crisis.

Julia had taken a deep breath and explained about how she'd always felt the odd one out, always wanted to wear girl's clothes. She told him about her mother dressing her in girly things in secret and the beatings her father gave her because she wasn't a proper boy in his eyes. She explained about the surgery that had given her the body she had always wanted, and about living a lie for the rest of her life. Scott listened, saying nothing. Finally, when she got to the end of her story – a newspaper threatening to expose her, the car crash that was meant to end her misery – he cleared his throat. She waited for him to tell her she was a disgusting, a freak; that she made him sick.

'And now – are you happy?'

Julia, her face streaked with tears, and feeling infinitely more miserable than she had for a long time at the prospect of losing the man she loved, nodded. 'Yes,' she said, her face crumpling again. 'I'm very happy.'

Scott had stared at the wall for a long time while Julia

held her breath. She knew she had lost him. Silence stretched between them.

'I need a bit of time to myself,' he had said, eventually, still staring at the wall.

After he'd gone she had crawled back to bed and cried until no more tears would come.

Julia powered along the corridor towards reception. After everything she had told him, he was still coming with her to the hospital as he'd said he would. That had to be a good sign. Then again, maybe he was just being kind. Perhaps once he knew she was a hundred per cent well, he'd be off. She started feeling queasy. Lesley was right. Her story was like something from one of the more lurid agony pages, and no matter how brave a face she put on, there was no guarantee it would work out well.

Sixty-Eight

Mike sat on a bench in the sun. It was a funny hotel. Nice enough building – reminded him of Chatsworth, although smaller, of course – and lovely grounds. Strange thing was, everyone had to muck in and help with the chores. It was the first time he'd been on holiday and had to mop the floor. Still, it seemed to be the same for everyone and nobody complained.

He watched a crow hopping about on the lawn. 'Stone the crows,' he said, amused. A woman in tracksuit pants and a white tunic emerged from the patio doors that led into the residents' sitting room. She came and sat beside him and held his hand. One of the chambermaids, as far as he could remember. The badge pinned to her tunic said 'Anita'. *Anita, I've just met a girl called Anita*, he hummed in his head. Hadn't he and Faye been to see *West Side Story*? He loved that song, 'Anita'. Only it wasn't 'Anita'. It was . . . no, he couldn't remember.

He turned to smile at the woman in the white tunic. She looked nothing like the girl, whatever she was called, in *West Side Story*. He'd got a call from work halfway through the show and left. He remembered now. Faye had gone mad. He chuckled to himself. Where was Faye anyway? Oh well, at least the staff at this place seemed friendly enough. Very attentive, always someone fussing about. Frankly, it was a bit over the top

369

at times. One of the blokes even helped him have a shower the other day.

'Your hands are cold,' the woman called Anita said, tucking a rug around him. 'Are you sure you don't want to come in?'

Mike gave her a broad smile. 'I'm taking the sun,' he said. 'Enjoying the great outdoors.'

She nodded. 'I'll come back for you at lunchtime.'

His gaze returned to the crow. It was hopping about and screeching. Another one jumped down from a nearby tree and they stood facing each other, beaks open, screaming. Mike got up. He wrapped the blanket round his shoulders and strolled across the lawn. As he stood under the tree, bird shit splattered on to the front of his sweatshirt. He raised his arms to the heavens. 'That's a sign of good luck,' he said, pleased, and walked on, sending the crows lurching off. The grass was nice and short. Perhaps the hotel guests took turns to cut it, he thought. He wouldn't mind a go on a sit-on lawnmower. They must have one with lawns this size. It was only a few days since he'd checked in, so he hadn't quite got the hang of how things worked yet.

He pulled the rug around him. He wished they'd hurry up and do his laundry, get his camouflage pants and khaki stuff back to him. His boots were gone too. He felt peculiar wearing a baggy tracksuit and slippers all the time. Still, everyone else seemed to be wearing them too. He glanced back at the building. Maybe it was some kind of spa where they gave you 'leisure suits' for the duration of your stay. He'd find out about treatments later. A massage would be nice.

He stood with his rug pulled over his shoulders and did a couple of lunges and some squats. Good idea to keep fitness levels up. Be battle-ready for the next mission. An image flashed through his head. He blinked several times, seeing himself in the executive corridor at Channel 6, hearing James Almond's voice coming from his office. Well, he was out of the picture now. Mike smiled and jogged on the spot a few times. His blanket slipped and he hitched it back round his shoulders, feeling a sense of satisfaction. Then he decided to spread the rug out on the grass and do a few sit-ups. It was shocking how out of shape he was. No wonder Faye had suggested a break, arranged it all.

He rubbed at his brow, disorientated, as if he was falling through space. He curled up in a ball as a peculiar not-quite-there sensation, something he couldn't quite put his finger on, took hold. He covered his head with his hands as it hit him again: dread and panic. He opened his eyes. The pleasant lawns had taken on a bleached, parched look. Something glinted in the trees. The scope on a high-powered rifle. Snipers. Shit! He flattened himself. If he stayed in the irrigation ditch he would be safe. Someone would come for him. He shielded his face with his hands. His helmet – where the fuck was his helmet? He felt someone drop down beside him. Thank God – cover. He rolled on to his back and stared at Anita, who was kneeling beside him. He blinked rapidly. 'Snipers,' he managed to say, his voice hoarse.

She placed a hand on his arm. 'I'm taking you inside now.'

Mike shook his head. 'Not safe.'

She gave him a reassuring smile. 'I did a recce,' she said, 'and we're fine. There's no one out there.' She held out her hand. 'It's OK. It's safe – I promise.'

Mike was shaking. 'I saw them – enemy snipers over by the trees.'

She kept hold of his hand. 'Trust me – it's OK.'

It wasn't, though. Mike was right. An enemy was indeed lurking in the trees at the edge of the lawn.

Sixty-Nine

It had taken Karen a while to come to terms with the news that Tabitha Tate was her daughter. At first she had wondered if the whole thing was some kind of elaborate prank. After all, following James Almond's revelations in court that she had been what he called 'a gymslip mum', a fair number of bogus 'daughters' had contacted Channel 6. It was easy enough to work out they weren't who they claimed to be. But she had always believed she would know her child the second she set eyes on her. For one brief moment it crossed her mind that Tabitha Tate was an advance party, checking Karen out on behalf of the real Amy. When she said as much, Tabitha – on-the-ball and ready-for-anything reporter that she was – simply produced her birth certificate and passport. Karen had to face the truth: Tabitha was Amy.

What troubled her was that her daughter was not at all how she had imagined she would be. True, they looked alike, not that she had noticed the resemblance before – she must have been going round with her eyes shut. Tabitha had the same fair complexion, green eyes and almost-black hair. In temperament, though, they were totally different. While Karen had practically fainted the day they'd met, Tabitha had maintained an almost icy composure. She seemed utterly unfazed to be facing her mother – her *real* mother – for the first time.

They had agreed to keep the discovery to themselves for the time being since Karen was in a state of shock. She needed time to get used to this new and unexpected state of affairs. The whole thing was so complicated, more so because of that whole business with Dave. Now that she knew the truth, Karen was going to have to make things right with him.

She checked the oven. She was doing a chicken casserole with cannellini beans she had made a hundred times before, and for starters they were going to have salmon and smoked cheese parcels with a watercress garnish and some amazing bread from a deli on the King's Road. A tenner for a loaf – it had better be good. There was a chocolate pud from Marks & Spencer if they were still hungry after all that.

She cast her eye over the table, lit the candles and poured herself a glass of wine to steady her nerves. She was wearing a red wraparound dress that showed off her curves and a new pair of strappy wedges, and had pulled her hair back off her face, the way Dave liked it. Time to mend bridges.

She heard the front door open and took a couple of deep breaths before he came in, loosening his tie, and slung his jacket on to the back of a chair.

He took in the sight of the table set for dinner, a vase of bright-yellow roses at one end, a dozen tea lights flickering in the centre, and gave Karen a quizzical look.

'I like what you're wearing,' he said.

'Thanks.'

She went up to him and put her arms round his waist.

Dave said, 'You smell nice.'

She gazed up at him. 'I'm sorry,' she said. 'For everything. Can we be friends again?' She pressed her body against him.

He put his hands on her breasts. Karen gave a sharp little intake of breath.

'Don't see why not,' he said.

She pressed her hands into his back. God, she'd missed him.

His hands were inside her dress, caressing bare flesh. 'Let's go upstairs.'

'No! We can't.'

He kept playing with her nipples. 'No? Sure?'

'Later.' She pulled away and tugged at her dress, covering herself up. 'First we have to have dinner.'

'Nah, bad idea.' He had hold of her wrist and was pulling her close again.

'We *have* to!'

Dave let her go and folded his arms. 'How come you've set three places?'

'Someone's coming.'

'Lesley had another heart attack?'

Karen gave him a weak smile and poured some wine. 'There's something I need to tell you. It's important.'

He took a drink. 'Go on, then.'

'It's going to be a shock, that's the thing, but it's nothing bad. I mean it might *seem* bad, but I don't want you getting the wrong end of the stick or anything because really it's all good. It will be, anyway.' She paused for breath. 'Once you get used to the idea. It might take a while, that's all.'

Dave was frowning again. 'You've lost me, Kaz.'

The doorbell went.

'I'll get it,' Karen said. Her voice sounded high and thin. She went into the hall, pulling the door shut behind her.

Dave slumped into a seat at the table and helped himself to

a hunk of bread. Voices reached him from the hall. He buttered the bread.

The door opened and Karen appeared, moving aside so Dave could see Tabitha Tate behind her. Tabitha was in a short black dress with a huge silver zip that looked like it should be at the back, and had her hair gathered up in a ponytail. Dave glanced at Karen, who was managing to chew her bottom lip – a sure sign she was nervous – and smile at the same time. Was this some kind of stitch-up? He put down his bread. Something began to register. He had never seen it before, but the resemblance between Karen and Tabitha was really quite striking. Before he could say so, Tabitha piped up.

'Hi, Dave – good to see you again. Bet there's not many blokes can say they've pulled a mother–daughter combo.'

Dave's brow furrowed. 'What . . . ?'

Tabitha gave him a brilliant smile. 'You know Amy, Karen's daughter?' She gave him a bright smile. 'Well, it's me.'

He looked at Karen. She looked ready to pass out.

Seventy

Julia was nervous. It was a week since she had seen Scott, and although they had chatted briefly on the phone and all appeared to be fine, she had been alarmed to get a postcard from him at her London flat just as she was getting ready to drive to The Nook for the weekend. The message was a brief and perplexing four words: *We need to talk*.

What was that supposed to mean? They were talking already. Weren't they? She had thought things were back on an even keel after that awful business when she owned up to being Alan Swales in another life.

The fact that Scott had kept her company at the hospital when she had her scan had given her fresh hope. Now she wondered if she had been kidding herself. Why would a man like him want to be with someone like her, now he'd had time to think things over? That's why they needed to talk. He was too decent to dump her without a word, no doubt wanted to tell her to her face that it was over.

She parked up and cut through the garden at the back. The kitchen door was open and Scott was in there. Jack Russell wandered out to greet her, stopping on the patio and stretching languidly before trotting over. She bent and scratched his head and he immediately rolled over and put his legs in the air.

'You're a silly thing,' she said, crouching down and rubbing his belly. When she looked up, Scott was in the doorway watching. She gave him an uncertain smile.

'He knows you're a soft touch,' he said, nodding at the little terrier, who was frantically pawing at the air, trying to get Julia's attention.

She smiled. No one had ever called Julia, acknowledged queen bitch of late-night TV, a soft touch. She stood up.

'I got your postcard.'

'I'm making prawn linguine,' he said.

They went in and he opened the fridge and took out a bottle of Bollinger. Julia gave him a quizzical look. He had style, she'd give him that. There he was, about to dump her, and yet he was going out of his way to make sure it was what they'd both refer to later as an amicable split. She put down her bag and watched him open the champagne, capturing the frothy liquid in a couple of flutes.

'You're going, aren't you?' she said, not able to contain herself. 'That's what this is about. The postcard, the champagne.' She gave him a fierce look. 'Well, it's your loss. I'm the best thing that's ever happened to you, and if you can't see it you're a moron.'

'Hang on a second—'

'It's no skin off my nose. I'm perfectly happy on my own.'

Scott folded his arms. 'Fine, be like that.'

'I will.'

Neither of them said anything.

Jack Russell nudged Julia's ankle. When she ignored him, he stood up on his hind legs.

'He's trying to tell you something.'

Out of the corner of her eye, Julia saw the little dog paw

the air. She tried not to look. Perhaps she would get a dog. At least they loved you no matter what secrets you had.

'Since you've clearly made up your mind, don't let me keep you,' she said, sounding as brusque as she could. She threw him a hostile look.

The corners of his mouth twitched. Was he laughing at her?

'Right,' he said. He went to the stove and turned down the heat under the pasta sauce. 'There's just one thing.'

Julia's heart was breaking. She hoped he wasn't going to say they could still be friends and he'd keep an eye on the place and cut the grass and whatnot when she wasn't there. She wouldn't be able to bear it.

He took something from his pocket.

'I got something for you, although, since you're throwing me out . . .' He gave a small smile, showing the chipped tooth she loved so much.

Julia was struggling to maintain her composure. She wished he would bloody well clear off and leave her to her misery.

'I've thought about everything you told me. Actually, I've thought of little else this week.' He frowned. 'And it's made it all clear.'

'There's no need to rub it in,' Julia snapped.

'And the thing is, I love you and I want to be with you. That's why I want to marry you.'

She gasped.

He opened a box and showed her a square-cut diamond on a platinum band. 'Say the word and I'll slip it on your finger,' he said. 'Will you marry me?'

Julia steadied herself on the edge of the table. Had he really just proposed? And there she was chucking him out! He stood in front of her holding out the glorious ring. She stared at it. It glinted back, tantalizingly. It was exquisite.

He snapped the box shut. 'Fair enough. I'll be off then.'

Jack Russell put a paw on her ankle. Julia felt dizzy. She recovered her composure and lunged at his departing back. 'No – stop! I will. Of course I will!'

'Something smells good.' Dave said as he watched Karen lift a casserole dish from the oven.

This evening, in an effort to impress, she had followed a Jamie Oliver chicken stew recipe she'd found in one of the Sunday papers. It seemed to require an awful lot of ingredients – by her standards, anyway – but the actual cooking hadn't been difficult, and when she tasted the sauce she was amazed. Had she really managed to produce something so good and with so little effort? She might actually get into this cooking lark.

Dave opened a bottle of red wine and poured each of them a glass. Karen placed the casserole on a hessian mat on the kitchen table and took another dish from the bottom of the oven.

'Creamy mash,' she said.

Dave grinned. 'Special occasion, is it?'

She wrapped her arms round his neck and gave him a hug. 'Just felt like spoiling you.'

He slid his hand up the back of her top and twanged her bra strap. 'I might spoil you in a bit.'

Karen giggled and squirmed free. '*After* you've had your dinner. I didn't slave over a hot stove for nothing, you know. I've done rhubarb crumble for pud.' She paused. 'Actually, I bought that.'

Dave gave her a wicked smile as he sat down. 'I already know what I'm having for afters.'

Karen shook her head and took the chair facing him. 'Actually, I did want to make things a bit special tonight.'

'Softening me up for something, are you?'

She took a deep breath. 'I just want you to know I appreciate you.'

Under the table, his hand stroked her leg. 'That's all right, then.'

'And there's something I need to tell you. Something important.'

He gave her a curious look. His hand was on her knee. 'You're not pregnant, are you?'

'No!'

'OK.'

Her cheeks were pink. 'Look, I know we've had our ups and downs, and I've been thinking about it, trying to work out how things got so out of hand.'

Dave smiled. 'You do a bit too much thinking, if you ask me.'

'I know. That's the problem, really. I'm always worrying and tying myself in knots about things . . . I've got all this stuff going on inside here.' She tapped the side of her head. 'The thing is, I almost lost you and I'm not letting that happen again. From now on, if something's bothering me I'm going to say so – and I want you to do the same. No more bottling things up.'

Dave nodded. 'Like what?'

'Anything.' She hesitated. 'I mean . . .'

'Go on.'

Karen gave him a long look. 'I really wish you wouldn't drink juice straight from the carton.'

He burst out laughing. 'OK, slapped wrist for me.'

'It drives me mad.'

He leaned forward in his chair and gazed at her. 'I wouldn't mind, you know.'

'What?'

'If you were pregnant.'

Karen felt her heart start to race. 'Really?'

'Why, would you?'

'No, no. I mean, I'd love it.'

He reached over the table and took her hand. 'We could have a go later – once we've eaten.'

Karen squeezed his hand. 'Afters?'

He grinned. 'That's right. Work up an appetite for the rhubarb crumble.'

She bent and kissed his hand. 'I'd like that.'

'The crumble?'

'The baby thing.'

'Yeah, I would as well.'

Seventy-One

For once, Faye was the first to arrive at the conference room. Paula, tapping away at her laptop, looked up and gave her a pitying smile.

'I won't harp on about all that stuff in the papers,' she said, sounding brisk. 'I'm sure you must be sick and tired of everyone going on about it.'

Faye shrugged. The truth was that she hadn't spoken to anyone since the papers had printed pictures of Mike at The Towers and suggested he was, as one tabloid put it, off his rocker. The photos hadn't helped. God knows what he thought he was doing clowning about and pulling weird faces. His top looked soiled as well. If Faye didn't know better, she'd say it was bird poo, although it could well have been the remains of his breakfast, as another tabloid had suggested. She was utterly mortified. It cost a fortune to stay at The Towers, so you'd think their highly trained staff could at least make sure the residents didn't make fools of themselves.

Ever since the pictures had surfaced, the press had been camped on her doorstep, and her mobile – how on earth had they got that number? – hadn't stopped ringing. Thankfully, Nick Green, Mike's editor, had sprung to his defence, saying it was customary for them to send reporters for some downtime at The Towers once they returned from what were considered traumatic postings. He said Mike would be back doing what he did best as soon as he'd enjoyed some well-earned leave.

'You're looking lovely, by the way,' Paula said. 'Is that a Missoni?'

Faye nodded. She was wearing a sheer knitted top that was actually a dress but was so short she'd paired it with skinny jeans and a pair of strappy heels. Fancy Paula recognizing a Missoni.

'Thanks,' Faye said. She didn't usually bother to check what Paula had on since she invariably went for the dowdy executive look she excelled at – a baggy top, often something chiffon or silk with a bow tied at the neck, a shapeless skirt and the ubiquitous flatties. Now, though, she realized Paula was wearing something fitted in charcoal grey with a slash-neck and three-quarter-length sleeves. It was hard to tell, since she had a cardi draped around her shoulders, but Faye could have sworn the editor was actually wearing a Victoria Beckham dress. No, it was probably the frumpy equivalent from some kind of outfitters for the more staid shopper. Then again, it did look like the real deal.

Before she had a chance to ask, the door opened and Lesley breezed in, giggling and breathless, with Karen on her heels.

'Hey,' Lesley said, waving. Her blonde hair was styled in a tousled plait over one shoulder. She was wearing cropped black pants and a grey vest with a black boyfriend blazer. Her face was dwarfed by an enormous pair of retro sunglasses with white frames. Her lips were a full and glossy bright orange. There was a flush to her cheeks that didn't look like blusher.

Karen looked suspiciously happy as well. She was in a jersey jumpsuit and her hair was tied back, which made her look like a teenager. Faye wondered if she had missed something. Neither of them had mentioned the stuff about Mike in the papers.

Lesley rootled about in her bag and brought out a packet of Twiglets. 'I slept for twelve hours last night. Can you believe it?'

Karen giggled. 'How come – did Dan wear you out first?'

Lesley's eyes widened. 'That's the thing. We hadn't even had sex. I was just exhausted.'

Paula looked up from her laptop. She was glad to see Lesley so happy and settled. Glad, too, that she had destroyed James Almond's secret files, including the one that could have wrecked Lesley's marriage. 'Please – we don't want to hear about your sex life.'

'I do!' Karen giggled again.

Faye watched the pair of them. What was going on? Had nobody seen the papers?

Julia breezed in wearing a short shift dress that showed off her long, toned legs, and towering heels. Lesley shot a jealous glance at the python-skin slingbacks as Julia strutted to the end of the room and took her usual seat opposite Paula. She beamed at the others.

Faye braced herself, waiting for her to come out with something cutting about the perils of having a basket-case husband. Or worse. Julia was humming to herself as she dug around in her bag for her lip gloss. Faye recognized the tune. She could have sworn it was 'You Raise Me Up'. She'd never have guessed Julia was a Westlife fan.

'You couldn't pour me a coffee, darling?' Julia gave Faye a radiant smile.

Faye held her breath. That was Julia all over, pretending to be extra nice and then delivering a killer remark when you least expected it.

'Sugar?'

Julia merely continued to hum and dabbed powder on the tip of her nose.

'Oh me too, while you're at it,' Lesley said, chomping on a Twiglet. 'Four sugars in mine.'

Faye gave her a bemused look. 'Four sugars!'

'I've got a sweet tooth all of a sudden.' She helped herself to another Twiglet. 'And a savoury one. I've suddenly gone mad for Marmite.'

Karen frowned. 'You *hate* Marmite.'

'Not any more.' She grinned at the others as Faye pushed her coffee towards her.

'*Four* sugars for you,' Faye said, slightly appalled. Lesley would be the size of a house in no time if she carried on wolfing down all that junk she seemed to have developed a taste for all of a sudden.

Lesley placed a protective hand flat on her tummy. 'I'm pregnant!'

There was a second or two of silence. Faye stared at her.

Paula gave her a broad smile. 'Well, I'm absolutely delighted for you, dear.'

Karen jumped up. 'My God, Lesley, that's amazing!'

She laughed. 'I'm three months gone!'

Karen rushed over and gave her a hug. 'I'm so thrilled for you.' She gazed around the room. 'Actually, I've got some news too. You know my baby was adopted years ago, and I've been looking for her for a long time? Well . . .' Karen hesitated. 'I've found her.'

Lesley looked astonished. 'You've found Amy – that's wonderful.'

'She's not called Amy, of course. I mean, the people who brought her up changed her name, not that it matters or anything, and—' She was gabbling.

Lesley cut in. 'What does she look like? Is she anything like you?'

Karen took a deep breath. 'Actually, yes. She's a lot like me.'

Julia interrupted. 'We're all very happy for you, but I also have some news.'

'Don't tell me *you've* got a secret love child somewhere,' Lesley said, her expression mischievous.

Julia ignored her. 'I'm getting married,' she said, thrusting forward her left hand to display the enormous sparkler on her engagement finger.

A stunned silence enveloped the room. Eventually, Paula rallied. 'Well, you've certainly kept that quiet. Congratulations. The ring is quite exquisite.'

Lesley recovered her composure. 'Do we know him? I assume it *is* a him . . .'

Julia gave her a frosty look. 'He's called Scott and he's gorgeous.'

Karen's jaw dropped. 'The guy who was taking care of you while you were recuperating? God, he *is* gorgeous.'

Lesley sniggered. 'I suppose *taking care of her* is one way of putting it.'

'Mock all you like,' Julia said, unfazed. 'We're in love and we're getting hitched.' She hesitated. 'You're all invited to the wedding, by the way.'

Karen went to give her a hug, but Julia put up a hand to stop her. 'No need to get all soppy,' she said.

'I'm really pleased for you,' Karen said, backing away. She would save the news that her daughter was actually Tabitha Tate for another day. 'You deserve it.'

Julia beamed. 'I do, don't I?'

Lesley stared at the ring. This Scott bloke must be loaded.

Faye felt something eating away at her as she watched them laughing and celebrating and Paula got on the phone to ask for champagne to be sent in. If she wanted, she could drop a bombshell of her own, tell them she'd found the statuette – the *murder weapon* – at Mike's place. Say how he'd had some kind of breakdown and had to be carted off to the loony bin in a straitjacket – that wasn't quite true, but never mind. That would wipe the smiles off their faces and make them pay some attention to her for a change.

'Hasn't anyone seen the papers?' she said, raising her voice above the chatter.

They all turned to face her. 'I know, poor Mike,' Lesley said. 'You must say if there's anything we can do,' she added as an afterthought.

'So anyway,' Julia said, butting in, 'I've seen the most amazing Vera Wang dress, but I'm just not sure. I might get Kyrie to make something for me.'

'Where did Davina McCall get her pregnancy clothes?' Lesley said.

'I'm sure she wore a lot of Diane Von Furstenberg, at least for the first few months,' Karen said.

Faye kept quiet. She had never felt more alone. As she gazed around the table, she realized there was no one she could turn to. At one time she'd have shared her secrets with Cheryl. For a while, when they were close, they had told each other everything. Well, almost everything. She fought back tears. A voice in her head goaded her, told her the only person to blame for the way her life had turned out was herself. Self-pity swallowed her up. What was the point of anything? Daisy, she told herself. Daisy was the point. She had to remember that, no matter how bad things got.

Seventy-Two

When the doorbell went, Faye wasn't planning to answer. It would only be some nosey journalist wanting to trick her into saying something that would give them the headline they were after – no doubt along the lines of HERO WAR REPORTER IN BATTLE FOR SANITY. Well, they could get lost. She topped up her wine. Sod the lot of them.

The bell went again. She put down her glass and ventured into the hall. Someone shouted through the letterbox.

'Faye – are you in? I just wanted a word. I won't keep you long, promise.'

The voice was familiar, but Faye couldn't quite place it. 'Hello,' she called back. 'Who's there?'

'It's me – Tabitha Tate from the newsroom. Can I come in?'

Faye froze. What did she want? Everyone now knew she was Karen's daughter, which had sent a few shockwaves around Channel 6. Of course the gossip mags had found out and plastered the pair of them all over the covers. Neither Karen nor Tabitha had given any interviews, not that you'd guess. The magazines and papers were full of 'exclusives' – all made up, with quotes from so-called friends of the pair – about the amazing mother–daughter reunion.

'Were you looking for Karen?' Faye said, confused. She really didn't want to let Tabitha in. For a start, she was still in her dressing gown, and the place was a mess. As usual, she had persuaded her mum to take Daisy so she could put her feet up.

'It's you I wanted a word with,' Tabitha said, sounding breezy. 'Five minutes, that's all.'

Faye unlocked the door and opened it a fraction. Tabitha, in a sloppy black sweater and cargo pants and some kind of satchel hitched over her shoulder, smiled up at her. 'Hi, all right if I come in?'

'No! I mean, it's not convenient.'

'Oh, OK.' Tabitha took a step back. 'It's just that it's a bit delicate.'

Faye held on to the door. 'Has something happened to Karen?'

'No, nothing like that.' Tabitha smiled. 'Actually, I wanted to ask about your husband.'

'Mike?'

'Look, I know he's in The Towers and he's clearly not well—'

'There's nothing wrong with him,' Faye said, feeling defensive. 'He's resting. You might need a spell in there yourself – if you ever do any *proper* reporting.'

Tabitha seemed taken aback. 'Sorry, I thought—'

'I can guess what you thought, same as all the other hacks breathing down my neck day in, day out. If you don't know, just make it up – isn't that how journalists operate these days? Anyway, what's Mike being in The Towers got to do with Channel 6?'

Tabitha shook her head. 'Nothing. Look, this is awkward. It would be better if I could come in.'

'I've told you. It's not convenient.'

Tabitha heaved her bag off her shoulder and rested it on

the step. 'The party, the night James Almond was murdered.'
Faye stared at her. 'I've been following the investigation, talking
to the police, wading through all the statements, you know . . .'

Faye's heart began to race.

'And . . . it struck me that Mike knew his way round the
building.' She hesitated. 'There's no easy way to say this. The
police reckon the same person who killed James also attacked
Cheryl West and, not to put too fine a point on it, Mike had
a motive. I mean, you were seeing Cheryl and James let the
world know.'

Faye clutched the door.

Tabitha shoved her hands in her pockets. 'It's not all that
far-fetched. I mean, he was familiar with the layout at Channel
6, he knew where Cheryl lived . . .'

Faye felt nauseous. 'Is that what the police are saying?'

'Actually, it's my theory. But . . . you know Mike best. You
don't think that might have tipped him over the edge – you
know, guilty conscience?'

Faye struggled for breath.

'Something went missing from James Almond's office the
night he was killed. A comedy award from the Domes. It was
probably the murder weapon.'

The colour drained from Faye's face. She wished she had
been able to get rid of that damned statuette at Mike's place.
'Would you please leave me alone?'

'But—'

'*Please* – just go.' She swayed slightly as she hung on to the
door.

Tabitha gave her a cool look, taking in the tangled hair and
the absence of make-up, the dressing gown.

'Just fuck off, will you,' Faye said, and banged the door shut.

'I only asked her about Mike, you know – said he might have done it,' Tabitha said.

Karen covered her face with her hands. 'No wonder she threw you out.'

'Threw me out? She never even let me in. She just stood there – in her dressing gown, by the way – looking as rough as anything. She's not a boozer, is she?'

Karen looked away. They were in the canteen at Channel 6. Faye had barely spoken a word in the production meeting. She said she wasn't sure she would get to Julia's wedding, made some excuse about not being able to get a babysitter, even though Julia said it was OK to bring Daisy. Karen wasn't sure what was more bizarre – Faye saying she might miss the wedding of the year, or Julia allowing a baby at her nuptials.

'The police have drawn a blank,' Tabitha was saying. 'I mean, it's not like it's case closed or anything, but the investigation's definitely winding down, it's obvious.'

'I suppose it's bound to at a certain point.'

Tabitha took a sip of her cappuccino. 'He could have done it, you know.'

'Who?'

'Mike Parry.'

Karen sighed. Tabitha was a lot more tenacious than she had been at that age. She could be quite exhausting. 'What on earth makes you think that?'

'One, he was at the party.'

'So was I.'

'Two, he knows his way round the building.'

'So do I.'

'Three, he disappeared. No one saw him when the owner was making his speech.'

'Yes, well, I left then too. Maybe he was in the other studio, or just getting some air.'

'Maybe. Personally, I doubt it. The main thing is he had motive for killing James and Cheryl.'

'You're starting to sound like someone off *CSI*.'

'Admit it, it's all completely plausible.'

Karen shuddered. 'Someone tampered with the shower in my dressing room. Someone gave Lesley a heart attack. Are you saying that was him too?'

Tabitha grinned. 'I love that – a heart attack.' She looked thoughtful. 'If you ask me, that was definitely Mike, taking evasive action, throwing everyone off the scent. It was only ever James and Cheryl he was interested in.'

Karen glanced at a nearby table where two guys in fine-knit cardigans and skinny jeans were deep in conversation. 'Keep your voice down – you don't know any of this. It's only a theory.'

'It's a good one, though,' Tabitha said. 'What's more, I bet Faye suspects him. I could tell by the way she was with me. She got the shock of her life when I turned up and came out with what she's already thinking.'

'I really think you have an overactive imagination.'

Tabitha shrugged. 'It doesn't matter in the end. It's not like there's any proof and he's gone bonkers anyway, so that's the end of that.'

'Poor Mike.'

'Or *clever* Mike. Maybe he's not bonkers at all, just faking a breakdown. No one's going to point the finger at a poor, traumatized war reporter, are they? Genius!'

Karen shook her head. 'Honestly, I've never heard anything so far-fetched – it's news you're supposed to be covering, not make-believe.'

'Seriously, most of the weird stuff I come across is a lot crazier than anything you'd make up.'

Seventy-Three

Julia was in the garden at The Nook, barefoot in a sheer cream slip, her face tilted towards the sun. There were only a few clouds dotting the sky – nothing to spoil her big day.

At the bottom of the garden a small marquee had been erected. Caterers were busy adding the finishing touches to the food for the reception. Julia sipped her coffee from an enamel mug – a gift from Scott that urged her to *KEEP CALM AND CARRY ON*. She smiled. She *was* calm, eerily so. She had a peculiar sense of inner peace and happiness that some might even call serenity. It was not a feeling she had ever experienced before. With a huge occasion looming, she would usually be on edge, wound-up, shouting and stamping her feet. She glanced down at her toes with their glossy red nails. The day before she had been for a super-luxury pedicure with a woman who was practically a legend in the world of celebrity foot care, and had emerged from the discreet little Mayfair salon practically walking on air. For as long as she could remember, Julia had hated her feet, thinking them big and clumsy-looking. Pedicures had always been a nightmare. Now, though, she was grateful to be able to walk again. It had been touch and go for a while. That crazy night when she had crashed her car in the Strand underpass no longer seemed real. It was as if it had happened to someone else.

She wriggled her toes in the damp, dewy grass and stretched, feeling the muscles in her back go taut. In a few hours she would walk down the aisle. She felt a shiver of anticipation and the hairs on her arms prickled. At the far end of the lawn a pair of blackbirds pecked at the ground, foraging for breakfast.

Scott padded out from the kitchen and wrapped his arms around her. 'You'll catch your death out here,' he said, nuzzling her neck.

She leaned against him. 'It's a lovely day. Perfect.'

He held her tight. 'Not getting cold feet?' He paused. 'That wasn't meant to be a joke.'

Julia laughed. 'I read somewhere that it's good for the soul to feel the bare earth beneath your feet.'

'OK.' He gave her a curious look.

Julia planted a kiss on the back of his hand. 'And I remember thinking at the time that it sounded like a right old load of New Age rubbish.'

'That sounds more like you.'

She gave him a dig in the ribs. '*Anyway*, I think there might actually be something to it. I mean, it really does feel good.' She wiggled her toes again. 'It's definitely giving me a warm feeling inside.'

'Sure that's not me?'

She twisted round and gave him a coy look. 'You're definitely helping, but, you know, I'm coming round to this barefoot lark.'

Scott hoisted her into his arms. 'I'm glad you're feeling all spiritual and connected to the earth, but I don't want you coming down with pneumonia before I get you down the aisle.'

Julia looped her arms round his neck. She gazed into eyes that were brighter than the blue sky and full of mirth. 'I'm not, by the way,' she said, her face serious.

Scott stopped in his tracks.

'Getting cold feet.'

He gave her a lingering kiss. Julia felt the earth spin.

'You know we're not supposed to see each other on the day of the wedding. Not until the church.'

Julia shrugged. 'I don't mind if you don't.'

'And definitely no sex before the ceremony. It's bad luck.'

Her eyes widened.

'I don't mind if you don't,' he said, carrying her inside.

'I still don't see why we had to spend the night in the middle of nowhere,' Lesley complained. 'I mean, it's not like we couldn't have driven down from London in time for the wedding.'

'Because Julia wanted us here and it's her big day,' Karen said. 'She wants us to go round and have a glass of bubbly with her, help her get ready.'

'I don't suppose it's strictly accurate to call it a wedding anyway,' Lesley said. 'Not when she's a—' She lowered her voice. 'You know.'

Karen sighed. 'It's a civil ceremony and a church blessing, so that's a proper wedding as far as I'm concerned.'

'Isn't life funny?' I mean, it's not so long ago that we were thinking about her funeral.'

'Lesley!'

'And here we are now, just hours away from probably the freakiest wedding I've ever been to in my life.'

'I don't think it's that unusual – look at Roy and Hayley on *Coronation Street*.'

Lesley grinned. 'That's what I mean. You're not telling me they're your idea of a normal couple?'

'They adore each other, you can tell. Have you seen the way he looks at her? It's obvious they're besotted.'

'It's not real, you know.'

Lesley glanced around the breakfast room of the country house hotel they'd spent the night in. Sunlight spilled through mullioned windows on to tables covered in stiff white cloths and laid with heavy silver cutlery. The oak-panelled walls were hung with tapestries. The floor, faded parquet, had creaked when Lesley clattered over it in her sky-high heels.

'Do you think Julia picked this place to punish us? I mean, it's not exactly Babington House. There's not even a spa.'

'I think it's lovely, full of character.'

'Don't tell me – it reminds you of something you saw in *Midsomer Murders*.' Karen opened her mouth to object, but Lesley kept on talking. 'It *is* weird, though, isn't it?' She checked her reflection in the shiny blade of her butter knife and ferreted in her bag for her lip gloss. 'Life, I mean. Just look at all that business with you and Tabitha.'

'I know. When I look at her now, I can't believe I didn't spot the resemblance straightaway.'

'Me neither.'

'Your turn to take on the perils of motherhood next.' Karen grimaced. 'Do you mind what you have?'

Lesley stroked her rounded tummy. 'I keep saying I want a girl, but I'll be happy whatever.' She gave Karen a contented smile.

The door opened and Faye came in wearing ripped skinny jeans, a tight vest with a neon palm tree on the front, monster wooden platforms and a pair of oversized D&G shades.

'Look out, here comes our very own celebrity mum of the year,' Lesley said. 'Quick, hide the sherry.'

An outdoorsy-looking couple in the corner stared as Faye clomped across the room. 'I'm starving,' she said, sitting next to Lesley and picking up the breakfast menu. 'I'm going to have everything.'

'Careful, you might get something disgusting like black pudding,' Lesley said.

'I love black pudding,' Faye replied, putting her menu aside. 'What's the coffee like?'

Lesley turned up her nose. 'Let's just say I'd be surprised if they've got an espresso machine in the kitchen.'

'So,' Karen said, 'the plan is we go round to Julia's after breakfast, have some fizz, calm her down – what's the betting she's in a right old state already? – and then it's off to the church. Dave and Dan are meeting us there.'

'Is it going to be just us?' Faye asked.

Karen shrugged. 'She said she wanted to keep it intimate. Just proper friends.'

Lesley pulled a face. 'What are we doing here, then?'

'It's a shame Paula couldn't make it,' Karen said.

'I know – two trannies together.' Lesley chuckled. 'Even more freaky.'

Karen gave her a stern look. 'Paula is *not* a tranny.'

'A sex-change whatsit then.'

Faye said, 'Has Paula really had a sex-change?'

'The shoes are a dead giveaway,' Lesley said. 'And her feet are enormous. She must wear size twelves.'

Karen's face was frantic. 'I hope you're not going to upset Julia with that kind of talk, today of all days.'

Lesley gave her a wicked smile. 'Course not. I'll be on my absolute best behaviour.'

Seventy-Four

'Not like that,' Julia said, glaring at Karen. 'I said a *teeny* bit of spray, just to hold the curls at the back in place.'

Karen flinched. She stood with the can of hairspray in her hand awaiting Julia's instructions.

'Let some air in, will you,' Julia snapped, wafting a hand in front of her face. 'Before you poison us all with the fumes.'

Karen edged past her and struggled with the stubborn sash window.

'Oh, for goodness' sake,' Julia said.

Lesley, perched on a brocade chaise longue at the end of the bed, chuckled. 'What's up? Pre-wedding nerves?'

Julia, her wedding dress hidden under her dressing gown, peered at her reflection in the dressing-table mirror. 'Not at all. I've nothing to be nervous about.' She turned and aimed a serene smile at Lesley as Karen continued to wrestle with the window. 'It might help if you undo the catch,' she said, her voice sweet, still gazing at Lesley.

Karen went pink. The window glided open.

'Is it going to be a real vicar and everything?' Lesley said.

Julia stiffened. 'Why wouldn't it be?'

'I just wondered if it's all legal and above board.' She gave Julia a meaningful look. 'Bearing in mind . . . *you know*.'

Julia dabbed her favourite Eau Du Soir perfume at the nape

of her neck. 'I was just about to ask if your so-called natural pregnancy is *above board*, as you put it, bearing in mind you went through the dreaded Change years ago.'

'Think what you like. I don't suppose *you'll* be giving birth any time soon.'

Karen stepped between them. 'Stop it, you two.' She gave Lesley a stern look. 'This is meant to be the happiest day of Julia's life, so no more sniping.'

Lesley gave a shrug. 'She knows I'm only teasing. Anyway, if anyone spoils her big day it won't be me.'

Julia's eyes narrowed.

'I mean, has anyone seen Faye since she offered to go downstairs for another bottle of champagne?'

Karen swallowed. 'Oh no – that was ages ago.'

'She'll be in a corner somewhere getting sloshed as we speak.'

Karen hurried from the room.

'Seriously, Julia, I'm pleased for you,' Lesley said once the two of them were alone.

Julia maintained an icy smile as she waited for Lesley to follow up with a snide comment.

Lesley beamed at her. 'I mean it. It's nice to see you looking so happy.'

Julia, bemused, braced herself for the inevitable insult.

'Tell you what, lovely – I'll get you another glass of champagne.' She got up, stooped, and planted a light kiss on Julia's head. 'You look amazing, by the way. He's a lucky guy,' she said.

Julia blinked, astonished. Lesley had better hurry up with that drink – she was going to need it.

*

'She's late,' Lesley said. 'Of course.'

The little church was filled with flowers and ribbons and hundreds of flickering candles. Red candles at that. Lesley was surprised they allowed such things in a place of worship. She was sure she'd read something in one of her magazines about coloured candles having different meanings, and red definitely signified lust. If she remembered rightly, the lighting of the candle represented the spark between a couple while the flame, erect and throbbing with heat, was symbolic of . . . oh well, never mind. Julia's vicar must be one of those progressive types.

Up a flight of wooden steps at the side of the altar, a solid woman in a long black skirt, cream satin blouse buttoned to the neck and a felt hat with flowers on the brim teased something haunting from the organ. Below, next to a painting of a figure in a flowing robe with a golden halo and birds perched on his outstretched arms, was a woman in a sober navy suit with a briefcase at her feet. The registrar, presumably.

'Bride's prerogative, arriving late,' Dan said, resting a hand on Lesley's thigh.

'No hanky-panky in church,' she said, giving him a playful slap.

'Weddings always make me randy.' His thumb strayed to the top of her leg.

'Stop it!'

The vicar, a lean figure with flowing white hair, looked up from his order of service and frowned.

Lesley flashed him a dazzling smile. 'You'll get us thrown out,' she hissed at Dan between clenched teeth.

Dave draped an arm round Karen's shoulder. 'Small turnout,' he said, gazing at the rows of empty pews.

'She only wanted us here,' Karen said.

'Who's that then?'

Karen followed his gaze to an elderly woman in a double-breasted camel coat buttoned right up, and a cream pillbox hat over short grey hair. 'Probably some local who comes to all the weddings.'

'Maybe it's Julia's mum.'

Karen frowned. 'No – she'd have said.'

He nodded at the brown and white terrier lying at the groom's feet, its chin supported by a kneeler. 'Who's he – the best man?'

Karen giggled. 'It's not exactly a conventional wedding. They're just doing it the way they want.'

'Don't blame them.'

Faye dug her elbow into Karen's side. 'What's the hold-up?'

'She'll be here in a minute.'

Faye slumped back in her seat, frowning. 'I'm dying of thirst here,' she said, sounding tetchy.

Earlier, Karen had found her on the patio at The Nook sinking the champagne she had gone to fetch.

Outside, Julia stood in the sunshine. Through the open door she could see the back of Scott's head. Her gaze went to the other side of the aisle, to Lesley in her fabulous Cozmo Jenks hat. Karen was a couple of seats along, hair tumbling over her shoulders in gleaming raven waves. Next to her, Faye shuffled in her seat. On her own in the front pew, her pillbox hat at a jaunty angle, was Julia's mother.

Julia smoothed the front of her dress, a simple strapless off-white sheath with a low-cut back and just the smallest hint of a train, and glanced at her bouquet, an enormous bunch of fragrant freesias. As she stepped into the porch, she lifted the front of her dress a fraction, revealing ivory peep-toe stilettos studded with Swarovski crystals. Underneath her dress she was wearing an exquisite Rigby & Peller basque with the date of her wedding day hand-stitched in blue on the underside. Julia had chosen to follow some of the traditions – those that appealed to her.

The vicar looked up and caught her eye. She nodded. For a moment all she heard was a blackbird singing to its mate in the churchyard, and then the first few notes of Wagner's *Bridal Chorus* seeped into the air. Scott got to his feet and turned to face her. Jack Russell ambled up the aisle, tail wagging, as Julia, euphoric, swept forward, not taking her eyes off her groom for a moment.

Lesley scrabbled about in her bag.

Dan grabbed her wrist. 'Leave it,' he said. 'Your lippy's fine.'

She blinked back tears. 'I'm looking for a hanky,' she said, unexpectedly overcome at the sight of the powerful current of love and longing surging between Julia and her husband-to-be.

Seventy-Five

'I'm telling you,' Tabitha said, barely able to contain herself. 'There's a statuette in Mike Parry's place.'

DI Tim Ellis leaned back in his chair and put his feet up on his desk. Tabitha glanced at the scruffy Vans and drainpipe jeans. Hardly what you might call formal detective garb, but still, it was the weekend and he was supposed to be off-duty.

'And how come you know this fascinating fact?'

'I saw it. Through the window at the back.'

DI Ellis looked sceptical. 'He's an award-winning reporter. He probably has any number of statuettes.'

'I know, but it looked . . . weird.'

'Weird.'

Tabitha took a deep breath. 'Dirty. Stained.'

'You could tell that by looking through the window, could you? Don't know why we bother with forensics.'

'OK, I'm guessing, but it was – well, messed-up.'

DI Ellis nodded. 'Messed-up, was it? Right.'

'Shouldn't you be arresting him or something?'

'Care to explain what you were doing snooping round his place?'

She looked away. 'It adds up. It had to be him. You should have seen the look on Faye Cole's face when I spelled it out to her.'

'You do know she rang the desk sergeant the other day, practically hysterical, and said you'd been harassing her.'

'It was a misunderstanding,' Tabitha said. 'She was probably sloshed anyway. Once she sobers up, she'll see I was doing her a favour. If your other half was a cold-blooded killer, wouldn't you want to know?'

DI Ellis got up and put his jacket on. It just so happened he had been about to have another chat with Mike Parry anyway. Something about Faye Cole's histrionics had aroused his suspicions. Considering she lived her life in the public eye, it all seemed rather over the top. Surely Tabitha turning up unannounced wasn't the worst thing that had ever happened to her.

'We'll bring him in, have a chat,' he said.

Tabitha held her breath.

'I don't expect he'll tell us anything, mind you. Word is he's not all there.'

'Not according to her,' Tabitha said. 'She reckons he's just resting up.'

'Want to stick around, see if you've got your scoop? Course, you do know that if you're wrong you'll end up with egg all over your face.'

Tabitha got out her phone. 'I'm a hundred per cent sure. It's a gut thing. I can feel it.' She could feel the adrenalin beginning to pump through her system. 'Can you hang on a bit? Give me a chance to rustle up a crew and get them over to The Towers to capture the moment when you bring Mike Parry out.'

DI Ellis smiled. 'It's not an arrest. We're questioning him, that's all.'

'I know, I know.' Tabitha's heart was thudding with excitement. She was on the verge of a massive scoop, she could feel it.

Even better, she was *part* of it.

Seventy-Six

Julia sat in the gazebo with Scott. Her husband. Several feet away on the patio, the sun sinking behind them, were Karen and Dave and, at their feet, Jack Russell, who nudged at their ankles with his nose every few seconds, begging them to throw a ball. Julia sipped at her champagne, utterly content, while Scott caressed her fingers and the two of them laughed at the antics of the little dog. Finally, Dave handed Karen his champagne and picked up the ball. Jack Russell sat up, alert, waiting for it to sail through the air.

'Look at that,' Julia said. 'Nobody's immune to the charms of Jack Russell.'

'Just like me with you, then,' Scott said.

Julia rested her head on his shoulder. At the far end of the garden her mum, still in her coat, inspected a rose bush. Opening up to Scott had meant Julia could let her mother back into her life from time to time. It didn't matter what she said, what secrets she might reveal. Scott knew them all anyway. At last, Julia could be herself. Her real self. No more lies, no more running away when anyone got too close and the threat of exposure loomed. With Scott, all the barriers that had made life such a tough, painful ordeal had been torn down. Maybe she would give up TV now, live a quiet life, turn her back on the vanity and celebrity nonsense she had seen as the be-all and end-all for so long. She could be happy here in her little hide-away with the man she loved. She let out a dreamy sigh.

'What's going on inside that head?'

'I was just thinking about telly and how pointless it all is. I might give up work.' She paused for a second. 'Be a house-wife instead – look after my gorgeous husband.'

'If that's what you want.'

'I can't think of anything I'd rather do.'

'OK. Except you'd miss it all in five minutes flat.'

Julia sat up and gazed at him. 'I wouldn't.'

'You love it and you're good at it.' He stroked her neck. 'Give yourself some thinking time, Mrs Walker – see how you feel after the honeymoon.'

She snuggled into him again. *Mrs Walker*. 'OK. You're the boss.' She couldn't help giggling. Had she – notorious ice queen and control freak – *really* just said that?

Tabitha had her scoop. Once Mike Parry started talking, he wouldn't shut up. It was clear he held a grudge against James Almond for making public the details of his wife's gay affair, and he made no attempt to disguise his bitterness towards Cheryl. She had corrupted his wife, was how he'd put it. He had been the one who'd tampered with the shower in Karen's dressing room and sent a pig's heart to Lesley, hoping the girls might point the finger at Julia, since she had always been mean to Faye.

His interview wavered between coherent when it came to his feelings and vague in terms of some of his actions. When DI Ellis asked him outright if he had murdered James Almond, he said, 'Well, someone had to.' The DI wanted to know if it was Mike who had attacked Cheryl. 'Affirmative. Mission accomplished,' he had said, raising a clenched fist.

Ellis had got a search warrant, which was when things finally became clear. The statuette in Mike's living room, which Ellis had spotted right away on a shelf with a clutch of awards for news reporting, had almost certainly been used to murder Cheryl West. As Tabitha said, it hadn't been cleaned up following the attack. As far as Ellis was concerned, the lab tests were a formality. A bloodstained rucksack had been bagged and taken away by forensics too. Ellis was certain Mike had killed Cheryl. That made sense.

However, something didn't feel quite right.

'What did you do with the other statuette? The one you took from James Almond's office?'

Mike gazed up at him. It was a while before he answered. 'I just wanted to put things right.'

Ellis leaned on the desk. 'The statuette – where is it?'

Mike chewed at his thumbnail. 'I lost my buddy in Afghanistan. Bloody good cameraman. Three kids. Couldn't do fuck-all about it.' He rubbed his face. Ellis had no idea where this was going. 'Sometimes you have to step up,' Mike said, 'do your bit, save someone else's skin.'

Ellis sat in the chair facing him. 'Mike, I know you've been through a tough time and I'm sorry about your buddy, I really am. But please – help me out here, will you? You haven't told me anything about the Channel 6 party and how you ended up in James Almond's office.' Ellis gave him a long look. 'So tell me. Put things right. What did you do with the other statuette?'

Mike mumbled something.

'What?'

'Classified information. Need to know.' He closed his eyes.

'If there's anything else you want to say, now's the time to speak up.'

'I got rid of it,' Mike said, his voice firm. 'The statuette. I used it to stab the evil prick and then I chucked it. Trust me – you'll never find it, so you might as well stop looking.'

Faye was in the marquee, well gone, picking at the icing on a piece of wedding cake, when her phone rang. It was a private number and she was tempted to ignore it, but since there was a slim chance it was her mother calling about Daisy, she decided it was best to answer.

At first she thought it was someone playing a prank, claiming to be a police officer, saying something about serious charges in relation to the murders of James Almond and Cheryl West. She went cold. Then she remembered her complaint about Tabitha Tate and wondered if the police had finally got their act together and arrested her. Karen wouldn't be happy. Faye glanced up and saw her canoodling with Dave on the patio. Well, tough. Faye pressed the phone to her ear. She was struggling to hear the man on the other end of the line.

'Can you say that again?' she said. 'I'm at a do and it's noisy.' In fact, apart from a girl in a black dress and white apron clearing away empties, Faye was alone in the marquee. She waved her glass and the girl plucked a bottle of champagne from an ice bucket and gave her a refill.

'I wanted to let you know we'll be bringing charges later today,' DI Ellis said.

'Oh good,' Faye said. 'Maybe she'll think twice about turning up on the doorstep upsetting people in future.'

There was a pause. 'I'm sorry – I'm not quite with you.'

'Tabitha Tate. What's she being charged with? Trespass? Breach of the peace?'

DI Ellis cleared his throat. 'I think we're at cross purposes.

We'll be charging your husband with the murders of James Almond and Cheryl West.' He waited for his words to sink in. 'A couple of hours ago we searched his property and recovered what we believe is the murder weapon, and that, together with his statement, means there's no doubt.' He decided not to mention that the statuette missing from James Almond's office had yet to be recovered.

Faye gripped the phone. The statuette. Her fingerprints would be all over it.

'I wanted to let you know, out of courtesy. Obviously, the media interest will be high and they're bound to turn up at your home and place of work, so you may want to go away for a few days.'

She stared into space.

'Ms Cole – are you still there?'

Faye struggled to speak. Eventually she managed to say, 'I'm still here.'

'I understand you and your husband are separated, but, as I say, that won't stop the press coming after you, so I wanted to give you a heads-up.'

Faye clicked her phone off and put it back in her bag. All she could think about was escaping before word got round. She headed up to the house.

Karen waved. 'Lovely spot, isn't it?'

Faye, fighting the urge to be sick, waved back. 'Yeah, great. Just nipping to the loo.'

She went inside, cut through the kitchen into the hall and hurried out of the front door. There was a shop in the village – they'd have the number of a cab firm. She'd go to her mum's, hide out there.

*

411

Karen's phone bleeped with a text message. Tabitha. She smiled at Dave. 'She says she hopes the wedding was fun and to give her a call.'

'Go on, then.'

'Oh, it can wait. She probably just wants the gossip.'

They were quiet for a moment before Dave said, 'I still think it's weird that Tabitha's your kid.'

'I know. Sometimes I look at her and can't get my head round it. I mean, she's so . . .' Karen searched for the right word.

'Stroppy?'

She dug him in the ribs. '*Strong*. Self-possessed.'

Dave grinned. 'I bet you were the same when you were her age.'

When Karen was twenty-something she was in a girl band having hit records and touring. Come to think of it, yes, in her Thunder Girls days she had heaps of self-belief. Not unlike Tabitha. It was only when Jason cheated on her with an air-head half her age that her confidence took a battering.

'Maybe,' she conceded.

Dave said, 'Bet you were never that ruthless, though.'

Karen pulled a face. 'It's being in news with all those cut-throat hacks that makes her like that.'

'I still can't believe she went round to Faye's and accused her old man of being a serial killer.'

'Yes, well, she knows she overstepped the mark there and she promised to back off.'

'She'll be round at his place right now going through the bins, snooping about to see if there's a window open so she can get inside and have a good old nosey while there's nobody at home – mark my words.'

Karen stared at him. 'She'd never do anything like that.'

'Bet you anything.' He chuckled. 'It's being in news that makes her like that,' he said, mimicking her. 'Tell you what – at least she's got that dickhead off our backs.'

Once Tabitha had come on the scene, the weekly delivery of white roses from Jason had dried up. He was utterly besotted with his daughter and therefore much too busy trying to make up for lost time to bother with Karen any more. And according to the papers, he was seeing some girl who'd been on *Big Brother*.

'You see,' Karen said. 'We should be grateful.'

'I am. So should he, mind. I was about ready to lamp him one, knock some sense into that thick skull of his.' He raised his glass. 'So, shall we drink to your strop— sorry, *strong* daughter?'

She touched her glass against his. 'Tabitha.'

Seventy-Seven

Tabitha had agonized over whether to ring Karen. In the end, not wanting to alarm her or cast a shadow over Julia's big day, she had waited as long as she could before sending an innocuous text. It was all so tricky. She really didn't want the wedding party switching on the TV and stumbling on the news that Mike had been charged with murder. The sight of Tabitha reporting live from the street in front of Mike's house – which now had a police officer posted outside and crime tape across the front door – wouldn't go down well. Still, at least DI Ellis had said he would call Faye and tell her what was going on. She would be with her friends when he delivered his bomb-shell. Tabitha couldn't help feeling bad for her. It would come as quite a shock. But not that much of a shock. When they'd had their little doorstep set-to Tabitha was pretty sure Faye knew more than she was letting on. Perhaps she would even end up being charged with something.

A voice in her earpiece told her to stand by, that they'd be coming to her live in fifteen seconds. The studio anchor said her name. She pushed a stray strand of hair behind her ear. The light on the front of the camera went on; the sudden glare making her blink.

'In ten,' the studio PA told her.

Tabitha straightened her shoulders and gave her cameraman the thumbs up.

'Five, four, three, two, one. Live on remote camera one.'

Tabitha gazed into the lens, her expression solemn. 'Police are still searching the property behind me, the home of award-winning war correspondent Mike Parry,' she began.

Faye directed the cab driver through the Channel 6 staff car park and got him to drop her at the back of the building, where she nipped in through the scene dock next to a deserted Studio 1. Even though she'd been drinking all day, the call from DI Ellis had sobered her up. She hurried past the props department, turned into the dressing-room corridor, key at the ready, and let herself into the first room on the left. Once inside, she bolted the door and leaned against it. She could feel her heart beating a bit too fast and told herself to take her time.

After a minute or so she got on to the table in the corner of the room, reached up and dislodged a ceiling tile marked with a tiny blue dot no one would see unless they were looking for it. She felt around inside the cavity until she touched something cool and smooth. Her heart hammered away as her hand closed around the base of the statuette that had gone missing from James Almond's office the night he was murdered. She couldn't leave it there now. It was too risky. She got down and shoved it inside her bag without looking at it. There had been no time to properly clean it up.

Thinking about that night, she retched and ran to the bathroom to throw up into the toilet. Kneeling on the cold floor, vomiting, with tears running down her cheeks, Faye considered going to the police and telling them what had happened. She couldn't just keep quiet. Then again, she had to. Daisy couldn't lose both her parents. Her head swam as she thought back to the night of the Channel 6 party, how she'd been coming back from the loo when she saw James Almond get in the lift and head for the executive floor. It was a spur-of-the-moment decision to follow him using the service lift, which creaked and clanged as it chugged to the top of the building. This was her chance to tell him what a mess her life was in thanks to him.

As she crept from the lift through the executive dining room and into the empty corridor with its glass-fronted offices and plush leather sofas, she had seen the light on in James's office. The door was not quite shut. For several seconds she stood frozen to the spot, her nerve starting to go. She looked over her shoulder. Strange – she could have sworn she was being watched. Just as she was about to turn round and go back the way she'd come, she heard laughter coming from James's office. She clenched her fists.

James Almond reclined in his restored executive chair and watched the new owner of Channel 6 make a beeline for one of the weather girls. It made him laugh out loud. 'Oh, for God's sake, show some originality,' he said.

He didn't notice Faye come into the room. She was standing in front of the desk by the time he swung round and saw her.

'Shit, you made me jump,' he said. He looked her up and down, not bothering to conceal his distaste. 'I don't recall inviting you.'

Faye's eyes were filled with hatred. 'You think you're so clever.' Her voice shook.

James gave her a nasty smile. 'That's because I am. Now get out. I'm busy.'

He turned back to the TV screen in the corner where Vladimir Vladislav had his hand on the bare back of the blonde weather girl. His hand slid down and patted her behind. James laughed. 'Naughty, naughty. What would Mrs Vladislav have to say about that?'

Faye took a step around the desk, stumbled and knocked the lamp. The light shone on to the wall behind James. Without looking at her, he made a tut-tut sound. 'I'll give you ten seconds to get out, you pathetic drunk. Go and find your loser friends.'

Faye blinked back tears. She would not cry. 'I had a good life until you came along,' she said.

'Oh, get the violins out.'

'Y-you ruined me.'

'Please, I can't possibly take all the credit.' His lip curled. 'Face it, Faye, you're rubbish.' He pointed at the bin beside his desk. 'That's where you belong. You're a rubbish presenter – hence no work. You're a rubbish wife – hence no husband. And you're a rubbish mother – where *is* your darling daughter, by the way?'

Faye's head felt as if it would burst. Her eyes darted to the row of awards – BAFTAS, Emmys, Domes – including one she and the others had won when *Girl Talk* was at the height of its success. He had no right to any of them.

James glanced at the screen. Vladislav's hand was inside the weather girl's dress. 'You really are a hopeless little tart. You couldn't even manage to give birth when you were meant to.'

Faye gasped. Tears ran down her face. She took a step forward. 'You cold bastard . . .'

James shot her a look. Watching the Russian get all touchy-feely with the weather girl was making him horny. He made a grab for Faye, lunging at her breasts, roughly tugging at the front of her dress. 'I never saw the appeal of you before,' he

417

said, breathing hard as she struggled to get away, the booze slowing her down. James held on, a vile sneer on his face, his eyes fixed on her cleavage. 'But you know what, Faye – I'm beginning to think I may have made a rare error of judgement where you're concerned.' He squeezed her breasts.

'Let go. You're hurting me.'

'Oh, don't go all coy. You follow me up here, half-pissed – what do you expect?' He yanked at her top, exposing bare flesh. 'Oh God, yes.' His mouth latched on to her nipple and he began to suck.

Faye reeled in horror. She struck out. James was strong. He would rape her and no one would care. No one ever cared. There was a painful pounding in her head, like a series of sharp jabs, making her dizzy and disorientated. She felt as if she was losing consciousness. An image of Daisy came to her as something inside went *snap* and she lashed out, blackness belching up to consume her . . .

Dazed, she took the service lift back to the ground floor and headed for her dressing room. Once inside with the door locked behind her, she realized she was still clutching the statuette. Her hands were bloody. She put the award down and went into the bathroom, where she scrubbed at her hands under the cold tap. As she studied her reflection in the mirror above the basin, it struck her that there was nothing in her expression to indicate what she had just done. Her eyes were dull, blank. It was as if she was in some kind of trance, not quite there. She had just killed a man.

Her hands shook under the jet of freezing water. She turned off the tap and dried them with toilet paper, then flushed it away. Her teeth were chattering. She would have to get rid of the statuette. Trembling, she gazed up at the ceiling from where she was perched on the edge of the sofa. The tiles looked loose, resting on a steel frame. She climbed on to the table. Not tall enough. She picked up a folding chair and used it to give her more height. Better. A tile shifted when she pressed on it, and she slid it to one side, creating a gap. Once the statuette was inside, she eased the tile back into position. Just to be sure she would remember which one it was, she took a blue felt-tip pen from her desk and made a small dot. Then she climbed down.

Her breathing was too rapid and she leaned against the wall, forcing herself to take slow, steady breaths. She put the chair back, washed her hands again and wiped the sink clean then flushed the sodden tissue away. And then she checked her reflection once more, straightened her hair and smoothed her dress. She would go back to the party.

As she had headed towards the studio, her legs threatening to buckle beneath her, one word had clattered about inside her head: Daisy, Daisy, Daisy.

Outside, the cab was waiting. She splashed her face with cold water and patted it dry with a paper towel. She needed to pull herself together now, be strong. Mike must have confessed to murdering James Almond as well as Cheryl, even though he knew she was responsible for James's death. What was it he'd said about how he'd seen her at the party but she hadn't seen him? He had known all along what she'd done, and this was his way of protecting her. Now it was down to her to help him. She would get the best lawyer and Mike would claim diminished responsibility due to Post-Traumatic Stress Disorder. No jury could fail to feel for him. She would stand up in court to declare her love for him and say she was standing by him. However long it took, she would wait for him.

She thought of him in his smelly fatigues opening tins of Carnation milk, their marriage in pieces, grieving for his dead cameraman, utterly, hopelessly lost, and it made her want to weep, despite what he had done to Cheryl. Faye had failed him. Mike was a decent man and a wonderful father. All this was her fault, and yet he had stepped up to take the rap so that she wouldn't have to.

Her eyes filled with tears. 'I'm so sorry, Mike,' she said. 'I'll make it up to you. I promise.'

Seventy-Eight

Julia was reclining with her feet up in her comfy first-class seat as the plane soared over the Atlantic. Her mood was thoroughly relaxed. Perhaps this was what people meant when they talked about wedded bliss. 'Tell me again,' she said.

'We're spending a few days in Grenada – in a tucked-away apartment with our own private pool and a secluded beach,' Scott said. 'There's a spa, even a Gary Rhodes restaurant if we feel like going mad. Then it's off to Bequia – *Beck-way* is how you say it – totally unspoiled and off the beaten track, so I hear.' He grinned. 'No TV where we're staying. How ever will you cope?'

Julia eased her seat back another couple of inches. 'I don't mind. It's not like I'm a telly addict.'

He laughed. 'No, course you're not. You only wanted to put it on last night.' He gave her a stern look. 'On our wedding night.'

'You'll just have to be firm with me,' Julia said, rubbing his ankle with her bare foot. 'I'll be too busy doing other things anyway to watch telly.'

'Exactly right.'

They were silent for a moment. 'I don't suppose . . .' She stopped herself.

'What?'

'I was going to say maybe we could watch the news now. A final catch-up, and that's it. I promise.'

Scott shook his head. 'It'll only be the usual doom and gloom.'

Julia gave him a pleading smile.

'Go on, then.'

She flicked to the news channel on the small screen in front of her. Scott returned to his *Lonely Planet* guide. The strains of Elgar's Cello Concerto drifted from his headphones.

A minute or two later Julia grabbed his arm. He turned and followed her gaze to the screen. There was Tabitha Tate gesturing at a white-painted terraced house behind her. The caption said: *LIVE: War reporter Mike Parry charged with murder of Channel 6 boss and Girl Talk host.*

Julia stared at the screen, speechless. Scott took her hand. Together they watched as Tabitha explained that Mike would appear in court in a few hours.

'*Oh my God* – it was soldier boy all along,' Julia said. 'I wonder if Faye was in on it.'

'I hardly—'

'Maybe that's why she turned to drink.' She flashed a triumphant smile.

'Julia—'

'Maybe *that's* why she packed him off to the loony bin!'

Just like that, the old Julia – the grade-A bitch who took great pleasure from the misfortunes of others – had surfaced, sending the new and more chilled version packing.

'At least she'll get a few covers at last. That's about the only reason the magazines would bother with her. Worth going to jail just for the exposure, I suppose.' She clapped her hands, her face a picture of delight, while Scott gazed at her, a frown darkening his features.

'She'll be moping about in black looking tragic, bet you anything.' She looked thoughtful. 'The press will be all over *Girl Talk* now.'

'We can always turn round when we get to the other end and go back.' His voice was cool. 'I'd hate you to miss all the attention.'

Julia pictured the media frenzy that would be under way right now. *Girl Talk* would be splashed across every magazine and tabloid newspaper. A jolt of excitement went through her. This was a one-off, a once-in-a-lifetime opportunity, whereas they could have their honeymoon any time. She was just about to say so when she caught the troubled expression in Scott's eyes and sanity returned.

'We're newlyweds,' she said after a pause. 'It's our first day as a married couple and we're going on our honeymoon. That's what matters.' She held his face in her hands. 'From now on you come first. Us. Our plans take priority.'

'Sure?'

'Totally. Hundred per cent.'

She had waited all her life for things to come right, and if she wasn't careful she could lose it all; happiness was such a precarious thing. Well, she would not let that happen. She closed her eyes and a film began to run in her head, transporting her to a pristine beach where polite little waves broke on the shore. Two figures drifted into frame. She smiled, seeing herself in close-up, tanned, relaxed, and happy – hand in hand with her husband.

extracts reading groups
competitions books new extracts
discounts extracts discounts events
competitions
books new reading groups
events extracts
new books
extracts new titles reading groups
interviews
events extracts events
discounts
new books events interviews new books
events new reading groups books
discounts extracts discounts
www.panmacmillan.com
extracts events reading groups
competitions books extracts new